First published:
2020 by Corrado Caldarella

ISBN: 9780645001075

Cover design by:
Ross Robinson Creative
PO Box 161
Malanda QLD 4885

Self-publishing support services by:
Intertype
U45, 125 Highbury Road
Burwood VIC 3125

Genre

Friendship/Adventure, Diary Style

Contents

Long ago tales were told by storytellers that were people who would enchant their listeners with legends of faraway lands. This is such a tale delivered on a day to day basis. The characters interact at given times but most of the adventure is unfolded by the storyteller. The telling is about a faraway corner of the Universe where life unfolds events as it does all over the Universe. We will ride shoulder with Jit, the main character, and share his experience as he undertakes this journey, with the other characters interjecting at times too. The storyteller hopes to enthral you with an other than ordinary life, in anything but an ordinary part of the Universe, set an extraordinary distance away.

Corrado

Geelok

Jit Unapell stood on the bridge of his ship and watched the stars slowly drift by. His ship, the Windchief, was the first of the 'Windchiefs' and despite her age, she was still in great order with ageless lines. However, no weapons came with the ship because like all Windchiefs, they have I.S.T shielding, (*Impenetrable Shielding Technology*) that's so effective none are needed. Only if the new owner should request them was it done. The Jorpahs were the makers of these fine crafts and were known throughout many Galaxies for their mastery. There were other fine ships to be bought too but if you had the money you bought the best. Jit had a couple of TX-5 Pulse Laser cannons put on his ship, but they were mostly used for target practise when meteors presented an obstacle.

At present, he was on his way to a small moon named Geelok. He's hoping to find an old friend he hasn't seen in a while. Around five year's Jit was thinking. Arrill Splitcloud is his friend's name and they'd known each other since their early school days. They parted company when Arrill met Leearnah and it became a serious thing for him. Jit was the best man at their wedding. Geelok was still another two hours away so he left Ladone to run the ship. Ladone was a hologram computer image that could run the entire ship on her own. Although she was a hologram, she didn't like it when you called her, "Just a hologram." She was not just Ladone she was also the Windchief.

In the galley, he made fresh coffee then took a seat at the dining table. In the centre was a popup hologram of his mother and father. They were smiling at him and both were long since deceased. He was almost twenty when his mother passed, then a short time later his dad did too. As Jit was the only child, all his parents had was left to him. After selling everything, he had enough to buy the Windchief and go into the transport business. Now he was self-employed and could finally be independent.

He lived on the ship as she was fully setup with a master cabin having all the comforts of home. There were two spare cabins all with their ensuites and a small kitchenette. Most of the ship was built for cargo but all the living areas including the bridge were luxury of the finest quality. You felt like you were in a palace more than an interstellar ship. There was a full gym as well as an extensive library and in the cargo hold, were four small ships. Two were fighters and the other two were commuter shuttles but could be turned into small cargo movers with some re-arranging inside.

The propulsion in the Windchief was a Rollollium drive system and a mystery to all but the Jorpahs. The engine room was a sealed unit with the same shield protection as the ship and only the Jorpahs were able to access it. The fuel cell lasted twenty years and when it was spent they would come out and fit the new one. If the ship broke down the Jorpahs would come out to fix it at no cost anywhere in the known galaxies. That's their guarantee and the age of the ship didn't matter. To date, no Windchief had been reported with any problem except a spent fuel cell.

He was bought out of his deep thoughts by Ladone who'd materialized in front of him announcing that they'd arrived in Geeloks orbit. She was wearing a yellow business suit this time with white shoes and a matching hat. He hardly ever saw her in the same outfit twice! He thanked her and she dematerialized again, leaving him alone with the memories of his smiling parents. He finished his coffee then prepared to go down to the cargo bay and use a shuttle for the trip to the moon's surface.

....

A sandstorm was building up on the horizon and it was moving fast in his direction. The sandstorms on Geelok could strip a man to the bone in moments if he was foolish enough to be caught out in one. Arrill had five minutes to get everything inside and lock the place down. He knew how fast these moved and the destruction they could leave in their wake. Already the wind was fierce, making movement a skill of balance. The storm door responded to his command and sealed him in shutting the noise out. It reminded Arrill of a tomb when it reached its zenith with a final clunk. There was another wall just inside the storm door which was made from tinted bifold glass doors for when the weather was fine, allowing light to stray in. At the top were slots that could be opened for a breeze to pass through as well.

Outside he could hear the storm trying desperately to take hold and tare the door from its path as the intensity built up. Many storms have tried but none have yet budged it. For the last year, he'd been living in this cave, his sanctuary. A hunting friend of his showed him the cave and all he had to do was make the door and point of entry tube or "Poet." That was the most time consuming and costly thing he needed to do. The Poet was for entering the cave if the front door was too blocked. The rest was easy with everything portable that could fold away.

A complication unfolded with his ex-wife and now he had to clear it up. Her brother Zarp was out to kill him for a beating she received, but not from him. The new guy she'd shacked up with gave her a real touch up and to his knowledge, she was laid up in hospital in a coma. He didn't even know the name of the guy who beat her up and to make matters worse he could've been from any part of the galaxy. Only when and if she comes out of the coma, will she be able to set things right, but until then, he was on the run and fearful for his life.

....

Down in the cargo bay, Jit settled into the pilot seat and did his pre-flight checks before he lowered the shield and exited into space. He darted down to the moon's surface and into Port Arczepp which was the only port on the small moon. He wondered yet again if Arrill was still on Geelok. His friend wanted to buy a Tavern the last time he spoke with him and if he did it should make it easier to find him. Jit could never understand why Arrill would pick this rock to settle on when there were so many other places that were not so hostile. Arczepp was a mining town that accommodated a hundred and fifty thousand people now. It grew quickly since the first explorer's arrived. The potential to get rich mining the ore and minerals drew the desperate from all over the galaxies. You had to be desperate to live in this place he thought! Being in the transport business allowed him the privilege to land in the mining docks and he soon settled into one of the bays assigned to him by tower control. He exited the shuttle and set the auto secure then went to arrange ground transport. The attendant at the office was professional in her work and with a minimum of fuss she had him in a vehicle.

The docks were only a short distance from town and as he entered the township's outer limits, he passed the large curved spires that stretched out on either side of the roadway and encircled the town. According to the sign he sighted the spires were the town's protective shielding when a sandstorm ventured to close. Within thirty minutes he was at the information booth to begin his search. Jit needed to find all the taverns in Port Arczepp and then visit each one until he found Arrill. That's providing he did buy a tavern. There were only a dozen which should make the going easy. Soon he had the list in front of him and he left to go to the first and closest tavern called, "The Settlers Bar."

On entering Jit walked into a poorly lit room with about two dozen or so people scattered around the place. Smoke swirled thickly in the air, clearly visible to all who entered the premises. Some patrons were at tables and some were at the bar while others were hunched over gaming machines. He walked up to the bar receiving very little attention from anyone as he passed through. The proprietor asked him what he'd like, and he ordered a drink then asked him if he knew Arrill. The guy seemed a bit nervous and was no help at all. He decided to let the matter go and ordered something to eat then went to sit at a vacant table. While he waited, he watched the people sitting around him. They were either talking or simply staring into their drinks. No one made any eye contact with him, yet he could feel someone's eyes staring at him. Yesterday's local paper sat on the seat beside him and he picked it up to read and rolled a cigarette at the same time. The news was the same predictable telling of tragedies, so he flicked through the pages looking for the local gossip at the back while he waited.

....

Inside the cave, the interior was still the same as when Arrill first moved in. All he had to do was set up lighting and a makeshift bathroom and kitchen area. His bed was the sofa and the ground was still sand that had been compacted with an additive to make it as hard as dirt. It wasn't a big space, but it was enough to meet his needs. He'd never planned on being in the cave this long and wondered how much longer he would have to endure this lifestyle. He poured himself a drink then went to his workshop which was just a bench and from a drawer, he retrieved a map he'd been studying. The map was payment for work he carried out. The old guy said it was genuine and all he had to offer. After looking at it, Arrill believed it to be genuine and took it as settlement hoping he hadn't been suckered. That was a couple of years back now and although he'd had it that long he didn't start studying it until he came to live in the cave.

In the year that he'd been working on it, he made slow progress and was now hooked on seeking what it hid. According to what he'd deciphered he had to go to the twelfth Galaxy and find a planet called Spee. He had a slight idea where the Galaxy was but finding the planet would be guesswork unless it was on the map and he hadn't deciphered that yet. The planet might even be a moon he thought to himself. If he was right about what he discovered, the next big problem was getting there. With no ship, he wasn't going anywhere! Even if he sold everything he had, it would only amount to half of what he needed to buy a spaceworthy ship. The situation seemed hopeless. What he needed was someone with the skills to figure the map out, but he didn't know anyone on Geelok nor was he at liberty to wander around and ask. The only person he knew that might be able to help him was a very long way away and getting there would require an interstellar ship. He worked on the map for another hour then stopped and went to fix a snack to eat while he watched the news. The news was the same depressing information as usual. It seemed that no one was interested in good news these days! Outside the storm was still tearing the place apart and it hadn't abated at all. Occasionally something would hit the door startling him, and he wondered where the projectiles might come from as he was a long way from anywhere.

The duration of the storms was unpredictable on Geelok and some had lasted for as long as a week. After being captive in the cave for too long, one could start to go a little crazy. He had supplies that would last him for a month if necessary, but he wasn't sure if he could handle a month trapped in the cave. When he finished eating, he went to do some maintenance work on his ground transporter ready for his next trip into Port Arczepp. The sands of Geelok were like graphite powder and without regular maintenance, the vehicle wouldn't last a second trip to town. He was four hundred kilometres from the Port and the last thing you needed was to break down. Nobody travelled to where Arrill was so help was unlikely in the event of a breakdown. When he was satisfied with the work he carried out, he decided to shower, then he sat back with a drink in his hand and looked at the map some more. With nothing coming to him he set the map aside and kicked back to watch a movie from his collection.

....

Jit was halfway through the paper when his food arrived. It looked great and his stomach growled in anticipation, he was hungrier than he'd realised. The bartender scuttled away after setting the plate down, hurrying to his position behind the bar. Jit watched him for a moment, then he concentrated on eating his beef stew and cheese bread. While he ate, he continued flicking through the paper, all the while feeling that someone was still observing him. Whenever he looked up though, he saw nobody looking in his direction. After finishing his meal, he went to pay, and to complement the chef then he stepped outside into the late afternoon air.

There was a bench seat further down the path and he ventured towards it intending on having a cigarette. While he sat there and enjoyed the cool evening breeze, he noticed a brothel across the road. The girls usually knew a lot about what goes on in a town so he thought it might be worth asking there. He crossed the road and walked down to it and upon entering he was greeted with a sweet aroma from incense in the premises and dim lighting with opulent surroundings. When he approached the counter, the Madam came out to enquire what his needs were. After a short chat, the woman told him that Arrill was on the run and hadn't been seen for quite some time. Rumour has it that he's living somewhere in the wastelands she informed him. He thanked her for the help and walked back outside where it had now become dark.

Jit decided to leave any further searching until the following day. Now that he knew Arrill won't be in the tavern business anymore this would make finding him a lot more difficult. He also wondered what sort of trouble he had got himself into to make him go into hiding. On his journey back to the shuttle he noticed a lot of traffic heading into town and on arriving at the Port he saw an interstellar passenger ship on the tarmac explaining where all the people came from. Once he was back on board his shuttle, he went to the small kitchenette to make a drink then went onlink to seek some information. If Arrill was in hiding and he still knew his friend, there was no doubt in Jit's mind that he would stay out for long periods. However, he would still need to get supplies. There were only two places he could shop to buy bulk supplies in Port Arczepp. He wrote them down and hoped that Arrill didn't shop elsewhere on Geelok. It was getting late by the time he finished so he called it a night and went to bed.

The following morning, he woke by 7.00 am but didn't rise out of bed until closer to eight. He went to freshen up, and then made coffee and breakfast in his tiny but functional kitchenette. While he ate, he thought about where to start first when he arrived in town. He formed a rough plan and by 9.00 am he stepped outside and was greeted by an already warm and fine day. He secured the shuttle and made his way into town still using the vehicle he hired. The interstellar ship was still on the tarmac and there were people in uniform running around preparing her for the next voyage. Long baggage carts snaked their way across the tarmac following no set path in particular. Jit wondered where her next destination might be as he passed the workers who only briefly looked his way. He waved at them and they nodded back as he passed into the giant shadow of the large craft. A half hour later and with little traffic he arrived in town and made his way to the first bulk buy store Arrill was likely to shop at. Port Arczepp was setup in a grid, which made navigating easy. The first place turned up nothing and again he could feel the reluctance of the owner wanting to divulge any information. Despite the size of the town it still seemed to have that small town caution to strangers. The next and last place he visited was on the other side of town and proved to be a little trickier to find as he had to drive up a narrow oneway lane to get to it. The car park of this establishment was a lot fuller he noticed suggesting a more popular place to shop. Inside, after passing through the double electric doors, he encountered floor to ceiling shelving stacked full of every imaginable food available. Rows and rows of it! Forklifts were buzzing around, busily preparing orders and restocking the shelves. This store was definitely the hub of the shopper looking for bulk purchases. Now all he needed was someone willing to part with some information. An employee with a pleasant manner soon guided him to the manager's office and he made his way through the tangle to get there. The place was huge! The manager was a burly looking man with an old but noticeable scar across his left cheek and nose. A nose that looked to have been broken many times. When he spoke, his voice betrayed his fearsome looks and he informed Jit that he did know Arrill but hadn't seen him for quite some time. He also told him that four managers ran the store and he could've come in when one of the others was on duty. If he wanted, he could come back and check with each of them the manager suggested. Jit thanked him and left his contact details and asked if he could pass them on to the other managers then made for the exit.

He went back to town and decided to continue checking the taverns. Maybe someone might divulge something if he persisted. He dug out of his pocket the list from the previous day and headed for the next place on it. The tavern he arrived at was called "The Crossed Arms" and he pulled into the parking lot on the side of the building and walked around to the front entrance. Upon entering he was welcomed by the smell of food and stale ale. There were a few patrons scattered about the place and gaming machines flashing colours offering the chance to win irresistible prizes. The atmosphere in this tavern was more relaxed than the one he entered the day before and even the bartender was friendlier. They struck up a good conversation, but he still wasn't any help in locating Arrill or giving any useful information. After finishing his drink, he left his contact details and went to check out some more taverns hoping to have better luck there. He thought it might be difficult to find Arrill but he wasn't prepared for this kind of difficulty! The next two places turned up nothing either and as he pulled up to another one on the list, he doubted he would do any better there.

In the car park, there were three people talking amongst themselves, and Jit parked in a space beside them. When he got out, he struck up a conversation with them that led to asking if any of them knew Arrill or his whereabouts. Only one of them did and he said he was last seen at one of the outposts in the desert region. They were getting ready for the journey out there and the driver asked Jit if he wanted to come along and see for himself. The driver's name was "Ishmak" and he was taking two female Jorpah's out there to entertain the miners. Ishmak had a ground transporter which mainly dealt in cargo, but he was also able to pop out foldaway seats and accommodate for passengers. With nothing to lose and some company, Jit said yes and climbed aboard. Within a few minutes they were underway and according to Ishmak, the journey would take a few hours to get there. He told Jit and the girls that he'd been living on Geelok for the past couple of years running cargo to all the different outposts on the moon. He went on to say that when he first arrived, he worked at the mines operating a front end loader and saved all he could so he could buy his transporter and then work for himself. Jit could relate to that! He had plenty of work and made a lot more than he did in the mines and was contemplating buying another transporter and putting an operator in it. The way he said it Jit was expecting Ishmak to ask him if he wanted to work for him but instead, he changed the subject and went on about the sandstorms. He told them how they would turn up unannounced and leave you stranded until they passed. His transporter had anchoring capability so it wouldn't be blown around the moon if they were caught unawares. It was compulsory on all transporters now after some went missing and were yet to be found. Jit wondered how bad the storms must be and hoped not to encounter any whilst on the moon. Then Ishmak changed the subject again and told Jit the last time Arrill was seen at the outpost was four or five weeks ago. Not much goes on in a small place that he didn't know about. Some distance out of Port Arczepp they passed another transporter heading into town. Ishmak didn't recall seeing that transporter around and wondered where he operated from. He knew most of the operators but that one eluded him.

....

It was the early hours of the morning when Arrill woke up. The DVD logo bounced around the screen on the television and he watched it for a moment while the fuzziness cleared from his head. When he checked the time, it was only 3.00 am in the morning so he turned off the television and slumped back to sleep. As he drifted back off to sleep, he remembered some of his dreams, but all were blurry except for a part where he was in absolute darkness. That he remembered well! The next time he awoke it was 8.00 am and by the silence in the cave, he knew the storm had lifted. His first attempt at standing failed miserably and he sat back down to nurse his pinging head. That homemade spirit was smooth going down but the next day it had claws that raked your brain and hung onto the back of your eyeballs. He soon managed an upright position and went to wash and make a much needed coffee.

Before doing that, he lowered the storm door to let in some fresh air and light. The day was clear and fine with a slight breeze carrying the smell of freshly disturbed sand inside. With his coffee in hand, he went outside to see what damage the storm had done to the world outside his cave. The storms had the ability to change the landscape dramatically. As he surveyed around he noticed a small mountain range where the day before it was just sand mounds. The sand was virgin bare except for some footprints left by the wildlife that scrounged for food and he was puzzled how they survived such conditions. Fortunately for Arrill, the storm blew in such a way that it didn't block the cave entrance. When that happened, it could take quite some time to clean it up depending on how bad it was. When he finished his drink, he went to make another one and made preparations for the trip into Port Arczepp. It would take close to four hours to get to town and that depended on how much the storm re-arranged the surroundings last night. By 9.00 am he was in the driver's seat and on his way.

The scene around him was mostly baron but in some places, along the way, there was an oasis that seemed to dodge the effect of the weather. It was almost as if they moved out of the way! Geelok was still a new discovery and Arrill believed the moon to have a personality of its own. Since he'd been living so close to the wilderness, he had the feeling the land around him was aware of his presence and showed him things about itself. He travelled for three hours before he saw the first sign of people. It was a transporter heading out to one of the outposts in the wastelands. A short time later he saw Port Arczepp on the horizon and the force field spires that protected it and knew he didn't have much further to go. As always, the closer he got to town the more apprehensive he became. He ran the gauntlet every time he came to stock up but so far, he had no trouble. He also changed his days around so there was no set pattern for anyone to follow. Maybe that helped too he convinced himself. He couldn't wait to get this mess all behind him and have his freedom again.

Leearnah was a Chungah as was her brother. The Chungahs were good and mostly violent free people but the bad ones were unforgiving and cruel. Leearnahs brother was the latter and he thrived on people's fear of him. If he saw Arrill he knew he'd be shot without a chance to explain. When he was close to town, he sent a coded message to his friend to open the door for him then he darkened the tint on the windows and drove in through the back and straight into the arranged parking spot which hid his vehicle from sight. Arrill had changed the look of his vehicle so no one would recognise it anymore, but it was still better to hide it he thought to himself. After securing his ride he went up the back entrance and into "The Crossed Arms Tavern". A few turns later he arrived at a lounge area where he helped himself to a drink and then took a seat on the comfy sofa. Being a long trip, it was nice to relax and stretch out in this secluded little haven. It wasn't a very large area and would only accommodate twenty people at most, but it had a great atmosphere. Only a few chosen people used this lounge as it was Neeok's private room and right now it was vacant.

Before very long his friend Neeok, the bartender

walked in and greeted him with a brief hug. He then went to make his drink and joined Arrill to catch up with events since they last spoke. There wasn't much to tell from Arrill's point of view and when Neeok told him some guy was looking for him he tensed up. When he told him his name was Jit Unapell the tension drained away and the feeling of hope replaced it. How many years had it been he thought to himself since he last saw Jit? This was no coincidence, of that he was certain. Neeok relayed what Jit had said and then passed the contact details to Arrill assuring him that he said nothing because he didn't know who he was. Arrill told him he did well and with that settled Neeok returned to work as his break time was over. After he left, Arrill went to make another drink and sat down to contemplate why Jit would be looking for him.

Old memories were awakened about the time they used to cruise around together and how simple life was back then. It was a great time and if he hadn't met Leearnah they would probably still be hanging out together. They were good friends and as close as brothers as far as he was concerned. He opened the note that Neeok handed him and in it was the means of identifying Jits shuttle, where it was, and how to get there. This changed his plans now so instead of getting supplies for the trip back to the cave he had to catch up with Jit and find out why he wanted to see him. Hope surged through him again giving him a new and much needed charge. While he thought about these matters the warning light in the lounge flashed warning Arrill to hide. It could only mean that Leearnahs brother was in the tavern or one of his cohorts and despite the lounge being a private room it was too risky to remain there. He left and went to the secret room concealed in the cellar which only he and Neeok knew about. He could feel the tension rising again so he took the bottle of scotch with him to help ease the feeling. The last thing he wanted was to drag Jit into his problem. After what seemed like many hours Neeok came down to inform him that

Leearnahs brother had moved on but that he knew Jit was in town looking for Arrill.

'Not much escapes that guy' said Neeok.

Arrill did not doubt that as he seemed to have ears and eyes in every part of Geelok. He decided he was hungry and ordered a feed which Neeok, in turn, went to arrange. He also thought it might be a good idea to wait out the rest of the day where he was and head out to find Jit at nightfall. So he remained in the hidden room where he could relax and poured himself another drink then hit the remote control which bought up the television concealed in a cabinet. He went through the channels until he found a movie channel to settle on and at the same time could feel his body beginning to relax with the help of the scotch. He was just about to doze off when Neeok came in with his meal. The food smelt great and the aroma filled the small room quickly. As he watched the television his mind kept straying to why Jit wanted to see him after all this time. What most astonished him was the timing! The afternoon slipped away quickly because Arrill fell asleep during the movie catching the credits at the end when he woke. As it was closing on time to leave he began to feel the tension rising with the prospect of going outside again. He looked over at the bottle of scotch but thought better of it. A clear head is what he needed right now.

....

Ishmak told his passengers stories about his experiences on Geelok since he'd been living there. Some were humorous while others sounded a bit exaggerated to Jit, but the girls were enthralled absorbing every word he spoke and hanging on for more. They were both extremely beautiful with Jit guessing them to be in their early to mid-twenties. Their perfect shaped legs were clad in pink and white striped leggings and both were wearing super short shorts and breast hugging tops that left little to the imagination. With Ishmak being the great entertainer he was, the journey passed quickly and it didn't seem long before they arrived at "Klesspar" their destination. Jit noticed as they drove through the quiet streets that a feeling of oppression hung heavy in the air. He could see by the way the girls looked around that he wasn't the only one thinking that. The feeling was further intensified when they entered the main street to reveal a ram shacked establishment of slap together buildings. Some sat empty and looked to have been that way for some time. Ishmak stopped out the front of the only tavern named "Klesspar Inn". The streets were wide and the few stragglers around watched them as they disembarked from the vehicle. Jit fast lost any hope of finding Arrill in this place. He helped the two girls with their suitcases and entered the Inn with them closely following. Ishmak had other business to attend to and told Jit he would be back when he was done and left.

Upon entering the Inn Jit was taken aback at how ornate and elegant the interior was inside. The bar was a horseshoe shape made of dark polished wood with swirling grains in it and what looked like a marble top. The marble, if it was marble was jet black with lapis blue stripes etched through it. There were tables with chairs scattered around the bar lounge for patrons and two walls were crowded with gaming machines. All attention was on them as they walked in and he could see everyone's eyes popping out of their heads when they saw the girls. A well dressed and buxom woman approached them from a side hallway that ran alongside the bar. She was attractive despite her age and walked with an air of confidence. She greeted Jit and then took the girls with her back the way she came. Now standing alone Jit felt awkward so he made his way to the bar nodding at people as he did so. Some responded in like and others never made eye contact at all. At the bar, he was stunned by a glamorous looking girl with a pretty face and alluring eyes that served him. Jit introduced himself and struck up a bit of a conversation with her which led up to asking her if she knew Arrill. She told him she had only been in Klesspar a week and was unfamiliar with anyone by that name. He thought about trying to describe Arrill to her but after five years he didn't know what he might look like either! He thanked her and went to sit at a table in the back of the room with his drink.

He wondered where Ishmak was and how long he'd be and was deep in thought when a machine to his right suddenly burst into song and colours as its player won a small cash prize. The winner did a short victory dance around his stool before resuming his position facing the machine and continued playing. Just as Jit was contemplating going outside for a smoke, the girls came back out and joined him at his table with their drinks. Jit finally introduced himself and the girls revealed their names to him, one being named "Nisteeva and the other Kalisafah". It seemed like they decided to stay awhile and see how things panned out they said to him. A few more people came in while they talked, and Jit thought again about where Ishmak was. Ten minutes later his thoughts were answered when he walked in and strolled up to their table.

He asked what they were all drinking and continued to the bar returning with the refreshments in no time. They chatted away for a while before Jit excused himself and went outside to have a smoke and walk up the street to check out the other shops. There were not many so it wasn't going to take long and he thought maybe someone might know Arrill if he saw the right person to ask. He found no one to ask and by the time he returned to the tavern he finished his smoke. He walked inside and found the girls laughing at Ishmaks stories again and took a seat at the table. They conversed for another hour before Ishmak said it was time to get going because if they left now they would arrive back in Geelok just on dark. He told Jit he didn't like driving at night as some of the wildlife could present a problem. Some of the things that came out were bigger than his transporter! They bid the girls farewell and said they hoped to see them again and were off.

Back in the transporter, Jit noticed a stack of boxes and drums occupying the space in the back. Must be cargo to go back to Geelok he thought to himself. He also noticed a strong pungent odour that he couldn't identify. Ishmak informed him that it was some herb used by the Chungahs in their cooking and despite the smell it was safe. It was grown on a few small farms out here for the demands in Geelok he went on to say. They were soon back in the arid wastelands where all one could see was an ocean of sand speckled here and there with low scraggly bushes. It was a boring landscape and fortunately for Jit his new friend always had something to talk about. He thought to himself that Ishmak should've been in the entertainment business because everything he talked about, he made interesting. For some of the journey, Jit nodded off which helped make the trip pass quicker. When he woke again, they were about an hour from Geelok and Ishmak just started talking again like a radio you'd switch on. Soon they could see the lights of Geelok on the horizon and Jit was welcoming a stretch and something to eat. He was feeling a little saddle sore from being in the seat for so long and was looking forward to some fresh air too.

In town, he was dropped off at his vehicle and Ishmak gave him his contact details in case he needed his help for anything. Thanking him he watched Ishmak round a bend and disappear into the night. The car park was abandoned except for his vehicle awaiting his return like a faithful dog. Being hungry he decided to look around for something to eat so he didn't have to worry about it back at the shuttle. There was no shortage of places to choose from in Geelok and everything was open all the time. He decided to walk and soon spotted a food parlour that served wild game meat and chose to be adventurous and try some. When he finished, he got up and went to pay at the little booth by the doorway then stepped out into the fresh evening air.

Across the road was a cinema with crowds jostling to get in and see the latest new movie. It had been some time since he went to the movies and he contemplated going to join them but decided he'd had enough of crowds and changed his mind. Besides he was here to find Arrill, not on vacation. He wondered how he was going to achieve that and how long it would take because everything so far had come to a dead end. He walked the short distance back to the hire vehicle and decided to have a drive around town for a look before heading back out to the shuttle. It was still early and there might even be the off chance he'd see Arrill. While he drove around, he became aware of another vehicle following closely behind him. Jit made a few turns to be sure then stopped at a shopping mall and pretended to go in for something. Whoever it was stayed in their vehicle waiting for him to come back out. He thought for a moment, then walked out a different exit and hailed down a cab, and asked the driver to take him to the port via the front of the mall. Sure enough, his follower was still sitting in his vehicle waiting for him to come back out. Jit recalled the feeling earlier on when he thought someone was watching him and wondered how long he'd been followed for. He also wondered if they knew he had a shuttle at the port. The driver dropped him a half hour later at his shuttle and after paying him he went in and planned what to do. As he was being followed, the last thing he wanted to do was bring more trouble to his friend.

....

It had been dark for a couple of hours now and Arrill

thought it would be safe to get going. Back at his transporter, he keyed in the passcode on the panel to let him out then got in and left the way he came with the gate closing automatically as he passed through it. While he negotiated the streets via back ways out to the port, he wondered how long Jit had been on Geelok and if he would be there when he arrived. He was feeling a little apprehensive about the meeting because of the length of time but soon dismissed the notion. He was so caught up in his thoughts about the matter that the journey passed unnoticed and he soon turned into the mining port. The last time he'd seen Jit he was bouncing around space with no direction in particular. After driving around a maze he came upon a bay with a solitary shuttle parked in it and figured it to be Jits. The shuttle was a fine looking craft although it was smaller than he expected. On closer approach, he saw someone looking out from the cockpit then move from sight. It then dawned on him that Jit might be travelling with company. He stopped his transporter just in front of the shuttle and shut down the engine, his heartbeat suddenly quickening a little. He sat there for a moment looking and waiting to see if anyone would come out and then stepped back to the exit and opened the door into the cool night air.

....

Jit was halfway through his drink when he saw lights reflecting through the cockpit from an approaching vehicle. He went to the hidden compartment to retrieve a pistol which he slid into the back of his pants. The vehicle out front was different from the one following him in town, this one was a transporter and he was sure it was the one he'd seen when travelling with Ishmak earlier on today. He watched for movement concealed behind the bulkhead and then saw the side door open and a lone figure stepped out. Five years may have passed since he'd seen Arrill but there was no mistaking his face in the dim lighting. He was a little nervous suddenly as he stepped out to greet him. They walked up to each other with Jit speaking first,

'How are you old friend, it's been too long hasn't it?'

They shook hands and briefly hugged before Arrill held him at arm's length just looking at Jit.

'I can't tell you how good it is to see an old friend' he blurted out emotionally.

He let Jit go and they went into the shuttle to continue talking as Jit could sense he was on edge. Inside he told Arrill to take a seat and went to make a drink after replacing the pistol in the hidden compartment. When he returned his friend was pacing. Jit placed the tray on the small table and sat down and Arrill sat down opposite him.

'Still have your coffee the same way?' Jit asked him.

Arrill replied with a nod and Jit poured out two cups and passed him one.

He looked at Arrill and said, 'Do you want to tell me what's going on then?'

In a torrent lasting a half hour, Jit was told everything that was bothering Arrill with no details spared. He understood now why he was so tense and told him to secure his transporter and they'd take off and go to his ship out in Geeloks orbit.

"My transporters already secured," said Arrill so Jit prepared for liftoff.

Arrill joined him in the front seat and felt more relaxed to be with someone he could trust. It seemed like only a week had passed since he last saw him and not all the years that had slipped away. They lifted off and Arrills transporter remained alone on the tarmac shrinking at an ever increasing rate as they climbed higher up and then streaked spaceward. As they lifted higher into the air, they could take in the whole of Geelok and it looked magical with the glowing lights illuminating the desert for miles around with an eerie glow. It was soon a vanishing speck as they entered the blackness of space and coming up fast in front of them a ship began to emerge. As they came closer Arrill realised that his friend had a Windchief and turned to look at him. Jit sat there with a smug smile on his face but kept his focus on the task at hand as he prepared to land in the cargo hold. He dropped the shield and floated into park next to shuttle two and set the craft down cutting all power as he did so. Arrill noticed the two fighters sitting opposite the shuttles and said,

'Nice little fighters you've got there, ever use them?'

Jit answered telling him he'd only used them so far to take out and play with. He then raised the shield and when the cargo bay was at normal atmosphere they climbed out and made for the bridge. Arrill followed him looking around at the wonder of his ship. She still looked like a new spacecraft and was quite spacious inside. In the glass lift, which was round, it gave you a 360 degree view of each of the four levels as you passed through them. When they arrived at the top floor and bridge, they were both greeted by Ladone. Jit introduced Arrill and told her he'd be staying for a while then told Arrill to make himself comfortable and went to the galley to get refreshments. Ladone continued talking to Arrill informing him about what she did and if he needed to know anything, he just had to call her name. She could appear in any part of the ship with any hands on work being carried out by service and maintenance bots at her control. She then vanished as she had appeared leaving Arrill standing alone to look around the bridge.

The view from the bridge was 180 degrees with monitors above the front windows giving views out the back making up the 360 degrees. The captain's chair was just behind two pilot seats and elevated a little higher. That arrangement was at the front of the bridge close to the out looking windows. The elevator was in the centre and the entire bridge was lit up by lights on consoles and in walls all with a purpose in mind. Although Arrill had heard about Windchief's he'd never been in one to see what they were like. So far, he was gobsmacked wherever he looked. Jit soon returned and found his friend sampling the captain's chair.

'Nice view he said' as he handed a cup to Arrill.

'Yes' replied Arrill, 'and quite an impressive ship!'

Jit continued to tell him how he bought the Windchief not so long ago after deciding to enter the transport business. He also told Arrill that he was at the unveiling of the Windchief Four not so long ago and it made his ship look like a tug. It was a stunning piece of engineering and art melded together to make an extraordinary craft.

They sat in the two pilot seats and that's when Jit told Arrill of his newfound plan. Arrill listened without interrupting him until he finished then let out a long breath at what Jit was considering undertaking. Arrill knew the contacts to do what he had proposed but also knew it would be suicide, or as close as one could get! Instead, he asked Jit to come back to his cave and he would show him something he acquired that could see them both set forever. If it turned out to be false, they could then try his idea. Jit agreed and let the matter go then went to dig out a drop he'd saved for a special time as this. He returned with two shot glasses and an odd shaped bottle. It was a gift from a customer he once did business for he told Arrill. The drink was fully mature at fifty years of age and every year past that, it became better and more sort after. The bottle he was about to open was already seventy two years old. The liquid that poured out was viscous and honey coloured with a pleasant smell that tickled the senses. The taste was like nothing Arrill had ever tried and the effect was instant. It totally relaxed him which was a feeling he'd not had since all the trouble with Leearnah started. They talked and drank until the early hours of the morning before Jit told him where his quarters were and retired to his cabin. For Jit the journey was made on rubbery legs that felt like they'd give way at any moment. In his cabin, he lay on his bed still clothed, and thought about what Arrill said until he slipped into unconsciousness.

....

Arrill watched his friend walk to the lift in an unsteady fashion then decided to call Ladone and asked her to bring up a display of the ship's layout so he could get familiar with his surroundings. Feeling like a hot drink he decided to go to the galley to make one. He was taken aback at how immaculate the place was and wondered if Jit ever cooked in it. After a short search, he found what he needed and made his drink. He returned to the bridge where he continued to study the ship's layout and despite her old age, she still had technology that surpassed his understanding. After being awake for another hour he could feel the numbness of the drink and weariness bear down on him, so he made his way to his quarters. Upon entering he saw the universal sleep sign on the far wall and went to depress the button which revealed a single bed. A light then flashed prompting a second push of the button for a double bed and ten seconds later it winked out. He sat on the bed and looked around for a minute then kicked off his boots and lay down letting out a long breath as he did so. He thought about all that happened for the day and how things were beginning to pan out. He also thought about having a shower, but sleep overcame him and for the first time in a long time he slept peacefully.

…………………………..

Jit awoke at eight am and lay in bed a little while before he got up and went to have a shower. He felt fresh and quite alert considering all he had to drink the night before. Once dressed in clean attire he went to bang on Arrills door and then he would start breakfast. He thought again about what Arrill said last night and was eager to see what he had up his sleeve. He was nearly finished making breakfast when Arrill walked into the galley still dressed in yesterday's clothes but with the smell of soap on him. He muttered a good morning greeting and went to sit at the dining table. Jit remembered that his friend wasn't a morning person, so he kept conversation to a minimum until he came right. He poured him a coffee then went to complete the cooking. When breakfast was done, they made their way to the cargo bay in preparation for the trip back down to Geelok. The journey down to the surface bought the feeling of anxiety back for Arrill and he tried not to show it. He had a sense of peace on the Windchief and enjoyed the freedom of it. Jit sensed his friends' unrest and assured him that everything would be fine.

They landed back at the mining port where Jit went to pay for the vehicle he hired and arrange for someone to pick it up from the shopping mall car park where he left it the night before. For an extra cost, it was all taken care of. They were soon underway again and the next stop would be Arrills cave. Arrill was at the controls and enjoyed the freedom of flying again. With the shuttle, it would take under an hour to get to his cave. He flew to what he guessed was fifty kilometres from home base before he switched on his homing device. Without it, there would be no way of finding his cave in this ever changing landscape. The changing landscape is what has kept him safe all this time because there were no distinguishing landmarks to adhere to. It was the perfect camouflage. He knew the direction based on his compass and the rest was up to the homing beacon.

It was only a short time later that it began to chime matching the rhythm of the flashing light on the device. All Jit could see below them was sand and more sand interspersed with low lying bushes here and there. Before long the signal remained constant suggesting their destination lay directly beneath them and Arrill commenced the landing procedure. It was on the ground that Jit could finally see the cave entrance which was cleverly concealed. When they stepped outside the first thing Jit could smell was hot sand carried on a hot breeze to match. For Arrill this was home and all too familiar. He led Jit to the side of the entrance and removed a false sand coloured rock concealing the hidden yellow button. At first, there was only silence and then Jit could hear a fluid running through pipes which finally cracked the door and sent it on a descent rapidly. It stopped level with the ground revealing a tinted glass wall and Arrills home. A cool rush of air advanced to greet them as they passed through the doorway in the glass wall.

'Quite a nice little set up you have here' he said to Arrill, how did you manage the isolation?'

'Mostly it was okay but there were times at first where it sent me close to insane' he replied.

Inside the cave, it was musty from being closed up and noticeably cooler than outside. He offered Jit a seat and went to make a drink for them both. Jit looked around while he waited and was impressed at what his friend had achieved in the cave. He also thought highly of Arrill being able to deal with this situation for a whole year on his own. Arrill soon returned with steaming hot coffee that filled the cave with its pleasant aroma quashing the musty smell of the cave quickly. He placed the cups on a small table then went to retrieve something from a workbench. On his return, he dropped on the table in front of Jit an old tatty looking piece of paper. At least that's what it looked like to Jit until he scooped it up and knew it wasn't paper he was holding, but some kind of parchment. It was soft and pliable despite its age and etched into it were lines and pictures he could make no sense of.

'What's this' he asked as he studied it closer?

'I believe it's a map to something, said Arrill, but I don't know what yet'.

Jits' questioning gaze led Arrill to divulge how he came upon the map and what he had deciphered so far. It was not what Jit had expected but he tried to remain optimistic because he could sense Arrill was. He told Jit that he knew someone that could unravel its secret and if it turned out to be a hoax, he would then try Jit's idea. Jit let out a sigh and ran his hands through his hair and agreed to give it a shot. With that settled Arrill then told him they would have to journey to "Kelpuk" in the eighth galaxy and look for a friend of his named "Fryppe" who was a leading expert in anything antique. It had been several years since Arrill last spoke with Fryppe, but they were the best of friends, and time shouldn't have changed that. Besides, he knew that solving a riddle was what Fryppe loved to do. Arrills biggest concern was, would Fryppe still be living where he was the last time he spoke with him? His next concern was his transporter which was still at the mining port. Jit suggested it would be a wise idea to collect the vehicle and return it to the cave because they could be away for quite some time. Arrill had to agree with his friend although he wasn't too pleased about going to the port again.

The day was still early so they secured the cave and flew back to get the transporter. Jit was at the controls this time and he calculated that Arrill should arrive back at the cave by five thirty pm. When they landed at the port Arrill handed Jit a homing beacon and told him the compass setting with apprehension plainly showing on his face. Jit wanted to say something but thought it best left alone. He watched his friend walk across the tarmac to his transporter and enter then he lifted off and headed out to his ship. As he rose into the air, he looked down to see Arrills transporter turn to face the ocean of sand that awaited him and wondered what was going through his mind. With that thought gone his attention returned to the map on the return journey to the Windchief. It may have been nothing but false hope, but Arrills belief in it was enough to compel him to give it a chance. He blocked the doubts that arose as he lowered the shield and made entry into the cargo bay. Within moments the yellow light flashed indicating it was safe to exit the shuttle. The only movement in the cargo bay apart from him was a service bot going about its work. In the elevator, he ascended to the top floor and exited onto the bridge and summoned Ladone then asked her to calculate the time it would take to get to "Kepluk" in the eighth galaxy. The reply was almost instant. At full power, she said it would take approximately six days and seven hours.

....

As Arrill drove off on another three and a half hour journey he hoped it would be the last time he had to undertake such an event. Although he didn't know what the map would reveal he took comfort in Jit's idea even if it boarded on suicide. He wanted to get off this rock whichever way he could. He also knew that Jit wasn't convinced of the map's authenticity but then he was the same when he first came upon it. It was only after he started to decipher some of it that he realised it was too complex to be a fraud. Somehow, he knew the map led to something, and whether this was true, or he wished it to be true, remained to be seen. Only time was going to prove him right or wrong. Along the way he thought about how long it would take to get to Kelpuk then there was always the chance that Fryppe may have moved on. He hoped not because he didn't know how Jit would feel about wandering around the stars looking for Fryppe. Suddenly there seemed so much to do! He thought about Leearnah laid up in hospital in a coma she may never come out of. He needed her to come out of the coma so the truth could be told. Despite the fact she left him he still had strong feelings for her, and it ached him that he couldn't go and see her. He wanted to find the abuser who hurt her and see justice done for the pain he afflicted on her and free him from the situation he was in. Whilst deep in his thoughts the homing beacon alerted him that he was close to his cave shocking him that the journey had passed so quickly.

On arriving he opened the storm door via remote in the transporter and one side of the glass wall lowered as well and he drove the vehicle straight in and parked her up. On checking the time, he found he still had half an hour before Jit would turn up and if he knew his friend to be the same, he would be on time. Jit was always on time! He went to make a drink and while he sipped away at it, he packed the things he might need for the duration of his time away. He looked around the cave and started to feel a sense of foreboding at the suddenness of leaving his long time sanctuary but at the same time, he was excited at the prospect of moving on and would come back later to clear things out and say goodbye. It was almost five thirty so Arrill poured himself another drink while he waited for Jit to show up.

....

Jit was occupied checking supplies when Ladone interrupted him reminding him of his schedule. Today she was dressed in a safari suit with high black boots and atop her head sat a broad brimmed hat. Around it was a white scarf tied in a knot at the back with the rest flowing down her back loosely. He had a brief chat with her before he went to the cargo bay and boarded the shuttle then proceeded with the starting up routine and lifted off. On entering the atmosphere, he activated the homing beacon Arrill had given him and followed the compass directions. On the descent, the signal guided him to his destination amongst the sea of sand. As he was landing, he saw Arrill come out with a bag in tow and turn around to secure the storm door to his cave. Jit kept the shuttle running and watched the door seal shut and his friend walk towards him with a slight smile on his face. He looked like he had the weight the world on his shoulders. After he heard him close the exit door Jit lifted off and Arrill dropped his bag on the floor then joined him in the cockpit.

'Well are you ready for this?' he asked Jit

'As ready as I'll ever be' he answered back and with that said they set off on their quest to "Kelpuk".

The journey back to the Windchief was made in silence and when they arrived, they went up to the bridge and Jit instructed Ladone to prepare for departure. Onboard, there was enough food, water, and supplies to last him and Arrill two years before they needed to re-stock the ship. With the prospect of leaving it was noticeably visible to Jit that Arrill relaxed and was happier. How he managed throughout the whole year proved to Jit that his friend was made of tough skin. He relayed to Arrill the length of the journey they were about to undertake as they watched the stars that were stationary now drifting by lazily. Jit sat down and informed him of the activities that were available onboard.

There were a first aid room and a fully equipped gym along with a picture theatre and a games room. Those were on the third floor along with the cabins. On the second floor was a fully loaded library with many books covering all sorts of topics. The Windchief was designed for interstellar travel and if the distance was too great you could also choose to go into stasis for the duration of the journey. The stasis room was also on the second floor and contained six chambers in all. When Jit finished explaining the layout Arrill excused himself and told him he wanted to check out the ship's library. He was hoping to find something that might help further his understanding of the map.

'I'll start dinner soon and will call you when it's ready' he called out to Arrill as he watched him descend through the floor to the second level.

His friend acknowledged with a nod and then was gone. Jit spun around in the captain's chair and looked out to space and marvelled at the beauty of it. It didn't matter how many times he travelled through this immense place it was always a thrill he never tired of. All the planets of different colours and sizes with moons circling them that seemed like you could reach out and touch them, yet they were a long way away oozing in a viscous slow motion. On the dark side of some planets, he could see city lights in huge clusters sparkling like jewels. Soon they would reach the outer rim of the galaxy then they would enter the expanse of clear space. That's when you really felt small and insignificant! Out there you could see all the galaxies suspended with vast gaps in between them and motion seemed to come to a halt. Right now, the Windchief was travelling at galatial speed, and at the outer rim, she would accelerate to full velocity. Even at full speed, it would take days before one noticed any progress in the expanse of clear space. So far to date only a small percentage of the universe had been mapped and that had taken centuries to achieve. Jit left his thoughts about the universe and went to the galley to begin dinner.

....

The elevator stopped at Arrills request on the second floor and in front of him on the wall was a large map of the floor layout displayed. The location of the library was spotted right away as it was the largest room on the whole floor. He walked down the corridor until he found a door with the picture of a book embossed on it and stepped inside. On entering, the first thing that hit his senses was the overpowering smell of books. Arrill loved the smell of books and breathed it in, a hundred memories flooding his mind at the same time. The next thing that staggered him was the volume of books in the library. The entire room was floor to ceiling with books filling every space to the brim. What an awesome collection he thought! There must've been many hundreds of them. When Jit mentioned a library, he thought it would be a pokey little room with maybe a few dozen books in it, not this! As he stepped on a pressure sensitive platform, he heard a sucking sound and an overhead voice informed him the books were now ready for retrieval. They were all held in place by an energy field that stopped them from being scattered around in the event of turbulence. Again, he marvelled at the Jorpahs and their attention to detail. On some of the more primitive planets, they were considered as gods.

In the centre of the room was a table and chair which

he sat at then fired up the computer and commenced his search for topics relating to maps of any distinction. Ten books came up on the matter and he managed to stream that down to four that seemed more likely to suit his needs. He pressed confirm on the keyboard and the books protruded out of the shelves a little, making it easy to find them. With the books in his possession, he went to the soft leather sofa to sit and see what information he could glean from them. He was deeply engrossed when he was interrupted by Jit's voice announcing dinner to be ready over the intercom. He left the books on the sofa and would return to them later then made his way up to the galley.

…………………………………..

Most of the food on the Windchief was already made and all it needed was to be bought out of TSC, *Time Still Containment*. Food could now be kept indefinitely since the invention of TSC and when it was served it was as if it had just been made. It revolutionised the entire food menu for space travel throughout all the known galaxies. When dinner was about to be served up Jit summoned Arrill via the intercom then went to get the wine he uncorked earlier on and poured a glass each. While they ate Jit asked him if there was anything in the library that was helping his cause.

'Not yet' replied Arrill juggling a mouthful of lasagne in his mouth. 'I've still got more books to look through so maybe something will be revealed in their pages'.

Jit poured more wine and listened to Arrill praise the extensive library on board the Winchief. He told him that everything, excluding the cannons, was on the ship when he bought her; and it was coming up to four years since he took possession of the vessel. He then relayed that in all that time he'd not had the slightest bit of trouble. He continued telling Arrill how successful the cargo business was when he first started the work, but as more and more people entered the same line of work it became more difficult to secure loads. The big boys wanted to own the entire cargo transport operations and, because they could afford the latest and fastest ships, they were shutting the smaller operators out of the large contracts. He went on to tell Arrill he'd been considering selling the Windchief and finding a nice place to settle and retire. The money he would get for the sale of his ship would be ample enough to see him through for the rest of his life. The other option he considered was buying a smaller ship and traveling the universe exploring the unknown. Arrill agreed that those two options were better than his idea to run the suicide mission he intended on. Jit laughed at the way his friend expressed his opinion then got up and went to get dessert. They were discussing what they'd do in Kelpuk when Ladone interrupted them announcing that they were about to enter "clear space". The next thing they felt was a slight wave of distortion as Ladone moved them to full speed for the long trip through the vast void before them. While they continued their conversation, Jit went to get the last of the spirit leftover from the day before. A few hours later when all the drink was consumed Jit bid Arrill good night and retired to his cabin. The ship was on autopilot with Ladone running the show and would remain that way for the next six days as they sped towards their destination in the eighth galaxy. In his cabin, Jit sat at the desk and added to his journal. Since catching back up with Arrill, the writing had been flowing easier with the changes that now took place. When he finished, he closed the log and spun around on the chair to look around his cabin. Deep down Jit wondered if he could ever sell his ship as the bond had become too strong. He banished the thought and prepared for bed. In bed, the spirit he consumed made his body feel weightless and that was his last thought.

………………………………..

Arrill bid Jit goodnight as he watched him walk past the main control panel and look to check something before boarding the lift and vanishing from sight. He looked back out to the blackness of space and the looming galaxies that hung in their orbit with mixed thoughts crowding his mind while his eyes grew heavy with sleep and slowly shut.

…………………………….

Jit woke at what would be 9.00 am if he were still in Geelok. They would follow the same time frame until they reached their destination in the eighth galaxy. He showered and dressed then went out to the bridge to check if all was well. Everything was always okay, but he still liked to look and satisfy his doubt. On entering the bridge, he found Arrill asleep still where he was when he went to bed last night. He chuckled to himself and let him be and continued to the galley to make coffee. Back on the bridge, he poured two cups then gave Arrill a push on the shoulder to wake him. It took a second push to achieve a result and in slow motion, he became alive again. He left Arrill to his drink as he'd need some time to fully wake up and went to make a start on some breakfast. He was almost completed with the task when Arrill wandered in and asked what the drink was called they polished off last night. Jit told him it was called "Bahjinika" and was made to an age old recipe by some out of the way religious cult in a place he'd forgotten the name of. He wished he'd paid more attention as it was a fine tasting drop which left you clear headed in the morning, unlike some other beverages. All that was left now was a dark glazed pottery bottle containing only memories.

While they ate an old memory surfaced and they laughed at their youth and the lack of life experience. When breakfast was over Arrill returned to the library to take up where he left off the day before and Jit decided to go and do an hour workout in the gym. He liked to maintain a certain level of fitness just for his mind's sake. All the equipment in the gym operated using resistance and you could choose for the computer to pick a random circuit or make one up yourself. He let the computer pick a circuit this time and walked over to the bike where the routine would commence first. He preferred to do it first thing in the day where he would be well rested from sleep and refreshed. When the hour was up, he went to his cabin to shower and change into clean clothes and returned to the bridge.

Out in the velvety blackness, the galaxies were a little larger as they progressed to their destination. Jit picked up the book he was partway through and continued where he left off. The story was a little slow going but he persevered in the hope it would pick up and get better. During reading, he was startled by a brief transmission that only lasted a couple of seconds. It was a tune accompanied by words that went... *"See you later alligator,"* and then went silent again. It was a phenomenon that only happened in clear space and he heard other ship pilots talk of the same encounters happening to them. This was the first time Jit had experienced such an event. No one knew what it was or what it meant, let alone where it came from. It was suspected to be the act of pranksters, but others believed they were messages from a faraway world. He dismissed further thoughts of it and returned to his book.

....

In the library, everything was as Arrill left it the day before. He took up his position on the couch and continued where he left off in the hope of finding some answers. With one book left to look through, he stopped because he was hungry and went to do something about it. He was surprised

Jit had not called him for lunch and wondered what he was doing and where he was. His thoughts were answered when he arrived at the bridge and found his friend asleep in the big chair with a book on his lap. He left him to his slumber and made his way to the galley to check out the menu and see what he could make for lunch.

……………………………..

Jit awoke at his name being called out and to the aroma of food. He thanked Arrill for making lunch and, while he ate, he asked if he'd ever heard the mysterious transmissions that travelled throughout clear space. Arrill replied by shaking his head but told Jit he had heard other people speak of such events. Jit conveyed his brief experience earlier on and they discussed the possibilities of what it could be. When lunch was over Arrill retired to the library once more to continue his searching. Jit sat on the bridge alone with his book on his lap and pondered the things he and Arrill discussed about the mysterious transmission of which any could be right. He then picked up his book and continued from where he left off immersing himself again in the tale. It was starting to gain momentum now.

……………………………

The days passed by quickly and with each passing day, the galaxies before them grew larger and larger until Ladone announced they were about to enter the outer rim of the eighth galaxy. On entering it the Windchief slowed down to galatial speed once more. Kelpuk was less than ten hours away now and they started preparations for the trip down to the surface. Arrill found nothing of any help in the books he searched through and the feeling of doubt about the map's authenticity kept tugging at him. Everything now depended on Fryppe and the hope he could make sense of the map, if any sense to it there was, and this all pended on finding him first.

…………………………………

Kelpuk

When the ship reached Kelpuk Ladone made the calculations setting them in orbit around the planet. Compared to Geelok it was a forest covered planet with huge rivers cutting ruts through the land. Kelpuk was also four times the size of Geelok with an equal area of land and water. This was Jit's first visit and Arrills second, although it was some time ago. With the map tucked into his pocket, he followed Jit to the elevator, and they descended to the cargo hold. Arrill was feeling a sense of excitement mixed with hope as they did so. Onboard, the shuttle Jit complied to take off procedure then lowered the shield and exited the Windchief. They were both looking forward to the break from the ship's confinement and the natural air of being outside. Although the Windchief duplicated everything perfectly the main obstacle was one's thinking.

As they approached the planet and began the descent through the atmosphere, they adjusted the time to Kelpuk time. It would be 8.00 am when they touched down in "Dongardiah", the biggest city on the planet. As the landscape drew upwards toward them the city layout was revealed in an octagonal fashion spreading outward from the centre. There were large trees scattered about with branches that stretched across the streets and rivers dissecting the city into pieces. On the outer edges of the city were the landing ports with four in all. Jit made for landing at port number two with instructions coming from ground control. They landed in a bay big enough to accommodate the shuttle and cut the power. The first thing Jit noticed was the cooler temperature compared to Geelok. They both pulled on another jacket then made their way to the vehicle hire booth. The vehicle they hired ran via a means of compressed air that drove fins at the wheels for movement. It was an old means of motion, but it was effective and clean. The motor was electric which ran the compressor and with one solar panel covering the entire roof it could power the vehicle indefinitely.

Jit drove and followed the signage that pointed the way to the information building towards the centre of town. There were bridges everywhere crossing the rivers that were part of the city and connected the maze of roadwork. The trees that looked large from the shuttle were huge from ground level and Jit guessed them to be many hundreds of years old. They were mindboggling in their size and dwarfed the buildings beneath them. The road system was two layered with a oneway direction going into the city and the top layer was a oneway direction going out of the city. They soon arrived at the information building and on entering the structure they could smell the lingering sterile odour of cleaning agents as they passed through the doors. At one of the information desks, Arrill sat down in front of the monitor and began the search for Fryppe's shop name and address to confirm he was still in the same place. While he searched Jit looked around at his surroundings and the people going about their business. Some were visitors like them while others worked in the building.

After some time Arrill was relieved to find his friend was still at the same business address and he printed out the details and stood to leave. Back outside they boarded the vehicle and Arrill set the information into the onboard computer and then followed the prompts to their destination. Jit was enjoying being a passenger and took in all the sights that surrounded them and relayed to Arrill how he could settle in a place like this. The parklands they passed along the way were a spectacle of vibrant colours with flowers he had never seen before. Some were the size of dinner plates while others were only visible due to being bunched up in clusters. Children played in the parks with an odd looking ball screaming and laughing as they kicked it to one another while others played on swings that looked more like sculpture than playthings.

Jit felt a real sense of kindred to the place as if he'd been here before and with each passing minute, he felt more at home on Kelpuk. The place was beautiful! They crossed over another of the many bridges and came into a large open area where the traffic went around a giant steel structure that looked like a machine of some kind. It was not operational anymore and at one time must've played a vital part in the development of the city. There was a plaque on it, but they were going too fast for him to catch what it said. After ducking and weaving through a few more streets they entered a plaza where Fryppes shop was located. The name of his shop was *"Yes and No Antiques"* and the wording on the front awning that stretched over the footpath was faded but still readable. All the shops were arranged in a square with the car park in the center courtyard. The entry point was also the exit. The place was already buzzing with activity and people were everywhere either shopping or tending to shops. They found a spot to park and entered with little room for error then squeezed out the doors.

The plaza had a real friendly atmosphere to it and felt more like a marketplace than a plaza. As they walked over to Fryppes shop Jit looked at the other shops with goods crowding their fronts on sale and merchants piling more things on the already bulging piles. The entry into Fryppes shop was through a wall of colourful beads hanging down like a waterfall threatening to entangle the passer through. The sound of the beads brought forth the assistant who was concealed in a back room and Jit looked to Arrill to see if it was Fryppe, but his friend gave no indication that he knew the person. The shop wasn't well lit, and it was cluttered with all manner of strange looking items. It also harboured a dank and musty smell no doubt from the old wares the shop exhibited. Arrill asked the smiling person waiting to serve them if the shop was still owned by Fryppe to which came the answer yes. They were also fortunate because Fryppe was back from a long away trip and returned home last night. The relief swept over them both but more so on Arrill who seemed tense. With Fryppe's home address in their possession, they thanked the assistant and negotiated a path through the tangling beads to the scents of outside again. Back in the car Arrill entered the address into the onboard computer then navigated his way around the oneway circuit and exited onto the main road again. Most of the houses along the way were concealed behind fences of vegetation but the ones that could be seen were three story premises with white plaster walls and roofs made up entirely of solar panels. The more Jit saw the more he wanted to find out about Kelpuk as it seemed to him that he stumbled upon a little paradise of sorts. They followed the computer prompts which took them in a roundabout fashion to the motorway that spanned above the city and went outwards towards the Mountains. Fryppe lived out in the country.

As they passed the sensors in the motorway the autopilot took over and the steering wheel folded away giving the driver the same room of comfort as the passenger. The view from the height of the road was of ancient forests that stretched skyward and vegetation so thick it would seem impossible to penetrate. They progressed toward the snow capped mountains that loomed higher and higher as they closed in looking like sentinels that stood to attention awaiting their arrival. After a half hour of driving the vehicle moved over to the farthest lane on the left and took the next exit. Upon entering the exit, the computer warned the driver to prepare for control then the steering wheel unfolded from its resting place. The road curved around and under the motorway and followed along the foothills of the looming giants on a tight but smooth road.

On Jit's side, they followed a sapphire blue river that was not much wider than the road but looked deep and cold. Along some parts of the water, there were rapids and the white plumes seemed vividly white compared to the deep dark blue. The valley was breathtaking! They passed some hairy cattle grazing in some far away paddock that looked up to see what the noise was then went back to their eating obviously used to vehicles. The paddocks were vivid green with patches of little yellow flowers breaking the green and speckling the hillside. Large rocks protruded here and there being the survivors from the mountain tops with smaller ones littered amongst them. Ahead the sky was spotted with large black birds with wingspans easily the length of a shuttle circling looking for prey. Jit wondered what kind of food they would eat and memorized to look up when he was outside.

The road soon curved to the right and on a track straight ahead the surface turned to white gravel indicating Fryppes driveway. His name emblazoned on an old unused farm implement as a letterbox confirmed it. The view from the house was extraordinary! The house itself was nestled tight into the forest with only the front part protruding out enough to notice it there. It was a log style structure with a covered veranda all around and sitting up on poles. As they pulled up a figure stepped out through a screen door onto the veranda and looked down at them. Judging by the smile on Arrills face Jit gathered it to be Fryppe. He wasn't what Jit expected at all when he saw him. He was short and stocky of build with powerful looking arms the size of Jits thighs. They were covered with all kinds of markings and atop his head, he sported a cap of many colours.

'Arrill, come on up my ole friend and bring your friend with you', hollered down Fryppe.

His voice boomed as if out of a barrel. They followed the path guiding the visitor to the front door with a track veering off it to the right leading to the back of the house. At the top of the veranda, Fryppe waited and hugged Arrill like a brother. Then Jit was introduced and received the same welcome. It was like being hugged by a bear. When they entered the house Fryppe introduced them to "Tortille" his wife. She was a tall thin woman that seemed to glide along as she moved. They were led to a seating area at the back of the house with the forest encroaching within a short distance of the glass wall. Jit sat down and watched through the window at small birds flitting around in the trees chasing bugs and making a feast of it.

In the midst of conversation, Tortille returned carrying a tray laden with coffee and Kelpuk delicacies that looked tempting. She placed the tray before them then disappeared into another room. Jit watched her fluid movements as if she was underwater and was almost hypnotised by them. The conversation for the first hour or so was more about pleasantries and catching up on all the events since Fryppe and Arrill last saw each other. Every so often Jit looked around the house and took in the surroundings while they talked. The inside of the house was very much like the shop with many objects to look upon and contemplate their function. When the coffee and cake were gone Fryppe went to a cabinet and pulled out a bottle and some small shot glasses then returned to his seat. While he poured them a serve, he went on to tell them the drink was a handed down recipe made by Kelpukian women for their husbands. As soon as a daughter marries the mother passes the recipe on in a longtime tradition. The drink was called "Junglemind." The men to this day still don't know the closely guarded secret of how it's made. He poured them another and then Arrill pulled out the map and placed it before Fryppe. While Jit sipped at his drink, he watched the change come over Fryppe when it registered what was in front of him. He picked it up and looked at Arrill and said,

'Is this real?'

'I don't know, replied Arrill, that's why we've come to see you'.

He turned it over in his hands feeling it as if in some way it authenticated it then placed it on the table again. Arrill went on to tell Fryppe how he came into possession of the map and how much he so far managed to decipher. Fryppe looked over and told him the map looked genuine enough but deciphering what was on it may take a while. He told them they were welcome to stay as his guests until he does. The conversation drifted to Jit's life and during the event, Tortille appeared with another tray loaded with filled rolls. Jit found it hard to not stare at her fluid motions as she placed the tray before them and floated away again. She was all bone to look at with a sharp face that was very attractive and thick black hair that flowed right down to her waist. She wore a brightly coloured dress that went right down to the ground making her look stretched out and her feet were bare and calloused from constant exposure. Fryppe talked about some of the things they used to get up to in their youth and from what Jit could piece together these guys knew each other since school days. When they finished eating Fryppe asked them to follow him then picked up the map and led them to his workplace.

They climbed a set of wooden steps that spiralled around until they reached the top floor of the house. Upon entering the room, they were met by the smell of paint and wood shavings mingled with other scents that were less potent. There was clutter everywhere on workbenches scattered around the room giving the impression of a productive area in progress. Fryppe cleared some space on one of the benches and spread the map out for further study. He remained silent while Jit and Arrill looked on then walked over to a desk and pulled a draw open rummaging through it looking for something. Not finding what he was seeking he shuffled to another bench and cleared things away on top of it unveiling the jewellers monocular he was searching for. While Fryppe and Arrill hunched over the map muttering incomprehensible things, Jit wandered around the workshop looking at the part finished projects on the benches.

The room itself was octagonal with small windows high at the top allowing the light to come in from all angles. The benches were situated all around the outer perimeter with the staircase coming up in the centre of the room. Tools were hanging from the walls and others resting on benches the like of which he had never seen before. Some of the works scattered about were still awaiting the masters finishing touch. As to what they were only Fryppe would know. On one bench sat a clock type device that was a mass of cogs and springs with its purpose firmly locked in Fryppes mind. At another bench, he stopped to look at a female form draped in some soft material made of pale yellow fabric standing half his height. She was beautiful as she stood in a twisted spiral with her arms stretched upwards to a point and her head bowed low. She must've been a completed work he thought to himself as he could see nothing wrong with it. She would make a fine addition in the Windchief he thought and wondered if she was for sale. He was taken aback at how beautiful and lifelike she was.

While he was contemplating where he would put her in the ship, he rejoined the others and according to Fryppe, Arrill was right in some of his decipherings except for the planet he called "Spee" which was called "Spollee." To Fryppes knowledge there was no such planet which meant they could've been looking forever for a planet that didn't exist. Afterward, Jit left Fryppe and Arrill to their work and decided to go outside for a look around. Fryppe warned him about going into the forest and told him to take a firearm in the event he should do so and relayed to him where to find one. Back down the spiralling wood staircase he soon found the cabinet and looked at the array of weapons displayed before him. On opening it he inspected some of them with no inkling at how they functioned. Absorbed in his intrigue he was distracted by movement at the corner of his eye and looked to see Tortille watching him from the shadow of another room. He smiled at her and was about to explain when she looked away and disappeared deeper into the shadows. There was something about her that was creepy he thought to himself and dismissed the event going back to what he was doing. He found a sidearm that was similar to the one he owned and loaded it then slipped it into his pocket and walked outside onto the veranda. He could still feel Tortilles eyes on him no doubt observing his every move.

The veranda had a small table on it surrounded by three chairs and along the wall leading up to the table was stacked an assortment of what looked like junk to Jit. Some of it was covered in a canvas sheet while some lay uncovered with thick dust and cobwebs gathered all over it. He walked down the stairs onto the lawn area and stood there for a moment deciding which direction to take. There was a cool breeze blowing that seemed to gather momentum as the day drew to an end. He chose to walk along the forest edge and on the way, he saw gaps cut into it indicating pathways made by whatever creatures lived in the entanglement. Everything grew vigorously and the leaves on the plants looked as if someone had polished them one at a time such was their gloss. There was an earthy smell permeating from deep within the forest and he could hear movement in there but couldn't see what it was. Then he was startled by the cry of a bird, or at least that's what he took it to be. Further cuts into the forest up ahead had prints left in them from creatures that dwelt yonder leaving Jit to wonder what manner of things lived in the wilderness before him and the warning words of Fryppe echoed back to him.

The sun was beginning to set behind the Mountains with a slowly stretching shadow that covered the house and aimed for the river. Jit remembered the large birds he saw when they first arrived and looked up to see what the sky held but it was clear of all obstacles with the colour of nightfall seeping into it. He decided to go down to the river and on passing the vehicle he stopped to get his jacket. His feet crunched loudly as he traversed the gravel driveway and when he was almost at the letterbox, he could hear a vehicle coming from further up the mountain road. It passed by and disappeared around the bend and the silence took over again. Down by the waters edge the reflection from the sunlight danced on the water with the final rhythm of nightfall approaching. A few cattle in the distance looked at him for a moment then went back to their ceaseless eating and fertilizing. The water was crystal clear and the view to the bottom was crisscrossed with all manner of fish ranging from small to large. Suddenly the breeze blew stronger and he decided it was a good time to head back to the house. The lengthening shadow had caught up to him and was speeding towards the paddocks on the other side with each passing minute. As he returned, he noticed the weather was changing as well, and looking like a storm might be brewing up.

When he entered the house, he returned the weapon he took and then climbed the stairs back to the top to see what progress Fryppe and Arrill had made. As he approached, they looked up briefly and asked him to join them. Fryppe showed him a part of the map and explained the importance of the discovery revealing a clue that was vital to continue deciphering it. Jit nodded but only in politeness as he had no idea what he was talking about. Arrill was looking like the winner of some grand prize as each new revelation bought them closer to what the map concealed. He had waited a long time for this moment. Jit watched them muttering to each other while he listened to the wind outside gathering momentum. Through the top windows, he could see the forest leaning heavily giving away the wind's direction while dark ominous clouds briskly gathered with the fading light. They all jumped when a rogue branch darting through the air like a missile and impacted on the side of the house rattling the windows. Fryppe left his position hovering over the map for a moment and went to switch on the lights and lowered shutters over the windows.

'The storms can get quite wild up here he went on to say' and returned to the map.

Then the rain came shooting like nails into the side of the house and melting on impact with the solid walls. The noise from the wind and rain consumed the entire workshop with only one's thoughts shouting louder in contest. Fryppe suddenly stood erect as if to reveal an important discovery but instead announced it was time for dinner. Retiring downstairs, they entered the dining room to find the table laden with a variety of hot and cold food and the aroma of fresh baked bread too. It was also quieter in this part of the house from the raging storm outside. Tortille didn't join them for dinner and while they ate Fryppe talked about some of the places he frequented to buy stock for his shop. It seemed to Jit that Fryppe had ventured to many faraway places in search of unusual items. He went on to say that not all the items in the shop were antiques and that some merely presented themselves as such hence the name of his shop is "Yes and No Antiques". The storm's intensity increased shifting the conversation to the weather for a period. However, the talk soon went back to the map and what Fryppe was beginning to piece together seemed to be leading to some sort of power source. He wasn't yet certain of what it was or could be used for, but he was certain it was ancient technology of some kind.

'It's possibly an ancient race of beings that live on Spollee or used to live there' he said.

Mostly it puzzled him how the map ended up on Geelok and in the possession of the previous owner. He knew very little about Spollee and had never been there although he had been to the Magnamere Galaxy searching for goods. Magnamere was the old name for what is now called the twelfth Galaxy. When dinner was over, he and Arrill went back to the workshop while Jit stayed and decided to see what was on the television. All this map stuff was out of his league and best left to the experts he thought. After figuring out the remote control functions he commenced flicking through the channels to see what they viewed as entertainment on Kelpuk.

Despite all the channels available, he found nothing that captured him which seemed to be the usual occurrence. He got up and ventured over to Fryppes movie collection to see what might be worth viewing there but that was in vain too. He looked around and saw a bookcase against one of the walls and went to see what was in there of interest. Most of the books referred to antiques and other information about the craftsmen who made the goods and when they were made, all of which was a valuable wealth of knowledge for Fryppe but held no interest whatsoever for Jit. He looked up at the old clock on the wall that suddenly caught his attention then wondered what became of Tortille as he hadn't seen her in a while. She didn't join them for dinner, and he wondered if she was avoiding them. Maybe it's got something to do with Arrill he considered. He banished the thought and looked at the clock again with it reading the time as 9.00 pm and made his way to the top room to see how the boys were coming along with the map. As he walked past the table, he noticed for the first time that it had been cleared but never saw Tortille do it.

In the workshop, the noise of the storm continued to dominate the room and Jit found Fryppe and Arrill hovering over the map with their lips moving but their voices drowned out. Joining them he waited for a progress report. So far things were the same with Fryppe admitting difficulty in the map's interpretation. It was like nothing he'd seen before and even what he thought was right might not be. They decided after a little while longer to call it a night and go back to it in the morning with a fresh mind. Fryppe showed Arrill and Jit to their rooms and bid them goodnight then shuffled up the hallway and rounded a bend disappearing. Jit and Arrills rooms were opposite each other and Jit said goodnight and decided to retire to bed too. He sat on the bed in his room and looked around at his surroundings. Here and there on the walls were little paintings hanging with words of comfort or encouragement written upon them. The bed was a single bed with a set of drawers beside it and when Jit lay down, he found the bed surprisingly comfortable. He undressed and slipped in between the cool sheets meanwhile outside the storm was still tearing the place apart with not a break since it started.

....

Arrill looked around his room and sat on the edge of the bed thinking about the map and what further secrets lay hidden in its symbols. Even Fryppe was having trouble with it which in a way made him feel better. It seems the old guy he got the map from was right about it being genuine and he wondered if he attempted trying to unravel its mysteries too. Surely he would've tried and, if he did, what could've happened that made him give it up? He undressed and got into bed still contemplating other techniques that might work when he was overcome by sleep and drifted off. The storm outside raged on reminding him of his cave which he found familiar and comforting.

....

Jit woke startled from sounds outside his room and then remembered where he was and relaxed. It was quiet in the room which meant the storm had passed. He slept so peacefully throughout the night and heard none of the storms at all. The Junglemind drink probably played a part in that. It wasn't like your usual drink and the effect was unnoticeable until you sat down to relax. Once he was dressed, he picked up the towel at the end of the bed and went to wash his face. Arrill must've already been up as he could hear Fryppe and him talking in the kitchen. When he washed and freshened up, he ventured down to join them.

'Good day to you all' he said to them.

Fryppe passed him the coffee pot and he poured himself a cup whilst listening to what they were talking about. Fryppe continued to say that any more progress to be made would have to be done at his shop where he had some more books that may help. He also told Arrill not to get his hopes up as the language and symbols on the map went back a very long time. Getting a foothold in any period was the biggest problem as, so far, he hadn't been able to find anything even remotely close to what was written on the map. They all agreed on one thing at least, the map was no doubt genuine. A wall clock chimed 8.00 am announcing the time of day while they ate some breakfast. Jit looked at his watch to see if the times were in sync.

When breakfast was completed, they helped clean up

then all went back up to the workshop. Upon entering Fryppe went to the switch that raised the shutters setting them in motion and allowing light to come streaming into the room exposing dust particles floating in the air. He picked up the map which lay where it was left the previous night and passed it back to Arrill.

'You might as well hold onto that while we're in transit' he said and led them back down the stairs.

Downstairs Fryppe went to a few different draws about the house looking for something then on finding it announced,

'Let's go!'

They agreed the previous night to go back to town in the hire vehicle and Fryppe could drive so Arrill could have a look around. It was harbouring on 9.00 am when they exited onto the veranda and were met by a slight cool breeze. The sun shone warmly making the breeze tolerable. At the vehicle, the shady side of it was still thick with unmelted frost and Fryppe went to get the hose and wash it off. Jit looked around and despite such a wild storm last night there was no debris around at all. It was warm in the vehicle when they opened it up and Jit sat in the back while Fryppe and Arrill took the front. They were soon crunching gravel with the journey to Dongardiah in motion. Jit said little in the back and mostly looked out the window and listened to the others talk. The mountains looked entirely different from the beginning of the day and the full light on them seemed to stretch them even higher towards the sky. They were truly majestic! Shadows leaned a different way painting the landscape all new to him and it was like seeing it for the first time again.

In what seemed like moments they were circling

around and back onto the motorway where the vehicle computer took over and Fryppe and Arrill spun their seats around to face Jit. While they drove along Fryppe played the tourist guide pointing out things and telling little stories about them. Jit found him to be a genuine person and liked him already. The offramp for Fryppes part of town soon came up and when he took over from the autopilot, he continued at speed with the ease of a person who'd done the run many times. When they arrived at the plaza, they entered a different way which was an underground arrangement with parking for shop owners plus the unloading of goods. They parked at a spot marked Y/NA and exited the vehicle with only a little space to squeeze out the door. The entire underground area smelled of vegetables that were being unloaded off a truck at the dock end. They walked to a door with an exit sign on it and going through it they climbed up a few flights of steps and appeared in a tight laneway behind the shops. Even on this side that is mostly hidden from the public, the buildings were tidy and the street was clean. A black and white cat sat on one of the walls in the sunshine looking down at them with eyes only half open having been disturbed from its slumber.

Fryppe dug out of his pocket the keys and opened the door. He went to a keypad and entered a code then a beep announced the place was all clear. As he led them to the small kitchenette, he flipped light switches along the way bringing daylight to the shop. Jit noticing the musty dank smell even stronger with the premises closed overnight. In a short time, Fryppe had the aroma of freshly made coffee to drown out the other odours. They took a seat at a small table and Fryppe left saying he'd be back and vanished into the shadows to switch on the rest of the lights and open the front door for trading. Arrill pulled the map out from inside his jacket and placed it on the table in front of him and stared at it quietly then looked up at Jit and said,

'Do you think the guy I got this from already tried to solve the map and turned up with nothing?'

Jit looked at his friend and wondered what to say as the question seemed more like a request to hear a positive comment,

'I really don't know Arrill and neither do you, so we'll just have to wait and see what destiny unravels' he replied.

They were about to discuss it further when Fryppe appeared back. He dropped a few old large books on the table making the table creak then picked up his cup and took a large gulp of coffee. The books numbered three in all and even from where Jit sat, he could smell their old age. They're probably worth a small fortune he thought to himself. Fryppe took a seat and passed them a book each and the idea was to flick through the pages looking to see if any of the symbols or language on the map were contained on their pages. The books were thick and it was going to take some time to achieve the task even with all three of them working at it. During the process, Fryppe had to occasionally go out to serve customers entering the shop for a look at what was on sale. The time quickly sped towards lunchtime and Jit was looking forward to a break from the work. He volunteered to buy lunch and walked through the shop out into the bright sunshine and bustling crowds of shoppers. It felt good to be outside. The place was a buzz of activity.

Fryppe recommended a deli/sandwich shop he frequented which Jit soon spotted. The shop was busy with people getting their lunches or picking up orders and only three people to tend to it all. Finally, he was served and ordered sandwiches to go. Back at Fryppes shop they made small talk and then had cake to finish off a satisfying lunch.

They had just cleaned up when the same assistant that Arrill and Jit spoke to the day before arrived to start work. Fryppe had arranged to do half a day and introduced him to them. His name was "Retkaz" and was born on Kelpuk and had always lived in Dongardiah he informed them after the introduction. Both Jit and Arrill told him a little about themselves then he wandered out to the shop to serve a customer who just entered through the noisy beads. Fryppe marked where they were up to in the books and bundled them atop each other and indicated for them to go.

'We'll go back home to do the rest of the searching' he suggested and with that said they left Retkaz to close up and went back to the underground car park.

It was warmer outside at this hour Jit noticed and peeled off his jacket carrying it over his left arm. The car park still had a lingering vegetable smell in the air as they traversed the expanse back to the vehicle. They were soon out onto the busy streets where Fryppe took them around a different way to show them parts of the city they hadn't seen yet. They soon discovered that not only bridges connected the rivers, but also underwater tunnels made of a glass looking material. One they entered was an elongated circle with a dual carriageway on both sides for two lanes of traffic with glass support beams in the centre. Jit looked up and through the glass and could see the distorted shapes of the buildings wobble and the sun bouncing around trying to find a spot to settle. With the vehicles being electric there was no pollution therefore no need for vents. The glass tube was supported by steel columns fixed to the riverbed not that far below them. Curious water creatures swam around but stayed well back being uncertain what to make of the glass serpent.

They exited into another part of Dongardiah that was made up of older style buildings but to look at seemed new.

The only way one knew they were older was because of their style and flair which was typical of the period and the obvious clash compared to the new structures. Despite the clash, everything was weaved into a harmonious rhythm by plants of different species and colour making the landscape and buildings flow together. The sense Jit felt was one of wellbeing and euphoria furthering his interest in Kelpuk. They soon stopped out the front of an old and regal looking building which Fryppe announced as the Museum. He disclosed he had a friend working there who had been studying odd languages all his life and he might be able to shed some light on their search. They took the walkway to the entrance and along the sides were planted rows of needle like trees that pointed skyward. The inside of the building was huge with glass cabinets everywhere containing all manner of relics from another time or place. The ceiling was high with other objects hanging from it to ponder at. Other things stood on display on the floor and some things you could interact with. Fryppe left them and went looking for his friend while Arrill and Jit passed the time at the cabinets and learned more about the city history.

On entering another room Jit noticed a drink vending machine and asked Arrill if he wanted something. He declined so he went to see what was on offer. When he approached the machine, he was astounded that the drinks were free! When he returned to where Arrill was he noticed a stunning looking woman standing alone near a glass cabinet smiling at him as if she knew him. He looked around to be certain it was him she was looking at then looked back at her and smiled in return. Their looks stayed connected until a dividing wall peeled them apart.

'I wonder who she was' he whispered to himself.

Arrill was behind a group of people trying to see what

the cabinet before them held but to no avail when Jit stepped up announcing his return. They found a bench seat along a wall out of the way where they took a seat to wait for Fryppe. Jit wondered how long he might be and was about to say something to Arrill when he spoke up.

'I wonder how long Fryppes' going to be?' he said to Jit.

'I was just thinking that' Jit replied with a shrug of his shoulders.

They only had to wait another few minutes before the burly figure of their friend came into view and they stood so he could spot them. He came over with a big smile on his face and told them his friend agreed to come over tonight with some papers which could prove to be helpful. He then led them out the entrance and they headed home.

They entered onto the motorway once again after negating the traffic and as the autopilot took them home Fryppe told them about his association with his friend from the Museum. He used to own an antique store some years back and they both met by competing for an item at an antique auction which Fryppe finally won the bid for. Looking outside Jit noticed ominous clouds gathering and wondered if another storm was on its way and how often the storms happen on Kelpuk. It was mid afternoon by the time they rolled off the motorway and Fryppe took the controls again. A short time later they were driving up the gravel driveway announcing their arrival to Tortille. When they stopped at the top, she was in the garden working in a pair of trousers and loose top with gloves on her hands pulling out plants and replacing them with others. Fryppe went up to hug her and give her a peck on the cheek while Jit and Arrill just smiled and said hello. He told Tortille they were having an extra guest tonight for dinner then rearranged the books he was holding and led Jit and Arrill into the house to continue searching the volumes. They chose to sit in the lounge room where it was more comfortable and while Jit and Arrill made a start back where they left off, Fryppe went to get snacks. All three of them worked at looking and comparing symbols and languages all afternoon and some symbols from the books came close but weren't identical enough to be a match. As for the language, it remained a mystery unto itself. After a period, Jit announced he was going out for a smoke and to have a break. All that looking at symbols and languages was straining his eyes.

Out on the veranda the sun had hidden behind the clouds and while he smoked, he thought more about what Arrill had said earlier on. Did the previous owner of the map try to find the map secret and if so, what did he conclude and how long did he work at it? You couldn't help but wonder. He hoped it wasn't just some madman's idea of a joke and everything on the map was a creation from an overactive mind. It wasn't a pleasant thought, but it was also quite possible! He dared not say what he thought to Arrill waiting instead at what time would unravel. He cleared his mind of it and finished his smoke then went back inside to continue searching. It was late in the afternoon when they had all finished looking and nothing was found in any of the three books about the secrets of the map. So far everything came to a dead end and with each failure, Jit could see the toll it was taking on Arrill. Around 6.30 pm they heard the sound of tyres crunching up the driveway and it seemed Fryppe's friend had arrived and hopefully he could shed some light on this mystery.

Fryppe got up to welcome his guest while Arrill and Jit sat in silence waiting. They could hear the two talking outside before they came back inside and entered the lounge.

'Arrill and Jit I'd like you to meet, "Tarmacuz"', said Fryppe.

They stood and shook hands with the man then took their seats again and listened to him and Fryppe talk a little before Fryppe passed him the map to inspect. Jit noticed him be a tall thin man wearing a smart business suit that looked like he'd just put it on. His manner was professional, and he spoke with an accent that he couldn't quite place. Tarmacuz studied the map for a few minutes then set it aside and opened the briefcase he carried in with him. He pulled out a pile of papers placing them before him and set the case back on the floor then started going through the papers. He worked as if he was alone muttering to himself under his breath and then laid a sheet on the table. He didn't have to say anything as they noticed symbols that matched the map on it, the images of which were firmly implanted in Jit's head after hours of searching and looking. There was silence for a moment as the realisation sunk into all heads then Tarmacuz said,

'The language I'm not familiar with, but the symbols are similar to the maps symbols.'

He went onto tell them that he would need some time to unravel the maps meaning as the language was complicated and extremely old. Before he could say another word Tortille appeared in the doorway for a moment and looked at Fryppe then walked away. Fryppe stood announcing dinner was ready and they should eat and continue work later. The table was laid in a smorgasbord fashion with all kinds of meats and vegetables served in plates of their own. It smelt great and Jit suddenly realised how hungry he was. They took a seat and began eating and talking and Jit wondered why Tortille didn't join them. He hadn't spoken a word to her since they arrived. The conversation shifted back to the map and Arrill told

Tarmacuz how he acquired it and how long it's been taunting him. Tarmacuz went onto say that however he came upon it it was a stroke of fate and could unlock something of extreme importance. Exactly what he wasn't sure of yet, but with his years of experience in these matters, they should be able to piece together enough to point a direction. They made small talk for a while with Arrill and Jit telling Tarmacuz a little about themselves and the kind of work they were in. Dinner lasted a good hour before they shifted from the table and went up to Fryppes workshop. Fryppe told them to go ahead and he'd be up soon with hot drinks. Arrill placed the map on a cleared bench and Tarmacuz soon hovered over it like a vulture at a meal. He pulled out a monocular and studied the symbols closer with the occasional word to himself confirming his thoughts. It was as if he were alone in the room.

When Fryppe returned they worked at the map late into the evening before Tarmacuz concluded a theory. It seemed they would have to travel to Spollee and find the location of where the map originated from to possibly get some better understanding of the languages written upon it. The symbols were a language too but with the little he had, it wasn't enough to conclude anything solid. What they had was a map with two languages on it and one language also being part directions possibly. With that said he told them he must leave and would enquire around the Museum tomorrow from some of his colleagues for any helpful information on Spollee. He apologised that he couldn't be of more help. Jit and Arrill shook his hand and thanked him then Fryppe walked out with him and they could be heard talking on the veranda before Tarmacuz finally left. When Fryppe returned he told them Tarmacuz would inform him immediately of any news about the map and he would relay the message to them straight away. It was late by this hour and Jit bid them goodnight and went to his room to retire. He lay on the bed thinking about the trip to Spollee wondering how long it would take to arrive and what they would find there. A nagging thought crossed his mind before he drifted off to sleep, had this journey taken place before, and if so, what was the outcome?

....

In his room, Arrill grabbed his towel and went to the bathroom for a quick face wash and to brush his teeth. Everything he'd done and heard through the day whirled around in his head and he wondered if he'd get any sleep at all. Back in his room, he hung the towel on the rail then lay down on the bed still clothed with only his boots removed. He hadn't been to Spollee before and wondered if Jit had and then he wondered what the place was like. He could soon feel the drowsiness of the day overcome him followed by the fall into a deep sleep.

....

The next day around 7.00 am, Jit woke and decided to get up and have a shower. Outside his room, the house was quiet with everyone still asleep. The shower did wonders and fully woke him with coffee the next concern on his mind. With cup in hand, he went to sit out on the veranda and have it while looking over the splendid valley before him. He could feel the crisp cold air working through his clothing as he sat in silence. By the time he finished his cuppa he heard walking in the house and went to see who was up. Fryppe was in the kitchen pouring two cuppas which he put onto a tray. They exchanged greetings then Fryppe excused himself and went back to his room. Jit concluded he wasn't working today and Retkaz must've been opening the shop. He poured another drink and went back onto the veranda to have a smoke and think about what they were going to do. It seemed they would be going to Spollee and there was no reason they couldn't get going today he concluded to himself. He decided to wait for Arrill to get up and discuss the idea with him.

It was 8.30 am when Arrill appeared from his room and Jit gave him time to have his cuppa and come alive before he started the discussion.

'We might as well start making our way to Spollee' he said to him.

Arrill looked up from his cup with that faraway look for a moment then slowly nodded his head in agreement.

'Have you been there?' he went on to ask him.

He shook his head and asked Jit the same question to which Jit said no. They were discussing the journey when Fryppe appeared with Tortille behind him and they sat on the lounge to hear what they had planned.

'We've decided to start the trip to Spollee,' Arrill told them, 'and we are going to leave shortly.'

Fryppe was going to tell them they could stay until Tarmacuz made contact, but he could see Arrill was restless and just nodded in agreement. Instead, he told them that as soon as he heard from him, he would let them know via the "link". Anyone anywhere in the known galaxies could be contacted via the link. By 9.30 Arrill and Jit thanked their friends for the warm welcome with Jit telling them they were great hosts then walked down the stairs to the vehicle parked on the lawn awaiting them.

'Did you remember to get the map?' Jit asked Arrill to which he patted his jacket pocket in response.

From the veranda, Fryppe hollered, 'Good luck my friends, and safe journey!'

They gave a final wave to Fryppe and Tortille then made their way back to the Port where their shuttle awaited their return. Arrill took the wheel again and along the way, they talked about what a nice place Dongardiah was and hoped to come back again soon. Jit found the place very appealing telling Arrill he could easily settle here. He then went on to tell Arrill he thought Fryppe was a good person and considered him a close friend already. Arrill agreed, saying he had that effect on people. Before too long they entered the spaceport and went to return the vehicle then they took the conveyer back to where the shuttle was parked. With Jit back at the controls, he went through the starting procedure and headed out into space. He was missing Ladone and his ship and looked forward to getting back.

Every Windchief came with a personality placed in a hologram that was unique to that ship only. No two were alike and he was happy with what he had. Behind them, Dongardiah shrank away like the setting sun and they were soon in the confines of space with the Windchief in view. Jit banked around on approach and entered the cargo bay and sat the shuttle in its usual position. With the light indicating it was safe to exit they emerged from the shuttle and went to the elevator and ascended to the bridge. The familiar smell of the ship was a welcome embrace for Jit knowing he was home again. As soon as they emerged on the bridge Ladone appeared to greet them. Today she wore a shoulder to floor length light blue dress with a split up the left leg to her upper thigh. On her feet, she was shod with shiny black steep stilettos with a heel that came down to a needle like point. Possible for her to wear as she weighed nothing! She looked stunning like she always did, and Jit was delighted to see her.

'You've been away a couple of days' she said, 'was your mission a success?'

He relayed the events telling her they had to go to Spollee so she started preparing the ship for the journey. It looked like they were going to be cooped up in the ship for another week according to Ladones calculation.

Spollee was in the twelfth galaxy where only a few planets were colonised in the entire galaxy. The Windchief started moving with the stars flowing past giving away motion as they prepared to enter deep space yet again. They sat at the bridge watching the last spirals of the eighth galaxy drift by like misty clouds in silence each lost in their thoughts. Before long they felt the shift to full velocity and the entry into the velvety blackness of clear space. Ladone appeared and asked him what he hoped to achieve on Spollee when they arrived to which he told her they were awaiting a message from Kelpuk that might give them a starting point.

'If the map comes from Spollee there must be some connection to a clue or person who can help find a clue' replied Ladone.

Jit agreed and liked the positive attitude as he was finding doubt kept trying to loom over the situation. When he finished talking, he decided to go to the gym for a stretch workout and maybe some light weights seeing though he hadn't done anything the last couple of days. He found his body craved the workout if he didn't stick to it regularly. They were partway through the second day of their journey when they received a reply via the Link from Fryppe. They were to go to the city of "Galasol" on Spollee and look for a professor Pepplplant who may be of assistance in their quest. According to Fryppe's message, Pepplplant was the friend of an associate whom Tarmacuz worked with when he was in the antique trade. Arrill sent a return message with their thanks and told him they'd keep in touch with the outcome.

He felt a sense of renewal from the news which perked both back up to continue the chase. Jit sat in the big chair on the bridge looking out at the endless blackness from time to time while he persisted with the book he was reading. He was a third of the way through it and getting better with the turning of each page. Arrill joined him and positioned himself in one of the seats before him and stared out at the blackness. Jit put the book down waiting for Arrill to say something.

'At least we have a place to start when we get to Spollee' he said.

Jit agreed it helped the confidence level some.

'If this map does lead to something what are your thoughts on what it might be?' he asked Jit.

'It's all a guess whatever any of us thinks but I'm hoping for a treasure of some kind that will make us wealthy' replied Jit.

'What about yourself?' he asked Arrill.

'Treasure too!' he said back.

He then went on to tell Jit that he wanted to clear his name back on Geelok and then go see Leearnah and help her in whatever way he could. Jit listened and could detect that Arrill still had feelings for Leearnah even after she left him for someone else. He realised that their breakup must've taken its toll on him and not enough time had passed to heal the wound. He reminisced on the thoughts of a broken heart and how it affected a person. It had been a long time now since he had the same experience and although the wound was well healed over, the memory was as fresh as the day it happened. It seems that when sad things happen, they are never forgotten! In the quiet Jit thought about the mysterious message he heard the last time he was in clear space and wondered if it would happen again. When they finished Arrill told him he was going to his cabin to lie down and nap for a while. Once he left Jit continued to read until he nodded off himself.

He dreamt he was running through a forest with something in pursuit but couldn't see what pursued him. Branches slapped at his face and arms as he barged through them and vines tangled his progress making him stumble often, then the ground gave way, opening up a hole before him which he fell into and was swallowed up. He woke up with a start his breathing heavy and looked around at his familiar surroundings then relaxed. The book had fallen from his lap and lay on the floor in front of him which he got up to retrieve and sat on the edge of the seat recovering from the experience. He sat there a while pondering what the dream meant. Arrill still hadn't surfaced yet and he wondered if he was dreaming strange occurrences too. He looked at the time and it was after 5.00 pm according to Kelpuk time and he thought about what to have for dinner. He went to shower then returned to the galley to set dinner in motion. And motion is what all meals are because the food rested already made in containers needing only to be bought out of TSC and served up. The food was kept in a large chilled pantry which when selected travelled upon a conveyer belt to the oven and heated the meal to eating temperature. There were also ingredients kept in TSC if one desired to cook a meal from scratch which is what Jit did sometimes. When the meal was close to serving, he summoned Arrill via intercom. Arrill strolled into the galley five minutes later looking like he just woke up.

'Sleep well?' asked Jit.

'I did,' replied Arrill, 'and I couldn't believe how long I slept' he added.

'I had a lot of dreams of which I can remember none'.

Jit went on to tell him about his dream and how vivid it was too. When dinner was over, they cleaned up and decided to catch a movie in the theatre room. The theatre room had seating for two dozen people with large comfortable chairs for long viewings and plenty of room to stretch out. There was a small kitchenette in the room so cold or hot drinks could be served, and it was also stocked with treats for movie watching. The Jorpahs spared no expense and covered every possible angle for a pleasant and comfortable experience. The screen was the regular size one would view at a movie theatre with surround sound that put you in the picture. They watched a movie lasting three hours and it was the story of a guy caught in the struggle between what society expected and what he wanted. It was one of Jit's favourite movies because it was very much about reality. Too often we do what pleases others at the expense of our happiness and freedom he thought to himself. It was late when the movie was over and Jit bid Arrill good night and went to his cabin. He was soon laid in bed with his arms folded behind his head looking at the ceiling thinking about Spollee and the map and other thoughts that flitted through his mind until he felt the pull of sleep drag him under and shut out the world.

....

Arrill sat in the theatre alone enjoying the quiet solitude a theatre can induce with only his thoughts to keep him company. The blank white screen stared back at him awaiting the next movie. He sat there for a time then got up and went to get a cold drink which he took to his room. With the long sleep he had earlier on he was now not tired and sat up looking at the map yet again. He turned it this way and that thinking it might reveal something they all missed but nothing came, and he put in on the cabinet next to his bed, kicked off his boots, and laid down. He thought about this professor Pepplplant and wondered what kind of a person he was and how much help he would be then he wondered how many more planets they might have to travel to on this quest. Arrill wasn't sure how Jit was taking all this but so far, he hadn't said anything and just went along with the outcome. He thought about how fortunate he was to have a friend like Jit and really hoped all this searching would pay off in a big way.

....

On the bridge, nothing stirred as all were asleep then in the stillness a crackle on the radio woke the silence with, *'beach, far away in time'* and all was silent again. The twelfth galaxy slowly crept towards the Windchief as she made her way through the viscous thick blackness all alone.

....

It was 9.00 am before Jit rose to start his day. He dressed leaving a shower until later and went to see what Arrill was up to assuming he'd be up by now. He found him on the bridge and talkative indicating he'd been awake some time.

'Sleep in did we?' he asked Jit.

He nodded and continued to the galley.

'I'll have one too if your making coffee' shouted Arrill after him.

Back on the bridge he passed a cup to Arrill and took a seat while the fuzziness of sleep cleared away.

'I already had breakfast' Arrill told him, 'so don't wait for me to eat if you are hungry.'

'I'm not just yet he replied, but I will have another cuppa.'

'What about you?'

Arrill held up his cup indicating a yes without saying anything. When they finished Jit told Arrill he was going for a workout then ventured down to the third floor. After an hour of intense training, he went to his cabin to shower then put on some clean clothes and went back to the bridge. Arrill was in the same position talking with Ladone when he returned. She was kitted out in a long tight white dress that hugged her frame to her waist then flowed outwards to the ground covering her feet. She wore a sparkling necklace that graced her delicate neck and shoulders, and on her hands, she wore white gloves. Her hair was up in a bun. In one word; stunning!

'Hi Ladone' he said when he entered.

She looked and smiled at him still talking and answering a question Arrill had asked. He took a seat next to Arrill and listened in to what they were talking about. When she finished, she winked out like she does leaving them in silence again.

'She's quite a piece of work isn't she' commented Arrill, to which Jit nodded telling him he was quite fond of her.

The time soon reached midday and by then Jit was hungry having skipped breakfast and went to sort something out to eat. Arrill offered to help but he declined and told him to relax. In the galley, he decided to cook something himself and retained from TSC the things he needed and set to work. He found it therapeutic putting food together to create a meal and today he made a dish he taught himself. It took a few attempts at getting it right over the years, but he now had it perfected and Arrill could be a test subject to confirm it. He'd not shared this dish with anyone yet fearing criticism. When it was ready, he served it with fresh bread at the dining table then hollered out to Arrill. He soon came wandering in saying it smelt good and that he was hungry too. His friend confirmed the food was good by clearing his plate in little time. When they cleaned up the mess Jit suggested a bit of time in the games room.

The games room had machines around the outer edges, against the walls, and in the middle was a pool table that could also double for other functions.

'Pool then' said Jit to which Arrill nodded in agreement.

They were closely matched but sometimes Arrill was in better form and just beat him. Ladone appeared and took a seat at a stool and watched them making the competition more intense. They played a couple of games with Arrill being one up on Jit then they went onto the other machines to pass some time. When a few hours had passed they went back to the bridge and sat at the front seats watching the faraway galaxies closing in ever so slowly. It was hard to imagine when looking out there that they were moving at such staggering speeds. The time crept to dinner time and Arrill went to prepare something giving Jit a break. Jit sat there alone in silence and pondered what it would be like moving at four times the speed they were going with the image of the new Windchief still firmly etched in his mind. She looked fast and cost a small fortune to own. Despite the ship being all that, he still wondered if he could part with his ship and more so, Ladone. He soon heard Arrill call out from the galley announcing dinner to be ready and swivelled around in the chair making his way there thinking how good it was to have someone else do dinner giving him the peace of mind.

Jit hadn't even reached the galley doorway when he could smell a familiar ole smell. On the bench just out of the oven were two pizzas with the cheese on top still sizzling and bubbling looking and smelling delicious.

'I can't remember how long it's been since I had pizza' he said to Arrill.

'It's been a while for me too' he replied.

They loaded the two pizzas and cold drinks onto a tray then took the elevator down to the third floor and went to the theatre to catch a movie. Although he didn't think he could, Jit managed to polish off a whole pizza to himself while Arrill was struggling through his last piece. They stopped for intermission and Jit dug out another bottle of something he had stashed away and two shot glasses. He poured a shot glass each of yellow liquid and passed one to Arrill. It was strong in the mouth and its vapour was breathtaking burning down your throat until it entered your stomach. The after taste was good and it lasted a while on the palate. He poured another each and they kicked back to relaxed watching some cop movie Arrill picked. They stayed in the theatre late into the night sitting there well after the movie to finish drinking the fine yellow liquid, which Jit told Arrill came from a bottle shop he passed by on one of his travels. He couldn't quite remember how long ago it was, but he could remember the shop was unique because it contained drinks from all parts of the galaxy. Despite it being small inside it had eight floors going down into the ground making it quite extensive in its range. The elevator in the centre was a large disk with a rail around it and went up and down the floors attached to a centre pole. He recalled coming upon the bottle of "Leebranawat" on the fifth floor down from the top. Arrill agreed it was a nice drop and despite them having finished the bottle they were still able to sit up and talk so long.

Jit was the first to rise and told Arril he was fit for bed and left with Arrill soon moving to do the same. When Jit arrived at his room, he sat on the bed for a minute caught off guard by the drink blasting his head from the effort. This stuff felt like you were okay sitting down but when you got up, look out! He kicked his boots off and stripped quickly then slumped into bed breathing heavily from the exertion. He didn't have much time to think about anything as he passed out soon after.

....

Arrill could hear Jit struggling up the hallway and managed a few steps before he struggled too. He suddenly felt twice as heavy and walking seemed to happen in slow motion from disobedient legs. What the heck was that stuff he thought to himself! In his room, he went to splash some water on his face but that helped none. On the way back to the bed he kicked off his boots leaving them where they landed and went to lay down half falling onto the bed when he was near it.

....

Jit woke the following day at 7.00 am then decided to get up and shower. When he arrived on the bridge Ladone greeted him as he passed her on the way to the galley. He greeted her back and when he entered the galley, she materialised in the room to continue chatting. You never knew what to expect from Ladone. With a brew made he sat at the dining table and wondered when Arrill was likely to be up. Ladone had dematerialised again leaving him with his thoughts. When he finished, he poured another cuppa and went to the bridge to sit and look out into the blackness and see how much progress they'd made. They were close to halfway to their destination and he thought about what they would encounter on Spollee and where they might have to go next. This was turning into quite an adventure and only a few days ago he would never have imagined himself doing this. He was disturbed from his thoughts by the elevator descending indicating Arrill was up.

....

The days rolled one into another and at the end of the sixth day, Ladone informed them they would arrive in Spollee orbit the following day around 11.00 am Spollee time. Jit adjusted his watch to match as he and Arrill sat in the front seats on the bridge watching the spiralling arms of the twelfth galaxy closing in. It was a beautiful sight to behold with orange red hues dotted by millions of stars and an outer rim of fine blue dust. They were still too far away to pinpoint the planet yet but in amongst the spiralling turmoil lay their next stop and Jit could feel the excitement of the unknown creep into him. He wondered if Arrill felt the same because for both of them this was a part of the Universe they'd never been to. As they slept that night the Windchief slowed down to galatial speed on her final approach to their destination.

....

Spollee

Jit awoke early from a restless night of sleep no doubt due to the new path they were about to undertake. He lay in bed a few moments gathering his thoughts then went to shower. Refreshed from the wash he dressed and went to the bridge to see what progress they'd made. Appearing on the bridge he first noticed the proximity of all the planets, moons, and stars after the long period in clear space. They filled the viewscreen and almost seemed like you could reach out and touch them. He was not long up when Arrill arrived on the bridge too.

'Good morning' he said to Jit as he went to get a cup and pour himself a cuppa too.

They both sat staring at the view before them, lost in awe and wonder. Ladone appeared and told them she already contacted Professor Pepplplant and that she was expecting them.

'She!' they both said at the same time in surprise.

They were to go to her estate which was not so far out of Galasol, a nearby city, and they could land on the pad near the house marked by a large orange circle. All the coordinates were already entered into the shuttle for the journey to the surface when they arrive in Spollee orbit, only a couple of hours away now. Jit asked her about the weather on Spollee so they could prepare for the conditions. From the information she relayed back it sounded like a temperate climate and in Galasol it would be the beginning of autumn. They took the elevator down to level three and went to change and prepare for meeting Pepplplant. Jit wondered what she might be like and look like, forming an image in his mind while he got ready. Once he dressed, he filled his pockets with all the bits and pieces he carried then went back to the bridge. It was always entertaining when they arrived in orbit around a planet. Jit sat there in silence watching the mass of Spollee hanging in front of him as the Windchief made the final approach for orbit. It was a big yellow cross brown and white planet larger than Kelpuk but not by a lot. Around the planet were several moons orbiting, each a different size with some having large pockmarks in them. One large sun heated the planet which was mostly orange and still a long way away from it. Ladone informed him orbit was established and at the same time Arrill turned up. They bid farewell to Ladone and went down to the cargo hold ready for the downward journey to the surface. Shuttle number two was prepped with the information so they buckled up and Jit went through the startup routine then lifted off and flew out the bay into space. Once again, he was able to see his ship from the outside and he checked her over satisfied.

'She's a beautiful ship,' said Arrill.

'I know, he replied, I love her more than my own life!'

Everything he had was in his ship and if he lost her, he might as well be dead. They entered the atmosphere descending through light clouds for a time before clearing them to see the landscape below. As soon as they did the radio caught their attention with traffic control wanting to know their intention in Galasol. Jit explained they were to meet with a professor Pepplplant and waited while they checked his story, then got the go ahead with a brief introduction to the rules. The landscape below them was mostly open grassland with patches of forest scattered about and water lay in large lakes making up half the landmass. Mountain ranges could be seen off to the horizon with their heights remaining hidden by the distance. They soon came upon Galasol which was right in the middle of a large forest. It was more of a very large town than a city with gardens mixed among the structures and the forest around the edge was broken in three places by roads for coming or going. It looked like a nice place to visit while they're here if they get the chance Jit thought to himself.

They continued past Galasol and could soon see a large house appearing before them and shortly afterward the orange circle was visible, and Jit made preparations for landing. As they came closer two people stepped out of the house to watch them land. A flag on a nearby pole fluttered furiously from the shuttle engines thrust as they lightly touched down and shut her off. After unbuckling Jit looked at Arrill and said, 'well, here we go,' and they made for the back exit.

They stepped out into a mild day with sunshine filtering through cloud gaps and took in the new scents of the land. The two people who stepped out of the house walked over revealing a man and woman. When they approached the man dressed in a suit introduced himself as "Shalby" then he turned around to introduce, "Miss Limtom Pepplplant". To Jit he seemed like the servant or butler by his manner. Jit took her extended hand and shook it lightly with Arrill following his lead. She was a plain looking woman but still attractive wearing long trousers with a short sleeve top revealing toned arms making Jit wonder what secrets she hid. Her hair was very light red bordering on orange and down to her shoulders with ice blue eyes to match. To look at Jit guessed her to be in her mid-twenties. After the introduction, they were led to the house which was more like a mansion. From the air, it was diamond shaped and at the widest part of the diamond two large towers were stretching up higher than the rest of the building, and at the tip ends were two smaller towers. The structure seemed to be made of stone mixed with lumber and had the appearance of being very old. It was four storeys high and higher at the towers which gave it a domineering presence over one. They entered via the main entrance even though they passed a back door and Jit figured his host wanted them to see the place in all its splendour.

When they entered he could see why. After passing through two large double doors they stood in the foyer which spilled them into a huge room with a flowing staircase rising to the second floor. The walls were covered with all manner of objects with some being in glass cabinets while others sat regally on their own atop pedestals. The chandelier was so big he wondered how the thin chain holding it managed, but there it stayed. The place must've been a cleaner's nightmare! Limtom led them through the house to the inner courtyard where carefully maintained gardens with waterfalls trickling down rock sculptures decorated the area. In the center of the garden was a large pond with a water feature and beside it was a covered area with a large table and chairs surrounding it. She led them under the cover and asked them to sit down while they waited for Shalby to return with refreshments.

Limtom went onto tell them she received a call from a colleague on Kelpuk, to which Arrill and Jit went onto explain telling her all the events since arriving at Kelpuk. She listened studiously as they unfolded the story and when they finished Shalby turned up with a large tray loaded with beverages, sandwiches, and cakes. He put it in the center of the table then stood to one side of Limtom like a machine awaiting further instructions. While they ate, she told them a little about her family history and how far back the generations went, and how they arrived on Spollee. After lunch Arrill retrieved the map from his top pocket and laid it down in front of her. She studied it for a while before saying,

'I'm afraid I can't tell you anything, but other old families are living in Galasol who might be able to assist. I will need some time to contact them and see what I can do for you.'

Then she went on to tell them they were more than welcome to stay as her guests in the meantime. In the ten bay garage were vehicles they could use and Shalby would assist them with any questions or needs they may have, to which he looked at them and gave a nod. With that said she excused herself telling them she had to make some calls and walked back to the house. Shalby then told them to follow him and he would show them to their rooms so they could get settled in. Both their rooms were situated on the third floor, one beside the other. They checked out the accommodation which was more like first class motel suites with a balcony that faced the inner courtyard offering a grand view of the entire area.

Down in the garage, they found an assortment of vehicles including a motorbike that was not ordinary. It was a beast and Jit couldn't imagine Limtom riding it. They decided to take a ride around the place on some dirt bikes and explore the property. They were having such a good time that when Jit looked at the hour it was getting late. After returning the bikes to where they found them, they entered the house and turned right then walked along the hallway spotting Shalby who was heading towards them. Jit thought they were probably late for dinner as it was getting onto 7.00 pm. He was right because Shalby nodded and asked them to follow him where the Miss awaited them in the dining room. After passing through a few rooms and at the end of one, Shalby threw open the high double doors in front of him and they were exposed to a room big enough for a family to live in. The table was long enough to seat twenty six people and Jit wondered how often the seats were all occupied. Limtom sat at the furthest end and she seemed so tiny in the distance. Jit spoke first,

'I'm sorry if we've kept you waiting.'

Arrill nodded his agreement and to their surprise, she smiled then said,

'Actually, you are perfectly on time as we eat at 7.00 pm'.

They took a seat and Jit briefly looked at his watch and it read 6.55 pm. He felt a huge relief they didn't make a bad impression on her. They talked over a glass of vintage red wine while dinner was on its way with the conversations being mixed and spontaneous. Soon another set of double doors opened at the opposite end of the room and in entered some servants with covered trays and desserts along with bowls of fruit and more wine. For three people there was enough food to feed them for a week Jit thought. For a good part of the meal, they made small talk and laughed at mishaps, and later when they got to dessert, Limtom informed them about what she found out since they last spoke.

Apparently, an uncle on her mother's side was clued up on symbols and languages and may be able to help but he was away until the following day. Limtom went on to tell them her uncle lived at the foot of the Mountains which was a day drive away. Jit was going to suggest using the shuttle but thought better of it in case Limtom had other plans arranged. They continued talking for a while further with her telling them a little more about herself. Her parents passed away from a vehicle collision just before she turned twenty years old and became the sole owner of the entire Pepplplant fortune. She was an only daughter and to Jit she seemed quite strong, yet lonely. She went on to tell them she'd been running the place for eight years and giving away her age at the same time. At 9.00 pm she stood and excused herself telling them she went to bed at such an hour every night. Jit and Arrill thanked her for the fine meal and said they would see her in the morning then watched her walk out a different door to the others. Jit didn't even notice the door until she stepped towards it.

'I should've asked her how to get back to our rooms' Jit said to Arrill.

'Shalby can't be too far away' he said back, and Jit nodded his head agreeing but wondering how to summon him.

They both decided to look for themselves with the advantage of at least knowing their rooms were on the third floor somewhere. The place was big on the outside but inside it seemed even bigger! As they ventured out the same doors they'd entered, they tried to pick familiar things to guide the way. The rooms they passed through had ample furnishings to fill the room yet plenty of space so one could move freely about. To Jit it seemed like they were rooms made to have crowds in them. Every room was different yet had the same touch to it suggesting it was created by the same mind. He had never been in a place this big before and it seemed staggering to him that one family would live in such an immense space. Fortunately for them after five minutes of wandering around lost Shalby found them and led them to their rooms. Jit thanked Shalby who bid him good night then entered his room. Inside, he could hear the muffled voices of Arrill and Shalby outside the door for a short time, then he heard Arrills door close and all was quiet. His room had a bathroom of its own, so he stripped and went to wash before bed. He was soon finished and as he lay in the bed with the finest linen wrapped around him he thought about Limtom and was beginning to take a liking to her. The events of the day came crashing down on him making him feel weary and in moments he slipped into oblivion.

....

After talking to Shalby a few more minutes Arrill entered his room and stood there with his back to the door a moment looking around the room in thought. His thoughts were map oriented wondering what obstacles might lay in their path next. He stepped over to the bed and sitting on the edge took off his boots then lay down for a moment. The intention was only for five minutes but all the drink got the better of him and put him under subtly and surely.

....

When Jit woke he looked at the time and it took a couple of attempts to focus before it read, 8.10 am. It startled him at first but then he remembered there was no set time to leave today and relaxed. It was quiet out in the walkway and he wondered if Arrill was up yet. He had a lot to drink the previous night, and by bedtime he was close to wrecked, so he might be still passed out in bed. He dressed in his same clothes, taking note to have a spare set at all times in the shuttle from now on. When he stepped into the walkway, he could hear footsteps far away but getting closer and he recognised them as Shalbys. In a few moments, he saw him coming and wondered how he knew Jit was ready to exit his room. When Shalby approached he bid him a welcome to the day and led him to breakfast with Limtom. Jit asked Shalby if Arrill was up yet to which the reply was,

'I'm afraid not sir.'

Breakfast was to be had in the sunroom which was at the front of the house being where the sun rose. The room was mostly glass and set with plants all around the outside giving the impression you were in the garden. A few windows were open a small amount allowing a cool but pleasant breeze to waft through the room. The mesmerising jingling of a wind chime could be heard coming from somewhere out in the garden.

Limtom was sitting at a large oval table with her back to him when he entered the room. Before her, was an assortment of covered warming trays with hot food in them. He greeted her and took the opposite seat feeling a little awkward at being alone with her. She told him to help himself and he suddenly realised how hungry he was. He picked up a plate from the pile and served himself then started chatting with Limtom while he ate. He told her how he lost his parents some time back and as she listened Jit could feel her understanding come across. Her light blue eyes that looked like the colour of Topaz were filled with compassion and he stared into them losing himself for a moment.

She was just about to say something when Arrill entered the room.

They exchanged greetings and he took a seat then Limtom extended the same courtesy to him as she did to Jit. For a moment they watched Arrill load his plate then she looked back at Jit, their eyes met, and she smiled then looked away again. She picked up the coffee pot and offered more coffee which they both accepted with thanks and the conversation shifted to Arrill. Breakfast lasted until close to 10.00 am before they finished and prepared to leave. Limtom led them to the garage and upon entering the now familiar area they saw Shalby under the bonnet of the car they were going to use checking the vital fluids before the journey. The vehicle had six doors and the three of them entered in the back and when Shalby was finished he sat at the wheel. It was pure luxury in the cabin with leather lounge seats in a bench style facing each other and the driver was in the front and separated from the back by a glass partition. Jit and Arrill sat in the back seat facing the front while Limtom sat opposite them facing the rear of the vehicle. There was plenty of legroom to stretch out and it was more like a small room than the cab of a vehicle. There was a television in one of the side panels along with a fully stocked minibar beside it. When they reached the end of the driveway, they turned right then accelerated up to speed with no sound and barely feeling any motion at all. The vehicle glided along effortlessly which was going to make the long trip to her cousin's place pleasant. Along the way, Jit asked Limtom about the unusual bike in the garage and she told him it belonged to her father who bought it as an investment because only a hand full were ever made. Then she went on to tell them she rode it often but liked the sidecar taken off as it was more fun.

Outside the windows, the day was sunny and fine with a pale blue sky overhead and the large orange sun climbing higher into it. The landscape changed as they made the passage to their destination with large areas of smooth rock that were still only mounds and not a thing growing on them. The rock was grey with black lines running through it in erratic patterns. It was so smooth it shone in the sunshine giving it an eerie look but at the same time intriguing. They passed more large lakes which flowed into each other with narrow flowing streams forming the connection. After they drove for a few hours they passed a roadside eatery appropriately called "The Road Side Inn" and Shalby pulled into the car park and under a large shady tree.

'We always stop here to eat when I'm en route to my cousin's place,' she informed them and waited for Shalby to open the door for her.

There were another few vehicles parked here and there and only the breeze could be heard blowing through the large tree that spread over them. It was quite serene and calming Jit thought to himself. Inside some people sat at tables scattered about the room eating and talking quietly then a man walked out from another room with arms outstretched wide calling Limtom and hugging her to himself. She introduced Jit and Arrill to him and then he led them to her usual table close by a window looking out the back of the property. The window was large giving an undisturbed view of the entire area bringing the outside in. Limtom's friend was named Elmbenn and he was short and round with a jolly attitude and permanent smile creasing his face. Not a string of hair graced his head, but he wore a tidy trimmed beard. After the introduction, he left again and was soon back with a bottle of local wine grow by his brother. He served four glasses then scurried away to the kitchen again. They found out some things about Shalby as they waited for lunch and that he used to be in the Special Forces according to his tales. An hour later they finished the meal and then had a coffee before they set off again. The road was mostly free of traffic with just the odd vehicle passing in the opposite direction making for a peaceful and quiet trip. Occasionally they would pass little cottages nestled upon a hilltop or some that were burrowed into the hillside with only the front visible. Cattle roamed the fields within groups eating while others lay on the ground chewing the cud watching them go by. The closer they arrived at the mountains, the more the landscape changed with many more trees growing in closer clusters. Some of them reached into the air two to three hundred feet. By late afternoon they were at the foothills of the majestic giants at last. The road came to a T intersection and they turned right and followed along the foothills climbing ever slowly until they happened upon a steep driveway running off to the left an hour later. Shalby exited the road and followed the driveway up and slowed down when they came to a large clearing which was a natural plateau and overlooked the entire valley before them. The view was amazing!

The house they stopped in front of was large, but by no means the size of Limtom's place. It was a two story affair made of the same rock as the mountain which caused it to blend into its surroundings. By the time they were out of the vehicle a well groomed and spoken fellow came out to meet them. He embraced Limtom kissing her on the cheek then turned to shake Jit and Arrills hand vigorously. Limtom introduced him as "Melparcan" or Mel for short. Shalby didn't stay and after they exited the vehicle he drove off and Jit watched the vehicle shrink away in the increasing darkness. Limtom went on to explain he had relatives living nearby and always called in on them when they ventured out this way. He would return later or in the morning, or sooner if she called for him. Mel led them around a path that crossed over a small footbridge which traversed an old pond with plants growing in it and deposited them at the main door to the house. Lighting hidden in the ground brought the gardens to life creating a magical experience of wonder as they made their way. The inside of the house was spacious as they walked to the dining room and all sat down at a large square table. In the center of it was a round flat dish with a mix of starters before one had dinner. Dinner must be close thought Jit. He looked at the time displayed on a wall clock and it read six fifteen pm. They all took a side each of the table and picked at the starters while Limtom and Mel caught up on events since they last saw each other. The conversation then moved to Mel telling Jit and Arrill a little about himself. He told them he had many years of experience dabbling in different languages from all around the planet and other worlds. He went on to say that some of the languages were very close looking but miles apart in meaning so it was important to identify what they had. He went on telling them he'd spent a considerable amount of time in the field too. The conversation stopped when a nearby door opened and a little old lady followed by a young girl came into the room with dishes and platters. During the meal Mel continued from where he left off and when he finished, they made some more small talk between the four of them. One conversation Jit and Arrill heard was of Limtom in an embarrassing moment to which she didn't prefer to remember or talk about. Jit and Arrill told Mel about themselves during the meal as well.

After dinner, they all adjourned to the sitting room to continue chatting. There was a large coffee table in the center of the room and on it sat an odd shaped ashtray and a box of long dark smokes. Mel picked the box up and offered them around with only himself and Jit lighting up. Once they were settled Arrill pulled out the map and passed it to Mel to look at. He put the map down for a moment and went to get some spectacles then took his position again to study it. The tension Jit could see in Arrill was visible on his face and he wondered how his friend was coping with all this. Even he was beginning to feel the strain from the uncertainty. Eventually, Mel said,

'I will need some time with this I'm afraid' saying it mostly to Arrill.

'Maybe even a few days' he continued.

Arrill said it would be fine as they had to know after coming this far. They all stayed gathered in the sitting room until late into the evening talking and having a hot drink before Limtom stood and excused herself saying she was tired and not used to being up so late. Shortly after she left Mel showed Jit and Arrill where their rooms were, and the bathroom then told them he was going to bed too and they could do as they pleased. Their rooms were on the ground floor of the house and next door to each other at one end of the building. Jit wished Arrill a good sleep and went to his room feeling ready for bed after the drink he had which made him feel drowsy. He stripped and lay in bed for a few moments thinking about what Mel said until sleep overcame him.

....

Arrill closed his bedroom door behind him and pulled his boots off then went to sit on a nearby chair. It had been a long day and he could now feel it weigh upon him. Would Mel find some answers he wondered and if so, what would it mean for them to do next. His final thought before falling into unconsciousness was of Jit and Limtom earlier on and what seemed to be developing between them, or maybe he was just imagining things.

....

Jit slept until seven thirty before he awoke feeling refreshed and a little startled from the different surroundings again. He lay under the covers for a moment missing his ship and his familiar cabin not to mention Ladone and her quirky outfits. Once out of bed he donned his clothes on again and decided to get new clothes today or wash what he was wearing as they were beginning to get grimy and he was feeling conscious about it. He picked up a towel that was provided on a dresser then went to the bathroom to freshen up. When he finished, he walked back down to where the dining room was and found Mel and Limtom talking amongst themselves at the table. They looked up at him upon entering the room and greeted him with Jit doing the like in return then sat down. The coffee pot was on the table, so he poured himself a serve and listened to the conversation they were having. It wasn't long afterward that Arrill made an entrance looking a little rough around the edges. He managed to croak a greeting then sat down and poured himself a coffee and sat in his chair quietly sipping away. Breakfast was soon served and occasionally Jit looked over to Limtom who seemed to avoid eye contact this morning for some reason. During the meal, they talked about what arrangements should be made if Mel needed the map for a few days. They agreed to go back with Limtom, and they could return when Mel had some news for them.

They would return with the shuttle as there was plenty of room to land on the plateau and it would cut the journey down by hours. They were just finishing off breakfast when they heard Shalby arrive back from visiting his family. Mel walked them to the front door and told them he'd be starting work on the map as soon as they left then wished them well, hugging Limtom and watched them navigate the path back to where Shalby waited. Shalby greeted them and opened the door for Limtom and inside she sat the same way as the inward journey. Inside the vehicle it was warm, and all the sounds of the outside were shutout as they descended the driveway back to the road and pointed for home. They talked for a part of the trip then Limtom wanted to watch a movie, so they passed a couple of hours viewing that. The movie was a romantic adventure which, to Jit's surprise, was quite good and very entertaining, keeping him on the edge of his seat often. Not at all what he expected!

At around twelve thirty he started getting hungry and wondered what they were going to do for lunch, surely the others must be hungry too by now, he thought to himself. Arrill sat quietly watching the movie but his thoughts were on the map. He hoped he could trust Mel and was a bit uneasy about leaving the map with him. It had never been out of his possession before and he was taking a great risk trusting someone he didn't know at all. Before leaving he contemplated staying with Mel but didn't want to give the impression he didn't trust him or Limtom. Then he wondered what Jit was thinking about all this as he hadn't said a real lot about the map lately. Limtom announced they would be having a picnic lunch at a favourite spot of hers which was close by. Jit wondered what they would eat when she continued telling them that Shalby had loaded a picnic hamper into the boot before coming to pick them up.

He soon felt the vehicle slow down and then Shalby turned left off the road onto a gravel track leading them through the fields. The gravel road could be heard rumbling underneath the vehicle with the occasional rock hitting the floor making a dull thud. Jit could see the mountains starting to shrink as they put a fair bit of distance between them and Mel's place in the few hours they'd been on the road. They were back to mostly flat land with the occasional tree here and there and the odd cluster of low bushes. They only grew to the height of a man and displayed medium size white flowers over them. Large rocks sat like sentries in the paddocks with some allowing vegetation to take hold and flourish somehow. Jit noticed one rock wore a colourful hat tilted to one side made of wildflowers almost looking deliberate in its making. They followed the gravel road until it rounded a large hill that concealed behind it a tiny hut with a small lake in the front. The hut had a low fence around it with pieces missing and in need of a coat of paint. A large tree grew at the back of the hut which covered half the roof and the rest stretched out over the back yard. Shalby stopped at the front and parked then hopped out and opened the door for Limton with Jit and Arrill getting out on the opposite side of the vehicle. The lakefront was close by with just a small amount of grass filling the gap between. Limtom led Arrill and Jit to the hut through the gate and along an old uneven stone path with tiny flowers growing in between the gaps to the front door. The dwelling was made from panels of wood laid horizontally with windows that seemed too large for the place. No doubt for the views, thought Jit. The wood panelling needed some paint too as it hadn't seen any for a long time judging by its condition. The planks were sawn rough with blade marks visible despite the time. They watched Limtom remove a false piece of planking to retrieve a hidden key allowing them entry. As they stepped over the threshold, she told them it was the house her mum grew up in when she was a child and it's been in the family ever since.

She never met her grandparents on her mother's side of the family she went on, as they died before she was born but her mum and dad frequented the hut often when she was little. It was quaint inside Jit thought and very humble compared to the mansion she lived in now. The whole hut would fit in one of her many large rooms easily he concluded. The walls were the same looking as the outside with pictures hanging from them and shelves stacked with old memorabilia and barely readable tins that once contained food. The furniture was sparse and very basic meeting the barest of needs with no thought for comfort at all. There were only two bedrooms with a bathroom at the end and the kitchen and lounge room were both together making one large room. They passed through the house and out the back door to the large tree that shaded the house. Under it sat an old picnic table that was now laden with all the food Shalby had placed on it from the vehicle.

A soft cool breeze blew, carrying on it the scent of the fields which was soothing and pleasant giving the feeling of a relaxed country setting. An old bent clothesline sat in the yard with wires missing from it and a bird perched on its top watching them with sharp eyes that didn't blink. The rest of the yard had signs of a once vegetable garden in one part and flower gardens in other parts with some flowers still blooming despite the neglect. On a stand sat an old water tank that would hold water no more due to the many small holes in it gathered there by time and the elements. Some were so large one could see the garden on the other side through it. At another end of the yard sat a shed that was closed in on three sides and barely standing with a lean giving away its age. In it were old farm tools and bits of machinery that served another era where they were the newest thing invented and very much needed. Now they sat there waiting for time to reduce them to what they once were.

The picnic table flourished with a variety of coloured bowls containing food in them looking itself like a flower garden. The tree covering the table was like a giant umbrella with small birds flitting around its branches seeming to complain about the intruders beneath them and not wanting to share their tree. While they ate, they listened to Limtom tell them about some of her childhood memories and reminisced with her as she drifted off occasionally deep in thought. She'd sit there staring straight ahead watching the movie of her life that only she could view, then come to life again and tell some more. When lunch was completed Jit excused himself and went for a walk around the lake but mostly to have a smoke. He saw a round rock and walked over to sit on it and rolled a cigarette. The big orange sun sat in the sky overhead warming him and the sound of wavelets lapping the shoreline seemed to play music of sorts with only the words missing. The lake was only small compared to some they passed along the way, but it was enough for supplying water and a nice spot to swim and refresh oneself. Around the edges in mottled patches grew thin spindly weeds that had a small round pod growing on top of the stem holding the secret to its hidden contents. A dilapidated walkway stretched a short distance into the lake where a boat could be launched or tied to with Jit doubting its ability to hold foot traffic any longer. He gathered this whole place was kept just for nostalgia.

On completing his smoke, he left the rock and finished walking around the lake startling a couple of small birds hiding in the reeds while making his way back to the others who were still sitting where he left them. Taking a seat, he poured himself a drink then listened in on the conversation

Arrill and Limtom were having. Around an hour and a half, after they first arrived, they helped carry some things back to the vehicle and then set off again. The return journey seemed to pass quicker than the trip out and they pulled into Limtoms driveway just as it was getting dark. Despite the comfort of the vehicle Jit was still aching for a stretch and walk around. On the way back from the hut they discussed their plans with Limtom and told her they would return to the Windchief to get a change of clothes and come back sometime in the morning. Jit contemplated asking her if she wanted to come up with them but she seemed far away and aloof for some reason, so he dismissed the idea. In the shuttle, he and Arrill strapped in and went through startup procedures then took off and headed once again out into space. He was looking forward to seeing his ship and Ladone as it wasn't often he would be away this long.

After they passed through the atmosphere and entered the blackness of space, they could see the speck of the Winchief in the distance. She grew large rapidly as they sped towards her and after dropping the shield, they entered the cargo hold and set the shuttle down next to number one. They exited and took the lift to the bridge where the moment they appeared Ladone did so too. Today she was geared up in a tennis outfit with a bandana wrapped around her head and the racquet slid down her back like a sword ready for action. Jit smiled to himself wondering where she'd play tennis and who with.

'I was wondering if you were going to come back' she went on to say.

Jit filled her in on the events that passed since he last saw her while Arrill speared bits of the telling in too. When they finished Jit excused himself and went to his cabin to shower and change his clothes. On completing the task, he felt refreshed and glad to have clean clothes on again then went back up to the bridge. Arrill was doing the same thing and hadn't made it back to the bridge yet so Jit decided to go to the galley and make something for dinner. Arrill soon joined him where they sat down to eat and talked some more about the map.

'It must've been difficult for you to leave the map out of your hands' Jit said to him.

'I didn't like the idea a great deal, but I had little choice in the matter' Arrill replied.

'Let's hope Mel can make some sense of it' he added.

When they finished, they both retired to the bridge to sit and continue talking while they had a drink. Jit managed to stay up until 10.00 pm before the full day caught up with him and he bid Arrill goodnight and went to his cabin. In the solitude of his room, he kicked off his boots and added to his journal entry then slid into bed. He lay there thinking about the day and only moments passed before weariness overtook him dragging him into a deep slumber.

....

Jit woke at 8.00 am and sat up feeling refreshed and a little hungry. He dressed and headed to the galley and arriving on the bridge he was greeted by Ladone. She informed him he was the first to wake this morning. He greeted her and went to the galley where she materialized and kept talking asking Jit what he was planning today.

'I'm not sure just yet Ladone' he said back to her while he prepared to make that vital first cuppa.

When it was ready, he went to sit at the dining table to have it and Ladone dematerialized leaving him alone with his thoughts. He waved over the sensor at the edge of the table and the hologram of his mum and dad appeared out of the center smiling at him. He missed them dearly, especially his mum. She was always taking his side and defending him when he was a child but if he crossed the line, she could also be a tyrant. Arrill was still asleep and Jit wondered how much more of the liqueur he had last night. That stuff is more like a body sleep tonic than anything else and if too much is consumed, you could sleep a whole day away. With that thought in mind, he decided not to wait for Arrill and cooked himself some breakfast. The smell of cooking bacon soon filled the air and when he had a satisfactory amount, he took a seat at the table again to eat. He had just finished when he heard Arrill greet Ladone on the bridge and a moment later he entered the galley.

'Good morning Jit' he croaked from a still partly sleeping head and went to get a cup.

'Good day to you Arrill, sleep well did we?' Jit said back.

'Like a dead man' came the muffled reply.

At the table, he took a seat and poured himself a cuppa.

'Hungry then?' Jit asked.

Arrill managed a nod of his head and Jit took away his empty plate and went to cook the same breakfast for Arrill. For a moment he watched his friend clear the plate in front of him in a methodical fashion before Ladone appeared again beside them. She was dressed in tight blue jeans today with a western shirt and sleeves rolled up to her elbows, and on her feet, she was shod with light brown boots that reached just under her knees. The boots had etchings all over them making them look swanky and eye catching. The shirt was unbuttoned to her cleavage line and around her waist, she wore a leather belt with a large blue stone in it. Her hair was up in a ponytail.

'Limtom called and asked if you would be so kind as to call her back when you are ready' she went on.

Jit thanked her and went out to the bridge to do just that leaving Ladone to chat with Arrill. He punched in her code and number and within moments the face of Limtom appeared before him on the big screen.

'Good morning Limtom' he said to which she replied in kind.

She went on to tell him that nothing was heard from Mel yet and at what time were they going to return to her place. Jit hadn't thought that far ahead yet and relayed he would call her before they left, to which she nodded and smiled then the screen went blank. He sat there for a little time staring at the blank screen deep in thought trying to understand Limtom. He almost sensed the feeling that she was disappointed that they weren't back at Galasol, yet yesterday he could hardly get her to look at him. While he was lost in a maze of thoughts Arrill came onto the bridge and thanked him for the great breakfast.

'So what's the plan for today?' he asked Jit and took a sip of coffee.

'What did you want to do?' he replied.

'I don't really care to be honest, so I'll leave it up to you' he passed back to Jit.

Then he added, 'besides, I thought you'd want to see

Limtom'.

Jit looked at his friend who stared back with a smirk on his face and couldn't think of anything to say, so smiled instead. He did like Limtom but was a bit confused about her feelings towards him. The time had crept past 10.00 am when Jit looked at his timepiece and he told Arrill he was going to the gym to do an hour workout and loosen his body. In the gym, he selected a program from the many choices on offer then walked over to the bike, hopped on, and started peddling. His thoughts went right back to Limtom.

....

Arrill sat on the bridge alone thinking about the map when Ladone appeared and asked him if he was thinking about the map. He replied by nodding his head and asked her if she could read minds. She answered by telling him that it was obvious the map was on his mind because his behaviour was the same as other times when he thought about it. She was no fool he thought to himself and smiled at her concern about the matter.

'Are you and Jit going back to the surface to see Limtom?' she then went on to ask him.

'I'm not sure what Jit wants to do' he replied to her.

'I think he likes Limtom' she then said, which surprised Arrill because of the way she said it, sensing a little hurt in her voice.
He looked at her thinking to himself how unique she was and could understand why Jit felt the way he did about her as he was becoming very fond of her too.

After the hour was up Jit was covered in sweat and went back to his cabin to shower and change into different clothes before heading back to the bridge. When he arrived, Arrill was still sitting where he left him talking with Ladone. She seemed to have taken to Arrill and they chatted like old friends he thought to himself, which pleased him as he wasn't sure how Arrill would find her when he first brought him on board. He greeted them and took a seat feeling the strain of the training he'd just completed but was also content with the progress he achieved.

'Have you decided what we're going to do yet?' Arrill went on to say and both he and Ladone waited for a reply.

'We could stay here and wait for Mel to uncover some meaning to the map or we could go down and wait at Limtom's place for the duration, what do you think?'

'I think we should return to Galasol and stay with Limtom seeing as though she has gone out of her way to help us so much' Arrill continued.'

Ladone said nothing waiting to hear what Jit would say and finally, he answered,

'Okay, we'll go back down to the surface and wait at Limtoms then.'

With that decision made he told Ladone to contact her and inform her of what they were going to do. While she took the task to hand both he and Arrill went to their cabins to pack a bag with clothes and other essentials that might be needed for the duration of their stay. Jit wondered how long it would be before they heard back from Mel and when he did reply he wondered what he would have to say. Arrill seemed to be staying calm he thought to himself, at least on the outside anyway. With all he thought he would need packed into a duffle bag he returned to the bridge where Arrill awaited with his bag in tow too. Ladone informed him that

Limtom was notified of their return and would be in town for the day on business, but the house was open and they could make themselves at home. They bid farewell to Ladone and took the elevator down to the cargo hold where they boarded the same shuttle they used the previous day. Arrill was at the controls this time and with the startup procedure completed they lifted off and exited the hold entering the star filled void of space once again.

The journey down was made in silence and, as they passed through the atmosphere and some light cloud cover, they could see Galasol as a speck far below. A large flock of birds could also be seen flying away from the shuttle some distance below too. They moved in perfect harmony seeming like one to Jit. Within a short time, they could see Limtom's place which grew as the shuttle neared them to their destination. Arrill landed in the same spot they stopped in previously and shut down the engines returning the peace and solitude the place beheld. It was just after midday when they touched down and exited the shuttle. On stepping outside they were welcomed by a warm sun and cool light breeze.

'I wonder if Shalbys about' Arrill asked Jit, to which Jit shrugged his shoulders in reply.

'He must be in town with Limtom' Arrill concluded and they both strode to the house and the front entrance.

Inside they retraced their steps to the courtyard and went to sit under the cover by the pool and watched the water fountain for a moment before Arrill interrupted the solitude,

'I wonder how Mel's coming along with the map' he said.

'I was just thinking the same thing' Jit said back to him while he pulled out his tobacco and rolled a smoke.

When he finished, he asked Arrill if he wanted a cuppa to which he nodded then asked Jit how he was going to find the kitchen.

'Already thought of that' said Jit and he got up and walked back the way they came. Instead of wandering around the house he went back to the shuttle and made coffee in the kitchenette on board.

'You found it' Arrill exclaimed, and Jit told him he made it in the shuttle, not wanting to wander around the house. There wasn't a soul in sight and they presumed the servants they saw the other night must only work sometimes. They enjoyed the relaxation and quiet while they drank coffee and talked about Limtom's house, and what a contrast it was compared to the hut they visited the day before. Both agreed the hut may have been a little rundown, but it had an all encompassing atmosphere of peace and solitude about it that was soothing on the body and mind. It would've been a great place to live as a child Jit thought to himself. As he sat there looking out over the gardens and estate, he imagined he was the owner and what it might feel like to have all this. Admittedly he had the Windchief which not many people owned and if he sold her he would be quite well off for the rest of his life, but what Limtom had was in a different league altogether. It would be a handful to handle it all he thought to himself, glad not to have such a responsibility to deal with.

'I wonder what time they will be back' Arrill said to him.

Jit looked at the time and it was just going onto 2.00 pm and relayed the time to Arrill. Then he told him that Limtom knew they were coming so she'll probably get back as soon as she can. From where he sat Jit looked up and could see his balcony and bedroom beyond. Some of the walls had vines growing on them that were covering a good portion of the walls taking away some of the harshnesses of the hard stone. It was cut neatly around doors and windows where it had spread the most making for a postcard look. The gardens were all filled with different coloured flowers that bobbled around in their groups fanned by the breeze, shaking their heads as if saying no to a question that wasn't asked. There were shrubs of varying colours and heights with sections of perfect lawn that were as soft as carpet to walk on and manicured to perfection. Everything had order and every space in the soil was filled with a plant of some kind filling any gaps. Statues stood in different positions around the courtyard with some clothed while others stood bare and shared the place with sculptures of varying kinds too. Some sculptures were driven by the breeze, while others were waterpropelled and entertaining in their simplicity. It looked so different from down here Jit thought, compared to viewing the gardens from the balcony. The afternoon drifted by and around 4.30 pm they heard a vehicle drive up the gravel driveway and knew it to be Limtom and Shalby back from Galasol. They both stared at the back door waiting for either one to appear and discover their position. Limtom was the first one out.

'There you both are, I thought you might be out here' she said as she made her way to the undercover area where they waited.

'Have you been here long?'

'We arrived around midday' Jit went on to tell her, with Arrill nodding his agreement too.

She sat down and told them she hadn't heard from Mel yet and would call him tonight and see if he's uncovered anything, then went on to tell them about her day like they were old friends from long ago. Shalby joined them a short time later and greeted Jit and Arrill in his usual manner that was polite and formal, then stood by Limtoms side waiting for her next need. Jit noticed Limtom looking at the coffee pot on the table and he explained to her why it was not a pot she recognized. She giggled slightly at his ingenuity then went on to another matter entirely. They listened to her chat away and Jit was becoming more certain with every passing moment that Limtom appeared a little eccentric. As a matter of fact, Shalby didn't seem quite right either, the way he just stood there perfectly still like one of the guards in a palace. Arrills words from earlier came back to him, 'we are on a different planet you know.'

When she finished spilling the events of her day, she asked them if they would like to adjourn inside and got up to lead the way. Jit picked up his coffee pot and cups and went to return them to the shuttle then joined the others inside following their voices to find his way. They sat in a lounge room that was close to the front entrance and the room could've easily accommodated fifty people with seating for all. He marvelled at how clean and tidy everything was with not a speck of dust to be seen anywhere. The time was just after 6.00 pm when Jit snuck a look and remembered that dinner was served at 7.00 pm in the Pepplplant household, which seemed forever away as he was already quite hungry. The breakfast he made this morning was all he and Arrill had eaten all day and if he was hungry Arrill must be feeling the same way too. They talked amongst each other for a little while before Limtom said she would call Mel to see if there was any progress made on the map. She got up and excused herself saying she would go to the study to make the call, while Jit and Arrill waited in the lounge room wondering what the outcome would be. She returned a little too quickly Jit thought, only to hear her say Mel didn't pick up and she would try again after dinner. The suspense was killing him and he couldn't even begin to imagine what Arrill was going through.

At 7.00 pm they followed Limtom to the dining room and, upon entering, they found the table was already laid out with food on it ready to eat. Shalby was the only person in the room and he waited for Limtom to be seated then left the room. Jit and Arrill took the same positions as the previous night waiting for Limtom to start first before they tucked in too. Shalby returned with a bottle of wine from the cellar that was covered in dust and according to Limtom was a fine vintage she found exquisite. He cleaned the bottle and uncorked it then let it sit on the table for a short breather before he served them a glass each. After the meal, they sat around the table talking for a while longer before retiring back to the lounge room and waiting for Limtom to return from trying to contact Mel again. It seemed to take forever before she returned and retook her seat while Jit and Arrill waited in suspense for a response.

'Mel has made some significant progress on one of the languages but as to the other he cannot find an inkling as to where it comes from or who wrote it' she told them.

'He believes it must be an ancient race of beings who may not exist anymore or if they do, they must be in some unknown galaxy' she went on to say.

'He said if you wanted to call in tomorrow, he would hopefully have more information as there were still more symbols to address.'

Both Jit and Arrill agreed with that motion and Jit noticed straight away that Arrill was perked up by the news. They asked Limtom if she wanted to tag along but she declined saying she had to go into Galasol again for other business and sounded genuinely disappointed she couldn't. When the wine bottle sat empty Jit noticed a stem in the bottle that looked like some kind of herb for infusion. He felt quite pleasantly relaxed with a slight fuzzy feeling in his head and a sense of enlightenment. From then on, the evening passed quickly with Limtom going to bed at 9.00 pm and they both remained up until near 10.00 pm before they decided to do the same. In his room, Jit washed then climbed into bed and lay there thinking about nothing in particular, until sleep claimed him.

....

Arrill leaned with his back against his bedroom door, glad of the solitude, and thought about what Mel had said. He looked about the room not seeing it, lost in visions of what might come next. Why was there a language on the map that no one seems to know he thought in his trance? Then there was the other language that may have a revelation and did the same hand write it too, and if so, why different?! He flicked off the door then went to wash and hit the sack. He laid in bed looking at the intricate patterns on the ceiling far above his head with many racing thoughts about the map, wondering if he was the first to come this far with it. Surely the old guy he received the map from must've tried looking too and it kept coming up in his mind why he would give the map away. The old guy may have had a debt to pay, but he could've kept the map to himself and none would be wiser. Endless questions came into his mind heading him for a sleepless night but instead, he stilled his mind and shut out the thoughts, and with the assistance from the wine he soon tumbled into a restful sleep.

....

Morning came quick for Jit and ten minutes later he decided a hot shower would do wonders and went to take that and begin the day. He looked at the time and it was just past 8.00 am. They hadn't talked about what time to leave today in last night's discussion, but it didn't matter because the distance would be covered in a couple of hours with the shuttle. Feeling a lot more alert and movement free he dressed and strolled down to the living room. As he neared the double doors, he heard voices reach out from the other side and upon entering was greeted by Arrill, Limtom, and the ever ready Shalby. They all greeted then he took a seat and served himself some breakfast. Everything was still hot and the others were only partway through their breakfasts having just started too. Limtom informed them she had to leave home at 10.00 am and soon excused herself to get ready. Jit and Arrill sat alone at the table with enough food still on it to feed ten people and continued talking. During the talk, Jit picked at some more food as did Arrill until Limtom re-entered the room. She sat at the edge of her seat to say goodbye for a moment then Shalby entered the room looking at her with the cue to go. She asked them to let her know what the outcome would be and to come back whenever they wanted then smiled and walked to where Shalby waited and they departed.
'We might as well leave too' said Jit a moment later to which Arrill responded by standing up and announcing he was ready to go.

They made their way back to the shuttle starting to get a feel for the place and as they buckled up they saw Limtom and Shalby drive up the driveway making for Galasol. Jit was piloting this time and they were soon skyward bound placing the coordinates into the computer and heading to Mel's place. The day was fine and clear and at an altitude of four thousand feet the scenery below was spectacular. The lakes glistened with the sunlight reflecting off them looking like giant gems of differing sizes set into the ground, while the roadways snaked to their destinations. Soon they saw beneath them the little roadside stop that was Elmbenns place and in moments it was gone from sight again. Shortly afterward they reached the hut Limtom owned and Jit pressed a button on the console to record its location in the computer to then be linked to the Windchief when they get back on board. It was a great little spot he thought and maybe Limtom would allow him the use of it some time for a retreat. Arrill watched the manoeuvre and gave a sly smile but said nothing. By this time the mountains were beginning to loom before them indicating their journey was close to an end. They were different to look at from this altitude but none of their majesty was stripped from them as they held Jit and Arrill in silent awe.

They soon spotted the dwelling where Mel lived cradled on the plateau against the flank of the giants that spiralled above it. Mel knew they were coming and Jit could make out the figure of the man as he prepared to touch down and end the journey that took just under three hours. They unbuckled and stepped out to be met by Mel with an extended hand which they shook then followed him inside where he told them lunch was ready. While they ate Mel told them the symbols he was able to decipher on the map were called hieroglyphics and belonged to a race that very little was known about. He could find no evidence or translation for the second language and wasn't even sure if it was written by the same beings. Jit and Arrill listened, spellbound by what Mel divulged whilst continuing to eat. He then went on to tell them that what he deciphered were just letters and numbers in no particular order that he could make sense of. He also told them the information was retrieved from personal ancient records held by some families he was acquainted with who collected antiquities of all nature meaning the decoding should be accurate and reliable.

When they finished eating Mel left the room briefly and returned with the map and a sheet of paper with the translation on it for the symbols and indicated for them to follow him. They retired to the lounge room where he placed the map on the coffee table and Jit and Arrill sat on the couch so they could both view the work at the same time. Mel sat opposite them in a big chair watching their reaction awaiting a response. All Jit saw was the same symbols or hieroglyphics that were on the map with either a number or letter beneath them meaning nothing to him at all. It seemed to him they exchanged one meaningless language for another! Mel spoke up again saying he thought they might be coordinates or something in that vicinity to which Arrill bobbed his head in agreement.

'It must mean something' Arrill finally said breaking the silence.

'I think Mel is right and they are coordinates to somewhere but where we don't know, at least not yet.'

'How are we going to find out the "where" part?', Jit went on to ask.

'I'll have a look at it later on and see what I can come up with and if all else fails we might have to contact Fryppe' said Arrill.

Jit took another look at the translation while they talked for another hour before Mel told them he had other important work to attend to. He told them to stay as long as they wanted before disappearing into another part of the house.

'What do you want to do?' Jit asked Arrill.

He sat there for a moment looking lost in thought before he focused on Jit and said,

'We should go back to the Windchief I think'.

With that said they called out to Mel who re-appeared a short moment later and told him of their plans. As they exited the house, they thanked him for everything and told him they would keep him informed of their progress as it unfolded. He said it was no trouble and if they needed his help to call anytime then bid them farewell and returned the way he came.

Once strapped back in the shuttle Jit powered up the engines then lifted off and pointed spaceward. It wasn't long before the fine lines of the Windchief could be made out and at an astounding pace they were soon entering the cargo bay and setting down next to shuttle one. It felt good to be on familiar ground Jit thought, with Arrill voicing the same thoughts out loud. Before leaving the shuttle, Jit punched another button sending the hut coordinates to the main computer of the ship then followed Arrill to the elevator. On the bridge the lovely Ladone waited to greet them, looking adorable as ever.

'So, tell me what news you have so far' she said to them.

Arrill went on to tell her what Mel said and showed her the translation to which she offered any help she could if he should need it. He thanked her saying he just might require her assistance and was glad for the offer. They talked variable possibilities about the decoded symbols coming up with many possibilities that seemed feasible, but none felt right or truly certain. Later on, Arrill excused himself saying he needed time alone to meditate on the matter, and went to his cabin. After he left Jit asked Ladone if the coordinates of the hut from the shuttle were stored onboard the main computer to which she confirmed with a nod.

'Why did you store that information?' she went on to ask.

It was a beautiful little haven he told her and would frequent the place if Limtom allowed it for some solitude and rest, providing he was in the vicinity of course. She made a little sound that sounded like "Oh" to Jit, then dematerialized and went wherever she goes when she is not visible. He sensed a little annoyance from her and smiled to himself pondering the very real person she seemed to portray. He'd spoken to holograms all his life in different situations, but none even came close to Ladone and her unique and very real persona. He thought back to when he first contemplated buying a ship and that very evening he found the Windchief for sale on elink. As soon as he saw the ship, he loved it immediately and arranged to have a look. He met the previous owner who was a female captain by the name of Rachel Kister. As lovely as Rachel was, she had a disposition with the male species and didn't want to sell the Windchief to Jit except that Ladone talked her into it. Right from the word go she liked him, and he felt the same too. It was a memorable time he would never forget, nor has he ever regretted. Whilst in his trance he was rattled back to the present by Ladone telling him Limtom was calling on the link. Her image appeared on the big screen still dressed the same as earlier on in the day.

'How did things go at Mel's place?' she inquired of Jit.

He went on to tell her step by step the day they had and was enjoying the chance to talk to her and seeing her again. She then talked a bit about her day then said goodnight reminding him they were welcome anytime and blinked out. He stared at the blank screen for a moment before becoming aware Ladone was standing near him.

'You two seem to be getting on' she said.

'Do you think so?' he replied.

'I can tell she likes you by the way she talks to you' she continued with.

He thought about what she said and maybe he was approaching Limtom the wrong way. Maybe he should just speak his mind to her and see what happens. Deep inside Jit knew the problem with that was how Ladone would respond to the situation. I guess she'd have to adapt because he wasn't planning on being alone forever, he thought to himself! For a moment he almost pressed the lit panel to connect him to Limtom and arrange to see her, then stopped midway frozen in thought. Maybe he should let things unfold a little more before he says anything, he concluded to himself and went to make a hot drink instead.

....

Arrill decided to go to the library instead of his room and relaxed on the couch with his head back and closed his eyes seeing if some spontaneous thought or vision might aspire. The numbers and letters did seem to present a position but how was it made understandable. A notion came to mind and he got up to find some star charts and see if anything on them might point a direction. The hours passed unaware as he lost himself in the search and was broken from his quest by Jit announcing dinner would be ready in ten minutes. The clock on the wall read 5.50 pm when he looked up at it and he told Jit he was on his way. He looked at the mess of maps everywhere and open books deciding to clean it up after dinner. He closed the door and walked to the elevator which still stood ready to take him to his desired floor.

……………….…………..

Jit woke up from a nap that came upon him while he sat on the bridge with his drink. He looked over at the cup which was still half full and long ago cold thinking about getting up to make another. Arrill must still be in his room he thought to himself then looked at the time which read 5.05 pm. It was close to dinner time and at the thought of it, his stomach suddenly felt ready to eat. The next big problem was what to eat! He loosened himself from the long seated position and wandered to the galley. He selected the desired meal on a panel located on the wall and pressed activate then went to sit at the table with his drink while the meal was made ready. At 5.50 pm he summoned Arrill in his room and received no answer, so went to ship com and repeated the call. His reply came back from the library informing Jit he was there. Five minutes later he heard the lift stop on the bridge and shortly after Arrill walked into the galley.

'How are things going with the translation?' Jit asked him as he went to get a cup.

'Nothing yet' said Arrill as he took a seat at the table.

The bell on the wall binged to let them know dinner was good to go and Jit went to get the meals and bought them to the table with the aroma quickly overpowering everything in the room. He then went to get the wine which he uncorked and sat down to eat. The hot and spicy Bolognese was delicious and the red wine complemented it like icing on a cake. Afterward, they went to sit on the bridge to relax and talk further.

'I was thinking I might contact Fryppe' said Arrill.

'Do you think he might be able to help?' Jit said back to him.

'I don't know but with one more mind chasing an answer it has to help some more' he said back.

'Maybe the contacts who knew nothing before might have more understanding of these hieroglyphics' he concluded.

Jit could see no harm in asking Fryppe as he already knew about the map and he might just be able to turn something over. Arrill asked Ladone who appeared at his request to patch him through to Fryppe on the link and she set to the task without delay. Despite the vast distance, they were connected in moments with Fryppe's face appearing on the big screen. He looked a little haggard as it was early morning in Kelpuk and he'd only just got out of bed. The timing was impeccable. While he wandered to the kitchen to make a drink Arrill told him what had happened so far with the news quickly bringing Fryppe out of his stupor. With coffee cup clasped in both hands, he sat listening to Arrill and occasionally looking at Jit too. After spilling all the news Fryppe asked him to send a copy of the translation to him and he would get to work on it right away.

They chatted a little longer then parted company with Arrill going to get the translation he left in the library and return to the bridge. He soon had a copy away travelling the vast distance in a matter of moments with a renewed hope from the experience. Once that was achieved, he told Jit he was going back to the library to clean up the mess he left and would return soon. Jit watched him descend in the elevator and noticed a spark of excitement in his friend's manner with the hope of something unfolding as each day passed by. He went to the console and asked Ladone to bring up the coordinates to the hut Limtom owned and as he looked at the settings, he saw something familiar. Going on memory alone he compared the numbers and letters and a thought came to mind. They were different numbers and letters but the order was close to the same which gave him an idea. Arrill reappeared on the bridge and Jit showed him what he discovered and after sending Fryppe a copy they both set to work at seeing where the coordinates might lead. Every planet had its own set of coordinates set for the size of the globe and sometimes they matched other planets, but they could also be galaxies apart. The ones Mel set out for them seemed right for Spollee and it was certainly the best place to start. Jit asked Ladone to print out a land map of the planet which soon unrolled from the printer and they set it before them and started marking out different spots according to the numbers and letters they had. The good thing with Spollee was that it was mainly landmass with water being in lakes all over the surface, there was no sea or ocean.

They worked for a couple of hours with Ladone popping in and out looking over their shoulders applying some of her expertise and when they finished, they had a map of Spollee with twenty X marks on it covering all the landmass and some lakes.

'If the map came from ancient beings, I wonder what the landmass on Spollee might've looked like a long time ago' said Jit.

'We'll never know until we have an approximate date and maybe that's what will be had at the end of these coordinates if we have them right' said Arrill back to him.

Right now, they had no idea who or what wrote the map Arrill was given but at least it seemed to be leading to something real and further convincing them it wasn't a fake.

It was well past 10.00 pm when the work was completed and both of them felt the strain of the day bare down on them, so they left the rest until morning and retired for the night.

....

The following day at 7.00 am it was Arrill who was up first and in the galley making a hot drink. By the time he had his first cuppa, he heard Jit greet Ladone coming onto the bridge. He walked into the galley and saw Arrill sitting at the table with the pot of coffee nearby and said to him,

'Sleep little did you?'

'Very little' Arrill replied.

Jit joined him at the dining table and poured himself a cuppa.

'Up for breakfast soon?' he asked Arrill, who said yes, but insisted he was making it this time.

He got up and took the empty coffee pot with him and made a start on breakfast. By the time it was close to ready Ladone had appeared to chat with them. Jit and Ladone talked about what he and Arrill were going to do for the day and she asked if he was going in with the shuttle or the Windchief. He decided to take the Windchief so that way if they found anything the ship would be nearby for whatever supplies they might need. The area that needed to be covered was extensive and would take quite some time Jit thought to himself. Arrill soon returned with a tray bearing a plate stacked with pancakes. Jit grabbed a plate and scooped a third of the stack and dumped them on his plate and told Arrill they were going to take the Windchief in to check out the marks on the map. Arrill nodded his agreement while he stuffed another mouthful of pancake into his face. They spoke little while they ate and pretty soon polished off the lot. Jit cleaned up and met Arrill out on the bridge where he was going over the work they accomplished the previous night.

'We should contact Fryppe and the other's telling them what we're about to undertake' Jit said as he approached.

He looked at the time and knew Mel and Limtom would be up by now and Fryppe would still be awake too. They were soon talking to the three which all appeared on the same screen using a third of the surface each and exchanged the information they concluded last night. While they saw to that, Ladone prepared the Windchief for planetary entry. The entry with the Winchief was a lot less turbulent than the small shuttle and they soon broke through the atmosphere with barely a rattle and beheld the land below pocked with blue spots marking the lakes. The mountain range from this height seemed meaningless despite its grandeur but its length was still impressive as it snaked along like a backbone for many thousands of kilometres. At the highest point, the mountains reached sixty thousand feet which were nearly double the height of the mountain that rose above Mel's plateau, and they were constantly covered in thick white ice. Most of the marks they calculated were on the mountains with different heights and distances separating them, but none covered such heights as the extreme tops. Some were on the flatlands and some were in the middle of lakes and they decided to start with the mountains first seeing though they had the greatest number of marks to be searched. Ladone piloted the ship at varying altitudes according to positions while Jit and Arrill positioned themselves with high powered binoculars and scanned the mountainside for anything unusual.

The first mark was soon beneath them with a height of two thousand feet and while Ladone held still on that position Jit and Arrill covered every spot possible within a two kilometre radius from the X spot. The ground before Jit was mostly bare of vegetation with past slides shaving some slopes smooth and steep. The shadow of the Windchief loomed large on the side of the slope with the day being sunny and fine for them. When they were convinced nothing was to be found they crossed out the mark on the map and moved to the next. Some lakes were close to them as they progressed and they decided to do them along the way instead of coming back later. To do the lakes they used the shuttle and at the mark, they lit up the spotlights to look in every dark nook and cranny with all kinds of sea creatures to be seen staring back. Some of the lakes on Spollee were huge and would take days to circumvent with a water vessel. It took longer to search the lakebeds, but it was just as good a spot to hide something as anywhere else, so it had to be eliminated from the search. At 1.00 pm they stopped for lunch and a break from the strain of searching. They didn't have any idea what they were looking for but just hoped something would stand out and they would know. Jit thought they might stumble upon a part of an old dwelling or town or maybe a path of some kind but so far nothing out of the ordinary was to be seen. It might even be a wreck of some type, the ideas seemed endless.

As they arrived at position three they took up their viewing places in readiness to scan the ground beneath them. The ground was a different colour from where they came from and some vegetation reached high altitudes with their effort at survival. Jit marvelled at a small group of trees that had managed an impossible stronghold in a cleft and grew quite large too. They looked like a tuft of hair on an otherwise bald face. Two and four legged creatures could be seen scuttling over the ground with incredible agility as they stuck to the steep slopes. Some stood their ground in defiance despite the size of the ship looking thoughtful as they stared back at Jit and Arrill. Spot number three turned out empty too and with a red strike through it, they moved on to the next location. On route to mark four, Ladone informed them that Limtom was on the link and next her face appeared on the screen.

'Have you found anything yet?' she asked with some excitement slipping in her voice.

Arrill left the talking up to Jit who told her what had happened so far and that they were on the way to spot number four to look. They talked until they arrived at the next location then cut contact and resumed scanning positions and raked the ground carefully. Ladone moved the ship ever slightly for maximum advantage giving them as much coverage as possible. Again they found nothing and crossed out spot number four and prepared to move on. The next location was further away than the last ones and took longer to get to but in due time they arrived and found this part of the range was a lot lower with more vegetation covering it. Despite it being lower it still boasted heights of twenty thousand feet at the highest point. The trees below were thick as carpet and seeing the ground was only achievable in few places such was their density. Some of them reached skyward up to five hundred feet yet they still looked like fragile sticks at the foot of the mountain that dwarfed them but also protected them.

With such thick cover, they had to go to the ground to see what may lay hidden beneath the trees. Even the shuttle was too big for this job and Jit had the perfect apparatus for work such as this. In the cargo hold there were closed in sections that contained a variety of gear like motorbikes and a digging machine with different attachments and best of all, "Jetpacks"! On opening the containment area, one backed onto the pack which was held at the correct height then strapped it on and released the holds, and walked away. They weighed as little as fifteen kilograms each and would lift a maximum load of two hundred kilos and ran by the same means that powered the ship, a fuel cell to be changed when required. With both soon geared up, they walked to the back of the hold overlooking the tree covered ground and prepared for lift off. Two metal arms folded out of the pack and fit under the user's armpits protruding out far enough to hold with the right side being the controller.

A toggle allowed movement in all directions. Jit was used to using his jetpack but before they stepped off the ship Arrill flew around the hold a little to get used to his. They were relatively simple to operate and once you had your balance it was all fun and excitement from thereon. Soon they were both hovering in the air between the Windchief and the tree carpet below. They descended through the canopy and under the trees was a whole new world that awaited them. They had coms on the packs so they could talk to each other without the need to shout or make hand signals. Under the highest trees was another canopy of trees that were lower and a different type and colour altogether. On passing through them one was visited by a view that took your breath away. Large areas of emerald green water lay in vast pools that were surrounded by jungle and huge rocks. The rocks must've fallen from the mountain tops long ago and settled in the places they stopped and littered the area like miniature mountains themselves. The water ran the same as the lowlands with wide streams connecting the pools. Rapids were made from rocks and other debris that tried to alter the water's path too. Here and there a slit of sunlight speared through to the ground looking like vegetation of some kind and supplying light to the surrounding area.

They lowered to the ground with Jit noticing the soft mulch compress under his weight and the smell of rotting vegetation strong in the air. A variety of coloured bugs flitted around from tree to tree and attached themselves to the trunks where one only noticed them due to their movement. Once situated in their place of choice the bugs camouflaged so well they seemed to vanish and become like the surface they made contact with. Small furry creatures scurried in the underbrush with Jit only catching a slight glimpse of colour and a shaking bush to announce their passage. A cacophony of sounds echoed through the thick forest with their faces hidden from them and at times they sounded musical and deliberate. Jit lifted off again and alighted on a large rock nearby preferring the solid ground beneath him and looked around to see if anything caught his attention. He watched Arrill for a moment hovering at twenty feet or so from the ground looking around the rocks and low shrubs then Jit lifted off deciding to look the same way. Even down at ground level, the plant life covered every available piece of dirt with the only uncovered parts being the water sections. Even there at the edges of the water there grew plants testing the gravity to impossible lengths creating a false ground of sorts. Everything felt and looked alive and the air was fresh and crisp. The closer Jit got to the foot of the mountain in his search, the more rocks there were, and the searching took more time. He looked to his right and could see Arrill bobbing up and down now fully confident in the use of the jetpack. They searched to the perimeter of the decided radius with nothing to be seen before they agreed to ascend back to the ship. Once back in the cargo hold they hung up the jetpack's then took the elevator to the bridge with both of them feeling weary from the day long search.

'That's five down' said Jit to Arrill and Ladone who eagerly awaited them on the bridge.

Arrill slumped down on the seat as did Jit. It felt good to get the weight off his feet and while he unwound, he listened to Arrill and Ladone talk but drifted off on his thoughts. Soon after Jit looked at the time and it was just after 6.00 pm and decided meatloaf would be good for dinner. When the selection was set on the TSC he returned to the bridge and waited with the others while the food was prepared. It didn't appear to take long before the chime announced the completion of their dinner and they both went to eat in the dining room. The next thought on Jit's mind after eating was to shower and he got up excusing himself and went to his cabin to do just that. The shower refreshed him considerably but did little to help his aching body and after he washed, he lay on his bed with the intention being short term. However, it was after midnight when he woke and slid under the cover's returning to sleep instantly.

....

Arrill watched Jit walk out the galley thinking the same thing about a shower, but didn't feel like getting up yet to do it. Ladone appeared beside him in a chatty mood distracting him slightly from his weariness suggesting other possible search manoeuvres and ideas. As helpful as she was trying to be, he found it hard to concentrate and take on board her information. She seemed to be more excited about the search than both he and Jit. Having heard enough Arrill told Ladone he was going to bed and made for the elevator.

In the peace and solitude of his cabin, he stripped and went to shower then slipped in between the covers. While he lay there with the weariness of the day pressing down on him, he thought about the next day and how many more places they had to look, and wondered if anything would come of all this. There was still the chance they were searching on the wrong planet or worse still, maybe their calculations were way out altogether. His tired mind soon stopped thinking and only played silent pictures before he slipped away into sleep.

……………………..

Jit awoke refreshed and alert by 7.00 am the following day. While he dressed, he thought about where they were up to in the search with mark number six coming to mind. Then he wondered if Arrill was up yet and went out to see but found only Ladone on the bridge to greet him. She was wearing a medieval dress this morning that covered her right to the ground with only bare shoulders exposed and a hefty view of cleavage that seemed to want to explode from their containment. Her hair was done in scrolls and was red with the dress being black on top and from the waist down a deep royal blue with a border of lace at the bottom edge in black too. She was like an ever changing picture that always surprised him with her talent for change and imagination. Jit was sure she was a hologram with an identity crisis and found it humorous. She perked the place up with her whacky behaviour. After exchanging greetings, he walked into the galley to make a cuppa. Ladone appeared there telling him that during the night she moved the ship into position to commence searching the next spot. He nodded and smiled wondering what, and if, they would find anything today.

It was 8.30 am before Arrill appeared in the galley and muttered a greeting whilst getting a cuppa and joining him at the table. Jit informed him they were at the next search location already and would start after breakfast which he got up to prepare. Upon finishing they cleaned up then retired to the bridge. The new search area was in a valley that was like a wedge taken out of the main body of the mountain. Steep impossible sides of slippery and loose rocks were precariously sitting in position daring any movement that would surely cause an avalanche. Jit scanned one side while

Arrill did the other and after careful screening, they found nothing in this spot either. With number six crossed off Ladone moved the Windchief to the next location which was on the flatlands for a change.

This time she landed the Windchief on the ground having plenty of room to do so and they searched the area on the motorbikes. Despite the ground looking grassy from the air, it was laden with small rocks concealed in the tussocks making for a skill of balance required to remain upright on the bike. It was a bit like riding a wild bull in a rodeo Jit thought as he bounced over the ground working hard at staying on the machine. Although the bike had great suspension his organs were still copping a hammering! Again, after a thorough search of the area, they uncovered nothing out of the ordinary and returned to the ship and stowed the bikes back away then crossed mark seven off the map. The storing system for the bikes had sensors that detect foreign matter and automatically cleansed the unit until it was contaminate free.

The Windchief soon lifted her bulk off the ground and when they arrived at mark number eight, they prepared the shuttle for underwater exploration as the next mark was in a lake. This lake was considerably smaller than the last one they looked over, but it was a lot deeper making the bottom murky with little light reaching down into the depths. Even the bright spotlights seemed to struggle to illuminate enough of the area to see anything. Occasionally a large boulder would present itself as a ghost out of the darkness giving cause for sudden manoeuvre. Large sea creatures lurked at the bottom with Jit being glad none of them decided to see if the shuttle was edible and continued their way with beady eyes that didn't blink. After an hour long search, mark number eight uncovered nothing either and they rose to the surface and boarded the ship. By this time, it was after midday and while they made the transit to mark number nine, they had something to eat. They were halfway through their meal when Ladone announced they had arrived at the next location. They finished lunch then went to the bridge to see what their next search spot presented them with.

They were back to the mountain range with this area sporting vegetation right up to its base and even climbing a little looking like ankle high socks. The growth wasn't as thick as spot number four but still had enough cover to warrant the use of the jetpacks again. Down in the hold they buckled up to the same packs and unfastened themselves in preparation for departure.

'Good to go' said Jit to Arrill, with him responding by winking and giving the thumbs up.

Jit noticed as he passed through the tree canopy that this type of tree had sharp needle like leaves that would cause concern on bare flesh. Even on his coverings, he could feel the sharp fingers trying to penetrate the material. Under the cover of the trees, it was mostly bare ground with holes in it dug by a creature of some kind that covered large portions of the ground. There was no water of any kind, yet it was damp and humid with a strange smell not encountered by Jit before. His senses screamed caution and he felt like they'd intruded somewhere they shouldn't have, yet nothing could be seen or heard from their vantage point. They were still at a height of fifty feet while they hovered and looked around at the bare ground that rose in parts and sunk in others making for hilly terrain. The soil was dark and indentations were cut into the ground that would fill with water when the rains came. Right now, they were dry with tree roots matting the area in search of water that was beneath the ground somewhere. The holes in the ground were round enough for a man to fit in them but it would be a tight squeeze and not something Jit was prepared to undertake. Something must make those holes, he thought to himself, and maybe they come out at night and hide in the holes during the day. One of the first things he was taught when he sat for his interstellar licence was, 'when on a different planet, think differently.' Following that you were shown consequences where things went wrong, with some being disturbing and others unforgettable.

'I wonder what those holes hide' said Arrill via the com.

His voice was as clear as if he stood right next to Jit.

'I don't know' said Jit back to him, waiting for the predictable next question.

'What should we do, they are in the search zone?' he returned.

Jit thought for a moment then said, 'we'll keep searching the ground until we make the full cover of the area then go back to the ship and send a couple of bots down to search the holes' he told him.

This way, at the very most, they might lose a couple of bots that could be replaced without too much trouble or cost. They spread out and stayed at their present height while they scanned every spot that came into view. The growth that climbed the foot of the mountain was a little thicker than the rest of the ground and sported no holes at all but had a steady cover of rocks over it ranging in size that would fit in a hand to boulders the size of the shuttle. Jit soon came upon a section of rocks that seemed to have been shaped by hand and went down closer to have a look. As he lowered to the ground, he had a good look about still feeling uneasy in the semi-darkness until he landed on soft moist soil. He sank into the ground a little as it took up his weight and felt uneven under his feet. He bent down to pick up one of the rocks and it had a distinct sharp edge on it like it was part of a larger piece that had broken off. It was well weathered suggesting it had been there a long time and scattered about were other pieces that looked the same but varied in sizes. He called Arrill on the com and he soon hovered into view and lowered himself to where Jit was.

'Find something?' he said as he stood beside him.

Jit passed him the rock he held and watched Arrill spin it round in his hands while he examined it.

'It looks like it's been here a long time' Arrill said to him.

'Yes, and there are more bits scattered around too' said Jit as he pointed to the ground.

Suddenly a folly of rocks slid from a point not far from them and they both looked up with surprise and watched the disturbed rocks settle in new positions. Nothing else moved and they looked at each other and lifted into the air with Arrill dropping the rock in his hand. It was only when they were above the ground that a four legged creature stalked out from behind a medium size rock and looked up at them. The hair on its back was standing in a threatening manner with teeth bared and a low guttural growl could be heard coming from it. It sniffed the ground where they'd stood and circled the area looking at them all the while then ran off into the mess of rocks which concealed it entirely.

They decided to head back to the ship after that experience and send the bots down to search through the holes. On passing through the canopy of trees Jit noticed heavy ominous clouds begin to form at the top of the mountain as they entered the cargo hold of the ship which hovered not far above them. Onboard the Windchief they stored the jetpacks away then went to the bridge where Ladone waited in anticipation for them. Jit greeted her and then asked her to send two search bots down to have a look through the tunnels in the ground. She complied and dispatched them with the large screen coming to life giving a view from their perspective via the onboard cameras. The screen was split in two and as they entered the holes the spotlight lit up showing a circular hole from each machine as they progressed through the ground. The holes were mostly smooth but sometimes roots protruded and were pushed out of the way as the machine moved forward against the resistance. Both bots eventually came to an intersection where other tunnels crisscrossed one another and it was looking like there was a labyrinth of tunnels down there. The walls of the tunnels became rocky and they changed direction at random going either up or down, left or right. On another smaller screen before them Ladone had the direction of the bots mapped out drawing their progress as they went and assisting in their return to the ship. A rumble was heard inside the ship and Ladone told them it was a thunderstorm building above the mountain. Jit wondered what the storms might be like as he hadn't encountered one on Spollee yet and recalled the wild experience at Fryppes place.

Without any warning, the ship was struck by a lightning bolt that diffused harmlessly but gave the ship a slight nudge which wasn't something that happened often.

'I hope this isn't some kind of burial ground or sacred site' said Arrill, startled by the strike too.

On looking out the forward viewing windows the mountain stretched above them and the clouds formed a dark hat around the monolith. Rain cascading down its side formed great waterfalls that looked like maiden's hair reaching the ground way below in mist form. It transformed the mountain completely making a breathtaking picture to behold and one not easily forgotten. Whatever made the tunnels had either long ago died out or was lost further in the catacombs that surpassed the radius of their search area. Jit told Ladone to withdraw the bots to which she attended straight away, and they watched on the screen as they made the exiting journey back to the ship. On exiting the holes, the bots showed a different landscape to the previous image. The water from the rain was filling the ruts in the ground and now forming wild mini rivers that tumbled over the once exposed tree roots. While they took in the scene before them Arrill suggested the possibility that the piece of rock Jit found may have come from somewhere above the mountain. The weather was too fierce to venture outside and look with escalating winds that changed directions at a whim and maddening lightning strikes that struck the ground at random with no pattern in mind. The bots were engaged for the search, but little could be made out as they were blown about in the fury, and the heavy rain made for a blurry view.

'We'll have to take a closer look when the weather abates' said Jit and told Ladone to bring the machines back in.

'I wonder how long this will last' Arrill spoke out expecting no answer in reply.

He no sooner finished speaking when Ladone announced a call coming through from Limtom and then her face appeared on the screen.

'How's the search going?' she asked them with a little girl's excitement in her voice.

They both told her the story of their progress so far taking turns at speaking then Jit asked her if she could catch Mel up on the news. She went on to tell them she spoke with Mel last night and he did ask after them and what progress they'd made. When they finished talking, Limtom's face blinked off screen and Ladone told Jit the bots were secure and asked him what he intended on doing. Outside the weather worsened with the rain swirling around driven by the winds and coming down in bucket's full. It had also gotten considerably dark despite the time being only mid afternoon as he watched the trees being thrashed about below.

'We should wait this out and have another look' Arrill said to him and he agreed, telling Ladone they would stay here until that suggestion was fulfilled.

Maybe higher up the mountainside, there might be some other clue to this journey that continues to pull them along, he thought to himself as he progressed to the gym for a workout. The hour passed rapidly with his mind thinking about the progress they'd made so far and his body working involuntarily with a rhythm born out of repetition. On finishing, he returned to the bridge where Arrill and Ladone talked away about search strategies and the likely outcome from all of this, meanwhile the storm outside continued to whip the landscape below with unrelenting fury. Before long nothing could be seen outside as darkness took over totally with the time passing 6.00 pm. While Arrill took care of dinner Jit went to his cabin to shower and change into clean clothes then returned to the galley where dinner was only a short wait away.

'So what's on for tonight?' asked Arrill.

Jit shrugged his shoulders then suggested a movie maybe, to which Arrill nodded then excused himself to go and shower first. In the theatre room, Jit prepared everything and chose an old favourite movie called "Stellar Wars." Despite its age, it still had the magic that drew one in. When

Arrill entered he flicked the remote to begin the movie and they kicked back in the comfortable recliners eating snacks and being reverberated in their seats due to the mind bending surround sound. Partway through the show, Jit paused for an intermission and went to dig out a bottle of something from his reserves. He returned a short while later with a tall slim bottle etched on the outside by laser depicting a scene that seemed ritualistic with people around a blazing fire dancing. The contents inside were pale orange with a pleasant fruity smell.

'Where do you get all these exotic drinks?' Arrill asked of him, to which Jit just smiled saying nothing further.

It was going onto 10.00 pm when the movie finished and after a long yawn, Jit bid Arrill a good night and made for his cabin, feeling a little woozy from the nectar he consumed. In his cabin, he kicked off his footwear and lay on the bed feeling numb from the neck down and light as a feather. He could still hear the storm raging outside such was its intensity and that was the last thing he recalled before slipping into a deep sleep.

……………………

Arrill remained in his seat for a while after Jit left enjoying the solitude which was only disturbed occasionally by the wild weather outside. He felt the weariness of the day weigh down on him and before he fell asleep on the recliner he got up and went to his cabin where he was soon horizontal and drifting off. Pictures flashed through his mind of treasure and gold, then a laughing old man running away from him, followed by darkness which completely engulfed him.

……………………

Jit woke from a restful night's sleep at 7.30 am but remained in bed a few more minutes before he got up and dressed, then ventured out to see if Arrill was up yet. On the bridge, the ever pleasant Ladone greeted him and informed him Arrill was still asleep and after greeting her he went to make a much needed drink. Outside the weather had cleared and all was calm, almost a spooky calm compared to the tempest of the previous day. He poured his drink then went to sit on the bridge and see what damage the storm had left in its wake. To his surprise nothing looked any different but then he couldn't see through the tree canopy clearly and it could be a whole new setting down there. Out the window, the mountain glowed with a pale orange colour from the early morning sunlight and the shadow of the Windchief marked its flank like a giant bruise. The waterfalls had depleted as quickly as they appeared with wet shiny surfaces still prominent and covering the mountain in patches. Everything had a clean look after the severe washing the storm had given the landscape and Jit wondered if the storm also uncovered anything else. He was deep in thought when he heard the elevator being summoned from below, and moments later he heard it dock at the top floor again. He greeted Arrill who stood there briefly as if wondering what to do next before he replied with a mumble of sorts then went to the galley.

He returned in a short time taking a seat and poured coffee for himself. Across the window flew some medium size birds that seemed to have plucked up the courage to venture close to the ship. Their wing movements were slow and easy as they passed by looking down in the hunt for food. Jit watched them sail past noiselessly admiring the stark colours they wore over them with feet dangling sharp claws that would render flesh to ribbons. While he watched them fly from sight he thought about some breakfast. When breakfast was over, and they were both ready they made their way to the cargo bay to buckle on the jetpacks then prepared to launch out for another look around at mark number nine before moving to ten. The air outside was cool on Jit's face causing him to shudder momentarily before the descent through the tree canopy distracted him requiring his full attention. They agreed to start the search from the ground again and work their way up the mountainside until they reached where they could go no further.

Things had changed below the canopy with large pools of water remaining behind from the storm and now the tree roots only stuck up in places where the water wasn't deep enough to engulf them. While Jit hovered around, he was aware that other things lived down here and kept a vigilant eye about him reminding Arrill to do the same. Most of the holes were now underwater where the ground was low laying, and a few remained undisturbed above ground with no sign of life still. They slowly scanned the ground as if for the first time and within a short while they reached the place where Jit found the rock that looked hand hewn. He could find no sign of any of the pieces though. They double checked in case they missed anything but still came up empty handed. Unperturbed they slowly escalated the mountainside scanning a section each as they gained altitude. Climbing higher they passed small holes in the mountainside that might've been caves but were too small for a person to enter and Jit wondered if they might be worth checking with the bots later. They speckled the mountainside and were only visible because they were now in such close proximity. They weren't discernible from onboard the ship. Some of them were elongated and barely more than a crack in the rock while others were rounder and could only be accessed by someone the size of a small child. Only flying creatures would be able to access most of the hollows such was their height with no footholds for even the most experienced land creatures.

During the search, Jit felt a cold draught lick his face yet could see no fissure to explain the phenomena and hovered closer to the side of the mountain where the draught was strongest. On closer inspection, he found a cavity hidden where the rock doubled over itself concealing the aperture when looking at the spot face on. If it wasn't for the draught, he would've missed it entirely it was so well camouflaged. The draught came and went almost as if the mountain itself was breathing and on closer approach, he saw a gap big enough for him to stand upright in but so narrow his shoulders almost touched both sides. The draught was cold and with it was a musty dank odour commonly experienced in caves. With his feet planted on firm rock, he looked into the blackness where he could see no further than the reach of his arm, then was startled from his reverie by the com crackling to life.

'Where are you?' crackled the voice of Arrill echoing in the tight space adding to the mystery of his surroundings.

For a moment he was considering to game with him but the concern in Arrills voice detoured him from such play. He backed out of his position a step and once again depended on the jetpack to hold him up. His eyes had to readjust to the brightness of outside as they were already conforming to the little light of the passageway. Arrill was not all that far away but looking in a different direction when Jit called to him via the com and watched him turn around and spot his location. In a few moments, he hovered beside Jit awaiting an explanation for his disappearance.

'I think I've found something,' he went on to tell him, 'but we'll have to go back to the ship to get torches so we can see.'

Arrill looked at him curiously, not saying anything waiting for further explanation, but instead, Jit turned and hovered over to the Windchief with Arrill close on his heels. Onboard, they hung the packs back up then took the elevator to the bridge where Ladone anxiously awaited them.

'Any success yet?' she inquired of them while their torsos were still emerging from the floor beneath.

Jit went on to tell them both what he'd found as they went to the galley to have a drink before going back out again. All the while they listened hanging onto every word in silence. When they finished, they made their way back to the cargo bay where Jit went to a supply cabinet and pulled out four torches. Two were large ones and two were smaller so they could fit in a pocket with the large torch clipping to one's belt. The torches were self power generating with the large ones having a handle on the side which could be wound, and the small torch charged by running a handle up and down the length of the body so it could remain portable and pocket size. A one minute charge action would run the implement for an hour and two hours for the smaller one with dependable light that never ran out. Jit strapped one to his belt with Arrill following suit and the small torch went into a pocket he could zip shut in the likelihood he should fall and lose one. Once they had the jetpacks back on, they exited the rear of the ship and hovered back to where Jit found the hidden entryway. Despite him knowing it was there it still took a little looking before he found it again. Arrill followed with no idea what he was doing until he saw him disappear right before his eyes into the rock wall. Back on the ledge Jit stepped in far enough for Arrill to gain a foothold as well then unclipped the big torch and wound the handle to amp it up ready for use.

'How did you ever find this?' said Arrill over the winding of torches.

'A breeze gave away its location' Jit said back wondering where the breeze came from in the first place.

When he turned the light on, its beam stretched into the darkness revealing a long passageway that leaned downwards on a slight angle remaining tight as far as the light penetrated. The breeze picked up a little and Jit noticed that the walls were uneven suggesting it was natural and not hewn by hand. With him leading the way they began the downward journey on an uneven and rocky path with the occasional bug scurrying to a place of safety. The air temperature remained cool on the gradual descent with the breeze growing stronger as it passed them, seeking an escape from where they came. The torch beam suddenly hit a wall in front of them looking like a dead end until they approached the wall then it suddenly turned a sharp right changing direction with an upward ascent now. Again, this path was only the width of their shoulders and a little above their heads, but it was smoother than the other path with more even ground beneath them. They came across a part of the path where the wind was a little more intense and on closer inspection, Jit noticed an opening the size of his head where the wind passed through. He looked up the small passageway and could see light reflecting off the wall further on and guessed it to be one of the many holes he observed from the outside of the mountain. It also explained how the wind was getting in. The path curved around to the left seeming to take the direction of going deeper into the mountain until they suddenly came to an abrupt end with no further to go.

'This is disappointing' said Arrill over Jit's shoulder, voicing his very same thought.

They shone the torchlight around until Jit fumbled his and dropped it. It bounced off the rock floor then flipped back into the wall in front of them and disappeared. At first, Jit thought it might be an entry like the one on the side of the mountain but when he kneeled to feel his way, he pushed his hand right through the wall before him. He stood up and did the same with his hand meeting a solid surface this time. He then lowered himself whilst patting his way until his hand passed through the wall once again. It was apparent that part of the wall was false giving the illusion of a deadend to shy away unwelcome intruders or thieves no doubt. Had it not been for his clumsiness they would've been walking away thinking it was a dead-end too. To get through the cavity they had to get down on hands and knees and crawl through the tight but otherwise passable gap. On the other side, the torch lay facing the length of the path awaiting them.

'I wonder how the illusion was created' said Arrill.

'It must be a hologram of some kind' Jit said back, with no other idea how it could be possible.

'One thing for sure, if it's been put there to mislead anyone then there must be a reason for that' Jit went onto say.

He picked up his torch and shone the beam around noticing that the walls were a little wider and higher in this part of the passageway then continued forward with a sense of caution pricking his conscience. Whatever this was they were walking into had to conceal something otherwise why bother going to all the trouble of misleading anyone for no reason at all he pondered. There was no breeze at all in this passageway and five minutes into the walk they came upon some steps that lead them down three flights then veered left and went down a further three flights. At the bottom, the path stayed straight for as far as the torch beam could reach and they continued following it further into the heart of the mountain. After walking a further five minutes they came to a small square room which contained three passageways before them, presenting them now with a new dilemma.

The room itself was bare of anything but had been hewn by hand with the walls smooth and flat and the ground done the same way. Torch beams crisscrossed each other in the small enclosure as they searched every corner hoping to find something that might give a direction for them to continue. After careful searching, all they had were the passageways in front of them and the decision of which one to pick.

'Do you think we should split up?' said Arrill with a little reluctance in his voice.

'I did think of that,' replied Jit, 'but I don't know if it's a good idea.'

They decided to stick together with the choice now being which passageway should they try first. They discussed all the possible ways one would do this and opted for the opposite finally choosing the left side passage.

'You know what I don't get' said Arrill, 'someone has obviously gone to a lot of trouble to do this, yet they've left not a mark or symbol anywhere'.

'At least not yet' concluded Jit as they stepped up to the passageway before them.

It was the same width as the paths that led to where they stopped but now the walls were cut and smooth all around looking very precise in their dimensions but not diminishing the claustrophobic effect at all. Jit stepped in first feeling like he was voluntarily walking into the gullet of some huge stone creature. The air around him smelt of damp rock but was still breathable. He concluded that these passageways must all be linked somehow to a larger area which must keep the air clean and safe to breathe. All of it was a guess of course but he also felt a strong pull dragging him along as if all this was meant to be. Up ahead the torch beam reached into the cavity as far as it could, revealing the dark swallowing throat ahead which kept going on. Soon the beam reached a larger area of darkness and the closer they approached the more it was revealed that the tunnel now split in three again. This time there was no small room but just the junction. At the juncture, they stood staring at the same situation as before and Jit took out a pad and pen deciding to draw a map for the return journey.

'This is getting a bit messy' he said thinking out aloud, with Arrill agreeing too.

'So are we going to stick to the same path as before?' Arrill asked while Jit retraced their steps from the outside of the mountain and drew them down in a manner he could follow.

'We might as well' he finally said and finished the line up to where they were currently standing.

By this time the light on the torches began to wane so they wound them up for another minute and prepared to go further into the heart of the unknown. Taking the left path Jit lead the way, once again feeling the closeness of the walls that only a moment ago gave him some room to move. The walls were still bare of any inscription or other sign of what hand might've done the work. They were so smooth and precise they looked manufactured in a factory and placed down, then covered with rock to conceal their existence.

'How are you holding up back there?' he said to Arrill.

'Truthfully, I can't believe after holding the map for so long wondering if it was anything real, that I'm now in this passageway doing this' he told Jit.

'It does seem surreal doesn't it' he replied.

Their conversation was cut short by the light of their torches casting a beam into darkness before them instead of reflecting off the stone. A few steps further on they came to a void and it was so immense the light of the torch faded into the blackness reaching no other side or thing to connect with.

'Now what,' said Arrill from behind Jit.

'Why would you cut a path all this way for nothing?' replied Jit, still shinning the torch around the void in the hope of catching something.

He shone the torch beam down in front of him and the rock wall cut down vertically with no bottom to be reached by its beam either. The darkness in front of him was so complete it seemed to eat up the light allowing it little reach at all.

Jit thought for a moment then said, 'we could do one of two things, go back to the ship and return with bigger lights; or I could jetpack out while you stay here with the light on for guidance back while I see if there is another side. Maybe the path continues over in front of us somewhere,' he finished off with.

They decided on trying the latter idea seeing as though they were already there, and Jit stepped out into the void turning around in mid air looking back at Arrill. All he could see was the bright beam with his silhouette in the background giving him a ghostly appearance.

'Well, here goes' he said and turned around to face the void then merged into it.

He kept his torch beam pointing ahead as he floated in the air and soon became aware of the fading light shining on him from behind and turned around to look. To his dismay, the light had faded to just speckles looking more like the stars in a night sky than the bright beam of just a moment ago. If he lost sight of the light, he could be lost forever in this place that seemed to have no end and absorbed all light. He started hovering back and almost immediately the light gained intensity and then became the bright beam it was before. Arrill moved back in the gap allowing room for Jit to step back in and could see he was alarmed.

'What happened?' he asked sounding a little panicked himself.

'This idea won't work' he told Arrill and explained that his light faded out after he only travelled a short distance.

If he hadn't noticed it and turned around, he might've been lost out there. They decided to go back to the ship to get bigger lights and this time Arrill led the way as they walked the same path backward. They walked in silence with each deep in thought about what lay at the end of all this and how far it would be to that point. Shortly afterward they arrived at the three way junction but noticed they exited from the middle path which wasn't the one they entered by. They looked at each other knowing it was not possible to be exiting out this way when the return trip to this point was straight like it was going in. Or so it seemed.

'What the heck's going on here?' said Arrill sounding frustrated.

'I don't know' replied Jit who took the lead and continued straight ahead wanting to get out now.

Arrill followed, and at a quicker pace, they soon arrived at the room where they first split off and this time, they exited the same way they entered.

'This whole place must be a puzzle of some kind' said Jit and he continued at a more sedate pace knowing he was back on the same path they entered.

Back at the cleft in the mountainside, it felt good to be back outside and the light of the sun took a moment to adjust to as they prepared to hover back to the ship. They were both hungry by now and when back on board they went to the galley to get something to eat prepared. They greeted Ladone on the bridge and she materialized in the galley to continued stalking them for information about their quest. Both took turns telling the story while one made a drink and the other prepared lunch. At the table, Jit continued telling her the final part where they exited from a different point and the rest of the path was the same until they exited the mountain. She listened intently not interrupting at all until he finished then told him how fortunate he was to be able to have such fun. He assured her the part in the blackness he experienced was nothing at all like fun and gave him a feeling of despair and fear that was almost palpable. She smiled saying nothing more before vanishing into her nether world and leaving them to eat. While they did so they talked about what might've caused them to exit through a different point from their entry as that was still bothering them most. The black impenetrable mist was of disturbing concern too, leaving them to wonder what mystery was contained in its shroud. When they were done with eating, they returned to the cargo hold where Jit went to get the heavy artillery of torches. The only problem with this torch was it needed a power source, as it was too big to run on windup power. He slid a battery into the slot then put a spare one on his side belt for backup. He decided to just take the one torch and once they were ready, they buckled into their jetpacks and took off for the mountain again feeling a familiarity beginning to form with it. Despite it being his third attempt, Jit still took a moment to find the cleft but soon did and entered with Arrill close behind. The walk to the first room where the passage opened to three points was made in silence with just their breathing being heard. At that point Jit looked at Arrill and took the left passageway as he did before and Arrill hesitated a second, looking at the middle passageway wondering where that would lead before he shot after Jit. It wasn't too long before they were back at the spot they decided to name "Blackcloud" and Jit switched on the big torch expecting wonders but was quickly let down. Despite all its power and luminous ability, it travelled only twice the distance of the other torch they used. Not giving up Jit told Arrill to hold the torch and he would try the same manoeuvre as before with the jetpack.

He did this but found he only managed to double the distance before that light also started to fade away. Still, his torch beam showed no sign of another side or entryway to continue the path they travelled on. He hovered back to where Arrill stood and when back on the solid ground told him that the light didn't go much further than the last one and they would need a new strategy. They sat in the narrow passageway facing each other and propped up the torches to make light then Jit pulled out the flask and poured a coffee each, filling the place with the aroma and making the atmosphere not so hostile.

'Got any ideas?' he said to Arrill as he slid along the floor, a cup full of coffee spilling some on the stone as he did so. The rock absorbed it and the small spill spread to a largish round mark.

They remained silent for a time thinking, then Arrill said, 'Maybe the void is of no consequence, and the path we seek lies elsewhere.'

There was more silence then he added, 'I had this bizarre thought that came to me, what if the passage we seek is the one that we exited out of and instead of exiting, we double back and see if it still brings us to this point?' he finished with.

'What did you have?' he then asked Jit.

'My idea wasn't as technical as that' he told Arrill, then went on to tell him that he thought of using Polonium thread to connect him to this side and just jet out in a straight line until he reached the other side. The beauty of Polonium thread is its strength and lightness making it possible to carry a five kilometre spool of the stuff. It just meant going back to the ship again to get it. They agreed on trying Arrills idea and when the coffee was gone, they stood to leave. They didn't walk for long before they reached the splice in the way but before exiting out, they turned and walked back the way they came. After walking for a little while Jit said, 'shouldn't we be back at Blackcloud by now!'

'I was thinking the same thing' said Arrill while they continued to move along.

Just as Jit was thinking Arrills idea was right they came to the void once again. He shone the torch around with the walls and floor looking the same but then noticed something unusual. They were standing in the same position where they had the coffee, yet the place where he spilt the coffee was dry and clean. He remembered the coffee leaving a stain after the fluid had soaked into the stone floor but here it was clean as if he hadn't spilt any.

'I think we might be in a different passageway after all' he said to Arrill.

'We walked further and the place where I spilled coffee is now clean, meaning we are at a different location.'

'So, you're saying we're at the void still but from a different angle' said Arrill.

'I think so' he replied trying to keep a sense of it all.

He turned around and faced the void and unshouldered the big torch then switched it on and shone the beam out into the murk before him. It was different at this point with the beam travelling further, yet it still made no contact with anything or another side. He turned around and handed the torch to Arrill and jetted out to try seeing how far he could cross before having to come back. He went a lot further this time but even with his torch beam reaching out as far as it could, nothing was still visible. Another idea came to him and went back to Arrill to tell him and set it in motion.

The idea was to set Arrill's torch on the path with the beam shining out so he could jet out to the maximum reach which in turn would give Jit a further reach too. A sort of light relay if you like. They tried this and Jit soon jetted on past Arrill who shone the large torch to give him some light to return and at the end of the reach Jit shone his torch beam around and this time contacted the other side of the gap. As he shone the beam around seeking entry into the wall, he gathered this to be some enormous cavern inside the mountain. He soon discovered a dark spot on the wall looking like a yawning mouth inviting them to enter if they dared. He called Arrill over via the com and as he drew near the beam of the large torch lit up the wall even more. The passageway lay below them and they had to descend into it making Jit wonder if his flight over he ascended some, although he felt certain he was hovering level.

They entered the passage with Jit going first again and Arrill cut the big torch. The passageway on this side was identical to the other side making it seem like the crossing of the void was just a daydream.

'I wonder if anyone has ever made it this far' Jit said to Arrill.

'With such an elaborate effort put into that void distraction thing, I would wonder too' he said back.

Thoughts of the previous map owner intruded his mind. Without the jetpacks, the journey would've had to be done another way which they were both at a loss for an explanation as to how.

'I was thinking, what would be at the end of the other passageways?' Jit said while he moved forward at a steady pace.

They both knew that they had to check out every pathway and follow it to its end to eliminate any uncovered ground. With no knowledge of what they were looking for they had no choice but to search everywhere! The excitement that something was coming of all this was mounting for them both. After walking a while, they came to more steps, but these were many and they climbed straight up on a sharp angle. Jit shone the torch beam up the stairs and the beam finished into the shadows further ahead of him as it had in the tunnels then commenced the climb upwards. They were quite steep, and he was soon breathing heavily reminding him of a workout in the gym. Arrills breathing could be heard over Jits as he laboured on the upward ascent, not in the best physical condition. Before long they appeared out of the floor in the centre of a large room and Arrill unslung the big torch and switched it on to light up the entire area leaving them stunned at what lay around them. The room had four doorways with one in each wall and the corners diagonal from each other were two large upright urns and in the other corners were two statues of part person part animal creatures that nearly touched the ceiling with their height. The ceiling was at least four to five feet above their heads. The urns were a dark colour with etchings all over them and two large handles for holding onto and the part person creatures looked male and female with heads Jit and Arrill had never seen before. The walls in the room were still bare but around each doorway ran a border of symbols and drawings of people dressed in clothing they'd not seen before and they studied them closer, one door at a time. Arrill pulled the camcorder from his utility belt and started filming the borders knowing they must be of some importance but not knowing what. When he finished with the doors, he also took shots of the figures and urns to send to Mel later.

Jit shone the torch beam up each doorway with the beam reaching once again into darkness revealing nothing other than smooth walls and the invitation beckoning one to enter. When he finished looking, he took out his pad and pen and drew down the way to where they were so far then re-pocketed them.

'Which way do we go now?' said Arrill as he packed the camcorder back on his belt and looked up.

Jit looked at the time and it was edging onto 4.00 pm and decided they should go back to the ship and return tomorrow and have a full day at it. They could contact Mel and send him the pics they took and see if he can unravel anything to help them in the next steps. Arrill agreed and they soon descended the stairs and headed back to the void to do a reversal of the way they came. Knowing the torch lay on the other side Jit just headed in a slightly upward direction until its beam became visible guiding him to the doorway. After the crossing, everything happened the same way as before with no surprises popping up.

The sun was over the mountain by the time they appeared at the cleft and the sight of the Windchief covered in shadows was good indeed. The air temperature was quite chilly Jit noticed, catching him by surprise and making him look forward to a hot drink. They made the short journey to the ship and in the cargo bay stripped off the jetpacks and made for the bridge.

'Ladones going to be chuffed when we tell her what we've found' said Arrill as they were elevated to the top floor.

Sure enough, she stood at the console in her usual position waiting for them to appear and fired away questions as soon as they were topside. Jit looked at Arrill and smiled while he went to make a drink and left him to deal with the barrage coming from Ladone. By the time he returned Arrill was just finishing the adventure telling. He passed a cup to him then asked Ladone to contact Mel and a few moments later he appeared on the big screen breathing heavily from the run to catch the call.

'I had a feeling it might be you two' he said and stopped for a second to catch his breath.

They both relayed what had happened so far then Arrill told him he was going to send some pics hoping they might give guidance in some way. During the exchange, Mel sat quietly just listening and nodding his head on occasion and when the Link sent the pics, he excused himself going into another room to get them. He walked back into the room ruffling paper as he looked at each picture of each door and studied them silently with a crumpled forehead deep in thought. Eventually, he told them he'd need some time to work on it and said he'd call back as soon as he had anything then winked out and was gone.

By this time the dinner that Jit set earlier was ready and while they ate, they talked about the day and the progress they made. Arrill seeming a lot chirpier than usual. It must be giving him quite a buzz thought Jit after he held the map for so long having no idea if it was worth anything or not. When they finished eating and cleaning up Jit told Arrill he was going to shower and made for his cabin. It felt good standing in the shower with hot water running over him. With clean clothes on he went back to the bridge passing Arrill on the way to his cabin to do the same. He sat in the captain's chair and looked out the window. Complete darkness now shrouded the land and the moons were beginning to reveal themselves rising from the horizon. They would soon cast a dim light over the land giving it an eerie appearance as the valley before him was lit up looking like the alien landscape that it was.

Lost in his thoughts he was suddenly interrupted by Ladone announcing that Limtom was on the link then her face appeared. He caught her up on events so far and she listened intently saying nothing but making facial movements when he relayed scary bits of the tale.

'This is fascinating' she went on to say then told Jit about her day and while she was doing so Arrill appeared greeting her as he took a seat.

They chatted for a while longer then she said she was bushed and had to eat yet before having an early night due to the stress of her day. When they parted, she gave Jit a long lingering look which was caught by both Arrill and Ladone. Arrill just gave him a sideways smile whereas Ladone dematerialized saying nothing at all.

'What should we do now?' said Jit looking at Arrill for a response and idea giving him a break from making decisions.

They agreed on watching a movie in the theatre, so they took the lift to the third floor and went to get comfortable and kick back for a while. The room darkened gradually, and the surround sound vibrated them in their seats as the movie shifted them from the events of the day and carried them off to an adventure of another kind. By the time the movie finished a couple of hours later, Jit was ready for bed, so he bid Arrill a good night and went to his cabin. In his room, he quickly jotted down a brief description of the day event in his journal then hopped into bed. While he lay there, he thought about Mel and what he would find then wondered how long it would take him to discover anything, and during all this, his eyelids became increasingly heavy. Just before he went under his last thought was of Limtom and the long lingering look she gave him until his eyes closed but her image lingered on.

……………………………..

Arrill sat in the silence enjoying the peace and quiet after the ruckus of the movie and thought about the events of the last few days. It didn't seem that long ago that he was sitting in a cave in the middle of a desert with no idea what to do and afraid for his life. Now he was on a planet a long way from Geelok with a map he held for some time and the beginnings of its secret slowly unfolding. Deep down inside he was filled with excitement but on the outside, he was bushed and mentally exhausted, so he got up with a little effort and went to his cabin. In his room he could feel the tiredness overwhelming him, so he stripped and slid under the covers and a few breaths later was off on the first dream that whisked him away.

....

Jit awoke just after 8.00 am and once he was dressed and washed he meandered up to the bridge where his first conversation for the day was with Ladone. He nearly tripped over his eyeballs when he saw her! She was geared up in the shortest possible skirt a girl could wear with lace stockings displaying a dragon down one side of them done in the same lacework and small black shoes with a moderate heel. Her top was a matching blue to the skirt that was low cut but still modest and her hair was tied up in a bun with some sticks sticking out of it. At least that's what they looked like to Jit! She wore a bulky necklace made of coloured beads and on both arms had matching bangles to complete her outfit. She was stunning as always but Jit felt something else was going on but couldn't quite put a finger on it.

They conversed in the same manner as always with her materializing in the galley when he ventured there to make coffee and continued probing him with what they were going to do today. He told her they would probably wait to hear back from Mel first and see what he would unravel from the pictures he was sent yesterday. At the dining table, he passed his hand over the sensor at the tables edge and his mum and dad popped up out of the centre smiling at him and he sat there sipping his drink and thinking about them. During his mesmerisation, he heard Arrill come onto the bridge, and at the same time, Ladone vanished. A moment later he entered the galley.

'Good morning' said Jit and Arrill surprised him by stringing together the same two words and greeting him back. He could hear him fumbling in the cupboard for a cup then he came and sat at the table and poured himself a coffee.

'I don't suppose Mel has called?' he finally said after a few sips of his drink.

'Not yet' returned Jit, leaving it short and easy.

He was starting to get hungry by now and decided to get up and do something for breakfast and left Arrill to his peace and quiet. They ate in silence until they were done then cleaned up and went back to the bridge. By this time Ladone was on the bridge and Jit heard Arrill near choke on a mouthful of coffee when he saw her. He looked over at Jit who just shrugged his shoulders in reply, and they took seats in front of the windows looking out at the new day beginning. The long stretched shadows of sunrise were slowly withdrawing as the sun rose to its zenith and warmed the day at the same time. The sky was speckled with clouds that drifted by rapidly on fierce winds that blew high up in the air, yet where they hovered it was little more than a breath according to the weather station on board. A flock of grey and bluebirds danced on the wind with their beaks moving for sound, but nothing heard. Jit watched them as they became specks on the horizon and then seemed to simply vanish from sight.

'Should we call Mel or wait a little longer?' Arrill interjected, snapping him from his meditation.

He looked at the time and it had just gone past 10 am, then he nodded and looked at Ladone who in turn fulfilled the request. After a short while, she announced that he was either not home or didn't hear the call and would keep trying until a connection was made.

'What should we do in the meantime?' said Arrill, and Jit looked at him with a mischievous look on his face.

'How about some adrenaline fun' he said back to Arrill who looked on eager to know more.

He went on to tell him that every so often he liked to take the fighters out for a spin and today was as good a day as any. He didn't need to say it twice as Arrill was up and fully awake at the thought of it and they were soon on the elevator platform and descending to the cargo hold. They geared up for the ride and Jit jumped in number one while Arrill settled into the seat of number two and prepared the machines for flight. With the customary pre-flight check carried out, Jit hovered out the bay door closely followed by Arrill, and once past the Windchief's shielding, he opened her up. He was snapped back into his seat with everything around him turning to a blur. In seconds the Windchief was out of sight as he skidded on the air at breakneck speed feeling himself come alive from the rush. Arrill was nowhere to be seen but Jit knew he was out there somewhere charging up on adrenaline too.

He bought his fighter down to three hundred feet above the ground and the feeling of speed was increased dramatically although he slowed down to a mere four hundred kilometres an hour. Wildlife didn't know which way to go and some ran left or right with others just diving into a nearby hole while some just lay squat on the ground in obvious panic from the sudden encounter. He was just considering a quick spin to the stratosphere when Ladone came online telling him Mel was trying to contact them. He told her he was on his way back and turned the nimble and extremely agile fighter around and headed back to the Windchief feeling a little disappointed at the interruption. When he arrived Arrill was just preparing to get out of the cockpit and he rested the craft beside number two and shut down the engine returning the cargo hold to peace and quiet.

'We should do that every morning' said Arrill when he climbed down from the cockpit to meet up with him.

Together they rode the elevator to the bridge keen to see what Mel had in store for them. At the top, they were connected by Ladone and in moments the familiar face appeared before them. They exchanged greetings then he got on with the translation of what they'd sent him. It seemed that the four doors were connected to the same positions as the four points of the compass meaning there was North, East, West, and South. He then went on to tell them the rest of the symbols were the same as the ones on the map that they couldn't decipher. No doubt what was written must've been of importance, but they had no way of knowing if it was detrimental in their search or not. With all said he told them he had to go as he was working on another translation of great importance.

They sat in silence for a moment with the information whirling around in their heads before Jit got up and went to get the map they marked with all the search spots. He spread it on the console and marked the point they were at then they searched to see if any of the other spots coincided with the same points of the compass. After some time working at it they found close instances but none were precise enough to mark as accurate compass points.

'What were you hoping to find?' Arrill finally asked him.

‘I thought that maybe another three points were spreading from this point making the four and completing a compass pattern’ he said back.

‘I think we should just go back to the room with the four doorways as they might be the four points and check each one first before we assume anything else’ Arrill finished off with.

‘I think your right’ agreed Jit and with that, he looked at the time which was nearing 11.00 am.

They decided to make something to take with them for lunch, so they didn’t have to return to the ship or go hungry later and settled on sandwiches and a flask of coffee. When they had everything they needed, Jit told Ladone what they planned then they took the elevator down to the cargo bay and strapped into the jetpacks ready for departure. The slight breeze of earlier on had picked up its pace a little making the use of the packs more challenging, especially when it came time to enter the cleft in the mountainside.

Regardless of the difficulty they were soon back in the confines of the narrow passageway and re-tracing their steps back to the room they left the day before. Navigating the void was as nerve wracking as previously, with both of them happy to be through it and on the other side. It wasn’t long until they were rising out of the floor in the center of the room and Arrill fired up the big torch lighting the place up. Even though it was their second visit, Jit could still feel a presence of some kind, like a lingering scent from a past visit. Although the big light lit up the place, they still used their small torches to scan every part of the room starting behind the urns and statues. They did each item one at a time dealing with the statues first. The motionless figures looked down on them with black beady eyes and arms folded in front of themselves ever still but giving the sense of realness. When they arrived at the urns, they thought about tipping them over but decided they might have something liquid in them and decided to look over the top instead. Although they weren't as high as the statues, they were still higher than either of them could reach so Jit got down on his hands and knees making a platform for Arrill to stand on. It was just high enough for him to look over the edge and with the torch he looked into the first urn.

'Well there's no liquid in this one but I do see something at the bottom' he said and hopped down to Jits relief.

They pulled the urn towards them and away from the corner then upended it with fine gritty material pouring out and spilling over the floor. It was black with the feel of fine sand but at the same time feeling artificial and warm to touch. The urn had a quarter of its height filled with the stuff and they decided it was for ballast seeing no other reason for it being there.

Arrill decided to tip all the contents out and sift through it with the feeling something else was at hand. They spread the smooth slippery matter over the floor thinning it out and his assumption turned out to be correct. In amongst the material Jit felt a hard object and on freeing it from the substance saw it to be a large emerald cut blue stone set in a silver casing with a small loop at one end. On turning it over he was able to see through the stone as it was exposed with the silver only making a border around it. When he held it up to the light the blue was deep and clear with not one inclusion making it rare indeed. At a guess, he estimated the stone to be in the vicinity of fifty karats. He passed it to Arrill who turned it over in the light examining it closer yet. With one urn done they soon had it back in place with as much content back in as possible before they lay the next one over to see what secret it unfolded.

After checking and double checking, the second urn turned out to be completely void of anything at all and after refilling it they stood that one back in place too. They looked at the stone again and Arrill said,

'It looks like a piece of jewellery of some kind.'

The loop had a wear mark on it from the stone once hanging on something but whatever that was was now long gone. Arrill slipped the stone into a pouch which also held the map and placed it back in his pocket then looked at Jit and said,

'So, which doorway do we go through first?'

Jit thought about it for a moment then took out of his pocket a compass and found the North position and faced the door the arrow pointed to.

'Well, this door is North which now leaves us with figuring out which is the right way' he went on to say.

'Got any ideas?' Arrill asked, sounding idealess himself.

'It's looking like just another guess' said Jit still not feeling the certainty like he did previously.

They discussed ideas and possibilities and came up with north being the head and going ahead seemed right so north they went. Before entering the doorway, Jit marked the other doorways with the rest of the compass positions then he stepped into the passageway and Arrill collecting the big torch followed close behind. The tunnel was the same as the others they'd walked through and after ten minutes of walking, they came to another room a little smaller than the one they came from.

In this room, there was only a stone block sitting in the center of it and nothing else. They walked around the block which was about three feet square and sitting up from the floor probably two feet. It almost looked like a table Jit thought to himself. He shone the torch up at the ceiling but even there it was clean with no signs or clues of any kind. He finally sat on the stone block and told Arrill they might as well eat to which he agreed and sat down on the block too. The additional weight was enough to sink the block into the floor catching them both by surprise with its sudden downward motion. Before they could react, the block was completely flat with the floor and then they heard a grinding of stone sounding up the passageway, then a heavy thud followed by a soft breeze blowing into the room. They sat still looking at each other waiting to see if anything else happened before Jit rose to his feet with Arrill doing likewise. They walked back out the passageway and a short distance in front of them spawned a set of steps going up on a forty five degree angle where a flat walkway was just a moment ago.

'This place is full of surprises isn't it?' said Arrill over Jit's shoulder.

Jit shined the torch up the stairs with the same scenario as before then begun climbing slowly as if testing each step first. He was aware the passageway they came through was now blocked and he hoped at the end of the steps there was a way to unblock it so they could get back out unless there was another way out. Up they went into the darkness using the small torch to see the way. A short while later they arrived in the centre of another room and when they fired up the big torch were met by a similar set up as the room with the four doorways. The difference was that this room had no doorways at all, only four objects were placed in the same order as the other room with the urns and statues. Again, there were two urns but different in colour and shape diagonal from each other and the other two corners had narrow but tall obelisks in them. They decided to eat first and when they finished, they went over the room with the small torches checking everything before doing a repeat action with the urns. These were empty of liquid too but when they laid them over instead of black gritty material, they had what looked like grain in them. The first one presented nothing after a thorough search but the second one had another emerald cut stone set in silver with the loop at one end of it. The only difference was the deep red colour compared to blue. They both examined it and again it was see through in the light and flawless in its clarity. Arrill added it to the pouch with the other stone and map then looked at Jit who was examining the obelisks again in case they missed anything.

'No doubt what we've found must be worth something, but I thought there might be a bigger haul than what we've turned over so far' he said to Arrill.

'I'm a bit perplexed too' returned Arrill 'but don't forget we still have more to check and maybe this is just the beginning of it all.'

'I hope your right' said Jit trying to remain optimistic.

Once they were satisfied the room was clean the next concern was how to get back to the first room which was now blocked by the stairway. There was nothing in the room that had anything in it which might've cleared the passageway, so they returned to the room with the block to have a better look around. They concluded there must be a way to get back out if there was no way forward from the room they left and hoped they were right. At the bottom of the stairway, they had a good look around to see if there was any tripping mechanism or lever, but nothing was to be seen and they made their way back to the room with the block. On entering they commenced searching the walls and floor and ceiling and it was during that time that Jit heard the grinding of stone against stone close by and turned around to see the block in the center of the room slowly rise of its own accord back to where it was before they sat on it. When it reached its zenith and stopped, they could hear the stairway lift with the sound of more stone grinding on stone, and then there was silence again. Jit looked at Arrill and said,

'It must be on a timer somehow which means if we were still in the room, we'd be trapped in there.'

'Unless another way out presented itself once the stairs went up' continued Arrill.

Content to be on their way they returned to the room with the four doors and picked the southern door to go through next.

'I hope this doesn't have to be done in a particular order' said Jit as he entered the passageway.

This passageway was the same as the last with smooth walls revealing nothing different than the others except the floor tilted ever so slightly downwards. A few minutes later they reached another room which was filled with water up to the passageway floor keeping secret what lay in its depth due to the black water, or at least what they thought was water. There was a strange smell lingering too, which they gathered was the liquid or whatever it was that lay before them. Jit shone the torch around and the beam exposed the same blank walls and ceiling, meaning the only other place to look was in the water itself. He unscrewed one of the cups from the flask and scooped out a cup full of it and even with the torch shining in the substance it was murky and once stirred emitted a foul smell.

'I doubt this is just water' he said to Arrill and poured the liquid back from where it came.

'So what should we do now?' Arrill asked of him.

He thought for a moment then said,

'Maybe we can leave this room until last and go do the other two passageways first.'

Arrill agreed seeing no other way short of climbing into the foul stuff and turned around to head back to the main room again. Back in the four door room, they chose the left doorway next which was west on the compass, and this time Arrill went in first. The passageway was still the same as the others but this time it rose slightly upwards as they progressed along with it for a little way and soon they entered a small room. This room also had no doors and the four objects in it were all urns, this time with each being a different height and shape yet they all carried the same colour. The big torch was set up after a battery change and with the room lit up, they started tipping urns over one at a time to see what was to be found in them. These urns also contained what looked like seeds and on closer inspection, they were double podded small things the size of rice and golden in colour. The first and last urn they searched revealed two more of the same emerald cut stones only one was yellow and the other green bringing the total to four stones now. With those two items safely stashed into the pouch, they backtracked to the main room again feeling a sense of achievement from finding something, even if it was only a small find. Jit let Arrill pass so he could go ahead of him into the third passageway being the east side of the compass.

Each time they crossed the room they had to look carefully because the hole in the centre they first came through seemed to camouflage itself and once Jit nearly stepped into it. After walking for ten minutes through mirror image walls they emerged into a room which contained nothing at all in it except a pockmarked wall in the middle that was two feet thick at most and reached right up to the ceiling looking more like support than anything else. The two ends didn't connect all the way, leaving a gap the same width as the passageways so you could walk around the wall at the same time. Arrill turned on the big torch which lit only half the room and after a thorough search of the walls, he moved the light to the other side of the centre wall to search there too. With nothing to be found, they looked at each other with questioning looks then decided to search the last thing in the room which was the centre wall.

The pockmarks were numerous but one by one they looked into each, hoping that something would unfold there. They were all the same size being circular and two centimetres in diameter, and about the same in-depth. If it wasn't for the block joins, it would've looked like a giant sponge sitting there. It was a slow pace poking every hole and looking at it with the torch, while Jit did one side and Arrill did the other. When they reached as high as they could they then had to have turns at being a platform while they finished the wall on both sides to the ceiling. It was on the last side that Jit found a different hole with its depth set way back so he couldn't reach it to see if there was anything in there.

'I found something' he told Arrill, 'but I need something long to poke in there and see what happens if anything happens!'

He hopped down from Arrill's back and after checking

if they had anything to go into the small hole, they found nothing that was thin enough or long enough.

'It's always something isn't it' said Jit a little exasperated.

He looked at the time which had become mid afternoon and guessed it to take a good hour and a half each way to get back to the same spot. They both agreed to leave it until the next day as there was no schedule to keep and they picked up the big torch and begun the trip back out. The journey back was the same as they came with no unexpected turns and the trip across Blackcloud was the usually uncomfortable sensation. The torch Arrill left in the passageway had run out of power but they were still able to find the other side of the void with little trouble now that they knew where it was. By the time they reached the cleft and could see the Windchief, it was going onto 5.00 pm and the weight of the jetpacks was becoming a burden on them both.

Back at the ship, it felt good to unstrap the packs, but it did nothing for the weariness they felt. When they reached the bridge Ladone waited for them and they greeted her then told her what had happened so far, with Arrill revealing the stones for her to have a look at. They took on a different appearance under the bright light of the bridge and all together they made a nice collection to possess. They went on to tell her about the foul smelling liquid in one of the rooms to which they weren't sure how to deal with. They decided to let the search go and think fresh in the morning then retired to their cabins to shower and change into clean gear. Jit was first back to the bridge and despite feeling better from the wash and clean clothes, he still felt the weariness of the day long hunt. After something to eat they retired to the bridge to sit down and look out at the growing darkness of days end. They'd not long taken the position when Ladone appeared and told them Limtom was on the link and a second later her face lit up the big screen. They re-told the same story they relayed to Ladone and Limtom was bursting with excitement from hearing the news. When she saw the stones, she was awed by them and wished she was with them to help too. They talked for a while and before she left they asked her to inform Mel of what they told her then she blinked off. Jit told Arrill he was having an early night and went to his cabin where he was asleep the moment he lay down.

…………………………..

Arrill sat up a while longer in the solitude of the ship with only his thoughts of the day spinning around in his head. In front of him he looked at the four coloured stones they found, wondering what other secrets the mountain held within its bowels and what length they had to go through to attain them. Soon he could feel sleep wanting to claim him and got up to make his way to his quarters before he fell asleep where he sat. His body was stiff all over making movement a will of the mind and, once in his room, he was soon in bed with the warmth of the covers soothing his sore muscles. He was asleep in moments.

…………………………….

Jit was first up in the morning and by the time he dressed and stepped onto the bridge, it was just going past 8.00 am. Ladone was there to greet him and he said hello on his way to the galley. Once he had his drink he went to sit on the bridge and look out at the new day unfold. A slight mist at the foot of the mountain slowly melted away with the heat of the sun and overhead the sky had a few small clouds hanging in the air moving slowly on a steady breeze. Thoughts of Limtom interjected his stillness for no apparent reason and he wondered what she was doing at the very same moment. He was broken from his trance when the elevator was summoned to the cabin deck meaning Arrill was up and on his way. Jit greeted him when he arrived on the bridge and received the usual grunt his friend made before he was fully awake and functioning properly. He went straight to the galley and soon returned with a cup of coffee in tow and what was left in the pot then took a seat. Ladone appeared soon afterward and they talked about what he and Arrill were going to do today with her giving ideas in an attempt to contribute to the search effort.

After breakfast, they cleaned up and made sandwiches to take with them and a flask of coffee because they could be gone all day again. With everything ready, they bid Ladone farewell then took the elevator to the cargo bay and Jit went to a cabinet looking for a device he knew he had that would suit the job they needed to attack. After some digging and searching, he pulled out a telescopic rod that could be adjusted at different lengths and slipped it into his utility belt then went to strap into his jetpack. As he slid it on the bruised muscles retaliated briefly then settled to the load. Arrill already had his on doing it while Jit looked for the rod and waited for him to finish before they exited the cargo bay. A slight breeze blew but presented no difficulty in the short distance to their location. The warm sun on Jits back felt good as he approached the cleft once again and located the entryway. Inside the mountain, they started the journey through the maze with torch beams guiding the way and within the given time arrived at the room they left the day before. With the big light bringing daylight to the otherwise dark room Arrill got down on all fours making a platform for Jit to stand on. With the telescopic rod extended all the way he poked it into the hole in the wall. It reached over half its length before contact was made with the end. At first, he poked lightly feeling no reaction from the other end of the rod then applied more pressure and felt the rod give way and sink into the cavity another few centimetres. For the first instant or two nothing happened but then they felt a slight tremor and a muffled sound which lasted a few moments, and all was quiet again. Jit stood motionless for a few seconds after the sound stopped and then stepped down from Arrills back looking around the room to see if anything was different. They checked the other side of the centre wall, but it was all the same there too with nothing changed from the way the room was before. Feeling a rise in concern having witnessed no change in the room they began to wonder if the way out was going to still be unaltered, so they picked up the big light and left the room.

Back in the four door room, everything was the same and they decided to go into the south passageway where all the water was. At the end of the passageway instead of being met by water up to the pathway, they found a deep well that encompassed the entire room with all the liquid now drained. Arrill turned on the big torch and shone it down the hole which was still wet with the fluid it once contained running down the walls and draining away into a smaller hole in the centre of the floor. Although the contents had drained away it did nothing to subdue the foul smell that lingered around in the closed space and if anything, it seemed more pungent. The drop to the bottom was at least four metres deep and stretched the same distance away from them with no evident means of getting to the bottom. For them, it was no problem having the jetpacks to assist, but without them, the climb would have to be done with ropes or a ladder. Arrill hovered down into the hole first and close behind him followed Jit with torch beam flicking all around the wet walls in the hope of locating something. When he reached the bottom, his feet stood on slimy slippery ground and the smell at the bottom was even stronger making breathing a little awkward. Arrill set the big torch down to light the place up and in the center of the floor was a cavity which no doubt allowed the fluid to drain away. The walls around them had a sticky film on the surface being the residue from the contents they recently held and in between the fingers, it felt like fine grease or something of the same nature. The foul smell was emitting from the substance because when smeared between the fingers, it released a greater concentration of the acrid stench.

'What is this stuff?' said Jit while he wiped his fingers against the wall again hoping to return it to its place of origin but only gathering more.

In the end, he wiped the substance on his clothing and refrained from touching it again. The walls were blank and the last place to look was down the drain hole which at first glance seemed vacant of anything until they shone the torch beam down inside it.

'This is one elaborate set up' said Jit as the beam exposed a narrow stairway descending into the blackness beyond.

'Those steps are going to be slippery' said Arrill as Jit prepared for the downward journey.

The space was tightly confined but enough to get through and when the steps petered out, they walked a few feet forward then they climbed back upwards. The climb up was longer than the climb down meaning they were at a higher level than the floor of the hole they came down in and soon popped up in another room, but a very small one. Jit also noticed the residue ceased after climbing up some of the steps which suggested the fluid only reached so far before it stopped. The small room was only two and a half metres square at most making for a cramped area with the two of them in it. The stairs came up at one end of the room, and at the far end against the wall sat a stone made chest with a thick stone lid on it and nothing else. The stone chest was the same as the walls being smooth and cut by the same method bearing no symbols or anything to say what was inside, or who made it. Opening it was simple with the lid giving little resistance before sliding away and exposing the contents it withheld. Sitting by itself in the middle of the chest was a small wooden box that Jit reached into and plucked out. The dimensions of the box were roughly twenty centimetres long by ten wide and the same in-depth and it weighed a considerable amount despite its small size. The wood, if it was wood, was polished to a high gloss finish and the swirling grains caused an optical illusion seeming like the pattern moved when viewed from different angles. With slightly trembling hands Jit pried the lid off, which fit with intricate precision, and inside was something wrapped in a deep blue velvety material. He pulled the item out and unwrapped the cloth to exhibit a golden coloured artefact of exquisite beauty. The shape closely resembled a key of sorts with coloured stones in the handle smaller in nature than the other stones they found but of the same colour and cut and number. Jit passed the piece to Arrill to look at and hold while he examined the box a little closer. It was made of one solid piece except for the lid, and even empty it weighed a considerable amount. The cloth was also some high quality fabric they had never encountered before.

'This is beautiful' exclaimed Arrill as he turned it over in his hands looking at every aspect of the piece.

Along the stem that ran down from the handle were branches that matched the stem but curved and twisted around in different patterns, giving it the look of a key or something that was the same. He re-wrapped the object and put it back in the box and because it was too big to go into the pouch, he placed it into the bag which carried their lunch and flask. Satisfied the contents of the room were discovered and all found they replaced the lid then backtracked to the room with the four doors and headed back to the void and made the crossing back to the other side of it. On solid ground again Jit led the way and in a short time, they arrived at the junction that exited the centre passageway. They then turned around and re-entered the centre entry to see if the tunnel changed and when they walked a little while they became aware the passageway was longer, meaning different too. Eventually, the passageway ended abruptly, seeming like the makers of the way changed their mind and gave up. The end of the work in front of them was still marked by the chisels that created the way and you could almost still hear them cutting stone like a ghost echo haunting the place. There were no signs of anything that suggested a way through and after a good look around, they headed back out. It was no surprise to them when they exited out the third entry and straight away entered the middle entry and repeated their steps. This time however they stopped just before they exited out the third entry and walked back the way they came. They were expecting to come to the void like what happened before and that did happen, but at the end of this passageway instead of a straight drop in front of them there lay a stairway going into the depths of the darkness. A very narrow and steep stairway!

'Obviously whoever made this place didn't think of jetpacks' said Arrill.

'Obviously not' agreed Jit, and took the first step down in confidence with the jetpack ready for use in an emergency.

The thrill of walking down a narrow way like this with little to be seen was exhilarating but only because of the safety of the packs. He wondered what lay at the bottom of the blackness and how far it might be to the bottom. Despite the safety of the jetpacks it was still an ominous voyage because even with the bright light you could only see a few steps ahead. The same thick mist hung in the air which caused no problem to breathe in but just affected visibility. The stairway levelled out after descending for ten minutes and they noticed the surface they walked on changed to a narrow plank of wood that looked the same colour as the box they found. Only this wood wasn't polished and as to what held it up, nothing was to be seen when the torch was shone under it and looked like it just floated on the mist. It must've been a test of courage Jit thought, because it did feel a little unnerving walking along it, even wearing jetpacks. They followed the wooden way into the darkness for ten minutes before they stepped once again onto stone steps and this time they climbed up. They continued upwards for a little way then arrived at another entry. Jit lead the way and they followed this passage for another ten minutes before they entered a large room. Of all the rooms they'd been to this had to be the largest by far. On shining the torch around they were met by the same blank walls, but the floor was etched out in what at first looked like patterns, and on closer inspection was a constellation chart.

'Do you recognize where this is?' Arrill asked Jit.

'Not by memory' he replied, 'but we'll take some pics and compare it to the charts we have onboard the ship and see what we come up with' he added.

Arrill pulled out the camcorder and rolled while Jit went over the walls and ceiling, double checking to make sure they missed nothing. As he did so he felt an elated feeling that slowly something was coming together, coupled with the excitement of still not knowing what. Convinced they had all the room contained, they turned around and made their way back. The trip back across the narrow bridge and steps was as nerve racking as previously and when they arrived back in the passageway on the other side of the void, they were relieved. When they exited from the path into the junction again, they came out the third exit as before then re-entered to see what happened next. After a short walk, they finally came to another dead end, with the way in front of them incomplete like the other tunnel end was. This wall also had chisel marks on it where the workers stopped and went no further. They decided two seemingly same dead ends were part of an elaborate puzzle system made to create confusion. They turned around after a careful look around to make sure nothing was overlooked and exited out the same passageway and were at the junction once again.

With everything searched and hopefully found, they made their way back to the first junction point which was the room with the three passageways in it. When they entered the room, they turned about to face the three openings with just the centre way and the way on the right, left to explore. Before going any further they stopped to eat as they were hungry and while they ate, they talked about what was found and why everything was spread out as it was. The time quickly passed and when they finished Jit entered the middle passageway with Arrill close in pursuit to see what they would come across this time. The passageway was the same as all the rest with the narrow close confined walls and low ceiling barely centimetres above their heads. At first, the way veered off to the right ever so slightly then continued straight and they walked along it for five or so minutes before it came to the end, which finished in a point with another passageway meeting it and completing the point, so it looked like an arrowhead. At the head of the point, there was a bulbous round section cut into the stone with the stonework cut leaving a pedestal that, at the top, had an angle cut into it. In the angled part was etched the outline of a planet and on the top right hand corner were some more symbols. They also noticed the planet had three marks like that from a chisel scratched into its surface seeming like an act of vandalism or unfinished work. Arrill produced the camcorder and rolled the information for further study later and while he did that, Jit searched around to see if there was anything to be found. Certain the search revealed nothing they went down the only way left to go and after the same length of time exited from the end passageway back into the room. They then entered the middle way again and before coming out the third way they doubled back again to see if the same thing happened as the other junction. This time they just passed the pedestal again and came back out the centre way with no change in the pathway at all. To be sure they entered the right passageway and tried that same method and exited out the same way with no change in that path either.

'Looks like these two passageways have nothing to be found' said Jit.

Arrill agreed and they started the walk back out to the Windchief. When they exited the cleft, it was mid afternoon and the sun was slowly making its way to the horizon drawing the end of day on the ground by the stretching shadows. Back on board the ship, they replaced the jetpacks in their positions and the torches in theirs, then they took the lift to the bridge where an anxious Ladone awaited them. They greeted her and while Arrill exchanged the events, Jit went to make a hot drink. When he returned to the bridge Arrill had the four coloured stones and the key displayed for Ladone to see. On the console, he was plugging in the camcorder to load the information they recorded so they could view it on the big screen. They waited for the picture to come up with what they thought was a constellation chart etched on the floor. It looked different to view from the angle of the screen compared to the floor and the three of them looked in silence for a while before Arrill noticed something familiar. He noticed a planet with the same symbols at the top right hand spot as the planet etched into the pedestal. Other planets on the chart had symbols too but they were marked differently with either more symbols, while others were not marked at all. All the symbols matched the language that couldn't be deciphered on the map and the four doors in the mountain.

'Looks like we have a star system and planet that are of relevance' said Jit while sipping his drink.

They then bought up the picture of the planet with the symbols to confirm the match and wondered why only this planet was etched into the stone. Arrill agreed, as did Ladone, leaving them with two more discussions to have…what about the last eleven spots they had yet to search, and how to find the constellation with the planet? After a short discussion, they agreed they should search the last eleven locations so they could eliminate any possibility of something else being missed and Jit instructed Ladone to make for position number ten. Surely there had to be more than this he thought to himself as the landscape out the window moved before him. While they journeyed to the location, they began searching star charts to see if they could pinpoint the constellation they pursued.

'There's one thing we have to take into consideration' said Arrill while they looked, 'and that's how much change has taken place in the constellation since this record was etched in stone?'

'Everything changes given enough time and for all, we know it could be many millennia since this was recorded. It could be the constellation we're already in with Spollee being the planet with the symbols' he finished with.

So, while Jit checked the charts, Arrill had the computer run possible changes in the system over different lengths of time. It was tedious work and they were so busy it seemed like only minutes had passed when Ladone announced their arrival at mark number ten. They checked the mark they'd stopped for and with careful looking found nothing out of the ordinary, so they jetted back through the tree canopy to the ship with another mark crossed off the list. Back on the bridge, Jit told Ladone to move to the next mark then asked her what progress she'd made with the constellation chart. Because they were gone only a short time, she hadn't achieved very much so Jit and Arrill picked up from where she left off and continued looking while they advanced to the next location. By the time they arrived at mark number eleven, it was getting dark, so they chose to look in the morning. The time soon reached 6.30 pm and Jit stopped work and went to prepare something for dinner. When the food was ready, Arrill joined him in the dining room where they ate and talked about the progress they'd made so far. After eating and feeling a little more perked up they went back to the bridge to continue their work. During the search, Limtom called to see how they were progressing, and Jit filled her in on what they'd found while she listened on saying nothing at all. When all was said, she told him about her day and Jit listened, feeling more like a couple exchanging daily events. There was no disputing the fact he had feelings for her because every time he saw her and spoke with her, he felt a kindred spirit connecting them. He just wasn't so sure if she felt the same way. When they finished talking, they parted company with a good bye and smile then the screen returned to star charts.

'You should just tell her how you feel' Arrill said while still doing his work and not looking up.

'I'm not really sure how she feels about me' Jit returned. 'Besides, she's seriously rich and might want someone of the same stature' he stopped at.

'You forget that you own an interstellar ship and a Windchief at that, which doesn't exactly make you poor' Arrill said back.

Jit agreed with him on his position, but it did nothing to fortify his belief that she might feel the same way about him. They searched right up until 10.00 pm before they both tired from the intense work and decided to call it a night and continue in the morrow. In his cabin, Jit showered and added to his diary then went to bed. His last thoughts before passing out from weariness were of Limtom, as he fell asleep with a smile creasing his lips.

....

Arrill looked at the collection of stones, map, and key he had in his possession, if it was a key. It wasn't the booty he was expecting but maybe there was more he told himself. He too wanted to own a Windchief and, if possible, he wanted the latest one out with enough left over so he didn't have to work again. Then there was the matter with Leearnah he wanted to settle too! His mind became foggy from the long day and he got up and went to his cabin where he laid on the bed and fell asleep still clothed with only his boots removed.

....

It was 6.00 am when Jit looked at the time, then rolled over, sleeping on and off until 7.00 am before he decided to get up. An air of excitement was in his moves as the map was beginning to show some signs of hope. Before long he ascended in the elevator to the bridge and was soon greeted by Ladone who appeared the same time he did. They exchanged greetings and when he went to the galley to make coffee she materialized there to continue chatting. He liked how they talked every morning and thought about Limtom and how it would be if she were on board then felt a prick of guilt for some odd reason. At the dining table, his mum and dad were ever smiling and not ageing in their hologram existence without a care in the Universe. He was partway through his first cuppa when he heard Arrill come onto the bridge and a few seconds later he entered the galley.

'Good morning' he managed, sounding like he was fully awake which caught Jit of guard momentarily.

'Good morning' he said back and waited for him to retrieve a cup and join him at the table.

As Arrill took a seat the hologram sank back into the centre of the table leaving a flat surface once again. They made some small talk and when they finished, they went to the bridge. At the window, they gazed out at the landscape before them, and at spot number eleven. After a careful search of the area, they concluded the place was vacant of anything relating to their search, so they ascended back up to the ship and crossed that one off the map too. Jit then instructed Ladone to move to spot number twelve and while they transited to the location, they went back to work seeing if they could match the constellation from inside the mountain. The busy-ness of the work kept them so occupied that they were soon interrupted by Ladone announcing arrival at their destination. Before long they were finished in spot number twelve and rose once again up to the ship where they returned torches and jetpacks to their positions then went to the bridge to continue their search from where they left off. Ladone moved the ship and it didn't take long to arrive at number thirteen because it was close by. In due time the search there revealed nothing, and they returned to the ship with another spot crossed off the list.

Without needing to be told, Ladone made for location number fourteen and seeing as the time was closing on midday they decided to stop and have some lunch. When they finished, they cleaned up then returned to the bridge and continued work.

'I hope this constellation we're looking for exists in the known parts of the Universe, said Jit, 'otherwise, we'll never know where to look'.

'I know, I thought of that too' replied Arrill, sounding depressed just at the thought of it.

Ladone interrupted them with the news that spot number fourteen was coming up beneath them and they left the console grateful for the break and went to look out the window. After another fruitless search of the area, they found nothing out of the ordinary and quickly returned on board where they replaced the gear they used then went up to the bridge. While Arrill went to make hot drinks, Jit launched back into the search. Ladone moved them to spot number fifteen while he looked and soon, he could smell the aroma of hot chocolate waft onto the bridge.

'Any progress yet?' he asked Jit as he placed the tray down on a cleared spot.

'Not yet' he returned and picked up the cup to take a sip.

They continued the work together and whilst doing so Jit had an interrupted thought about Limtom for no apparent reason. He couldn't get the thought about her out of his head until Ladone announced arrival at mark number fifteen. Leaving their work, they looked out the front screen to see what lay before them and were met by a white flat plain surface devoid of anything but ice as far as the eye could see. There wasn't even a mound to be spotted. It was just flat and level and lifeless and very white. They concluded after a short dialogue that if nothing could be seen then there was nothing to find and Jit instructed Ladone to move to spot number sixteen.

'I wonder if the ice melts up here' said Arrill, considering some hidden way beneath it that became exposed at certain times only.

'Do you think there could be something underneath the ice?' Jit asked him back.

'I'm not sure what to think' he said in reply.

'Personally, I believe we've found all to be found on Spollee, and our next destination is to find that planet marked on the constellation chart and pedestal' Jit returned.

They agreed that the next move to find the planet seemed obvious, but they also needed to know they did all that could be done on Spollee before moving on, so with a few more locations left to go, they set off for number seventeen and to complete the mission. While Ladone sped them to the next site they continued the work sorting through star charts. It was beginning to get late in the afternoon when they arrived at spot number seventeen and on gazing out the window, they beheld a landscape in total contrast from where they'd just come. They donned on the jetpacks and went for a look but were soon back on board having found nothing there either. They packed what they used away and went up to the bridge where Ladone was busy at work still matching star charts.

'Find anything that matches yet?' Jit asked her.
'Some charts have come close but weren't close enough to be an exact match' she replied to him.

'Oh, by the way, Limtom called looking for you and I told her you were busy and would contact her when you could,' she went on to say.

Just the mention of her name made Jit feel elated and he connected the Link and waited for her to appear on the screen. Arrill decided to leave them to talk and went to the galley to prepare dinner and Ladone also vanished appearing in the galley to talk with him. When her features emerged before him, she looked even more beautiful than usual and almost seemed like she'd dolled herself up for the occasion.

'Where are you up to now in your search?' she asked in a soft alluring voice.

Jit filled her in on what they achieved and, as he spoke to her, he looked deep into her eyes and she looked back the same way. Before they knew it, they were just staring at each other in a hypnotic daze. He snapped out of it, feeling a bit embarrassed at letting his guard down, and she responded the same way. They then made some small talk until they bid each other a good night and parted company. The star charts reappeared on the screen and for the moment Jit found no interest in looking at them at all and went to the galley to see what Arrill was preparing for dinner.

'Did you tell her how you feel?' Arrill asked him as soon as he entered through the doorway.

'No, but I'm more certain that she feels the same way about me now' he said back.

Ladone said nothing and just listened for a little then she dematerialized saying she was going back to look at charts. The meal was great and was served with a fizzy drink called Belhop, which was pleasantly refreshing and low in alcohol content. Just as well, thought Jit, if they were to do any work afterward. They made light conversation while they ate with Arrill drilling Jit about Limtom for most of it. Had it been anyone else he would've told him to butt out by now, but he knew Arrill meant well. It was good to be hanging out together like the old days when they were younger and careless. Now they had wisdom that comes from years of life and they were in a better financial position too. When the meal was over, they went back to work on the charts. Jit told Arrill to go start while he cleaned up then joined him and Ladone on the bridge later. Outside the window was complete darkness by now and all that could be seen was the reflection of the bridge and them at work on it.

Jit found his thoughts wandered in the direction of Limtom for a moment and wished they were talking on the Link again. He'd been alone for some years now and has been a little cautious in his moves, but this girl seemed to have power over him because every time he saw her, what he felt became more apparent.

'Are you still with us?' came the interruption from Arrill that broke the spell over him.

'Yes, did you say something?' he shot back in defence.

In front of them on the screen was the closest match they had so far with only a few planets off by a scarce amount. He agreed it was the best so far and they logged it with a file number and would come back to it later. They decided to check all the known charts available to them and narrow down the odds. Then, in the end, they would search the most likely constellations first. They worked right up until 10.00 pm before tiredness became a barrier, causing them to shut down for the night and going off to bed. Jit wanted to shower when he stepped into his cabin but decided to leave it until the morning. He was only horizontal with his thoughts a scant moment before he sunk into a deep and heavy sleep.

....

Arrill sat on the edge of his bed and shook his boots off then laid down still clothed with the intent of getting undressed in a moment, but instead, the culmination of the long day and the pasta plus the Belhop took their toll, and he unawares fell into a comatose sleep.

....

Ladone continued searching after Jit and Arrill went to bed and a half hour into it she changed the screen to the recorded conversation Jit had with Limtom and stood there to watch and listen to it. When it finished, she plotted a course to spot number eighteen and moved the ship away at a slow pace deep in thoughts of her own. Below is the darkness of the night and concealed in the long growth of the wildflowers, the Windchief was watched by the eyes of creatures that could see in the dark as she lit up and ghosted away.

....

Jit startled awake by a dream that seemed so real but as soon as he woke, he forgot it in its entirety with just fragments floating in his mind. He got up and went to shower and feeling refreshed he went to the bridge, where faithful Ladone waited to greet him. She looked great in a flower patterned dress that stopped short of passing her knees. The top just covered her cleavage leaving a valley to be seen and two flimsy straps curved over her delicate shoulders adjoining the back of the dress. Her shoes were white with flat heels and adorning them were gold stripes that curved this way and that connecting with the soles. Her hair hung free falling over her shoulders and back. He told her she looked great and smiled, then went to the galley to make coffee and prepare for the day. Arrill was still asleep he was informed by Ladone who appeared in the galley too. She told him they'd arrived at spot number eighteen which she set in motion through the night. Jit hadn't even noticed, but then he didn't look too carefully out the window with coffee being his first concern of the morning. When it was made, he walked back out to the bridge to see what lay before him outside.

A large body of water sprawled in front of him and encircling it like a ring was a forest of vegetation. The trees protruded high into the air and there were many, making the pond seem like the hole in a donut. The risen sun over their tops lit up the water that was emerald green, and mist hovered lightly over the canopy of trees in streaks that looked like brush strokes. It looked so serene, Jit thought to himself, watching an alien world reveal another morning to alien eyes. The Windchief hovered at her usual one hundred metres and according to the weather station on the console, there was a slight breeze and the temperature was still cool but gradually rising. The ground was contoured as far as the eye could see with the trees thinning out the further away from the pond they stretched. Ladone appeared beside him and said…

'You should've been here to see the sunrise earlier on. As it came up it started as an explosion of fire then rounded off and when it crossed the canopy, it drew a long thick finger of fire along the tops of the trees reflecting off their shiny foliage. I was hypnotized by it' she closed with.

Jit just looked at her seeing what she saw by the description she gave then said, 'The way you just described it, I saw it anyway' and smiled back at her.

'I love this life Ladone' he said to her, and they just stood together in silence looking at the day that grew brighter by the minute.

They were both shaken from their reverie by the elevator going down and at the same time, Ladone vanished too. Soon the head of Arrill appeared out of the floor followed by the rest of him except his vocal cords. Jit received the usual grunt after greeting him then he wandered down to the galley to get coffee, shuffling his feet as he went. Time just doesn't change some things he thought to himself as he watched his friend walk along and vanish into the galley. He could hear cups tinkling then silence again, followed by shuffling as he returned to the bridge. They sat in silence looking at the day that further unfolded before them then Jit went to prepare breakfast leaving Arrill with the view. After eating they cleaned up then went back out to the bridge where Ladone was searching through more charts. She greeted Arrill who replied in kind then they told her they were going out to see what was at spot number eighteen. Not surprising they found nothing of interest and ascended back up to the ship. Back in the cargo hold, they set the jetpacks back in place then went up to the bridge. Ladone turned around to greet them from her work and asked what they found, and they relayed their experience while she listened on.

Deciding to move along, Jit told her to execute the move and they continued going through the charts. By the time Ladone announced arrival at location number nineteen they'd searched all the available charts with only one constellation matching the closest to the picture taken in the mountain. They left further work on the puzzle for the moment and went to look out the window and see what was before them this time. The sight they met was one of splendour with the largest body of water they'd seen so far.

From it and spiralling high into the air were rock formations that could be best described as small mountains giving the impression of small islands. Vegetation grew precariously defying gravity and clung onto the steep sides partway up the spirals, with just the tops left bare exposing the rock beneath. There were many of these protruding from the water which looked more like a small sea compared to a lake. The water was choppy from a moderate wind that curved the tops of the surface creating foamy white caps.

Yet again there was nothing of interest in the lake and they soon returned to the ship. Back in the cargo bay, Arrill set the shuttle down and they were soon traveling on the elevator to the bridge with lunch on their mind. Ladone was in her usual spot waiting for a report which they delivered to her then Jit instructed her to move to position twenty which was the last one to search and they went back to the galley. After eating they returned to the bridge to await the last destination. Whilst in transit they went to work on the constellation they would soon be departing for and bought up the chart that was the closest match and reviewed it again. It was a definite close match which meant they'd be leaving the twelfth galaxy for the fifteenth galaxy with the trickiest part being, finding the planet. All they had was the picture Arrill took meaning it'll have to be done on comparison when they arrive there.

Deep in their work, they were soon interrupted by Ladone informing them of their arrival at the final destination. They walked to the window as they'd done many times already and in front of them were rolling green hills spotted by lakes that were the same as the ones around Galasol, meaning they must've been close to Limtoms place too. It seemed a bit odd, Jit thought to himself that Ladone hadn't mentioned that. Above the marked zone, they took the lift down and strapped into the jetpacks then made the trip down to the surface. The area revealed nothing of significance, and they were soon ascending back to the ship with the last position crossed off the map too. Jit was glad it was finally over. Once the jetpacks were secure in their containment area, they made their way back up to the bridge to see Ladone and tell her the news. When they finished conveying the events to her Jit looked at the time which was well past 4.00 pm and he wondered what Limtom might be doing. He asked Ladone to establish the Link and waited for her to answer. Instead, it was Shalby who filled the screen and genuinely welcomed them with a warm greeting then informed Jit, the Miss was out on the bike. Jit imagined her flapping in the wind trying to hold onto the handlebars on that brute of a machine and it formed a comical picture in his mind. He asked Shalby to pass the message on for her to call when she returned to which he nodded then blinked out again. With that settled he decided to go to the gym for a workout as he'd been so busy lately, he neither had the time nor the inclination to do so. In the gym he picked a circuit from the choice on offer and while he went through the routine, he thought about Limtom and what he would say to her. They were about to leave the galaxy and he needed to talk with her otherwise it would hound him wherever he went. He also wanted to ask her if he could visit the hut she owned in the country when the whim took his fancy.

With the workout over, he went to his cabin to shower and change into clean clothes. Once he was done, he returned to the bridge where Arrill sat talking with Ladone. Jit joined them and they watched the long shadows of days end begin to stretch over the land below shrouding the place in darkness. Soon the Link indicated an incoming call and Jit went to the screen to take it. Arrill remained with Ladone at the front looking out the window and continued their talking. Jit was soon back catching them off guard with his sudden appearance. He asked Ladone to set them on course for the Pepplplant Estate as he calculated they could be there in time for dinner, to which they were invited. They'd be there in two hours or so travelling at interplanetary speed and that gave Jit time to go change into something a little more appropriate. Arrill hadn't even showered yet and went to prepare too.

When they arrived at the estate the Windchief hovered at the usual hundred metres as there wasn't enough clear area to land the ship, and they went down in the shuttle once again. Shalby met them in the same place as the first time they came and guided them indoors.

'An impressive ship sir' he said as they approached, to which Jit replied,

'Yes, I'm rather fond of her too!'

The Windchief did make an impressive sight hovering in the air, above the estate matching the mansion in glamour. At the dining room, Shalby opened the doors and they stepped into the room where the table was already laden with covered crockery dishes and platters awaiting them. Limtom was in the room at her end of the table and stood to meet them, looking stunning in an apricot coloured gown that hugged her from the waist up to cover her cleavage, and from the waist down flared out reaching to the ground and covering her shoes. Her hair was up in a bun and from her ears hung petite ear jewellery and around her bare upper part, she wore a golden chain with a large yellow gem cut into the shape of a leaf hanging from it. The gem was exquisite with its brilliance catching the eye, but it paled in comparison to the bigger gem he was looking at. She greeted them and invited them to take seats which they did in the same order as the last time they sat at the table. From the proximity, Jit could smell a wonderful sweet fragrance crossing his senses from Limtom and it complimented her perfectly. Despite her petite feminine frame, her shoulders were toned like her arms but not so much that it took away her femininity. She was really beautiful, and he felt good being in her company again.

Through dinner, they mostly chatted about the adventure around Spollee and what they saw giving her more details which made the time pass rapidly. When they finished dinner and dessert, fresh coffee was bought to the table by Shalby. Also provided was a case of cigars. Jit took one out then looked at Arrill who shook his head in reply. He then looked at Limtom but more to see if it was okay to light up and she surprised him by taking one too. The aroma from the cigars mixed with the coffee and set the mood for more conversation which was relaxed by now as Limtom had a few wines and was less formal. It did nothing to diminish her beauty though. Cigar smoke curled high into the air weaving threads from invisible fingers and Jit watched his smoke entwine with hers and together they became one in a hypnotic dance. His eyes then locked onto Limtoms and she was looking straight at him through the dance with eyes that startled him. Despite her being humanoid she was still alien to him and right now he was reminded of that because her eyes were like he'd not seen before. They were fully dilated and all one colour with a depth like two universes. In their depths, he saw a reflection of his completeness and at that moment knew himself. With much effort, he tore himself from the intense pull her eyes had and looked at her whole face and smiled like he'd known her forever and when she returned the smile, in it he saw their life together.

How long they'd been this way was hard to tell but when he looked to where Arrill was sitting, his seat was vacant. He then looked around the room and noticed Shalby was also missing from the room. He looked back at Limtom who was still looking at him and nearly fell into her eyes again before he spoke and responded to a reply from her. They spoke and drank coffee while they smoked their cigars until late into the night before Limtom stood and looked down at him, then reached for his hand which he gave willingly. He followed her through the endless rooms of the mansion holding her hand while she led the way and eventually, they stopped at a pair of doors. She turned around with her back to the doors and looked at him then stepped close and whispered into his ear, 'I haven't done this before' and opened the door pulling him in with her. While he floated behind her, the words she spoke into his ear swirled around in his mind filling him with a deep desire for her and at the bedside, she stopped and turned to face him again. Taking both his hands in hers she guided them to the back of her dress where he found the zip that concealed her treasures and with a gentle but slightly trembling hand lowered the zip which allowed the dress to give way and fall to the ground. Underneath she was completely naked and as he gazed at her perfection, there was nothing he wanted more right then than to be with her and lost in her love. They spent most of the night and into the early hours of the morning entwined in each other until they fell into a deep and complete sleep in the afterglow of their union.

....

From the moment they lit the cigars, it was like a drug of some kind as Arrill watched Jit and Limtom behave as if no one else was in the room. He looked over at Shalby who was thinking the same thing by the way he looked back and he stood and quietly walked over to him. By this time, it was closing in on 10.00 pm and he told Shalby he was going back to the ship. Shalby offered the room he stayed in previously to which Arrill declined in favour of a familiar bed and found his way out to the shuttle. Shalby parted too and went about his business feeling happy that his little girl may have found someone to make her happy. Back on board the ship Arrill felt sharp loneliness and thought about Leearnah and missed her greatly. The elevator carried him to his floor, and he went to his cabin with thoughts of their time together to accompany him and follow him into the deep slumber that overcame him the moment he lay on the bed.

…………………………

Ladone heard the shuttle come on board and knew only Arrill came out from it. She was hoping to talk to him before he went to sleep, but soon realised he wasn't coming onto the bridge and dematerialized, anticipating morning to talk with him then.

…………………………..

Jit woke at some early hour with Limtom curled up in the fold of his body. He squeezed her close and kissed the back of her neck and shoulder softly taking in the fragrant perfume that still lingered on her. She made a little sound of delight and snuggled in closer and they slept in each other's embrace until day broke. The sunlight filtered through the slits in the drapes and bathed them and upon looking at the time it was 8.00 am. They were soon up and showered together, then dressed and made their way to the dining room. Looking out from the floor to ceiling windows, the sun was shining, and the day was clear and crisp looking. After taking their seats Shalby entered the room with a tray in tow carrying a pot of coffee. They greeted him and he responded in kind then left them to enjoy each other's company while they talked about the next part of the search.

It was going to be in the fifteenth galaxy, he told her, and far away from Spollee. The excitement of the search seemed wane now that he'd been intimate with Limtom and they fully bonded together. Already he couldn't imagine not being around her, so he expressed his desire for her to come with him. Surprisingly, she complied asking for a day to arrange matters in her absence to which Jit just smiled as he leaned over to kiss her. Every time their lips touched, he could feel a current flow between them that could only be described as electric. Shalby soon returned with breakfast on a push trolley and once the table was laden, he trundled off again leaving the way he came. They'd just started their meal when the holovision popped up from the center of the table and it was Arrill, seeing if it was safe to come down. Jit gathered he'd been up for a while to have a sense of humour at this hour of the morning. Limtom took a moment to get it, then giggled quietly while Jit told him breakfast was still hot and to come right away.

In less than five minutes Arrill was sitting at the table with them and they continued talking about the next part of the trip. He told Arrill that Limtom was coming with them to which he approved, saying it was a good idea. Jit knew Arrill would be okay with her coming along but he wasn't sure how Ladone would respond to the news. Maybe he might have to go up first on his own and tell her rather than just appear with Limtom and make it awkward. When breakfast was over, he left Limtom to do her organising while he and Arrill went back to the ship to prepare the way for the journey, and Limtom. With the shuttle back in position, they ascended in the elevator to the bridge where Ladone waited for them. Jit wished her a good morning and they spoke together for a little while avoiding the obvious until Arrill left saying he was going to make a drink leaving the floor for Jit.

'Limtoms coming along for the next part of the trip and I

thought I should tell you before bringing her up' he blurted out to her.

'I knew sooner or later this would eventuate and to be honest, I'm looking forward to having female company' she said back catching him off guard altogether.

'How long have you known I had feelings for her?' he asked.

'Since you first met her I saw a change in you, and every time you spoke with her from then on you changed a little more each time' she replied. 'I knew it was only a matter of time' she finished with.

When Arrill returned they talked about their departure and made plans they could execute when they were ready to go. He told them Limtom needed a day to organise her affairs and that they should be good to go the following morning sometime. According to Ladones calculation, it would take four days to get to the fifteenth galaxy then they'd have to find what quadrant the planet they searched for was in. With that settled Jit went to his cabin to change into more comfortable clothes and while he did, he looked around at his cabin thinking how it will be with Limtom living with him in such close quarters. His cabin was certainly large enough for two people but compared to the rooms in Limtoms mansion, it was only the size of a broom closet. Then his thoughts drifted off, thinking how he liked the idea of such close quarters with her. He felt ninety percent certain that she was going to like it too. He was deep in thought when Ladone distracted him over the com and told him Limtom was on Link. He asked her to connect her to his cabin and the monitor on the wall flicked to life, filling the screen with her face and making everything else in the room look dull.

'I know it's only been a little time but I miss you already' she said to him.

Jit went on to tell her he was just daydreaming with thoughts about her when she called and they laughed at each other's flighty behaviour.

'Come up and see the ship', he said to her, 'Ladone is keen to meet you and I can show you around.'

She nodded eagerly and told him she was on the way outside to wait for him. Jit leaped from the bed and went straight to the cargo bay and informed Ladone when he sat in the pilot seat of his intention. As he lowered the shuttle down to the ground, he saw Limtom looking up with a smile on her face, looking as radiant as any of the flowers in their beds. When the shuttle touched down, he swung around and went to open the side door and let her in. They met with a kiss and he guided her to her seat and they took off again. As they rose, she complemented Jit on the fine ship he owned and to Jits amazement she knew the Windchief was the cream of all space crafts. In the cargo bay, he sidled next to the other shuttle and then led her out the side door and into the large bay area. Deciding to introduce her to Ladone first, they took the elevator to the bridge and all the while Limtom looked around in wonder like a small child. On the bridge waited Arrill and Ladone and when they appeared, he introduced her to Ladone. They exchanged pleasantries and Jit could tell after the first few minutes that Ladone liked her, which relieved him straight away. When they finished talking and the formalities were over, he took her by the hand again and gave her the tour of the ship. While they were at the top, he showed her the galley and its workings then they went down a floor and he escorted her through the library and stasis room, with her stunned by the opulence throughout the ship. The next floor down he guided her through the first-aid room and the gym, then the theatre and games room and finishing with the living quarters. He then took her back to the cargo hold and showed her all the different gadgets he had down there including the fighters. She was awed at the fighters with their sleek fast lines matched with astonishing good looks. She asked if he ever used them, to which he told her he did but mostly to have fun with. Again, she surprised him by telling him she could fly too. He invited her some time to go out with him for a play and she was eager for that any time she said, gripping his hand tightly. The time was drawing near midday and he asked her if she wanted to have lunch onboard which she agreed to and they made their way back to the bridge. Along the way, she asked him how long they'd be away to which Jit couldn't answer. Already it's been over four weeks since he first met up with Arrill and the quest began, he thought to himself. And all they had so far were four stones and a gold key of sorts along with a constellation and a single planet. He knew Arrill wanted to find more treasure but as for Jit, he found his treasure and he wasn't letting go of her, then squeezed her hand and she looked up at him and smiled squeezing his hand back.

On the bridge, Arrill and Ladone were discussing scenarios for when they arrived at the fifteenth galaxy and they walked up to join them. Jit and Arrill left the girls to talk and get to know one another and went to prepare something for lunch. When everything was ready, they went back out to the bridge to find the girls laughing and chatting like friends from long ago. As soon as Jit walked up to Limtom she clung to him like her life depended on it. Holding her close he asked Ladone to extend the captain's deck. He didn't bother with it usually but today was a special occasion. Arrill and Limtom stood in awed silence as they watched the front windows on the bridge slide into one another and conceal in the wall and immediately the cool breeze of the day flowed in giving the whole place a surreal charge. The front panel beneath the windows then fell in silence and from it extended the floor with the panels clicking in place until it reached its end. From the ends of the perimeter where the floor finished extended the rail which folded up at the right height making the railing around the edge of the quite large deck. Finally, from the center of the floor parted two panels and from there protruded a round table with a thick center column and stopped at the required height. Out from the sides of the column extended long arms with six in total and they reached out unfolding until they made the skeletal frame of a seat. Next, the membrane that stretched over the frame inflated making the cushioning for a very comfortable chair, and lastly, from the center of the table extended a pole that flared out at the right height and became an umbrella shading them.

'How impressive' said Limtom, dragging Jit out with her onto the deck where the breeze was stronger and blew her hair wildly across her beautiful face.

The view was stunning from their vantage with green lush hills rolling off into the distance and the Pepplplant Estate lay spread out below looking smallish from their height. The sun shone with the sky mostly clear, except for a few streaky light clouds. Arrill offered to get the lunch and Jit sat down with Limtom and they chatted until Arrill returned with the trolley. He placed all the food on the table as well as the wine then pushed the trolley to the side and took a seat. Jit poured wine for them all and while they ate, they made small talk taking turns and talking about whatever came to mind. When they finished eating Jit and Arrill cleared the table and Arrill took the trolley back out, while Jit went to get the case of cigars. He offered one to Limtom who reached over and picked two out. Large thick plumes of smoke rose into the air and were quickly carried away by the breeze and barely hanging around long enough to even notice the aroma.

Arrill was soon back and took his seat and they passed

the afternoon talking like old friends and Limtom fitted in as if she'd always been there. Ladone called out to Limtom from the bridge informing her Shalby was on Link needing her attention. She excused herself and went to the screen. They talked about Limtom and how she fit in so well and were glad Ladone got on with her. She soon returned to the deck informing them she had to go back down as some matters required her attention. They left Arrill on the deck with the breeze and solitude and went down to the cargo bay to board the shuttle and were soon descending to the green lawn and gardens of the estate below.

'Can you stay with me?' she asked Jit, to which he smiled and took her hand.

He wondered what the life of a girl like Limtom would be like. All the responsibility she must have to keep a place like this going. Some of the matters she attended to were carried out on the Link while she conversed with different figureheads concerning her affairs. He was introduced to some influential people even if it was via the Link. In her office, Jit wandered around looking at her certificates of achievement hanging on the walls, and he realised Limtom was a lot more than met the eye. He looked at her, busily away in her normal surrounding signing papers and she suddenly looked up directly at him as if he'd called her name. It was uncanny how she did that. When she was finished, they walked to the sunroom where Shalby served tea and biscuits while they discussed what she might need to bring on the journey. Jit told her to prepare for anything up to a month away which surprised her a little, as she'd never been away from the house that long before. He comforted her telling her that any business matters could be settled on the Link with the hands on stuff dealt by her on her return. With all matters soon settled and Shalby left in charge, she told Jit all she had to do was pack and they could go whenever he wished. They agreed to leave right away, and she went to her room to pack. Jit called up Arrill and Ladone informing them of the news and told Ladone to prepare the ship for departure. A half hour later Limtom stood ready with two cases carried out by Shalby. They went out to the shuttle where Jit shook Shalbys hand and Limtom threw her arms around him giving him a hug and kiss on the cheek. With her bags on board, he secured the door and they rose into the air leaving the small shrinking shape of Shalby looking up at them. On the bridge, Jit found the captain's deck withdrawn and everything as normal and told Ladone to part for the fifteenth galaxy. It wasn't long before they looked back at Spollee with Limtom in awe as she'd never been off planet before. Jit went to stand next to her and she clutched him close while still looking at her planet slowly diminishing in size as they moved to galatial speed.

'Don't be afraid' he whispered into her ear while he held her close and comforted her. Will you be alright while I go and prepare dinner?' he then asked.

She chose to join him in the preparation, and they went to the galley leaving Arrill and Ladone on the bridge to chat amongst themselves. In the galley, he showed her how to select and prepare meals that were all ready to go or ingredients to prepare a meal manually. He let her pick dinner and followed her while she learned the workings of things which she picked up after being shown only once. She was not only beautiful but sharp as a razor too! When the meal was ready, she called out to Arrill who soon came wandering in sniffing the air as he walked through the galley door.

'Mmm, something smells good he complimented' with his nose still sampling the air.

She told him it was an old recipe handed down from her mum who got it from her mum and so on down the line. They sat at the dining table and feasted on the fine meal and talked whilst doing so. Afterward, they made a drink that they took out to the bridge and watched the galaxy slipping away from them until they reached clear space. At that point, Ladone moved the ship to full speed making Limtom squeal a little from the effect on her body. The step into clear space was the same viscous sensation of oozing through the darkness with the sense of movement removed altogether. With a four day journey ahead of them and the Windchief streaking to her destination, Jit went back down to the cargo hold and retrieved Limtoms bags bringing them to his cabin which would now be their cabin. She accompanied him and, in the cabin, he cleared some drawers making room for her to unpack and get settled in. He left her to unpacking and went to set up the theatre for a movie for when she was finished, then returned to find she'd placed her personal belongings around the cabin giving the place the look only a female can bring to an otherwise dull room. They'd settled in together so easily and comfortably and Jit couldn't imagine her not being around anymore. On her side of the bed, she placed a holo disc which displayed her mum and dad holding each other smiling at her, reminding Jit of his parents and how proud his mum would be of her. The empty bags were stored in a closet and out of the way and with that done they went to the bridge to see if Arrill was going to join them for the movie. He declined as Jit suspected he would, and they went back to the theatre room where Jit served some snacks for the show then hit the remote. The chairs in the theatre could be single or coupled together if so desired, which Jit arranged in such a fashion so he could be close to Limtom.

The movie lasted until 9.30 pm and Limtom expressed her genuine enjoyment at the show she'd never seen before. They went to the bridge to see what Arrill and Ladone were doing and found everything was quiet. Ladone showed up telling them Arrill was in the games room. Jit told her to let him know they were going to bed and they took the elevator down to the cabin deck and went to their room. Inside they undressed and slipped into bed and were soon asleep cuddled up together.

....

Arrill talked for a while with Ladone then told her he was going to the games room to spend some time. As he walked past the theatre, he could hear the speakers booming through the walls and wondered what Jit and Limtom were watching. In the games room, he took a seat at a flying game and had to chase a slippery character called Nettnott through the skies until he shot enough of his plane for it to fall from the air, announcing him king of the skies. It took a long time and, had it not been for his skill as a pilot already, he would never have defeated the guy making the game impossible for a novice. When he finished with that machine he'd had enough and went back to the bridge. On passing the theatre he heard it quiet and wondered where Jit and Limtom were. Arriving at the bridge Ladone told him they'd gone to bed a little while ago and he decided it was time for him to get to bed too. He bid Ladone goodnight then went to his cabin where he went for a quick wash then slipped into bed. As he lay there his thoughts about the map were suddenly replaced with thoughts of Leearnah. He held onto them until sleep claimed him shortly thereafter.

....

At 8.00 am Jit awoke and as soon as he stirred Limtom woke too. They rose to shower, dress, and take the lift to the bridge to see if Arrill was up yet. Ladone greeted them when they emerged from the centre of the floor and told them that

Arrill was not up yet. They went to the galley where Jit set to making coffee and Limtom took a seat at the dining table talking with him while he went about the task. She watched his moves as he glided around the familiar space with precision and was soon back at the table. Whilst sipping their drink Jit told her that Arrill wasn't a morning person and to keep talk light with him until he fully woke up. She smiled telling him she had a friend she'd known since school days who was the same and couldn't string more than two words together until an hour after rising from her bed. Jokingly he asked her where she lived and said they'd make a good pair in the morning together then they laughed lightly at the thought of it. Soon after they heard Arrill arrive on the bridge and a moment later he walked into the room. They exchanged greetings while he went to get coffee. After breakfast, they returned to the bridge and Limtom went to the window to look out at clear space. She couldn't believe something was so immense that even at the speed they were moving, it seemed like they were at a standstill.

Jit remembered when he first tried to comprehend clear space and how it messed with his head too. Now he knows you get through it and everything moves normal again. What ever normal is. While Limtom was off in her daydream he bought up the planet Arrill took the picture of and studied it for a while trying to see if anything came to him. The three scrape marks that looked like chisel scars were the most dominant apart from the symbols at the top corner. It would've been great right from the beginning if they knew what the symbols said. The scratch marks just seemed strange to him as they were out of place on the otherwise perfect workmanship in the masonry. What could they mean he thought to himself and while he was deep in thought he felt Limtom snuggle up beside him and ask him what he was studying. He showed her what he was looking at and they talked further about it tossing ideas around to see if anything presented itself, but nothing came to mind. Arrill and Ladone joined them a little later and all four of them discussed possibilities and scenarios for some time.

When they finished Jit told them he was going for a workout in the gym and Limtom decided to join him too. In the gym, he picked his circuit and Limtom chose one to suit her and while they worked out at various machines, they made eyes at each other making a game of it. He watched her workout and she breezed through the circuit with hardly any heavy breathing during the hour long exercise. When they finished, they went to their cabin to shower and change for lunch then returned to the bridge to join the others. With Limtom now familiar with the workings of the galley she offered to make lunch and left them to talk while she set to the task. Jit watched her walk away and before she disappeared up the corridor, she turned around to look at him and smiled. There seemed to be a way she knew when he was looking at her and it was almost as if she could read his mind, he thought to himself. The three of them talked about Limtom with Ladone expressing how she liked her and was glad to have her on board. She went onto say that she treated her like a real person and not like… "Just a hologram." They both knew to think of Ladone as just a hologram was to start on the wrong foot. Limtom seemed to know that too.

She was certainly more than a hologram to Jit and by now Arrill thought the same too. They moved onto other topics and were laughing at the picture Jit painted telling them of petite Limtom on that beast of a motorbike when she called to them from the galley saying lunch was ready. While they conversed, they found that despite them all being from different places, they had a lot in common which unfolded as they exchanged stories and events. The meal was great and when it was over, they retired back to the bridge to talk with Ladone. Later on, Jit asked Limtom if she wanted to join him in the games room to pass some time. Arrill declined the idea having spent last night in there and left them to it choosing to talk with Ladone instead. They took the elevator down to the third floor and in the games room, they searched together for a game they could both play and challenge each other. The time passed quickly and around 4.00 pm they'd had enough and went back to their cabin for a nap.

They lay on the bed together sharing stories about each other until the time slipped away to 5.30 pm and they decided to go back to the bridge. Only Ladone greeted them and she informed them that Arrill was in the library doing some more research. As time was nearing dinner time Jit decided to go and sort out what to have for dinner leaving the girls to talk and bond some more. While the food was preparing from TSC he walked out to see Limtom and Ladone locked in a game of chess with both closely matched in the skill. Limtom briefly looked up and smiled then went back to her concentrating. She was a fierce competitor which he especially noticed when they were in the games room. Despite the game being a close one, she was still beaten by Ladone to which she grinned and said she'd get her next time. When dinner was ready, he called Arrill who still hadn't emerged from the library, and they went to the dining room where Jit began serving the steaming delicious stew that filled the galley with its aroma. He just finished serving Arrills bowl when he walked in and took his seat. During the meal, they made light conversation about their destination and what was to come of it. When they finished Jit made coffee and they sat around the table talking for a while.

They'd been traveling a day now with three to go and when they arrive, they had no idea how much longer it would take to find the planet they sought. They spoke of matters such as this until they decided to all catch a movie and sauntered to the theatre room and settled into positions. Arrill picked the movie which was a secret agent mission that even Jit hadn't seen before. Right from the start it was good and kept a grip on him right until the end. By the time it finished, it was late and Jit and Limtom bid Arrill good night and retired to their quarters.

……………………..…..

Arrill sat in the theatre for a little while longer and poured himself another drink then decided to go back to the library to finish what he was doing before he stopped for dinner. In the room, he picked up the book he was looking at and continued searching through pictures of different kinds of keys to see if he could find anything that came close to the key they found in the mountain. That's providing it was a key! It was a shot in the dark with the idea coming to him during the day while they talked about other things. He checked right until the early hours of the morning going through everything Jit had in the library and found nothing that even came close. Feeling exhausted he went to his cabin where he called it a night and went to bed.

………………………

It was Limtom getting up that woke Jit the following morning. He watched her with half open eyes and had a stretch then waited for her to return so he could do the same now that his plumbing was awake too. When he returned, he whispered good morning into her ear as he slid back in beside her. Around 8.00 am they decided to get up with the need for coffee forcing the move. After showering and dressing they walked up to the bridge where only Ladone waited to greet them. They said good morning and Jit left them talking and went to make the brew and think about what to have for breakfast. Soon the task was done, and he went back out to the bridge and when the first cup was down, he revisited the galley and set to work on breaky. While he was in the process of making it, he heard Arrill come onto the bridge then he appeared in the galley looking for a cup. They said a brief greeting to each other, and he walked back out looking for the pot of coffee. Jit made more breakfast to ensure there was enough for the three of them and when it was ready, he called them to the galley and set the food out. The conversation during the meal was light with mostly Jit and Limtom talking. They talked about the map and treasure and the progress they'd made so far until the coffee was all gone then they cleaned up and retired to the bridge once again.

Outside the window, the velvety blackness of clear space continued to engulf them and in the far distance some galaxies could be seen but at present, they were just spots staining the blackness. Later they decided to go to the gym for a workout and Arrill asked if he could join them too. Jit showed Arrill the workings of the selections recommending a light workout as his body wasn't used to training, and when he was set Limtom chose her routine then Jit found one suitable for his requirement and joined them too. Arrill was soon sweating and breathing heavy but he kept at it wiping his brow often until he completed the hour long trial. He sat on the bench when he finished and watched Jit and Limtom until they were done and then they all retired to their cabins to shower and change and meet back at the bridge. When they arrived, they found Ladone waiting for them and she told Limtom that Shalby called needing her attention for a matter he couldn't confirm without her authority. Arrill soon joined them and they left Limtom to talk in private and went to the galley. The matter was settled quickly as they'd just made the tea and poured a cup each when Limtom joined them saying a woman's work was never done. She filled a cup for herself and they went back out to the bridge to talk with Ladone.

The Jorphah's performed a ceremony when they built their ship's which was carried out when the craft was finished. In a way, they give the ship a soul which is the hologram, and bind them together in a tradition they follow. His ships proper name is "Windchief Ladone" and that's how she is registered in their logs.

The time soon reached midday but neither of them was hungry yet with breakfast being so late, so they just went to make a light snack. The rest of the day passed the same way as the day before and soon day two was completed with three going past rapidly too. On the fourth day when they woke up and went to look out the window, they could see the fifteenth galaxy clearly and it seemed like you could reach out and drag it inside. Jit looked out in wonderment and for the briefest moment, the galaxy reminded him of one of the sea creatures in the dark depths of the waters back on Spollee. By days end they'd be there and then the search for the planet they had to find would begin.

'It's so beautiful Jit' said Limtom as he passed her a cup of coffee. 'Do you do this all the time?' she asked.

He went on to tell her that before he caught back up with Arrill, he used to transport cargo so he still got around but mostly within the galaxies. It was hard to secure work across clear space because it took his ship too long to cross the expanses compared to the new ships. He worked whatever galaxy was on offer and still managed to do okay out of it but what he was doing with Arrill was all new. He was about to continue when they heard the elevator move to bring Arrill up. The usual grunt escaped from him as he went to the galley to get a cup then returned to fill it after Jit told him the pot was on the console. Ladone had cleared out by this time leaving the three of them watching the approaching galaxy in awe. Jit remembered something he kept forgetting to ask Arrill, which was how he knew back in the mountain to backtrack on the passageways. Arrill replied by telling him it was a spontaneous reaction that came as if he knew all the time... more like recalling a forgotten memory. Jit decided to hit the gym for an hour and only Limtom offered to join him with Arrill still sore from the previous workout. As they made their way there, she told him how she was enjoying herself being with him and he smiled at her and told her the feeling was very much mutual. When they completed the circuit, they headed back to their cabin to shower. However, once inside they were soon consumed in each other's passion, falling onto the bed and continuing a much more enjoyable workout. Later on, they lay in each other's embrace, spent from the rush of passion until they could move, and went to shower. It was nearing midday by the time they returned to the bridge and Arrill was in the galley preparing something for lunch while Ladone stood at her usual spot and greeted them.

'That was a long workout' she said to which Jit just agreed, giving her a questioning look and sly smile.

They took a seat at the window looking out at the galaxy which had swelled even bigger by now and they both took in the awesome view that played before them. They were there for just a few moments before Arrill yelled out from the galley doorway calling them for lunch. Even before Jit reached the entry, he could smell pizza and asked Limtom if she'd ever had pizza. She told him she'd never even heard the name before and asked what it was. Despite her not knowing about pizza she still sniffed the air and commented on how pleasant the aroma was. Jit explained briefly about the delicacy and told her that Arrill made some of the best he'd ever eaten. At the dining table, they awaited Arrill who soon turned up with two pizza's still hot and bubbling on the tray. Jit hooked in pulling a slice free from one of them with the elastic cheese refusing to let go until almost at his mouth. All the while Limtom looked on with wide eyes of astonishment. She tried a piece and once she tasted it her eyes went wide, and a sound of surprise escaped her. Jit smiled at her while stuffing another piece into his mouth thinking how Arrill should've gone into the pizza business instead of a tavern. It was around 4.00 pm Spollee time when Ladone bought the ship out of full speed, reducing their progress to galatial speed once again. Limtom was speechless with every new experience looking like a child in wonder as the Universe unfolded its magic before her. During their journey over to the fifteenth galaxy, they agreed on seeking the most inhabited planet in the system and starting there. Ladone went about finding the most densely populated world and set course for a place called "Posskeddar." On route, they synchronised their times to match the planet which meant when they arrived it would be midday, Posskeddar time. That should make for a bit of confusion Jit thought as he finished setting his timepiece. They were still two hours away from their destination and along the way they checked to see what the weather would be like, and where the spaceports were located. Jit also asked Ladone to check whether they could accommodate for the Windchief or not.

Posskeddar

By dinner time they were in orbit around Posskeddar with the time being just after midday on the surface. Having been confined to the ship for four days they decided to have dinner/lunch on the planet. The city they were about to descend to was able to accommodate for the Windchief and they were soon to touch down in the city of "Kradbok." Ladone prepared the ship for entry and they took their seats at the window and watched the new world unfold before them. This was one of Jit's highlights and he always felt a renewed sense of wonder when he took in a new world. Kradbok control instructed Ladone where she could land and which way to face the ship on touch down and all the other rules that came with a society based structure. When they broke through the stratosphere, they then passed through thick lemon coloured clouds for a little way and on the other side, the city of Kradbok was laid out before them still looking smallish from their height. As they descended the ports could be seen with two in total and several different size ships scattered on the tarmac. The city itself was a sprawling metropolis of highrise towers with roads spiralling in every direction and disappearing in the distance as they converged on the country and mountainous region. As they came closer to the ground, lots of large parks could be seen scattered all over the city with vegetation that must've once covered the ground in abundance, thriving now in the confined space left for them. Large masses of people moved about with the time being midday bringing them out seeking sustenance.

The Windchief settled her mass slowly on tarmac one and shut down with ground crew tending to other ships looking up and checking her out. She still had style his baby and lines that were magic turning heads with her charm.
'We have arrived in Kradbok' announced Jit and stood looking at the others.

'Now we need a plan of action', said Arrill, 'and the library would be a good place to start' he finished with.

They agreed with him and went down to see what life on Kradbok was like. They exited the Windchief looking very small beneath her shadow and made their way to customs to continue with the rules. Surprisingly they went through with little fuss and walked to the office for vehicle hire to secure a ride. Again, with little fuss, they were departing from the port with the onboard navigation system giving Jit instructions on how to get to the library. When they arrived at the building, they could find no parking, so they had to go to the closest multistory carpark and walk back. They parked and along the way they decided to stop in at an eatery to try some Kradbok cuisine as the smell of all the cooking foods in the place was making them hungry. Little carts were everywhere with merchants selling their homemade specialties, cooked like mamma used too. Café's had people spilling out from them onto the footpaths with foot traffic walking around them to get past. The place was a buzz of activity. They walked past some buskers playing odd shaped string instruments with a sound that was both hypnotic and entrancing at the same time. The musicians moved to the rhythm of their music and occasionally looked up at the passersby hoping their work would procure a small contribution. They listened to them for a little while before hunger pushed them on and they finally spotted a place that had vacant seats for all three of them. The place was called "Jaks Staks" which was a steak house more than anything else. The name associated with the chef's steak tower that boasted six different kinds of steak cooked how the customer wants and each weighing in at two fifty grams making a 1.5kg feed. If you could eat it all in one sitting it was on the house the board proclaimed. Jit couldn't imagine eating all that steak in one go and wondered how many had walked away not paying. They sat at a round table and waited for service which was a bit slow in coming but eventually a polite young waiter approached them apologizing for the delay.

The day soon cleared of cloud cover and became sunny and the temperature was mild with a slight breeze wafting by. The air smelt quite fresh for a city and seemed clear like mountain air. The atmosphere in the place was friendly and relaxed despite there being hundreds of people around. When their meals arrived, Jit made eyes at Limtom while he ate and she made eyes back with Arrill just rolling his eyes at the pair of them. After eating they decided to continue to the library. The footpath they walked along was wide and although there were a lot of people using it you could still move about comfortably without bumping into anyone. Trees big enough to shade the walkway grew at intervals keeping the way mostly under a cover of greenery and birds perched in their branches made the path treacherous. They were only a few more minutes in transit before they came upon the library.

The building was modern with smoked glass and steel making up most of it. Due to its aesthetic design, the structure had little space to accommodate paper books therefore it was an electronic library with whatever book available on Posskeddar at your fingertips. Inside they found a vacant monitor to use and the three of them crowded around it. They entered the words 'local planets' in the search engine and begun the process of comparing what was on file with what they were looking for. They worked at it like one mind and narrowed things down for maximum information. While they did their work an automated drink machine made its arrival known and Limtom ordered three coffees to perk them up while they worked. The vending machine ran on a set circuit around the library floors serving only coffee, and good coffee at that thought Jit expecting something less. The work took them into mid afternoon before they found a planet that was no doubt the right one. The three marks they thought were a mistake of the chisel in the picture they had turned out to be three huge chasms on a planet named "Cartergole." It also was in the fifteenth galaxy and with further research, they discovered it was more the size of a moon but still classed as a planet. It remained uninhabited by the modern world and its technology. According to what they read the only inhabitants were local native people who'd lived there for many generations continuing in the old ways and shunning technology altogether. They took all the information they could find that would be useful to them and upon looking at the time it was 4.00 pm. All of them were feeling fatigued because if they were still following Spollee time they would be in bed by now.

'What do you want to do now?' Jit asked them, getting shoulder shrugs in reply.

They decided to go to one of the Bars that littered the city for a drink which might revive them to think about their next move. Coming upon a place called "The Shooting Vine" they entered a loosely packed environment with dim lighting and mostly friendly patrons that smiled at them as they entered. They smiled back while they made their way to an empty small square table against one of the walls at the back of the establishment. With their positions secured Arrill went to the bar to get them a drink and soon returned with the house favourite. According to the bartender, it was a fruit cocktail with a local drink spiking it giving it a nice punch. It tasted great with fruity flavours that woke the tastebuds and moments after it went down it rushed back to one's head and lifted your feelings, making you smile without control. Jit felt tired no more and understood now why all the patrons smiled a lot.

'This drink is great isn't it?' he said without really expecting an answer but got approving nods and sounds from Arrill and Limtom.

When they finished, he went to get another round finding out what the beverage was called at the same time as he wanted a bottle of it in his special cabinet on board the ship. The bartender told him it was a local drop made to an ancient recipe that hasn't changed and went by the name of "Abbeymoss." Jit purchased a bottle there and then and returned to the table with it and three more rounds joining the others who were locked in conversation. He studied the bottle and its ornate workmanship. It was made from some kind of pottery with the contents unseen. The bottom was round, and it bell shaped up for two thirds its height before it narrowed to a long and twisted spout with the cap on top. Decorations were imprinted on the surface of the pottery depicting flowers and other herbs making an attractive and unusual bottle for his collection.

It was around 5.30 pm by the time they stepped out of the bar and into the cooler late afternoon air. They all felt revitalised from the drink with weariness a thing of the past deciding to take a different route to the parking lot where they left the ground vehicle. The way they took was long and as they progressed evening fell, and the city began to light up changing its aspect entirely. Lights shimmered that were only a short time ago invisible on the towers taking the lights to the night sky above them creating a wonderment of colours. All the shops and eateries and bars lit up with a myriad of splendour that turned the whole city into a fun park. Along with the feeling from the Abbeymoss they were in the mood to do the town and searched for a place to have dinner then go wandering. They agreed along the way to leave going to Cartergole until tomorrow in favour of taking in the sights instead. They soon found a place that looked enticing and entered the establishment and was welcomed by the smell of fine cuisine. The layout inside the place was three tiered with floors changing heights as they made their way to the back. Polished wood made up the floors that looked like dark glass and with each change of floor they descended eight steps to the next level which was a repeat of the previous floor and only the settings were different. The roof remained the same height all the way which made it quite high by the time they stepped onto the bottom floor area giving the place a palatial feel. The lighting was splashed around on the walls and concealed in patterns making them part of the design looking masterful and working effectively. Spotting a table that suited them they took a seat and a short time afterward a female waitress appeared with the menus. She left them to decide, saying she'd call back when they were ready, and scooted off to the kitchen again. They made their choice and ordered and asked for a round of Abbeymoss. The waitress smiled and left soon returning with the same cocktail but in a different style of glass. While they sipped their drink, they talked about what they were going to do the next day, and during moments of silence, they finished looking around at their surroundings. Hanging from the ceiling was a messy yet deliberate network of pipework that was a piece of art and sculpture at the same time. The thicknesses of the pipework varied in roundness and throughout it, protruded things like a knife blade with no handle plunged into the steel, then there were old vehicle parts hanging from it that were painted and creating a contrast of images. Other things also protruded to which Jit had no idea of what function they once performed. The longer one looked at the work the more the eye seemed to come upon, revealing itself like magic of some kind.

Soon their meals were delivered by the same waitress whom Jit noticed smiled a lot at Arrill. When Jit finished, he summoned the waiter for another round of Abbeymoss. He'd never felt so good and couldn't stop smiling all the time. When they finished, they paid then went back outside and found a bench to sit on and watch the crowds. Young people skidded around the gathered mobs on fancy cut boards with wheels and street entertainers stood on some corners enchanting the passerby. The place was alive with more throngs of people than during the daytime. A short while afterward they made their way through the masses trying to remember the way back to the parking lot. It took some time, but they eventually found it. By this time fatigue was setting in again hitting them all at the same time. Once they were in their seats, they followed the instructions back to the Port. When they arrived, they found large ships were either loading or unloading cargo with much more activity than when they arrived earlier in the day. Jit stopped the vehicle beneath the Windchief, and they piled out and made their way to the bridge. On the bridge Ladone greeted them and they talked for a little while before weariness took over them again forcing them to their cabins.

....

The following morning after Jit and Limtom showered and dressed they went to the bridge to see if Arrill was up yet. To both their surprise he was…and was perky, meaning he'd been up a while. They both greeted him and Ladone then sat around talking about the plan for the day. Outside reflected the previous day with good weather and mild conditions. While Arrill was up first he pinpointed the way to Cartergole. Ladone predicted that they would be there around 5.00 pm if they left right away. Jit told her to prepare the ship for departure and went to return the vehicle they hired.

Within half an hour they were lifting off the tarmac and climbing into the skies of Posskeddar, about to leave its atmosphere and enter space again. They sat together watching the small planet grow smaller on the monitors as Ladone moved the ship to galatial speed. Jit couldn't help noticing whenever he smiled that his face muscles hurt, which was the result from last night and all the Abbeymoss they consumed. The bottle he bought was in his cabinet and he wondered if maybe he should've purchased a case of it. When they finished their coffee, Jit and Limtom went to have breakfast leaving Arrill who'd already had his on the bridge talking with Ladone. When everything was ready, they sat down at the table to eat and made light conversation. They talked about his parents and it was a good time of further bonding between them as they exchanged stories. While they were washing up Arrill came in and told them he found out the chasms on the planet were enormous with the centre chasm nearly half bigger than the other two. The big one bottomed out at three kilometres deep with its widest point five, and approximately one hundred and fifty kilometres long. It was going to be spectacular to see in person he assured them.

They all deferred to the bridge and sat at the window to watch the movement outside while they discussed some more of what they would do when they arrived at Cartergole. They agreed on leaving the Windchief in orbit, so they attracted less attention seeing though they didn't know what to expect from the locals. Hopefully, they wouldn't bump into any but there was no specific information as to the numbers of inhabitants or their locations. There were no towns or community structures like most cultures have. The people just lived in the forests and on the land like the rest of the life on the planet.

They then talked about what best mode to get to the surface with tossing up between using the shuttle or a fighter. The fighter had the advantage of speed and agility. They settled on taking a shuttle in the end because the aggressive look of the fighter might start them off on the wrong foot if they did run into locals. Plus, they'd have plenty of room for storage should they need it. The time sped away and around 1.00 pm they all went to the galley to have something for lunch. When they finished, they went to the cargo bay and prepared shuttle number two with what they might need. After they loaded all they could think of they returned to the bridge to watch their progress. The spectacle before them played out in stars and planets with suns that followed their moves and gave life. They oozed past lazily giving the sensation of movement even if it was at a slow pace. Limtom was speechless as she took in the grandeur of it all never having experienced intricacy on such a scale. Ladones prediction panned out accurately and they arrived in Cartergoles orbit just after 5.00 pm.

....

Cartergole

From where they orbited, they looked down at the three chasms, and even from their height in space, they were impressive. The sun was moving around to the other side of the planet which meant it was going to be dark on the surface soon and seemed to match time closely with Posskeddar. They sat for a while and watched the darkness stretch over the planet like a consuming fog until the chasms blended in with the shadow needing scrutiny to perceive at all. There were a few small moons around Cartergole that looked more like meteors than any moon and numbered three in total. Around six thirty the three of them went to the galley for dinner. Arrill had Limtom in hysterics telling her a story about Jit which he preferred not mentioned but didn't mind at the same time. They decided to eat on the bridge and while they did, they looked out at the changing shuffle of the Universe. After the meal, Limtom made contact with Mel on Spollee. He looked like he hadn't slept in days, having bags under his eyes and his hair was ruffled like he'd been out in the wind. They caught him up to speed on everything since they last conversed and before leaving told them to stay in touch then faded out. Shortly after the Link chimed again and this time it was Shalby checking up to see how they were going. Jit noticed he seemed to care for Limtom just like a dad would, and she responded like he was. He liked Shalby and thought he would've made a great dad because he was always there for her. Now Jit was always there for her and with each passing day, his love for her grew greater and greater with no set limit. He watched the interaction between them and could sense the deep mutual love and respect they held for each other. While they talked, he and Arrill went to make coffee and by the time they returned with it, she sat there alone deep in thought.

During their cuppa they discussed what to do for the

evening and when they finished, they made their way to the theatre. This time Limtom picked a movie from the collection and before setting it to run Jit selected some snacks to go with the show. He just sat down with all the goodies when Arrill asked him if they could have some Abbeymoss too. Jumping up at an excellent idea he went to get the bottle and three glasses and made a mix about the same as the one he saw made at the Shooting Vine. The movie Limtom picked was a romantic love story that Jit had seen before on his own but not with female company. He picked up on things that eluded him previously making the movie seem like it was almost about them. The feeling of Abbeymoss made the experience intense at times, causing them to squeeze each other in response. It was an unforgettable experience and the time passed quickly. When it finished, they sat in the theatre talking for a while longer enjoying the good atmosphere and feeling. Another hour passed before they decided to get to bed as they had a full day on the morrow with absolutely no idea what to expect from it.

They'd talked about going into the three chasms first starting with the big one and see if there was anything that showed them what to do or the next step. With no understanding of the symbols in the picture, they didn't know how to pinpoint a starting place. Despite that, Jit felt and knew Arrill did too, that some unknown thing was making the way and would continue to do so until this was over. Finding the cleft in the mountain was meant to be and so was the way through the first trick in the passageway. For whatever reason, this was happening Jit wanted to complete it and see what unfolded. The experience has so far topped anything he had ever done and finding Limtom was no coincidence. Before he realised it the closing door of their cabin snapped him out of it with the trip to their room un-noticed. They were soon in bed snuggled up and he whispered into her ear the thoughts he had of her walking back to the cabin.

…………………………

In his quarters Arrill went to wash his face and use the bathroom. He was still feeling the effects of the Abbeymoss having had one more than the others. He thought about the next day and the trek they'd made to this far away place so far and then wondered what more lay waiting for them. What would they find on the surface and what about these people that live like the other life on the planet? He undressed and slid into bed thinking about…what if this, and what if that situation, when sleep snuck up and sped him away from the thoughts. However, there was one thought that blinked at him before he went out, and in it, he saw a hand he was holding and although he couldn't see the face, he knew the feel of that hand.

…………………………

Jit and Limtom woke at the same time which touched at 8.00 am. When they were ready, they took the elevator to the bridge finding Ladone there to greet them. They returned the courtesy and continued to the galley where Ladone appeared in the mood for chatting. Fortunately, Limtom was a morning person and seemed not bothered by her brain having to work so early. With coffee in hand, they went to sit on the bridge and watch the day begin on Cartergole. It was a reversal of when they arrived with the sun this time ruling the planet. The three chasms lit up as the sun stretched across them, pushing the shadow away and when fully exposed they did look like three enormous scratch marks. What did the four stones mean and the key, if it was a key! Then there was the map ending up in Arrills possession that bought them all this way. The more Jit thought about it the more surreal it all seemed. From this height, nothing could be seen moving on the ground and in the sky, only some clouds ambled around changing shapes by the moulding winds. It was a spectacular sight to behold and they said very little with both caught up in the wonder of it all. Soon though they heard the elevator being summoned and knew Arrill was on his way. When he appeared, he greeted them like he'd been awake a while and went to get a cup. Back on the bridge he joined them and looked out at the sight too. Despite it being a small planet, it still had an ocean that covered thirty percent of it. The land varied in its formation with flat areas of grassland and small mounds with higher mountains bundled together in great clusters. They looked like islands growing from the ground and the green sea around them were the grasslands. Vegetation covered a lot of the ground and in the chasms, they were bald down the steep sides, and at the bottom, it was best described as wild woods. It was too difficult to tell from where they sat but they were soon to find out. When they finished their drink, they decided to have breakfast and prepare for the trip to the surface. In the galley everyone had a job to do with Arrill helping Jit make the breakfast while Limtom put something together for lunch they could take with them. At the dining table, they ate and made light banter going through mental lists hoping to forget nothing needed for the journey. When they were done eating, they cleaned up and made their way down to the cargo bay. The shuttle was all prepped for the expedition and when they were all strapped into their seats, Jit went through the pre-checks then they hovered out into the blackness of space leaving the Windchief and Ladone awaiting their return. The ship was a few thousand kilometres above the surface of the planet and as they descended towards the chasms, they grew in size revealing what couldn't be seen from the orbit they maintained. A short time later they were approaching the largest chasm looking more impressive with each closing minute.

The smaller chasms separated the middle chasm by two or three kilometres Jit estimated, and despite being smaller they were no less spectacular. Now that they were closer, they could make out waterways that flowed over the precipice of the large chasm dropping to the depths below turning to mist soon after spilling over the edges. The smaller chasms had the same events happening with all the waters coming from the mountain clusters carried there by narrow rivulets that cut through the grasslands. Ponds could be seen spread around giving away their positions by the sun reflecting off them making them appear to be mirrors hidden in the grass. Before sinking into the largest chasm, they flew around surveying what lay beneath them seeing no movement of any kind in the grassland. Although he couldn't see anything Jit had the drilling feeling one gets when being watched and had no doubt their presence was being witnessed.

He moved the shuttle to the middle of the centre chasm and they slowly descended taking in the spectacular scenery in silence as they lowered to the bottom. The walls were sheer drops for most of the way until they connected with the vegetation that met up with them around one hundred metres from the ground level. From where the vegetation began it sloped away to the centre of the chasm and levelled off again with ponds of water scattered about and some clear open paddocks accommodating the area too. Grass eating beasts could be seen with their heads bent at the task and Jit wondered how they were able to get to the bottom of the chasm with no visible way down from the top. Once at the bottom he found a large clearing that looked safe and settled the shuttle down.

'Why are we landing?' asked Arrill.

Limtom looked at Jit awaiting his response too. He

went on to tell them he just wanted to stand outside and take in the splendour of where they were and feel the place before they started looking around. Jit stepped out first and the air that hit him was still cool and crisp with a pleasant country smell about it. Limtom followed him next and just before Arrill stepped out he slid a shotgun into the holster that held it diagonally across his back. The sun was shining brightly, and the sky was a pale blue with the clouds of before gone altogether. The view from this angle was gobsmacking with the sheer straight sides of the chasm walls dwarfing everything around them in their grandeur. They were perfectly vertical right down to the beginning of the greenery and were visible as far as the eye could see stretching in both directions. He'd never stood in a place like it. It was breathtaking!

'This is absolutely stunning' said Limtom who cradled up beside him wanting to share the moment.

He held her close agreeing with just a sound whilst still absorbing the awe of what he was seeing. The grass they stood on was cut low making visibility possible for a good radius and he noticed as it got to the edges of the woods it was a lot higher. The beasts that ate the grass must've had a reason for staying away from the edges he pondered to himself. Some of the trees bordering the edges had vines hanging from them with large red tubular flowers draped at erratic intervals. From their center protruded a long tongue black in colour and split at the end making two. Sounds could be heard from creatures in the woods, but none could be seen with a good many sounds coming from the treetops. When they were satisfied with seeing the place from the ground level, they boarded the shuttle and began the search deciding to skirt around the edge of the chasm in a circle and work their way to the centre in a grid pattern. It was one hundred and fifty kilometres long and five wide, so it was going to take a while as they had to go slow enough to spot anything. If there was anything in this chasm at all! What they searched for may well be in one of the other chasms but eliminating the big one first seemed the right choice.

Jit picked a side to start on and while they floated above the canopy of the woods Arrill looked out one side while Limtom looked out the other. It was difficult in some places to see the ground through the trees but mostly they were able to see enough to notice anything outstanding. The progress was slow and in the given time they reached where the walls of the chasm met before going back the way they came but on the other side. The sheerness of the walls was consistent with no means of access to the top from the bottom to be seen yet. There had to be a way for the animals to get down to the bottom Jit thought and searched for that too. A safe open spot near a pond looked okay for lunch and he landed the shuttle and they went out to sit by the water to eat and take in some more of the splendour. The pond was the same size as the one at Limtoms hut in the country back on Spollee, with the grass encroaching right up to the water's edge.

Jit couldn't see the bottom when he looked in the water nor could he see anything else moving in it. Around the edges spaced here and there were clusters of uneven mushrooms growing that were mostly white but had a baked golden top with a sprinkling of pepper on them. It was so peaceful here and the feeling of isolation was notable he thought to himself and pondered what it would be like to live here. When they finished the sandwiches, they had a drink and cake to round things off then they boarded the shuttle again and continued their search. They had no idea what to look for and while they did look, Jit found he was thinking of all possible scenarios that might assist. If the last place they found was in the cleft of a mountain this could be the same. He knew one thing for sure, and that was they had their work cut out for them. They continued all the rest of the way around the rim until it met again at the other end and by then it was starting to get too dark to see well. They ascended back to the ship looking forward to a shower and giving their eyes a rest. Limtom complained of a slight headache with the excessive strain on them from searching.

....

As the alien craft returned from whence it came many eyes watched it with a multitude of thoughts considered. The main thought was what they wanted. They looked harmless enough and were searching for something without a doubt. From when they were seen coming down out of the sky they were watched with ancient eyes of wisdom. The same eyes were soon closed for the night leaving concern about the strangers until the following day, if they should return.

....

By the time they docked back in the cargo hold the hour had reached 5.30 pm. They disembarked and took the elevator to the cabin level where they went to shower and freshen up first before going onto the bridge. When Jit and Limtom arrived on the bridge Arrill was already there talking to Ladone and filling her in with what they did on the surface. They left him to talk with her while they went to prepare something to eat. When dinner was ready, they all sat in the dining room to take the meal, and while they did, they talked about the day they had. After eating they cleaned up then went to the bridge to join Ladone who'd appeared again from her netherworld. They talked amongst each other for some time then Jit and Limtom went to watch a movie and unwind before bedtime. Arrill stayed to chat with Ladone leaving them to have some space for each other. He was happy for Jit but also felt a twinge of jealousy that wouldn't go away.

The movie they watched was based on a true story about a guy who went to live in the wilderness deciding he wanted no part of society anymore. Limtom had never even heard of it let alone seen it before and she snuggled up to Jit tightly while they watched it together and ate snacks. The ending disappointed her though, thinking it was sad that he died alone from a mistake he'd made. Jit agreed having felt the same thing too when he first watched the movie some time back and told her that it was the reality of going back to nature. It was nearing 10.00 pm by the time the movie finished and they both retired to bed.

....

Arrill talked with Ladone a while longer after Jit and Limtom went to the theatre then decided to go to the games room to pass some time. His mind was restless and since Limtom had joined them he found he missed Leearnah more than ever. He played the game he favoured the most and instead of doing great like he usually did he did poorly with his mind just not in it. He ambled around the machines trying others but gave up and went to the library instead to sit and think. Moments later he got up and went to the kitchenette and made a hot drink then returned to the couch and ponder the thoughts that rushed around his mind. Around 11.00 pm he'd had enough then made way to his cabin. The theatre was quiet by this hour and he knew Jit and Limtom had gone to bed too. He was soon in bed looking up at the ceiling with his thoughts still racing and wondered if he would get to sleep at all. However, the exhaustion from the day caught up to him unawares and his eyes closed with a heavy finality to them.

....

Jit and Limtom were awake around 8.00 am. They soon arose and dressed then ventured up to the bridge. They greeted Ladone who pointed at the galley indicating Arrill was up, and only just! Jit smiled at her and kept going with Limtom in tow. Arrill was sitting at the table with the pot of coffee in front of him still full. He looked up and managed a good morning then poured his cuppa and put the pot down indicating for them to use. They sat around the table in their thoughts for a little while and after a few mouthfuls, Arrill startled them by asking what the plan for the day was. They talked about that until they finished their cuppa then breakfast was made. By the time they'd eaten everyone was firing on all cylinders and preparing to head out. Limtom had more sandwiches made and Jit noticed another container with the contents remaining secret. In the shuttle, Jit went through the usual procedure then exited the Windchief and sunk to the planet below to continue their search where they left off.

When they arrived, Jit showed Limtom what to do at the controls knowing she'd be a natural at it and let her fly for a while and he searched instead. They finished the first circuit of the grid they marked out then moved to the next. With the place being five kilometres wide they couldn't look properly in one swoop. Now as they scanned the ground below, they were closer to the bottom of the chasm where it begins to level out, but the landscape remained the same with dense woods and some parts being too thick to see through. Limtom flew great and Jit forgot after a while that she'd not done it before. The time passed quickly, and they were soon looking for a safe place to land and eat lunch. Jit took over the controls for the landing and they were soon on the ground with some large rocks scattered around. They were still a good distance from the shuttle eliminating the possibility of anyone or anything sneaking up. Outside of the shuttle the air was cool and refreshing with new beast droppings tainting the air quality. Scattered around was the evidence to confirm this and they found a spot where there had been less activity to eat.

The day was almost the same as the previous day with the sun shining down lighting the whole chasm up and warming it at the same time. They were sitting on a knoll overlooking the field that stretched out before them and in the distance not too far away they could see beasts eating the grass that grew faster than they could mow it down. There was a slow breeze that wafted by every so often carrying in it quite a chill. They ate sandwiches and talked then Limtom opened the container she'd bought with them which held a selection of fine cakes making up the dessert. When they were done, they recommenced the search. Jit guided Limtom through the lift off letting her fly again and they started back from where they stopped. They flew at around fifty to sixty metres from the ground which allowed enough height to clear most of the treetops and the higher trees they just went around. On the ground, small creatures could be seen scampering around seeking shelter from the ominous shadow that crossed over them. The grass eating beasts barely flinched as they went over their heads. None of them had yet seen anything to give away the presence of the local natives that were said to live here. The greater part of the landmass was above the chasm and would sustain life easier Jit thought but that didn't mean no one could survive down here. It was a huge area and could easily support a good sized community.

He concluded that after the circuit they were on they would have one more run up the centre of the chasm which would then complete it. The day was filled with a repeat of the previous day and by days end they'd completed the second run. With just the centre left to go, they left it until the following day as the light was growing dim and it would soon be gone altogether. Jit took over the controls again and they climbed back into the sky looking forward to getting out of the confines of the cramped shuttle.

…………………………

They were expected today and when they descended from the sky many eyes were in place to observe them from every angle and watch what they did. They scoured closer to the centre as they passed around the chasm further proving they were searching for something. They were the same in number with the same one carrying a weapon at his back as the day before. Warriors scanned the ground where they stopped to eat with not a skerrick to be seen anywhere except where the craft pressed the grass flat. Were they here seeking the temple of old, and if so, how did they come upon the information about it? The night was coming fast and the eyes that watched them closed again anticipating the visit that was undoubtedly to come on the new day.

…………………………

Once they were docked into position in the cargo bay they disembarked and boarded the elevator and went to the bridge to greet Ladone. Limtom went to make them a drink while Jit and Arrill shared the events of the day with her as she listened intently saying little in between. Limtom was soon returning with a pitcher filled with juice and joined the conversation. The time was closing in at 5.00 pm making it a little earlier than yesterday when they stopped. When they finished their drink Jit and Limtom went to their cabin to shower and change leaving Arrill to continue chatting with Ladone. Once they were done, they returned to the bridge finding the space quiet with only them on it. Ladone soon appeared again and they talked with her discussing the next day's plan until Arrill arrived back on the bridge from showering too. It was dinner time by then and they preoccupied themselves with the task of making something to eat while they continued discussing their moves for the next day. When dinner was over, they all cleaned up getting it done in little time then made another drink and went back to the bridge.

Outside the window, the planet was now shrouded in darkness with the chasms mixing in and vanishing from easy sight. In the silence of his thoughts, Jit wondered about the symbols and their meaning that were scratched next to the planet in the picture they took. He went to the big screen and bought the picture up and just looked at it for a while. Limtom walked over shortly after and asked him what he felt. He told her he was hoping something might just come to mind. Unfortunately, nothing did and after a time he shut it down and they discussed what to do before bedtime. They decided to play cards for a short time and set up the console as a table then got chairs and while Arrill set up the game Jit went to get some glasses and a drink. Just as Jit suspected, Limtom was an ace at cards keeping him and Arrill on their toes. The night slipped away quickly with Limtom and Arrill just coming out in front of Jit in the games. Around 10.00 pm he and Limtom bid Arrill a good night and took the lift down to the cabin level and went to bed.

....

Arrill watched them sink below the floor and prepared for bed too. He cleared the console and put things away then took the glasses to the galley. Ladone appeared and he talked with her a little before he bid her farewell and waited for the lift to return. In his cabin, he thought about what they achieved today while he undressed and climbed into bed. While he lay there waiting for sleep to claim him, he spent the moment reminiscing the times he shared with Leearnah. For some reason, he couldn't stop thoughts of her popping into his mind.

…………………………..

It was just past 8.00 am when Jit and Limtom stepped onto the bridge dressed and ready for a hot drink. Ladone appeared and they welcomed her as she did them then appeared in the galley to continue chatting while Jit made coffee. When it was ready, they went back to the bridge to watch the day unfold on Cartergole. A lot of cloud cover blocked their view meaning it wasn't going to be a sunny day on the surface. A short time later they heard the lift summoned to pick up Arrill. Moments later he protruded through the floor and bid them hello. He went to the galley to get a coffee for himself then came back to the bridge and joined them. Afterward, they ate breakfast and when done, they prepared for the trip back down to the planet and to finish where they left off yesterday. Arrill took the controls this time and they were soon banking left out of the cargo bay and descending to the surface. The cloud cover when they passed through it was thick with rain beginning and lightning flashes could be seen lighting up the surrounding area making for a wet day on Cartergole.

After clearing the clouds, the first thing that met them was the sheer walls of the chasm that were now shining wet with all the rain giving the place a different perspective from the previous day. It was pouring down which was going to impede the search from the poor conditions. All the while lightning flashed across the sky giving light to the ominously dark chasm. And if the rain and lightning weren't enough there was also a strong wind gusting, making it trying for shuttle control. Arrill landed where they finished off the day before with the rain smashing into the shuttle horizontally from the strong wind. While it did, they discussed what they should do. The wind blew fiercely rocking the shuttle with its gusts and they decided to wait a while and see if the worst of it passed over. Through the cockpit window, they watched the deluge pour down the glass as if they were under a waterfall which blurred the vision of the field out yonder. It continued the same for well over an hour before it abated to showers with the lightning gone altogether. The rumbling thunder could still be heard on occasion far off in the distance and the wind settled a little but was still strong enough to make low flying hazardous. They tossed up whether to wait longer or just leave it until the next day and decided on waiting a little longer. It was all to no avail though as the heavy rain came back in torrents like earlier on causing them to abandon the search completely for the day.

With that decision made Arrill took off again and they made the upward trip back to the ship. Onboard they went up to the bridge and Ladone was there to meet them enquiring what happened. They filled her in of the atrocious conditions on the surface saying it was too precarious to attempt a search and so returned. The time was bordering on midday and as Limtom had made lunch for down on the surface they ate the sandwiches on the bridge and made a pot of tea to have along with it. While they ate from the safety and calm of the ship, they observed the roiling clouds that kept the surface in turmoil still. Jit hoped that Cartergole didn't have weather conditions lasting long periods which they didn't know about. There was very little information about the planet available, meaning everything was going to be a new experience for them all.

The afternoon slipped away with little change on the

surface and by dinner time there was nothing to see as darkness had settled over the land and from their vantage, they occasionally spotted a lightning bolt snake across the darkness in the blink of an eye. After dinner, they returned to the bridge and Ladone informed them that Fryppe was on Link and then his face filled the screen in front of them. They spoke with him for a considerable length of time as they hadn't spoken with him for a while and caught him up with the progress they'd made to date. Tortille could be seen in the background moving ghost-like as usual and reminding Jit of her unusual behaviour. When they finished their conversation, they bid each other farewell and once again the screen went blank and silent. It was still too early for bed, so they went to catch a movie before calling it a night. By ten thirty the Windchiefs occupants were all asleep with just Ladone skulking about with sleep being an unnecessary function for her.

....

Jit was first to wake in the morning disturbing Limtom while he rose to go to the bathroom. A brief look at the time revealed it to be just past 5.00 am. When he slid back into bed Limtom was sound asleep again and he cuddled up to her joining her in moments. The next time they woke it was seven thirty and they got up to begin the day. Both were curious to see if the weather had abated on the surface below. When they stepped onto the bridge, they greeted Ladone then continued to the galley. Arrill wasn't up yet and Jit guessed him to be present shortly. They returned to the bridge to have their cuppa and see what Cartergole looked like weather wise. To their astonishment the day was clear, and the stretching rays of the sun clawed its way across the land waking up a new day. Even from the height they were at, they could still see the reflection of the sun rays bouncing off the sheer wet walls of the chasms. It was magical and the awe of it kept them silent as they took in the unfolding.

Arrill arrived on the bridge just before nine greeting them on the way to the galley. Back on the bridge, he joined them at the window gazing down at the brilliant day beginning below. It was an isolated place this, with a few scattered planets far off having small mining colonies and the closest large civilized world being where they came from, Posskeddar. Jit wondered how often anyone came here and if they did at all. There was no sign they'd yet seen on the surface to indicate any inhabitants were there or have been there. How many more worlds out there were void of people he wondered before Limtom stood up saying something about breakfast. Just the mention of it set his stomach going and he joined her in the making of it. When they finished eating, they prepared for the trip down to the planet. Limtom made some sandwiches while Jit helped and Arrill cleaned up the breakfast clutter.

It was 10.00 am when they exited the ship and lowered down to the surface once again. As they descended into the large chasm the walls glistened from the wetness that still clung to them and the falls that spilled water over the edges ran like maiden's hair until the drop atomised the water turning it into a fine mist that blended with the moisture on the walls. A slight breeze curled the atomised mist spreading wide and far and giving away the winds invisible motion. For all the rain that fell the day before there was no buildup or flooding of any kind making Jit wonder where all the water went to. They soon approached where they left off the day before and Arrill stayed at the controls while Jit and Limtom continued looking the ground over, taking one side each. During the search, Jit noticed that nothing walked on the ground, not even the grass eating beasts, which gave the place an eerie presence of a kind. It was as if the rain had washed everything away leaving a new land to behold. They hovered at the same height as previously skipping any tree that stood in their path slowly scouring the ground whilst running up the centre of the chasm. They searched thoroughly until the time quickly arrived at midday then located a position to set down and eat. When they stepped on the ground it remained moist and sponge like under their feet. With the ground to wet to sit on Jit grabbed a few fold out seats and they basked in the warm sunshine while they ate. After a short while, they bundled back into the shuttle and continued their search. Arrill let Limtom fly this time and took her position searching while they moved ahead.

By mid afternoon, they'd completed searching the big chasm with just the two small ones left to do. Limtom lifted the shuttle out of the chasm and they decided to take the left one next and search there. The smaller chasms were only three kilometres wide at the widest point and around one hundred kilometres long with the depth roughly the same as the big one. They started at one end and did a repeat of the same manoeuvre they carried out previously but when they reached the bottom they noticed the smaller chasm was darker because it wasn't as wide which gave them little time to look before it got too dark to see properly. They skirted the rim following the sheer wall looking through the canopy with the landscape matching the other chasm almost exactly. They searched until the darkness beneath the canopy hid too much from them and had to leave the rest until the following day. Limtom kept control of the shuttle and when they were close to the ship Jit took over to dock the bird.

....

Again, they were observed by hidden eyes and the same eyes now knew these strangers were looking for something and they feared what their intentions were. The temple of the ancients was a sacred place and none knew of it, so how did these three know and why did they seek it? There could be no other reason for them coming to this out of the way world. The council of elders would have to meet and discuss what to do. This was most unexpected with the entire community in a stir about the visitors. The chief turned to go to his favourite meditation place and put the thought forward.

....

Once the shuttle was docked into position Jit shut down the engines and they disembarked and took the lift to the bridge. Ladone waited in her usual position looking quite nice. She was dressed in a flowered dress that just passed her knees with a broad brim white hat sporting a ribbon around it in white too. She wore white shoes that exposed most of her feet and her legs were covered with striped stockings that disappeared under her dress. Even Limtom complemented her outfit astonished at her appearance. Jit was used to her dressing in the unexpected but had noticed in the last week or so that she seemed to have lost interest in doing so. She still dressed great but not the way she did before. He and Limtom left Arrill to fill Ladone in on all the fine details while they went to their cabin to shower and change. After showering they returned to the galley to prepare dinner. Arrill was still in his cabin. A short while later he walked in, smelling of cologne and dressed casually. Jit poured him a glass of wine and he joined them at the table. The four of them talked until the meal was ready and during the meal, they discussed the following day's plan. It was around 9.00 pm when they finally retired back to the bridge and Arrill suggested a few hands at cards before bed. They all agreed and set up the console and played a few games until near 11.00 pm. Jit was feeling the long day and told Arrill he was going to bed with Limtom quitting too, feeling fatigued as well.

....

Arrill remained up a little longer before he returned the console to normal and put everything away. While he did, he talked with Ladone until he finished then said good night and waited for the lift to come and get him.

....

While all aboard the Windchief retired for the night and slumbered, down on the planet a group of council elders met in a large cave and discussed how to confront this new situation that had transpired. The fires that lit the cave and kept it warm made dancing shadows on the walls with looming shapes that bent around all they covered. The elders were made up of men and women totalling fourteen in all and while they talked, they drank from a pottery vessel which they passed around. Late into the night, their meeting would go and hopefully, in the end, they will have found a way to resolve the new problem that had befallen them.

....

Around 8.00 am both Jit and Limtom rose for the day and dressed, with their next destination being the galley. Arriving on the bridge Ladone greeted them with her usual pleasant manner and they bid her the same back. Soon Arrill presented himself with a weak but audible good morning then rustled up a cup and joined them at the table listening to the conversation. Later, they had breakfast and when they finished eating, they prepared something for lunch to take with them, then made their way to the cargo bay. A brief look out the bridge window confirmed a glorious day on the surface of the planet. Jit let Limtom fly out and showed her through the startup procedure even though she'd watched him on several occasions. Her memory was as amazing as her skills and they were soon exiting the ship and descending to the surface of Cartergole. Within a short time, they were back where they left off and continued scouring the landscape below them. Being smaller than the middle chasm this one didn't have so many open fields making the search still slow going. Some of the canopy was difficult to see through with just glances in between the branches. When they reached the meeting point of the chasm tip they continued back along the wall on the other side to the other end, thus completing a full circuit. They made half the distance to the other end when lunchtime fell upon them and they looked for a place to settle down and get out to eat and have a stretch.

....

The warriors were in position, knowing by now that the strangers were coming back, they waited at an open area they hoped was best. Like eyes in the forest, they blended in becoming invisible to the untrained eye. When the hour drew near for the craft to touch the land they would prepare for the meeting, and soon after the lookout bought news of that moment, then they waited.

....

They spotted a decent size clearing with a small brook running through it coming from further up the way they'd come. It looked peaceful and serene so Limtom turned the shuttle around and prepared to land. As they lowered to the ground Jit and Arrill scanned all around taking advantage of the height and could see nothing move at all except the leaves of the trees flickering in the breeze. Once down they exited into the sunshine feeling its warmth on their skin and looked around. The place was beautiful with large trees growing that didn't exceed in height anymore than twenty or thirty metres. Their branches spread wide covering a large area out from the trunk. The clearing they were in was small compared to the other ones they stopped at but by now they were feeling more relaxed having only seen a few animals and birds. The brook bubbled away with crystal clear water that bounced over the rocks. Under the trees lay the shadows from the branches above, and the ground was littered with small undergrowth that changed in species and heights. The grass beneath their feet was still damp from the early mist that covered it and in prolific numbers, small five petal flowers of orange waved as the breeze stroked past them. After a stretch, Jit went to get the seats and they sat facing the brook to eat and take in the splendour of their surroundings. Some birds flew out of a tree and took to the sky catching their attention and they watched them soon to be lost in the woods beyond. While they ate the conversation was about the parts of the woods they couldn't see through too well and if they should recheck later with jetpacks. Limtoms eyes lit up at the mention of jetpacks. They locked eyes for a moment and at that moment they spoke volumes. When the sandwiches were gone Jit poured coffee for them all and Limtom had some cakes to go with it. The breeze picked up its pace for a burst feeling fresh on the face and then Jit felt a tiny sting on his neck and the last thing he remembered was reaching up to feel where he was stung.

…………………………..

The warriors stayed amongst the trees and despite their stealth movements a flock of birds scooted out from the branches of a nearby tree freezing them all in motion. The strangers watched them but seemed unperturbed by the birds admiring them instead. They continued closing in on the three and stopped to observe two of them blow smoke from themselves as a fire would. They watched fascinated by this for a moment then lined up their blow dart pipes and with pinpoint accuracy, they spiked them in the neck, and in seconds they slumped from their seats and fell to the ground motionless. They stood their ground for a time to be certain the drug from the darts worked on them. These were strangers and they knew nothing about them meaning they didn't know how or if the darts would even have an affect on them. After a length of time squandered away, they moved in slowly looking wearily at the bulk of the shuttle uncertain if it would move on them. They stepped on the ground still in stealth in case the intruders pretended to be immobile until they reached proximity. The leader poked at Jit's leg with his foot while all the others stood prepared for any motion. A second prod convinced them they were doused out and then they looked them over. The one who carried a weapon previously didn't wear it this day which made them think they were not robbers and didn't give the impression they were warlike. The leader felt a little calmer and instructed the pole bearers to come forward with the wave of his hand. They lay beside each of them a two pole device with skins stretched between them and lifted each person onto one and carried them away. The leader lingered until last and briefly poked his head in the open shuttle door to see the inside of this strange beast they rode. Nothing moved and it smelt otherworldly. An impulse passed him to step right in and was about to when his name was called, and he turned around to leave. The chairs sat empty now with a coffee flask on the ground and cups that remained where they dropped. Through familiar trails, they walked until they reached the hidden entrance to their cave and as they entered the priestess approached and performed her cleaning ritual before they could go further. When she finished, she brushed each one's upper arm with lavender coloured oil and stepped aside. The warriors continued deeper into the cave until they reached the chambers for the council elders and secured the strangers before leaving them to wait for questioning when they awake.

....

Jit opened his eyes feeling slow in his movements and his vision was blurry. A few moments later he gained full motor control of his body and his next immediate concern was Limtom. He was restrained by manacles on his wrists and ankles which were connected to a lug in the ground via a vine and allowed some freedom to move. It was enough for him to reach Limtom who was still out and when he looked over at Arrill he was coming around too. He also noticed something on her arm and touched it and it smeared a little leaving a film on his finger. He bought the finger to his nose but could only smell a slight mouldy scent and wondered what it was. He had the same mark on his arm and looking over at Arrill he saw he wore the same too. In a little while, Limtom began moving and coming around as well. A look at his timepiece told him they'd been out for close to five hours.

Their surroundings were a large cave that was lit by fire torches placed around the walls and some small fires burnt in holes in the ground giving more light to the enclosure. When Limtom was more alert she snuggled close to Jit and he felt her tremble slightly as she pressed herself against him. Holding her close to him as best he could, he consoled her and looked at Arrill who was awake too and looking around the cave with escape in his eyes. Many questions went through Jit's mind wondering who their captors were and what they wanted. It seemed they may have upset the locals after all. He went to move and change position but Limtom gripped him with a panicked grip as if he was going to leave her and looked up at him. He could see the fear in her eyes, and it grieved his heart to know she was suffering and blamed himself for bringing her here. The cave they were in was bare, with only the fires burning for light and heat.

There was no furniture or anything that resembled a place that was lived in and he speculated how long they might be here and what would become of them. It seemed obvious the inhabitants of Cartergole were behind this and he tried to think what they might have done to warrant this attack on them. He was also beginning to get hungry as the time neared their dinner time and tried to remain calm while he held Limtom who was still fiercely gripped to him. It was after 6.00 pm before they finally heard some commotion and looked up to see for the first time who their captors were.

At first, Jit thought the bad light was the problem with what he was seeing but as the procession came closer, he realised he was seeing fine. The tallest amongst them was no more than five feet and he was at the front of the line and looked to be in charge. The rest followed behind making fourteen all up and when they stood before them, the leader motioned to one in the group and said something. The one he spoke to undid their bonds setting them free to move and stand up and when they did they felt awkward because they towered over them all. Their captors were dressed in furs mostly with different colours on some of them and headgear adorned their heads as well. No shoes clad their feet and they were so calloused they looked like shoes.

'Why have you come here to our land?' spoke the leader catching them completely off guard that they could understand him.

Jit spoke up first and introduced himself and the others then looked at Arrill letting him take over the conversation. The leader introduced himself as "Wisplok" the chief of all the people who lived on Cartergole then motioned for Arrill to continue and sat crosslegged on the ground with the others doing the same. Jit, Arrill, and Limtom did the same too and right from the beginning, he told the story to Wisplok about the old guy he got the map from and all the rest since Jit arrived until the present. During their exchange, other people of the tribe came in bearing platters filled with fruits and nuts placing them before them. Jit was quite hungry by this time and even though he recognised none of the fruits, he picked one up that Wisplok ate and tried it. Limtom reached for one next never letting her grip go from Jit and ate in silence. When Arrill finished relaying all the events they waited to see what Wisplok would say. He spoke to the others in another language they couldn't understand and one of them got up and walked out of the meeting. They watched the person disappear into the shadows then looked back in anticipation of the outcome. Wisplok indicated for them to have more fruit which they did and while they ate, he told them about his people and how they rarely get to see strangers. Because of this, the entire settlement was in a buzz with the children the most difficult to constrain. He then went on to say that the Spirits gave a sign they were no threat and could be treated as guests which took a huge load off their minds. Jit felt Limtom relax instantly now that she knew there was no danger but still held onto him tightly. With the threat gone they could now talk and begin to form a friendship and both sides had many questions to ask. The first thing Jit asked was why they had a mark on them and was told it was a sign for all the people to know they were clean. Then he enquired about the shuttle and was told it remained as it was before they were carried away.

Jit looked at the time and it was just past 7.00 pm and knew it would be dark outside and wondered what might enter the open shuttle and make a home of it. After explaining his concern to Wisplok he dispatched a couple of warriors to shut the exit up because they would do him the honour to come and meet the rest of the community. With that situation under control, Wisplok stood as did the other elders and indicated for the three of them to follow. When they reached the passageways Jit immediately noticed the familiar masonry stonework as the mountain cleft back on Spollee. The only difference here was the paths were wider and much higher above their heads. The lights in the passageways were not fire torches like the cave but round and stick like with most of their lengths lit up. They protruded from the walls high up and to look at they were a tinge of blue, but on the ground and their surroundings they lit the place up like the midday sun. Jit couldn't see any means to what kept them lit and asked their guide what made them work. He told them the passageways and where they were going was all part of the ancient's work, and the cave they were in was their ancestor's habitat from a very long time ago. How they worked was just accepted and they never questioned the hand of the ancients. They wandered through an endless maze of passageways turning right and left until they arrived at an exit and spread out before them was a spectacle leaving them awed and speechless.

'Where are we?' asked Jit stunned at what he beheld.

Wisplok went on to explain that they existed in between the walls that separated the small chasm they were caught in and the large chasm in the center. Jit looked at him in wonderment trying to comprehend the scale of what he said. The sight before him was best described as a miniature city built inside a mountain. It's any wonder very little was known about the people of Cartergole he thought to himself. The cavern they looked out over was enormous with dwellings built all around the edges and sunk into the rock. In the centre was the dominating feature being a strangely shaped structure much like the one on the end of the key they found only many times larger. It had an equal length square bottom that rose high with the four sides meeting to a point at the top. It was glass smooth and resembled the key end perfectly. The colour of the structure was flat white, and no joining marks could be seen making it look like it was made of one solid piece. The lighting that lit this gigantic area was the same as the lighting in the passageways only they hung down from the ceiling like stalactites and were a lot thicker in roundness to accommodate the large area they had to light up. The size of the place was staggering, freezing them where they stood as they tried to absorb it all.

Below them were hundreds of faces looking up having gathered with the expectation of seeing the strangers. They felt like celebrities with all the attention they were receiving, and it made Jit feel a little awkward from all the exposure. To their right and left from where they stood were steps that angled downwards to the ground below which was at least thirty metres from where they were. From ground to ceiling Jit estimated the height to be in the vicinity of a hundred metres, maybe more. Wisplok told them the structure before them that dominated the centre was the Temple of the ancients and their sacred site. He then led them down the right side steps and they descended to the ground level. The steps were two metres wide, but the edge had no side rail which meant a lethal drop if one went over. When they reached half the height down, the steps spilled onto a landing then they turned left and followed another set down to the bottom.

By the time they reached the bottom all the crowd had gathered and wanted to touch them as if to be sure they were real. It was a humbling experience for the three of them and one they would not quickly forget. They all chatted away in their language smiling and bowing with the children touching them and quickly pulling their hand back in case they got in trouble. Wisplok led the way and they followed until they walked past the Temple. At close quarters it was even more impressive with the walls showing only a fine line where the pieces joined to make the structure. The line looked like it was drawn on rather than two points meeting at a joint. He wanted to touch the walls and feel them but dared not until they got to know their hosts a little better. If it's sacred to them it might be offensive for a stranger to defile their temple by touching it, even if they were considered clean. Despite everything being carved from rock, there were large Parks with trees growing and all kinds of vegetation comparing to the landscape outside. It was breathtaking that all this could be under the ground.

There was one Park directly under the way they came in with the temple in the centre and another Park at the opposite end. All around the edges were housing and meeting places with walkways between them and the Parks. Around the Temple was a large clear area and all the ground was the same rock that had been worked to create this magnificence. To think they flew over the top of all this a few times and never dreamt this would be under here. They eventually stopped out the front of one of the buildings and Wisplok stepped in inviting them to follow. It must've been a meeting house of some kind as there were cushions everywhere on the floor, with raised platforms that were tables scattered at random and varying in sizes. They followed the chief to the largest table and sat cross legged around it while the rest of the place quickly filled up and the bustling settled down to whispers. Soon bearers of fruit and nut trays entered and filled all the tables with an assortment of colours and smells, and they were encouraged to take and eat. While they did, a conversation took place with Wisplok seeming to be the only one speaking the same language as theirs. During the talks, more people entered carrying a large pottery urn that was fitted with a tap on the bottom, and from it, they filled small vessels with some liquid Jit couldn't see. The vessels were passed around with each person taking a sip and passing it onto the next person beside them. When it came to be Jits turn he smelled the milky liquid and was surprised at the pleasant fruity aroma that rose from the drink and put it to his lips and took a sip.

As he was the first one of the three to try it the room fell silent awaiting the response which he relayed with a nod of approval and a pleasing sound to accompany it. It was delicious with a slightly bitter after tang that compelled one to want more. The idea was to take a sip and pass it on, so he did as the rest did and waited for the next pass to take a bigger gulp. He went on to ask their host why only he could speak the same language as they could, and he told them because he was the chief, he had to know the main languages spoken in this sector. Even though he may never need to use them he was still required to know for situations just like the one they were in now. Jit told him they were informed of inhabitants living on the planet but after not seeing anything relating to people, they forgot all about the inhabitants altogether thinking they may live up on the top lands. That's why they dropped their guard which hadn't turned out so bad anyway.

They may never have found this place providing it was what they were looking for, and if they did, they couldn't be sure of the response they may have received. Despite the people's small size and basic weapons, they were still captured with no effort at all. Soon the vessel with the milky liquid passed by again and Jit could see now why it was passed around. During the time it took for the next sip to come his way he could feel the effects from the first sip which took some time in coming. It felt good though and they were relaxed by this time with a mood settling like they'd all been friends for a long time. Limtom was so relaxed she realised her vice like grip on him and behaved like normal. For a while there she was really scared, and he could feel it even without looking at her.

Wisplok went on to tell them about the history of Cartergole which for a long time was just passed on from one generation to another until records started to be kept. Much information was lost during the long period, but a considerable amount was retained too. According to their history, four visitors arrived on Cartergole but it was lost as to why they came and where they came from or how long ago. They co-existed with their ancestors and built the Temple which resides in the square. Also lost was the reason for building it underground when there was so much room above. He told them that they carved out an already existing cavern to accommodate everything they saw since they entered the Temple city. The original cave they were prisoners in was just one of many caves that littered these lands which were honeycombed with them. Some were small and some were large, but the city was by far the largest cavity they knew about. How it was done was lost to them too.

Jit was thinking Laser technology of some kind must've been used for doing the main work, with the fine detail done by hand maybe. As the evening wore on and grew late, people started thinning out taking the children home to bed and doing the same themselves. Soon there were only the three of them and the elders around the table talking and exchanging stories a while longer before they were shown to the guest quarters which were above them on another floor. By this time, they were all feeling the weariness of the day bare down on them, but they still sat up to discuss some things. The first thing to mention was how the Temple was the same shape as the end of the key to which Arrill said he'd noticed too. If the Temple was what they came to seek then they'd have to find a means to get a close look at it without offending their new friends. They agreed to discuss it in the morning with Wisplok, giving in to the overwhelming tiredness and went to bed. The bed arrangement was the same as the cushions but just a lot bigger with soft furs to cover oneself. They all slept in the same room with Limtom snuggled up to Jit on one large cushion and Arrill asleep on another nearby. With the place, quiet Jit could just make out a low hum emanating from somewhere around him before he slipped into unconsciousness.

…………………………..

The first sounds woke Jit at 6.00 am according to his timepiece and he felt quite alert considering the early hour. Limtom was still snuggled up to him sleeping peacefully like a baby and Arrill was still motionless too. It was around eight when they were ready to exit their quarters and went down to the meeting room where they stepped outside the building into the open courtyard. Even after already seeing everything yesterday they were still awestruck by the magnitude of what lay around them. The people that walked past them bowed and said something they couldn't understand, and they replied with a bow and smiled back. Not many wandered around and they thought it might be because it was still too early. From where they stood, they could see the Temple walls stretching up to its point high above them. Jit felt comfortable enough to start walking towards the large area around the Temple and thus bringing them in close contact with it. From the little he saw when they walked past it yesterday, he hadn't yet been able to make out any entry point to the structure. Surely it couldn't just be a monument he thought to himself.

The open area they came to was spacious with trees planted around in raised circular beds with a variety of coloured flowers growing around them and spilling over the edges. Benches were scattered about for people to sit on and very small birds flitted around that looked like bugs at first sight. They finally stood at the foot of the temple on one side and Jit estimated it to be around eighty metres from point to point and the height he guessed to be thirty metres. It was quite large and was the dominant feature in the city. Being as close as they were Jit noticed how smooth and glassy the surface of the structure was and wanted to reach out and touch it but didn't. The colour of the material used was a milky white with white stripes that swirled around in it that was only a shade different so they could be noticed. To stare at they almost looked like they moved to replicate clouds in the sky.

He'd never seen anything like it except for the small version on the end of the key they had. Because of its smallness he hardly even paid any attention to the shape but when seen on a scale like this it made a different impression. They started walking around the Temple with access being around it and behaved like tourists while all three scanned the walls to see if there was anything to show an entryway. As they did people walked by bowing slightly and smiling making them feel like they were part of the place and accepted in the city. If only all places were the same, he thought as he extended the same courtesy back to them. They'd soon covered two sides of the Temple with nothing to be seen other than the same flat white wall and lines where the joins met. Where the Temple met the ground the join there was the same as the ones on the walls making it seem like it was cut from the rock it sat on despite the colour difference. Such precision seemed impossible, yet someone knew how to do it. While he scanned, he thought about the four that came to Cartergole and wondered from where they came in the expanse of the Universe. Maybe they came from another Universe altogether he concluded as they reached the end of the third side of the Temple. Still, nothing presented itself as an entry of any kind, so they continued the same way along the last side. To look at it was impossible to tell one side from the other as they all looked identical. Jit became aware of the need for coffee as they'd had none since their capture and once he thought about it the desire became great, especially for the first one of the day. The closest place for that was the shuttle and he had no idea how to get to the outside just yet. None of them had any idea how far inside the mountain they were. All he remembered was the gap between the chasms was a few kilometres wide and they were somewhere in amongst it. More people walked past with smiles and bows exchanged and a short time later they reached the end of the last side with no results. There had to be an entry if this was a temple Jit thought to himself. He was distracted from his train of thought by Arrill and Limtom finally expressing their desire for coffee too. The next thing they dealt with was to find Wisplok and explain they needed to get to the shuttle. Jit doubted the people of Cartergole even heard of coffee, let alone drank it. They looked around and by this time more people began to wander around and they asked some of them how to find Wisplok. They were failing miserably when Jit noticed his headgear above the crowd coming their way. When he approached them, he said something to the villagers, and they bowed with a smile then went about their affairs. After they exchanged greetings Wisplok told them if they were hungry to follow him to the eatery, but they made their more immediate concern known to him and he called some warriors over to assist. He spoke some words to them then told Jit and the others to follow and they would be escorted to the shuttle. Before they left, he also informed them they were welcome whenever they wanted. Jit told him they would be back afterward and Wisplok smiled and continued to the eatery while they followed the warriors to the main entrance of the city.

They climbed back up the flight of steps they descended the day before and as they did Jit looked back at the Temple wondering how to gain access to the inside, if there was an inside. Through the doorway, they followed their guides with Jit trying to make a mental note of the way but soon giving up from the complexity of it all. A short while later they passed the cave they were kept in when first captured then they walked for another ten or fifteen minutes before they could see daylight up ahead. It was closing on 10.00 am when they stepped out into the sunshine with another fine day on Cartergole to be had. The air smelt of woods and wildflowers as they exited the cave and being still early there was a cool snap to the breeze that blew from the direction of the woods. Jit looked back to remember where the entrance to the mountain was and despite still being close to it, he already had trouble seeing the way due to its perfect camouflaging. It was the same arrangement as the cleft in the mountain back on Spollee, but this entry was at ground level and a lot bigger. They would never have seen it from the shuttle no matter how hard they looked. The trail leading up to the entrance was all rock so it didn't leave a track of any kind that could be spotted and followed. Once they were out in the open the shuttle was only a little way away and when they were upon it the warriors said something they couldn't understand and bowed then went back the way they came.

The chairs remained where they left them and, on the ground, they picked up cups and flask then went into the shuttle and got to work. Soon the aroma of coffee filled the shuttle and when it was made, they sat inside to drink it. While they did Jit linked with the ship and bought Ladone up to speed on what was going on. Even though his heart belonged to Limtom he was certainly happy to see Ladone as he loved her dearly too. When he finished, he fell back into talking with the others and they discussed what to do next. The most logical move was to go back and talk some more with Wisplok and slowly work their way into the community and gain their trust even further. Already these people made them feel welcome and the last thing they wanted to do was step on that trust and hurt them. When they finished a second cuppa, they went out to gather the chairs and return them to their places then they made the trek back to the hidden entrance. While they walked along Jit hoped someone would be there to guide them back in, otherwise, they would soon be lost in the maze of passageways. He also looked at the mark on his arm which was fading and wondered if they would have to undergo another cleaning ceremony. They hadn't travelled far before out of thin air two warriors appeared and all Jit could do was make hand signals to indicate they wanted to see Wisplok. It was a spectacle to see but the warriors seemed to understand, and one led while the other bought up the rear and followed them to the entrance.

At that point, another warrior took over and the two went back to wherever it was they were hiding. Being as small as they were, they could hide in many places in the woods. During the walk back to the city, they were passed by people carrying empty large platters going out the way they came. They bowed and smiled as they passed, then continued with their chatter which couldn't be understood by the three. Soon they could see the entrance to the city up ahead and when they entered the doorway the sight still awed them despite having seen it already. Jit looked at the Temple that drew all attention on first entry then scanned the Parks and walkways with no sight of Wisplok to be viewed. They followed their guide down the flight of steps until they reached the bottom then he stopped to talk to someone else briefly and continued to the far end Park. The Park was quite big and as they approached it they stepped up a few steps and onto it as it was raised from the ground some metre or so. It was as beautiful as any Park one would go to outside. Children were playing on swings and other playthings screaming and shouting as they always do. Trees grew up to fifteen metres high and were spread out like umbrellas with benches for sitting on outnumbering them by three times.

Water features lay here and there playing their melody and it was at one of the water features they spotted Wisplok sitting cross legged before it. When they approached, he looked up and invited them to join him then sent the warrior away. They all sat facing the water feature while they talked and Jit found the melody from the running water quite soothing. The feature was just simple in its design but in its simplicity, one could lose themselves in the waters chorus. They made small talk for a little while before Jit asked Wisplok if there was a way into the Temple. He sat quietly for a moment as if thinking about what to say then looked at Jit and said he didn't know. He went on to tell them that for many generations they believed there to be something inside the Temple but a way in had not been found yet. He then went on to tell them the council of elders was divided in the idea of finding a way. Some were afraid of what might be inside and were happy the way things were. Jit had to admit that life on Cartergole looked pretty good from what he'd seen so far. Even though a lot of people lived here the place remained uncrowded and spacious.

How they never spotted anyone from the shuttle is a testament to their hiding abilities. They ate fruit and nuts which must grow outside and seemed to be their main food source and all the people they'd encountered so far genuinely looked happy. Arrill asked Wisplok what they'd done to find a way into the Temple and he told them they checked every side from top to bottom, finding nothing at all. Just smooth walls that looked all the same as each other. They were so caught up in the conversation that before they knew it a long gong was heard and Wisplok stood and told them to follow him. As they walked, he told them it was time to have lunch and they would eat at the eatery which is what the people who are inside do. Once seated the conversation returned to the Temple and Wisplok told them he was watching them this morning when they walked around the edges knowing their thoughts just from their actions. He went on to tell them there were other things he would tell them but first, it had to be discussed by the council. He wasn't at liberty to make the call on his thoughts alone. They said nothing while he talked and wondered what other things he might be referring to with the mind conjuring up all kinds of possibilities. He told them the council was meeting tonight and the matter would be bought up then and he might have an answer in the morning. They weren't invited to the meeting so Jit guessed it to be a private affair and told Wisplok they would go after lunch and come back the next day. Wisplok explained they could stay if they wanted but Jit said they needed to get back to the ship as they had some matters of their own to attend to. Lunch lasted a good hour and when they were ready to go Wisplok called a warrior and instructed him to lead them back to their shuttle. They thanked their host and told him they'd be back in the morning around 10.00 am and made to leave. Some of the crowds eating had dispersed but the place was still quite full and as they exited the smiles and nods were countless. Jit found them to be very humble people and despite the language barrier, he felt they were welcome as certain as if they'd spoken it.

In the allotted time they reached the outside again and the shadow of days end was already beginning to stretch across the gap of the chasm. The sky above was still clear with flocks of birds the only mark in its perfection. It was hard to tell if the birds were high up in the sky or just small birds to begin with as Jit watched them bob out of sight. Within a short time, they reached the shuttle and the warrior bowed saying something then he stood back and waited, obviously wanting to watch the shuttle lift off. Once inside and strapped in Jit went through the startup routine and they were soon underway. The warrior below them sank to a speck and soon vanished, all the while not moving from his position, head cranked skyward.

'I wonder what thoughts are going through that warrior's mind' Jit said to Arrill.

'Complete wonderment I would imagine' he replied.

The shadow from days end was rapidly crossing the chasm they exited with the middle one next in its line of sight. From high up, they could observe its plight as it oozed across the land bringing darkness and the cold with it. In the cargo bay he set down next to shuttle number one then shut down the engines and they all made for the cabin deck with showers and clean clothing in mind. When Jit and Limtom were washed and dressed they made their way back to the bridge. As they appeared, they found Arrill was already there talking with Ladone. They greeted her and joined the conversation explaining in more detail their experience on the surface. During the gathering, Jit went to make a drink appreciating the convenience of the galley and all it offered. Although their capture was only for a short period, it made him aware of how quickly and unexpectedly things can change. Back out on the bridge, they talked about the key they found and the similarity between it and the Temple knowing it had some purpose, otherwise, why would it be where they found it? They pondered why the key was on another planet and so far away from Cartergole and what purpose did the stones they found serve. Hopefully, they might have some more progress after the council meeting then they moved on to talking about what Wisplok meant when he said there were "other things" he would tell them. He knew more, and Jit was itching to find out what it was just as Arrill was too. Dinner time was soon upon them and Jit was in the mood for a roast after all the fruit and nuts he'd had, and the others agreed, laughing at the same time. When it was ready, they ate in the dining room with Ladone joining them so they could continue their discussions during the meal. Once the meal was over, they played a few hands of cards and around 10.00 pm Jit and Limtom bid them goodnight and retired to their cabin.

....

Arrill stayed up a little while longer then admitted defeat from weariness and made for bed too. He said good night to Ladone and waited for the elevator to come and get him. While he lay in bed, he ran through all the happenings since Jit arrived on Geelok. He thought about his cave and Leearnah and his last thought before he succumbed to sleep was of him and Leearnah when they were together.

....

Limtom slipping back into bed was the first thing that awoke Jit in the morning. They fell back to sleep and finally rose from bed around 8.00 am to have a shower and dress. Next, they ventured to the bridge to see if Arrill was up yet. On arriving they found the ever faithful and pleasant Ladone at her post, whom they greeted warmly. While the girls talked Jit went to make the morning reviver. Back on the bridge, he handed one to Limtom then went to look out the window and see what the day on Cartergole was going to be like. The time was closing in on 9.00 am and the sun was still un-wrapping the darkness from the planet as it stretched forth fully exposing the chasms at the same time. They never ceased to amaze Jit, because they looked like an impossibly large bird scratched the ground with one claw while still in flight. Another glorious day looked to be set for the place and from this stance, it was hard to believe any population existed on the surface at all. But its secrets they now knew, and Jit thought it wise to keep this knowledge to himself, hoping the others would do the same. His thoughts were jostled by Limtom slipping her arm through his and locking close to him, now sharing the view.

They remained that way until the elevator was summoned and soon, they were presented with Arrill in their midst. He went to the galley to get a cuppa and was soon back and joined them at the window in silence. When they finished, they had some breakfast then they prepared for the trip back to the surface. It had just gone past 10.00 am making them late and Jit hoped Wisplok wasn't waiting on them. He didn't like being late. Down in the cargo bay, they buckled into their seats, and after Arrill ran the systems check they hovered out the bay and banked round to the planet starting the descent. In little time he landed in the same position as the previous day and even before they touched down, they could see two warriors awaiting their arrival. When they stepped outside the day was warm with the sun sparkling off the brook and the leaves in the nearby trees rustling from a slight breeze that pushed through them. The warriors bowed and smiled saying something at the same time which Jit took as a request to follow them or a greeting. They traipsed behind them with the scenery now becoming familiar to them from repetition and in a short time they were at the hidden entrance to the city. The bright light of the sun was replaced by the blue tinged lights in the passageway with only the warmth missing as they zigzagged through the maze network. Each time Jit walked the passageways he became more familiar with the way. Shortly they came upon the entry and soon stepped onto the landing overlooking the city once again. Still, it was a sight to behold and they took a moment to do so before gliding down the stairs after their escorts.

Things on the ground seemed the same as the day before with people going about their daily lives giving them a courteous bow and smile, and children were still fascinated by them and followed close by in small groups giggling and pointing at them. Jit thought they might be going to the Park again but before reaching the steps to climb up onto it they turned into a doorway that entered Wisploks residence. After walking through a short hallway, they stepped into a large rectangular room sparse of furniture except lots of cushions for sitting on. They live simply Jit thought to himself. Wisplok sat cross legged on a cushion at the table and when they entered, he called them to sit and join him. He was sipping some hot herb drink and poured them a serve in small vessels then handed them around. Jit bought the vessel to his nose and noticed it smelt a lot like the juice they had the day before and assumed it was the same with the only difference this time, being hot. Despite the smell being the same, it was different when tasted. It had a spicy flavour to it and the texture was a little syrupy running smooth down the throat refreshing one as it went. After a few sips, he also noticed it had a calming effect which felt pleasant and making for a great mood. They made small talk for a while and then Wisplok divulged the happenings of the meeting the night before. They were startled at what they heard, especially Arrill. He went on to tell them that others had come before them spanning back many generations and assumed they seeked the secrets of the Temple. None were approved by the Spirits, so they remained hidden from the previous visitors. The city was safe with the hidden entrance concealing any habitation at all. They would come and look around the same as you all did, then they would leave and continue searching the upper lands.

This time however things were different he continued, and told them that when they very first landed, they were watched, and from their demeanour displayed no threat or bad intentions on the first appearance. Then when the council met over the situation and the Spirits were consulted there was a sign that sealed the decision, and that was to contact you. The three of them sat motionless as they hung on every word spoken as if in a spell. On he continued with yet more captivating revelations telling them there was a hidden panel which was discovered by accident on one of the sides of the Temple. It was only small and when discovered he could make no sense of it at all. Maybe they could make more sense of it he said then went on to tell them the conditions put down by the council. The time slipped away quickly, and they soon heard the gong for the midday meal. Wisplok spoke to a nearby warrior who walked out, then continued from where he left off.

He'd just finished the last of what he had to say when four people walked in with platters filled with foods. It was all laid out on the table, along with some juice then they were gone again. While they ate, they discussed one of the conditions, which was the hour they could approach the Temple to see the panel. It had to be early hours of the morning when all were asleep and Wisplok was coming along with them as well. They talked all through their lunchtime and when the meal was over more of the hot herb tea was bought to the table. Jit asked Wisplok if he could smoke suddenly feeling like one and permission was given, and he looked at Limtom. She smiled at him and he rolled two and passed her one then asked Wisplok if he wanted to try one. He declined after observing Arrills disapproving facial gestures but watched them with fascination when they lit up.

He asked questions about the art of smoking and why they did it with Jit just saying he liked it and never thought of it as an art. While they did so they continued talking and arranging a good time to check the panel which they agreed would be 2.00 am. Wisplok informed them the main lights in the city turn down at 11.00 pm and imitate a full moon effect until the sun comes up outside, then they go bright again. He told them everything just worked automatically and has done so ever since it was built many generations ago. Something must've powered all these lights thought Jit, and he had no doubt the answer lay in the Temple. It was still twelve hours away before they could see the panel and Jit told Wisplok they would have to go to the shuttle to get some things they might need for later. He asked them if they needed a guide out and they felt confident that between the three of them they should be okay. They finished their vessel of herb tea then told him they would be back soon. He told them he'd be either at his home or in the Park when they returned and bowed his head to them as they departed.

They were soon climbing the steps back up to the exit and with surprisingly little effort found their way back to the outside. The shadows were clawing their way back over the land, but complete darkness was still a little way off yet. When they arrived at the shuttle, they put together some torches and other things like a spool of Polonium thread and some snacks as well as a flask of coffee. Everything they could think of went into backpacks and they slung them over their shoulders and prepared for the trip back to the city. This time when they arrived at the secret entrance there were no warriors to meet them so they continued straight in and gathered they were part of the place now and could be trusted. The maze back presented no problem and they soon exited onto the platform overlooking the city. They stopped for a moment to look over the sight and Jit wondered what the people were like who made this place. It was spectacular! At the bottom of the steps they made their way to Wisploks place and before they reached his doorway, they heard him call to them from the Park. They looked up to see him waving to get their attention and they stepped up onto the Parkland welcoming the soft grass under their feet. Apart from Parks, everything else in the city was rock to walk on.

He told them to follow him and he led them around the park which covered a large area at the end of the city. It was easy to forget you were inside a cavern until you looked upwards then you were dazzled by the lights with their blue tinge that shone like the sun. Wisplok told them the gardens were never watered, nor the lawn, yet everything remained green and grew vigorously. Everything behaved just as if it was outside. Jit thought again about the builders of all this and how he would like to meet them if they existed somewhere. Their technology must be impressive if they can turn a cavern into an amazing place like this. They passed a large pond and although Jit couldn't see anything, he knew something lived in the water as it rippled from movement beneath its surface. Whatever it was couldn't have presented too much of a threat as children played at one end of the pond splashing water at each other. He watched them play for a moment and remembered those days when life was just playing, eating, and sleeping.

They continued and came to a large water feature and paused for a while to watch its workings. It was made up of three upright slabs of rock with water spewing out the top and running down the sides. The sides had different shaped protrusions that were part of the slabs and it changed the water's path making fingers that played a watery tune on its way to the bottom. A loud watery tune! The slabs Jit estimated to be at least twenty metres high and if a breeze had been blowing, they would get wet from the mist that arose from the waters activity. Wisplok told them that when the lights turn down at night the look of the feature seems to change and it's quite an enchanting experience that he recommended to them. Soon they moved on and the noise from the tumbling water slinked off behind them becoming a whisper in the past. Their host was a man of many stories, keeping them entertained while they circumnavigated the park.

Occasionally people walked past and smiled saying something to them with its meaning only understood by Wisplok. Here and there were sculptures with abstract dimensions to their pose. Some were complex while others were simple yet no less thought provoking in their simplicity.

They followed their host until they finished where they began then he invited them into his home for tea. Inside they unslung the backpacks and left them in a corner for later then joined their host at the table. Jit checked the time and it was just past 4.00 pm meaning they still had a fair while to wait before they could see where this panel was and what it did. It must've been extremely well concealed because the three of them looked thoroughly as they scanned the walls but saw nothing that suggested a panel or anything for that matter.

Someone soon entered carrying with them a pot of tea with vessels for drinking and placed them on the table smiling and bowing all the while. They spent the rest of the afternoon chatting away with their host, exchanging stories about their lives. He was astonished when Jit told him about the Windchief and that he made a home of it. Wisplok told them that many nights did he go out and stare at the stars wondering what lay beyond their small world. Jit told him that only a small amount of the Universe had been mapped to date with experts saying there are more Universes to be found too. He then went on to tell him that the planet they came from was so far away it couldn't even be seen as a star. As he unfolded the story to Wisplok he could see that his host couldn't even understand the concept of space, let alone clear space. They lived a simple life these people and Jit thought to himself that they were better off the way they were. He'd not seen one unhappy person since they contacted them. They were still like warriors of the land, yet they lived in a city with technology they just accepted like the sun coming up. The afternoon slipped away quickly, and they soon heard the gong announcing dinner time. Wisplok stood and without needing to be called they followed, and he led them to the meeting room they first met in. When they arrived others were gathering too, and as soon as they saw the chief, they stepped aside allowing him entry and greeting him by bowing and smiling. At the same table as previously, they sat on cushions and waited for the food to arrive which wasn't long in coming. The place slowly filled up with the noise level rising a little, but not so much they had to shout to hear one another.

They kept conversation away from their quest to come and chatted about where they came from. They told Wisplok about planets far away and he was completely intrigued by the stories probing deeper to learn more. Limtom was fascinated by them too as this was her first time off-world. They both sat there like a couple of children listening intently as Jit and Arrill spilled their tales. They remained in the meeting room until 8.00 pm before they left and went back to Wisploks abode. A good portion of the people had left too and there was only a hand full of stragglers still at their spots drinking a clear liquid which was agreeing with them very well. Back at their host's home, they took up positions as previously and Wisplok wanted to hear more stories about the stars with Limtom showing an eager face for more too. During the talks, a young female entered with a pottery jug and drinking vessels placing them on the table and bowing before she left with a smile. She looked at Arrill a little longer than the rest and Jit caught the moment.

She was stunning with thick black hair that stretched long down her back and bushy eyelashes with big brown eyes that could end a war. As the people of Cartergole were only small in stature it was hard to guess her age. The drink she left for them was the same clear liquid the people in the meeting room were drinking, or it at least looked the same to Jit. It had no particular taste and was nearly like water, but the effect wasn't like water. It seemed to stimulate the mind making talking a lot easier as they remembered things otherwise hard to recall. In such a state the time went by quickly and it soon reached 11.00 pm when the lights dimmed to full moon mode. Jit looked at Limtom and they excused themselves and left for a romantic walk. He led her to the three large slabs they were at earlier on which Wisplok said was a spectacle when the lights went down. Everything around them had that low light like a full moon yet they could see everywhere with no effort. Even from a distance, they could see the three structures and at night they glowed with a low light that made them look like an apparition. The water still flowed over their surface and the mist could be seen giving them the ghostly look. As they approached and stood at the foot of them, they were an awesome sight and the water seemed to play a different tune which was almost hypnotic adding to the magic of it all. They found a spot on the lawn under a tree to sit and take in the moment while the water played its melody.

The shadow from the tree was still cast about them but it moved none and the lawn was speckled from its form. It was a little spooky with the glowing slabs standing like guardians and the crashing water delivering their voices finishing with the mist symbolising their fuming mood. The time slipped away quickly and at twelve thirty they made their way back to Wisplok's place to get ready for later. Jit could feel the suspense building from the anticipation. When they arrived Arrill and Wisplok were still seated the same as when they left. Jit told their host they went to see the rock slabs and the time passed as if they were there only a few minutes. Wisplok told them it had that effect on a person and it was one of his favourite meditation spots either at night or during the day. He also told them on another occasion they should go to the Park under the entry to the city and have a look at the structure there at night. It was a water feature too but shaped differently with a magic all its own. He said he frequented that spot quite often as well. As the hour neared 2.00 am they began to prepare themselves going over what they discussed earlier on in the day. When the time was right to go they slung their packs on and with Wisplok leading the way they exited his premises, had a good look around to be sure all was quiet, then walked the short distance to the Temple that awaited in the subdued light.

At the Temple, they walked to one corner of the structure and Wisplok had another look around before crouching down and sliding out a corner piece that worked like a drawer. It was close to ground level and the piece still held the corner shape in it and when fully extended only revealed a slot in its otherwise smooth surface. The fit from its home position was so perfect that it was impossible to know it was there unless told or found accidentally. Wisplok told them earlier on that the method of its discovery was lost over time but he believed a child found it by accident whilst playing near the Temple. It was known for many generations, but no one knew what it was and if it was anything of importance. At first, it would've looked like it was broken but on closer inspection, that theory was dismissed. Although the light was dim it was still enough to see by, and they all stared on in silence until Arrill pulled out the key they had and leaned over to see if it slid into the slot. The slot just looked like a thin line and the key slid into it until it could go no further but didn't sit flat and stuck up a little. All that stuck out of the slot now was the handle of the key.

Nothing happened so he tried turning the key clockwise then anti-clockwise and still nothing happened. They all looked at each other for a moment then Jit suggested taking the key out and trying it the other way around. Arrill did this and immediately there was a difference with the key sitting flat in its position then the sides at the top of the key folded outwards exposing a button in the center looking like an open flower. The button pulsed with a faint light a few moments after. They were all frozen at the revelation! They looked at Wisplok and he slowly lifted his arm and reached to the button, hesitated a further moment then pushed down. He pulled his hand away with nothing happening at first but then the sides on the key handle retracted back to the way they were, and the panel slipped back into place and sealed shut with the key still in it. They looked at the panel then at each other then back at the panel and nothing was happening. They stepped back to see the sides of the Temple, but nothing appeared or changed. Arrill then suggested a look around the entire Temple in case entry was on one of the other sides. They left Wisplok at the panel and walked at a quick pace around the other side of the Temple with nothing on that side and one side left to check.

As they turned around the point, for the briefest moment Jit thought he saw something, but he was uncertain what because all he saw now was another side the same as the rest. He was sure he'd seen something almost like a shadow! They returned to where they left Wisplok and even before they arrived, they saw him waving franticly at them. They quickened their pace and when at his side they saw the panel had ejected again. Arrill reached in and pulled the key out examining it seeing no change from when he last saw it. Wisplok told them the panel just slid out of its own accord, but he was too concerned to touch it. Limtom suggested the entry might be on a timer and after what Jit thought he saw he concluded she might be right. Arrill put the key back in and they followed the same procedure and this time when the panel slid in, they made fast tracks to the side Jit thought he saw something. The theory proved correct and they soon saw an opening that was shaped the same as the Temple, only upside down with the point facing downwards.

They stepped inside with Arrill leading the way and as soon as they were all in, the point of entry sealed up and they couldn't see the courtyard anymore. At once the walls glowed softly making enough light to see by. The walls were the same inside as they were outside and the glow that emitted from them made it seem like the entire Temple was a giant lamp. Before they moved off a panel slid out from the wall and in it was the key Arrill placed in the lock outside. He withdrew it and returned it to his pouch along with the other items and they followed the path before them. The panel slid back in as they walked away in silence with each one deep in thoughts of their own. Jit wondered how long ago it was that anyone walked inside the Temple as they progressed forward. Everything looked sterile and pure. The passageway was only wide enough for a single file so Arrill led the way with Wisplok behind him then followed Limtom and Jit bringing up the rear. They soon arrived in a room that must've been the centre of the Temple and its size Jit estimated to be around five metres square. There was nothing at all in the room except more symbols they only recognised from the repetition of seeing. As to what they said, they knew not still. They looked back the way they came and could only see the passageway with no change, so they proceeded to look around the room considering another hidden panel somewhere to be found. After a thorough search of all the walls, they checked the ceiling and floor with nothing either. They decided to check the walls again and this time moved around one place, so they checked the person's wall next to them. Sometimes what one misses, another may spot was the theory. And so it worked because after a short time Limtom said she found something, which drew them all to her position to see. In the centre of one of the symbols which mostly represented the letter O was an indentation barely visible due to its shallowness. On closer inspection Arrill immediately noticed a familiar shape to the hollow. It was the exact shape as the stones he carried so he pulled one out to check his assumption. The stone he tried was the green one which was first picked from the pouch and true to his guess, it fit so perfectly he had to pluck it back out with a knife blade to assist its removal. Nothing happened while the stone sat in the hollow which allowed for the stone to fit only one way. With the green stone done the next one Arrill placed down was the blue stone. They waited with anticipation for a short time until they soon realised nothing was going to happen then he tried the red stone and they waited some more. Still, nothing happened so Arrill placed the yellow stone in the dent with the hope something would happen, and it did. At first the yellow stone pulsed with a faint glow then the entire room vibrated, and they noticed the passageway they came in through, slowly moved up to the ceiling then disappeared as the room descended downwards. They stood their ground looking around and at each other with questioning looks mixed with concern until the vibrating stopped and the room went silent. During the transit down Limtom locked onto Jit with the same fierceness when they were captured by Wisplok and his warriors. They waited for a little time with nothing happening then they walked around the room wondering what to do next. Arrill guessed taking the stone back out might make something happen but after he did, the room remained the same. They scanned the walls again looking carefully for anything different from before but came up empty. Jit thought of something and told Arrill to try the other stones in place of the yellow one. He tried the blue one and all was the same then he inserted the red one and still nothing happened then as he pressed the green stone in, he prepared for what might come. The stone glowed but it didn't pulse like the yellow stone and after waiting some time he felt an impulse to press the stone. As he did, a passageway appeared resembling the one they entered the room from with the exception being it was on a different wall. Arrill gave Jit the thumbs up and walked into the passageway and the others followed closely behind. The first thing Jit noticed when he stepped into the passage was it tilted downwards on an angle. It soon came to a vee point then doubled back but continued down on an angle. They travelled about the same distance before they came to the end and the passageway spilled into a large room that was lit by the same lighting method as the city itself.

Again, these lights were in the ceiling but bulging out like a ball part protruding from a flat surface. The only thing that sat in the middle of the room was a chair and they approached it cautiously until they stood before it. The chair beckoned one to sit in it and they looked at Wisplok who in turn told them the Spirits sent them, so it was up to one of them to take the seat. The next choice was easy as all this was Arrills project and they stood back to give him room while he stood there for a moment in consternation. The seat itself looked like a pilot seat propped up in the centre by a shaft that rose from the ground. It had a high back with a headrest and its colour was equivalent to a pale blue sky. He slowly sat down as if to feel if it would hold his weight then fully stretched out and relaxed. As he did the chair spun around a little startling them all then slanted back and at the same time piercing the back of his neck with a needle that immobilised him immediately. The others weren't aware of the piercing and just watched him as he sat motionless waiting for him to say something or do something. Moments passed before Arrill spoke something none of them could understand and from the ground in front of the chair extended a stone pedestal with an angle sloped on it and three familiar indentations in it. Wisplok, Limtom, and Jit still had no idea that Arrill had been affected by anything and looked on with expectancy. Arrill had never felt his mind clearer than it did right now and knew whatever was injected into him was the cause of it. The needle had retracted by this time and movement to his body returned to normal. He remained as he was then reached into the pouch and pulled out the three remaining stones and sat forward to place them in their positions. He didn't need to guess because he knew the combination. It was as if he always knew but didn't require the information until now. The blue stone went first followed by the red and the yellow dropped in last.

As soon as the last stone went in, they all glowed to life and Arrill knew the next step was pushing the stones in the right sequence, which he knew too. Jit, Limtom, and Wisplok looked on without saying anything held in a spell and were astonished by what Arrill was doing and having no idea how he knew. After Arrill pushed in the right order the chair spun around a little further to a different position, so the pedestal was now beside him. Once again from the ground arose a larger pedestal that represented more of a console because of its size. When it stopped at its zenith the lights immediately dimmed down bringing the room into complete darkness except for the console. All Jit could see were the same symbols they'd seen on the map and in the mountain and now here.

'I can read what it says,' Arrill said to them.

'How?' exclaimed Jit.

Arrill then proceeded to tell them about the needle that stabbed him, and they were in disbelieve he didn't say something. He continued by telling them that as soon as he was pricked by the needle, he felt a calming that suppressed any concern about the matter and now could understand what the symbols meant. He fixed the backrest in a position for him to use the console and took in the sight that lay before him. Jit watched him navigate through the advanced piece of alien technology as he'd just come back from a lunch break. He touched the symbols using two of his fingers together and using both hands as if typing. Every so often he would turn to the pedestal with the stones in it and touch one of them or all of them in sequence. It was a dazzling spectacle to watch and they waited for what was to come. Arrill interrupted their trance by telling them that the people who left this information had mapped fifty eight percent of the Universe. To both Arrill and Jit's knowledge, only ten to fifteen percent of the Universe was mapped so far to date. Arrill touched symbols and the floor and walls including the ceiling became alive with stars and galaxies and it was so real it felt like one was floating in space. He went on to tell them that each quadrant could be selected and bought up to inspect and then he could pick galaxies and planets and anything he wanted to know. As he spoke the floor and walls and ceiling changed with different quadrants and different galaxies opening travel to so much more of the Universe. Information like this was priceless!

Jit asked him to see if he could find out who these aliens were and Arrill searched until he found one of many journals and touched another symbol which bought up in front of the console a holographic screen. They all looked on with expectancy waiting for Arrill as he read and relayed important information to them. The aliens were known as the "Suevons" with four of them making the total. They were two couples that were all scientists running an experiment that went wrong, delivering them into orbit around Cartergole. The experiment was conducted aboard their ship while they were trying to develop a faster means of space travel and they were extremely fortunate they weren't all killed. Equipment that could not be replaced was destroyed in the explosion leaving them stranded where they were. According to the records that was over three thousand years ago, and they hadn't the slightest idea where they'd arrived. They were a peaceful race of beings that had an unquenching desire for knowledge and exploration. They came to the surface of the planet and that was when they met Wisploks ancestors who were also a peaceful race of people. A strong bond soon developed between them and they settled on Cartergole which had a different name back then. They referred to the place as Yuplar. They looked like the people of Yuplar and had only one thing that differed, and that was they lived to a thousand years.

They left after being on Yuplar four hundred years seeking a planet they referred to as Stellstone and were seeking the Garden of Destiny. Only two of them went there while the other two went to a different place but there was no reference to where they went or their names for some reason. The two seeking Stellstone were named Adam Lorave and Evelyn Tomherone. Arrill stopped and told them there was endless information that would take a long time to read and if they wanted to record the charts for the Universe, he'd have to come back with the portable computer to download it all. Jit looked at the time and 4.00 am stared back at him, so they decided to go and come back the next night. If they left now no one would see them exit the Temple thus keeping its secret which was a condition set by the council.

The trip back out took less time and was a reversal of the trip in and they soon exited into the dim lights of the city and watched the doorway vanish before their eyes and become one of the sides again. They walked around to the panel and retrieved the key and watched it close and blend into the side again then returned to Wisploks home. When they arrived in the house, they were all suddenly aware of how tired they were and took off their backpacks and Jit pulled out the coffee flask. They sat on the cushions around the table and Wisplok watched them pour the black liquid into cups. Despite the colour looking ominous he found the aroma quite pleasant and tried a sip from the cup full Jit offered him. After the first sip, he displayed an agreeable face and continued sipping listening to them talk. They chatted until daybreak which wasn't long in coming and when it had arrived the three of them told their host they were going back to the ship and would return in the evening. Wisplok said that would be fine and they stood to leave. With backpacks in place, they made their way back to the shuttle. Weariness suddenly tolled on them again and all Jit wanted to do was go to bed and rest his body and mind. When they arrived at the shuttle Arrill took the controls and flew them back to the Windchief and they were soon in the familiar surroundings of the ship. They were so tired they didn't make it to the bridge, instead stopping at the cabin level and going straight to their quarters. In their cabin, Jit and Limtom were quick about getting to bed and it was only seconds after they lay down that sleep swept over them.

……………………………

In his cabin, Arrill sat on the edge of his bed for a moment thinking once again of the events that had passed in the last few weeks. He undressed and thought about the old guy who gave him the map and wondered what he would say if he was told what he gave away. Despite being tired he felt clear minded with the weariness being mainly in his body. As he lay in bed drifting off to sleep, he pondered where all this was going to end and when.

……………………………………

Ladone waited for some time before she realised that no one was coming up to the bridge. The time was just after 7.00 am and she wondered what happened guessing at a variety of possibilities. She knew they would eventually show up, so she went back to her netherworld to await their arrival.

……………………………………

Jit woke from a peaceful sleep and looked at the time which read a little past 2.00 pm. Limtom slept on undisturbed beside him. A little later they got up and showered then went to the bridge to see if Arrill was up yet. He was and had been for the past hour and they greeted him and Ladone before getting coffee. Back out on the bridge, they joined the conversation that Arrill and Ladone were engaged in. Arrill had briefed Ladone on everything that happened in the

Temple and she was ecstatic at the news. When they finished, they made something to eat and while they ate, they discussed the trip back to the surface. Arrill told them he had everything he needed prepared and when they were done eating, they returned to the bridge. Ladone was in her usual place of choice and they filled her in on what was going to happen next then made ready for the trip down to Cartergole. Arrill double checked to make sure he had everything he needed in the backpack and slung it on then they took the elevator down to the cargo bay. They told Ladone they would be back around the same time as this morning before slipping from sight as they descended to the shuttle. Limtom took the controls when they were on board and with the startup procedure completed, they set off to their destination. Since starting, Limtom was now an apt hand at shuttle flight and Cartergole was becoming like a second home to them all. By the time they landed in the same position as previously it was going on six thirty and darkness was rapidly consuming the valley. They quickly made their way back to the entrance of the city arriving there as darkness closed in and covered the chasm.

They walked the now familiar path to the city feeling like the locals and in a short time arrived at the landing overlooking the city. The place was deserted and upon looking at the time they gathered that everyone was at dinner. They took the stairs to the bottom and then proceeded to look for Wisplok and after checking his home and not being there they checked the first eating place they came upon. As soon as they entered the premises, they were greeted by smiling faces which they returned as they bowed then made their way to where Wisplok sat. Other elders sat with him and as they took a cushion and made themselves comfortable the conversation switched to them. Wisplok asked if they wanted food to help themselves but they declined, telling him they'd already eaten before coming back to the city. Next came around the vessels with the same fruity drink they encountered on their first visit and of that they partook. The evening drifted by and as it did people got up to leave and the noise level in the room dropped with each evacuation. Soon everyone was gone except the ones gathered around the table they sat at. The drink went from the fruity one they were consuming to the other type that loosened one's tongue making conversation easy. Jit asked Wisplok what the drink was named, and he told them it was difficult to translate into normal dialect but the closest he could get was "Enndrope".

As the evening wore on the elders left one by one until only the four of them remained. They did so until around 10.00 pm before they went back to Wisplok's home. Jit was feeling light on his feet which he had no doubt came from the drink he consumed. They followed Wisplok indoors and he invited them to take a seat then went to do something leaving them to talk amongst themselves. He returned shortly after and joined them at the table, and they discussed and planned for their move back into the Temple later on. When the time reached 11.00 pm the lights dimmed to full moon mode and as they agreed to go at one in the morning instead of two like last night Jit took Limtom to see the water feature in the garden under the entry. Wisplok told them they wouldn't be disappointed, and they were soon strolling down the path to the other garden passing the Temple along the way. The place was quiet and only they walked the path. Despite having been to the city a few times they'd never yet been to the Park under the main entry. It too was raised above the ground like the Park at the other end consisting of the same growth of trees scattered around with benches for sitting on and children's playthings littering the area. After following the path, a little further they could see the water feature playing just down the way. This one was a lot different than the other water feature and as much fascinating to look upon.

The feature in the other garden was high where this

one was long wasting little on height. It ran a length of twenty metres Jit estimated with the height being no more than five metres. Water ran from one end to the other and all the water fell into a pond at the bottom which collected the liquid before sending it back to the top to begin its course again. The course was made up of a vee-shaped stone that looked the same as the Temple with its smooth finish and marble look. The vee-shaped was peppered with small holes that allowed the water to run through to the pool below but because the volume of water was greater than what could drain away, it still made it to the end of the trough and flowed into the pool below too. In the pool lay lights that lit the water and the sound of it running was soothing and meditative. An hour quickly passed, and they decided to make their way back as they were leaving in a little while. While they walked back Jit thought about all that's happened since he and Arrill started this voyage. It seemed like just yesterday that they were talking about it and now they were nearing an end. For him, he found his treasure and squeezed Limtoms hand. For Arrill there was the map covering nearly sixty percent of the Universe for his treasure plus he could understand the language as well.

When they entered the house Arrill and Wisplok were laughing at something they were talking about. Wisplok asked them what they thought of the water feature and which they preferred, and Jit told him they were both great with each being unique making it hard to favour one above the other. 'A good and wise answer'...was the reply that came from Wisplok. With the time to go soon upon them, Arrill hoisted on his backpack and the four of them prepared to leave. Everything was silent outside and not a soul was in sight with the people of the city all asleep by now. They quickly and quietly made their way to the Temple and at the corner that hid the panel Arrill activated it and inserted the key. All of them had soon entered the Temple once again and shortly after, the way closed blocking the outside from view. Inside the key popped out to be retrieved and with Arrill in possession of it again they followed the same procedure back to the room with the chair in it. Jit noticed there was no odour of any kind in the passageway and not even in the room when they entered it. If the walls could glow for light, they could also keep the air clean he gathered.

As the room they entered descended, Jit tried to calculate the distance, but it was difficult to estimate the rate they were falling so at best he guessed four or five metres. They were soon in the last room with the chair awaiting their arrival and Arrill went to take the seat and begin collecting all the information. This time no needle pierced him as if the chair recognised him unless it only happened once, he thought. He was able to copy all he wanted down to the laptop and could leave everything as it was for Wisplok and the council. The council did not need star charts so they wouldn't be of value to the group in the same sense as it would be to them. For someone with an interstellar ship, it was on par with a mountain of gold. Once he had all the information, he could study it and discover its secrets back on the ship in his own time. Jit walked around the room while he waited and wondered how many worlds awaited discovery. He felt like a smoke but refrained from the act and continued pacing instead. It took two hours to gather all Arrill wanted and once it was all collected, they left. The trip back was the same and this time when the key was retrieved by Arrill he put it in the pouch with the stones and the map and handed it over to Wisplok. He'd told them earlier that the council will keep the knowledge of the Temple from the people for the time being. Now that he knew how to access the room below, he could learn the language and find out more about his ancestors in his own time.

It was just after 4.00 am when they entered the house

and sat at the table. Wisplok went to make tea and not too long after they were sipping a strong smelling but not unpleasant herbal tea which Jit found revived him considerably. Wisplok went on to tell them he knew they were good people even before the Spirits told him and that they were welcome to stay if they wanted or come and go as they pleased. He also told them to refrain from telling anyone else about this world. Their talk until daylight was about their newfound friendship and what they were going to do now that the journey was over. At 6.00 am they stood to leave and thanked their host for his understanding and kindness. They told him they'd do their best to stay in touch which in this case meant coming to visit as they had no Link hook up in Cartergole. Now with the star charts, they had in their possession they could end up anywhere in the Universe.

When they stepped outside the cold air hit them with force as they were used to the temperate climate in the city. It was always constant in there and out here the early morning breeze was sharp and cut through their garments like a flame to butter. As they walked to the waiting shuttle long plumes of steamed breath poured from their mouths and wafted over their shoulders making them look like a locomotive charging along. On their approach to the shuttle, they found it bathed in heavy dew and looked like an icicle sitting on the ground. Inside was impossibly colder than outside having had all night to chill everything so it was like entering a freezer. Jit took the controls and fired the bird up and got the heaters going and by the time they lifted off the shuttle was beginning to warm up. On rising, they looked at the chasms which were still in shadows and Jit wondered if he would ever be back to see them again. He felt a real attachment to the people of Cartergole and in a short time, they knew each other a strong bond had formed already. He could see now how the Suevons could've easily loved these people. Soon the Windchief was in sight and the chasms were once again just three scratch marks on the planet below them. In the cargo bay, Jit landed beside the other shuttle and they disembarked and took the elevator to the bridge. The time had just crossed 7.00 am and when they popped up on the bridge Ladone was there to meet them. Jit was always glad to see her, and this morning was no different. They greeted her and told of their adventure and once Ladone was all up to date the next point of the conversation was what they were to do now.

Arrill needed to get back to Geelok and Limtom had her home to stop at too, so they decided to make their way to Spollee which Ladone said would be close to five days' journey from where they were. Jit instructed her to leave and they set off for Spollee and the vastness of clear space yet again. In the monitors above the front window, they watched the planet of Cartergole shrink quickly behind them as the Windchief moved to galatial speed. They remained silent as the planet soon turned into a speck matching the other countless specks in the ocean of blackness. Once they were on their way Jit and Limtom decided to go and have a nap as weariness weighed down on them again, so they excused themselves and left Arrill and Ladone to talk while they went to their cabin. They didn't get into bed choosing to lay on top still clothed and cuddled each other with Limtom falling asleep in his arms first. As her breathing grew in intensity Jit knew that they would soon have to talk about what to do now that they were a couple. As he drifted off to sleep, he was certain of one thing, they had a strong connection to each other, and he could not be without her nor did he want to be.

....

Arrill watched them go and even though he'd been up as long as they had, he was overcome by the excitement of what he possessed making sleep impossible with his mind racing as it was. He decided to retire to the library to begin studying what he retrieved from the Temple. In the library, he fired up the laptop to begin sifting through the information he collected. He wasn't too long into the work before he felt the ship move to full speed as they entered clear space once again. An hour later he felt the weariness fall over him like a shadow and set the computer to the side and decided to go and have a nap. By the time he reached his cabin and kicked his boots off, he slumped onto the bed still clothed and fell into an instant deep and restful sleep.

……………………………..

It was late in the afternoon when Jit awoke and thoughts he had before going to bed quickly rematerialized and started him thinking again. Limtom stirred and rolled over to face him still sleepy and snuggled up to him and recommenced her deep breathing. It was around 6.00 pm when they emerged onto the bridge where only Ladone was there to meet them. They greeted her and when they looked out the window they looked into the inky ooze of clear space.

………………………………

The days rolled along with them doing the same routine as they did when in clear space and by the end of the fourth day, they could see the galaxy that hid Spollee in its numerous speckles. They should arrive at Spollee after lunch the following day Jit estimated. Limtom called Shalby on the Link and informed him they'd be home soon, and Jit could see he was delighted to hear the news. Along the journey back they also contacted Fryppe and Mel to catch them up on what had happened to date.

Back at Spollee

It was around 3.00 pm when they arrived at Spollee with the hour already set to Spollee time. Having decided to leave the Windchief in orbit Ladone set the position for the duration of their stay. Limtom went to their cabin and took some of her close things leaving the rest behind. Jit asked her if she wanted to take the shuttle down and her eyes lit up with a sparkle like two stars. In the shuttle, she vaulted into the pilot seat like an acrobat and started the procedure before the flight. As they entered the atmosphere and broke through it they could see the remnants of a fine day drawing to an end on Spollee. Soon they spotted the Pepplplant mansion like a stain on the greenery and before long, it loomed before them as Limtom skillfully landed the shuttle in the designated area. Shalby could be seen standing in waiting with his hair thrashing about from the storm the engines whipped up. As soon as Limtom stepped out of the shuttle she ran straight to him and they embraced in their greeting. Both he and Arrill shook hands with him again then they went into the house where he had tea ready. They made their way to the kitchen and sat around the large table to talk and catch up on more events since their parting. When they finished telling Shalby about their trip they discussed Limtom's business matters since she left. After they settled business matters Shalby went to prepare dinner so it would be ready by 7.00 pm.

He follows a tight schedule Jit remembered which was part of his military training he gathered and had seeped into every part of his life. He recalled Limtom telling him how punctual he always was, and you could set your timepiece by his movements. The three of them left Shalby to his mechanised routine and retired to one of the lounge rooms to wait until dinner was ready. Their conversation was about what Arrill was going to do and he told Limtom more details about his time on Geelok. They further discussed different strategies for gaining information when he returned to the moon and he was hopeful that Leearnah might even be out of the coma by this time. Either that or she was gone all together which meant they may never find who caused this grief in her life and his. As Jit listened to his friend talking about her he could sense that he still loved her deeply and the pain of it all showed on his face despite his efforts to hide any emotion. He wanted to help him resolve this mess and put some peace back into his life. Engrossed in the discussions they lost track of time until Shalby called out and said dinner was ready and to take a seat in the dining room. Shalby joined them for the meal which was the first time he did, and they engaged in a variety of talks with some being of his military days.

To look at he didn't seem the type but as he divulged his experiences, he took on a different manner exposing the secrets he shaded from everyone. The more Jit got to know him the more he liked him, and he was a wealth of knowledge in matters he knew nothing about. Arrill spilled his situation to Shalby which for him was the first time of hearing his woes and assured Arrill he could help in finding the culprit who messed up his girl. He told him he had influential contacts in many places and finding people was one of his specialties. As he spoke Jit got the feeling that the family he went to see when he departed at Mel's place was probably his brothers in arms more than his mum and dad. Arrill took on a lighter disposition from hearing what Shalby said restoring his hope of a resolution to the situation that's been troubling him for a long time now. The evening wore on and when they retired from the table, they went back to the lounge room to take a rest. Around 9.00 pm Arrill told them he was going back to the ship because he wanted to get back to work on the information he gathered from the Temple. Jit decided to stay the night with Limtom, so he bid his friend good night and they watched him make his way until he was out of sight. Shortly afterward they heard the shuttle lift off and within moments the silence of the night cascaded upon everything again.

Shalby was off doing something he didn't mention which left them all alone, so they retired to the TV lounge and relaxed to catch a movie. Watching the movie snuggled up together he thought about how Arrill looked rejuvenated after talking to Shalby. It would be great to see him and Leearnah together again and he remembered how they looked so right for each other when he was the best man at their wedding. When the movie was finished, they sat up talking a while longer about whatever came to mind whilst sharing a cigar. Shalby stuck his head in sometime later telling them he was going to bed and they bid him goodnight then prepared to do the same themselves.

....

After Arrill landed in the cargo bay and shut the shuttle down he took the elevator to the bridge and there awaiting him was Ladone. He was forming a strong bond with her and understood further how Jit could be so attached to her. He told her Jit was staying at the mansion and talked with her for some time then said he was going to the library to do some work. It was 10.00 pm when he entered the library and spread on the lounge was the laptop he left when he was last at it. His first task was to make coffee and while doing it he thought to himself that he never drank so much coffee until meeting up with Jit again. He was soon comfortable on the lounge then switched on the laptop and took up where he left off. There was so much information they retrieved from the Temple and the disclosure of the Universe before him was immense and complicated. He set those aside and started peering through the journals which exposed the Suevons down to their daily activities. It made for fascinating reading now that he could understand the symbols and he almost felt like he was sharing the experience with them from their writings.

It was during this work that he stumbled upon the writings of a room they referred to as "The Vault of Prosperity" and according to his understanding was located in the mountain where they first found the key and gemstones. The contents of the vault were called "Tinallah Berr" and he wondered what it was and if it was of any value. Soon he felt the weight of weariness drag him down and looking at the time was shocked to see it was 1.00 am in the morning. He was so absorbed in the work that it felt like only a short time had elapsed. Excitement built up in him as he once again set the laptop on the lounge and made the way to his cabin and bed.

....

Jit and Limtom woke at 8.00 am and after dressing they made their way to the kitchen. Upon entering the room, they were greeted with the smell of hot breakfast being cooked and Shalby welcoming them at the same time. When the pleasantries were exchanged, he pointed to the pot of fresh coffee just made and Limtom poured a cup each for all of them and they talked until breakfast was completed. They ate at the table in the kitchen which was less formal and during the meal the talk was about Limtom and what she was going to do now that she was back. Shalby offered to run things for her if she wanted to wander the stars a while longer and Jit hoped that she would take him up on the offer. He wanted her to come with him when they went back to Geelok. During their discussions, they heard the shuttle touchdown and a few moments later Arrill entered. He greeted them all and took a seat then put the laptop on the table in a clear spot and piled onto a plate some breakfast. Whilst eating Arrill told them what he discovered when he was at his work last night which astounded them all.

He then asked if any of them had ever heard of something called Tinallah Berr to which they shook heads and waited for further explanation. He went on to tell them that there was no reference yet to finding this room but no doubt it was in the writings somewhere and all he had to do was find it. When breakfast was over, they sat around talking further, and when they finished Shalby told them to go and he would clean up. They retired to the lounge room where Arrill went back to work sifting through the journals while Jit and Limtom discussed further what she was going to do. With this new revelation unfolding, she said she wanted to come along this time and Jit smiled with the received information. Arrill took notes as he searched through the maze of symbols and they decided to go for a walk and told him they'd be back shortly. Shalby entered the room just as they were exiting and told him they'd be back in a while and he nodded and went to see how Arrill was coming along.

The day outside was sunny with a light breeze brushing past them as they walked to the front gate and continued along the road hand in hand. A vehicle soon approached and as it passed, they waved at the occupants who returned the gesture, and soon it was gone and the serenity was restored. Small clouds speckled the sky and a flock of birds could be seen far ahead and heading mountainwards with a lone bird behind seeming to struggle to keep up. The breeze picked up on occasion then settled back to a puff with its movements recorded on the bending wildflowers that exposed its path as it swept across the fields. They walked for a good twenty minutes along the roadside not seeing another vehicle before Limtom ducked under a wooden fence and they entered a large field. It was part of the Pepplplant estate too and they strode through the knee high grass that grew lush and unbounding. Large trees rose and dotted the area with unseen birds hidden in the branches screeching their protest at the intruders. They passed a small pond and approaching the water's edge they took a seat on the grass and listened to the wavelets lapping the shore. Later they talked about each other and what they were going to do and Limtom made it clear that she never wanted to be separated from Jit. On hearing her words, he fought to control his emotions as she spoke with the same intent that he had. Together they enjoyed their surroundings for a while before they rose and walked back to the mansion through the fields of grass and wildflowers that poured forth a sweet and subtle fragrance into the air. Everything was clear with the sun shining in all its glory and Jit felt great to be alive.

The way they returned delivered them to the back of the mansion and Jit soon spotted the shuttle sitting on the landing pad waiting faithfully for its next duty. They slinked past the craft and entered the house and by this time it was closing on midday. Arrill remained where they left him buried deep in his work and Shalby was off preparing lunch for them all. Jit sat down to see how Arrill was progressing and Limtom went to see Shalby and discuss some matters with him. He sat on the lounge not saying anything for a while and eventually Arrill spoke telling him he found some clues which were set in a cryptic pattern. Placing it aside for the moment he asked Jit when they should leave for spot number nine. They would need the Windchief for the job so they would have to head back out to get her then enter back where location number nine was. Lunch was about to be served so they agreed on going after eating and as they'd just finished discussing the matter, Limtom called to them for lunch. Whilst eating they discussed Limtom coming along with them and depending on what happened at the mountain they may go from there straight to Geelok. Shalby was happy to keep the train on track while she was away and told her he was envious that he couldn't join them. Jit did a rough calculation and estimated even if they left now, they wouldn't get to number nine until late in the afternoon meaning they couldn't do anything until the morning.

The time raced away, and they bid Shalby farewell once again and boarded the shuttle with Limtom at the controls. In little time they started climbing skyward and gained speed towards the Windchief. In the cargo hold, she skillfully settled the shuttle down beside the other one and then shut everything down. The three of them were soon on the elevator and ascending to the bridge where Ladone keenly awaited them. They exchanged greetings then filled her in on events and when they delivered the details Jit told her to make way for spot number nine. With the record on file, she placed the coordinates and the ship moved towards their destination. It was around 6.00 pm when they arrived at the location and Ladone set the ship in the same position as previously and told them they were secured. Looking out the window at the mountain Jit felt a familiarity and connection with it and wondered what the age old monolith hid from them still. It loomed in front of them and it was basked in shadows and the fast diminishing remnants of daylight. The trees down below could be seen bending over from the wind that blew and he hoped it wouldn't be too strong in the morning otherwise using the jetpacks wouldn't be possible. Limtom came up beside him and slipped her arm through his to watch the spectacle and while they stared at the darkening landscape Arrill went to get dinner sorted. When darkness completely engulfed the window, they went to see if Arrill needed some help. He had everything under control, so they sat at the dining table to talk while the food was cooking. The conversation was about the journey into the mountain in the morning with Limtom expressing her excitement at the prospect of it all. After dinner was over Jit made coffee and Arrill excused himself taking his cup with him and going to the library to continue his work. Jit left the girls talking while he went to the cargo bay to prepare and check things for the morning. Feeling satisfied that everything was good to go he returned to the bridge and joined the girls in conversation. With them engrossed in clothes talk he soon parted and decided to go to the gym for a workout seeing though he hadn't been for a while. On completion, he went to his cabin to shower and change then went back to the bridge hoping the girls were talking about something other than clothing.

Before reaching the bridge however he stopped at the library level to check in on Arrill and see how he was coming along with the new language he'd picked up. When he entered the library the first thing that hit him was the smell of books and he found it a pleasant smell reminding him of times in study for exams. Arrill looked up from the lounge and greeted him and Jit asked him how things were going as he walked over and took a seat.

'I think I've got it all' he said to Jit and then explained what he had.

He told him that in one of the journals he found an encrypted message that gave him the first clue which led him to believe they had to return to the mountain. The next part had him stuck for a while but then he put it together. However, the last part was still eluding him as to what it meant. He then turned the laptop so Jit could see the screen and on it, he read….

"Where the unfound lay,
there must you return.
Two paths that meet at
the end of the world,
With end in sight…fear not,
a covered mark exposes the plot."

He stared at it a while then asked Arrill if he translated it right. He assured him that he'd checked it several times and it was right. He slid the laptop over onto his lap and told him to read it over a few times and went to make a drink. Jit could see how Arrill concluded to return to the mountain from the first sentence he read, but the rest was lost to him especially the very last part of the message which seemed incomplete to him. Arrill returned and asked if he thought any different after reading it a few times. Jit told him he grasped the first bit but the rest was beyond him. He was just about to explain further when they were interrupted by the speaker which was Ladone wondering where they were. Jit looked at the time and was startled that it was so late already. They said they were on the way up and left the library. Arrill told Jit he'd explain the rest tomorrow and they were on the tail end of the discussion when they appeared on the bridge. The girls were still talking but not about clothes and they joined them in the conversation for a while before Jit and Limtom said they were going to bed. In their cabin, Jit lay with Limtom falling asleep quickly by his side, and thought about the message Arrill showed him. He tried to unravel its meaning but failed as sleep lured him elsewhere.

…………………………..

Arrill chatted with Ladone a little while longer, then felt the weariness of the day press down on him so he bid her good night and went to bed too. In his cabin, he thought about a shower first but was too tired and just kicked off his boots and undressed. Sliding into bed he kept running the last part of the message over and over in his mind trying to make sense of what it meant but sleep whisked him away before he could accomplish the task.

………………………..

It was 7.00 am when Jit opened his eyes and thoughts of the day ahead intruded his mind at once. Shortly afterwards they both got up and after showering and dressing appropriately they exited the cabin. Surprisingly Ladone wasn't on the bridge to meet them and they could soon hear her talking with Arrill in the galley meaning Arrill must've been up for a while. When they entered the room, he was sitting at the dining table engaged in conversation with her. They greeted each other and Jit went to get cups then joined them at the table. When they finished their drinks, they all decided to retire to the bridge and see what the day outside presented. They went to the window to see that the mountain was basking in the rising sunlight. At its ankle floated the morning mist which was stubborn in its removal and still blanketing the trees with only the tallest ones defying its embrace. A few fluffy clouds lazily meandered along high above them and shrunk as their destination consumed them. Not to far away they watched a solitary bird flap effortlessly with no sound, chasing the clouds for a moment then changed direction and darted groundward with breakfast in sight far below. They looked on in silence and watched it perform and execute the manoeuvre with precision and finality born from repetition, necessity, and instinct. The small creature had no reprieve from the onslaught and its limp body hung from razor sharp claws as the bird took to the air again to find a haven for feasting.

The wind had died down since the previous evening and remained calm according to the weather station on board. Hunger soon attacked them all and Arrill offered to make breakfast while Jit took Limtom down to the cargo bay to give her a crash course in jetpack handling. In the cargo bay, he backed her into position and buckled her into one of the four jetpacks then unfastened her from the wall and explained what to do. With Limtom being as sharp as she was, he only needed to tell her the operation of the unit once then he watched her float around in the cargo bay getting familiar with the feel of the device. With no wind to compensate for she was quick at picking it up and then started having fun like the child she could be. It was one of the cute things about her he adored. She whizzed around squealing and laughing as she ducked high and low while Jit looked on amused by her behaviour. Arrill showed up announcing breakfast was ready and stood to watch Limtom for a while smiling and shaking his head at her tomfoolery.

She set down near the stand for the jetpacks and Jit assisted her in removing the unit and they met with Arrill who waited for them on the elevator. The smell of bacon and eggs could be smelt hanging in the air as soon as they arrived on the bridge. At the dining table, the food was already piled on a large platter and after taking a seat they ate heartily making small talk at the same time. Once breakfast was completed, they finished their juice and cleaned up. With the three of them on the task it was soon over then they went to the bridge to inform Ladone they were about to leave. A final run through the checklist confirmed they were ready then they went down to the cargo hold to strap into the jetpacks. With the things prepared in a small bag the night before Jit secured it to his belt and they stepped to the edge of the loading ramp and looked down at the ground below.

Jit sensed Limtom's concern and assured her it was okay and Arrill assisted by showing her the technique to try. He lifted off the floor a few centimetres then hovered out and floated into the cool morning air and turned around in mid-flight to beckon her out. All the while he told her that he knew nothing about the handling of a jetpack until he met up with Jit. She followed his example and once past the ledge she seemed to have gained her confidence and was okay. Arrill led the way and Jit closely followed Limtom assuring her via the comlink that she was doing great. Below them, the mist from earlier on was mostly evaporated with just a few wisps hanging on tenaciously to the heads of some lower trees stretching with reluctance at letting go. At the face of the mountain Arrill soon found the cleft and straddled into the familiar gap. Limtom entered with precision like she'd done it many times. She moved forward and close behind her Jit landed and once again was crowded by rock. He hadn't missed the confines of such proximity at all!

He passed torches to them and they wound them up then started forward retracing their steps of before. As they walked, he asked Arrill if he knew what to do and he replied telling him he'd show them when they got a little closer. Soon they arrived at the part of the path where they had to get on all fours to pass through the hologram gap. Once through it, they weren't long in approaching the steps which finally delivered them to the room with the three passageways in it. Jit immediately enjoyed the space around him and took in a breath of air with room to move. By the time he exhaled, Arrill walked straight into the middle passageway without a word and they quickly followed. In the given time they arrived once again at the pedestal with the other passage leading away to the third entry of the room they'd just come from.

It was then that Arrill showed them the two paths that led to the end of the World which was the planet Cartergole etched in the pedestal in front of them. It made sense to Jit once it was exposed and then he asked Arrill what the symbols meant on the pedestal now that he could understand them. He told them that it was the same name he read in the Temple which was the original name of Cartergole. The symbols translated said, "Yuplar." The part now that he still hadn't worked out was the last part of the message which was…

"with end in sight, fear not…..a mark covered, exposes the plot."

It was apparent to them that when they first came here, they must've missed something despite Jit being certain they looked closely. With an extra pair of eyes, they scanned every millimetre of the surrounding walls and the pedestal looking for something that might be covering something else. Arrill touched the symbols on the pedestal and the etching of the planet hoping something would be exposed but after a while, they stopped defeated, but not out. With three minds working at it the problem still seemed to defy them and they sat on the ground to throw ideas around which led to all sorts of stupid suggestions. Silence took watch for a spell while each one of them tossed thoughts around in the privacy of their minds. Jit realised he had nothing and was just about to break the silence when Arrill stiffened like something had stung him then said, 'It can't be that simple surely' and stood up.

Jit and Limtom were on their feet at the same time and watched Arrill step up to the pedestal and stand before it for a moment before he placed his palm over the three marks that symbolised the chasms on Cartergole. Nothing happened so he tried just covering one mark at a time leaving the centre one until last and still nothing happened. As the middle was the largest scratch, he turned his hand to a karate chop and filled the gap perfectly. Almost immediately a rumbling could be heard that sounded far away then the entire pedestal pulled away from them and hinged to the left and sunk into the wall revealing a hidden passageway.

'Wow, you're good at this' said Jit stunned at the spectacle that just played out.

Limtom stood speechless for a moment then said,

'You two have the best life!'

With the shock of the moment drained away Arrill led them down the same narrow passageway as the others with the path heading downwards on a slight angle. They walked for close to ten minutes before they finally arrived at what could be best described as a stone doorway. Above the top were symbols played out and Arrill looked up and translated, 'Vault of Prosperity.' He then looked at them and said,

'Now we just have to figure out how to get past this obstacle.'

He had no message for this situation and Jit suggested that it might be in another journal. Arrill nodded his head in agreement because he only looked through some of the journals and there were a lot more to go yet. The door blocking their way had no other symbols on it apart from the name but wasn't bare either. Instead, there were pictures of things like urns, staffs, stars, and boxes like the one they found with the key in it and other things too. The door sealed so well it looked like a dead end but then the pedestal was just the same and they didn't have an inkling that it would move. Jit watched Arrill stare at the door then touch some of the pictures seeing if anything moved or showed a sign of doing anything relevant. When he was satisfied that there was nothing before him his shoulders drooped in defeat and a loud sigh of frustration escaped from him. The answer had to be in one of the other journals he told himself and they turned around to make their way back to the outside. They soon passed the pedestal and when they were back out in the split passageway, they expected the pedestal to close back up, but it remained where it was. They continued until they came to the open room then slipped straight back into the next passage and soon arrived at the cleft and daylight again. It was bright compared to torchlight and they had to wait for their eyes to adjust squinting in the meantime. They soon floated towards the ship and Limtom was playing along the way by dropping low and swirling around and making fun of it. She was having a great time Jit thought to himself and he liked the idea of that.

The time was nearing midday and despite the hour, the air was still crisp on the skin. In the cargo bay, they unloaded the packs into their places then Jit left the bag with the torches on a bench as they took the lift to the bridge. When they popped up top Ladone was waiting for them and started with the questions straight after the greetings. As it was just after midday Jit left Limtom and Arrill to explain what happened while he went to rustle up something to eat. It didn't take long to get it ready then he called out to them and they all congregated around the dining table to eat and discuss the blocked passageway. They still came up empty-handed despite their best effort at finding a solution. It was agreed that there had to be something more in another journal that only Arrill would be able to find as he was the only one who could understand the symbols.

When lunch was finished Limtom got up and took away the dishes then returned with a pitcher of juice and they sat around a while longer talking about what might be on the other side of the doorway they were stuck at. They also wondered if any other surprises were blocking the way once they got through that one. When they finished Arrill departed for the library where his laptop was and made a start on searching the other journals. It had become an obsession for him now to beat this. Being unable to help him, Jit and Limtom decided to go to the gym and punish their muscles for an hour. After the hour-long workout, they retired to their cabin to shower and then lay down for a nap. It wasn't until two hours had passed before they woke to feel refreshed and ready to start again.

They stopped at the library to check on Arrill and when they looked in, he wasn't there and only the laptop sat open on the lounge. It stared at them with a blank screen, so they assumed he was on the bridge and went to check there. On the bridge, Ladone appeared and they asked her where Arrill was and she relayed the message he left for them. He didn't want to disturb them, but he didn't want to wait either, so he went back to the wall blocking their way to check something. Jit asked her how long ago it was since he left, and she replied telling him it was a little under an hour ago. Although they'd had no incident in the mountain so far, he still felt a rising concern which Limtom voiced too and they decided to go down to the cargo bay and strap on their jetpacks and go after him. It was only a short time before they both exited the back of the bay with Jit scooping up the bag with the torches along the way. At the cleft, he entered first and as Limtom did the same behind him he fished out the torches.

One was missing with the whereabouts known and after they wound their ones up, they set off. With the path now being familiar, they progressed rapidly and were soon where the pedestal once stood. When they arrived at that point everything was the same as when they left earlier on. They continued down the path and a few minutes into it they saw light reflecting toward them undoubtedly from Arrill. Jit called out and Arrill replied telling them he opened the door and was coming to get them. The excitement in his voice was unmistakable and he soon stood before them and said,

'We are possibly the richest people in all the known galaxies!'

Then he went on to remind Jit about the idea he had

when they first met and that the Vault of Prosperity containing the Tinallah Ber was a vault full of Chelinah Crystals.

Jit gaped in disbelief then said,

'How many are there?'

Arrill just beamed a smile and turned around beckoning them to follow. They nearly had to run to keep up with him. They quickly arrived where the way was blocked, and they could see the obstacle lay slid into the wall to the left of them as they entered the vault and stared around in awe. Arrill was right Jit thought to himself. They were probably now the wealthiest people anywhere.

Before him, he beheld a room around thirty metres by fifty metres in size and a height of maybe five metres. It was filled with mesh cages containing Chelinah Crystals. It was staggering as they shone the torch beams around getting a kaleidoscope effect from the reflection off the crystals. Chelinah Crystals were the most valued commodity in all the known galaxies and the Jorpahs were the greatest users of them which they used in the builds of their Windchiefs and shielding. Mostly it was for making the windows which were able to withstand the immense pressures. They were as good as currency in any region of the Galaxies. One cage full of the crystals was enough to see any one of them set for the rest of their life. Once the realization set in that he wasn't dreaming he asked Arrill how he opened the doorway. He went on to explain that he was reading through the journals more or less speed reading and it was nothing he read that helped him but more a dormant memory that awoke as if he always held it. It was the same feeling that came upon him when they were in the mountain the first time at the three junction split. He then went on to tell them the answer was on the pedestal again and all he had to do was to follow the same step as the first time only this time where the pedestal now sat. When he covered the middle mark, he heard the door sliding down the passageway and knew he'd succeeded.

They stood in silence for a moment before Limtom asked them what they planned to do now. The time was nearing dinner time, so they decided to go back to the ship and discuss options over a meal. As they made their way back and passed the pedestal, it this time hinged back from the wall and slid back into position sealing the entrance and returning everything the way it was. The walk back to the ship was made in silence as everyone was deep in their own thoughts now that they were wealthy beyond imagining. At least that's what Jit was thinking! By the time they reached the cleft once again the day was at its end and long shadows ate away at the landscape below. The air temperature had dropped and as they hovered to the ship the cold bit right through their garments chilling them quickly. Back onboard the Windchief, they warmed up in no time and after putting everything away they stepped onto the lift and made for the bridge. The ever pleasant Ladone awaited them and Limtom was the first to burst forward with the news. Jit noticed again how the two of them were like sisters now and she too treated Ladone like a crew member. They were both so excited with one encouraging the other that Jit and Arrill couldn't get a word in at all. Having given up on trying they went to the galley to prepare dinner.

'The girls seem to really like each other' said Arrill.

'I was just thinking that a moment ago' replied Jit.

Jit then went on to ask him how he felt about going back to Geelok and what he might find when he gets there. Arrill replied by saying that things were different now because he had money and with that, he could plan other ways of doing things. They talked about the Suevons while they did their work and wondered how long it took them to amass such a huge quantity of the crystals and where they harvested them. Although Jit had seen the room, he still found it hard to believe that such wealth was now in their hands. After dinner, Jit picked out a bottle of red wine he had saved for a special occasion. There was no more special occasion than today! The wine cabinet on the ship was more like a dummy waiter which served your request from a cellar like room and delivered the request to the galley or the theatre room. Jit had a large collection of fine wines in the cellar and an electronic display panel on the wall served as a menu for the stock he had on board. It also kept a tally of diminishing supplies. He corked the bottle and set it on the table and while they ate the talk was about what to do with their newfound fortune. To remove it all would take a long time and despite the cargo hold being as big as it was on the Windchief it would take two loads to collect it all Jit guessed. Just five cages full of Chelinah Crystals could purchase the new Windchief Four outright such was the value of them. They concluded the best thing was to leave them where they were, and they could just take as they wanted. After all, they'd been sitting there for a very long time with no one discovering them until they did, so it was probably the safest place of all. Only the three of them knew where the treasure lay, and Jit knew he could trust Arrill with his life, and despite knowing Limtom only a short time he had no doubt she was in the same category as Arrill. Besides, she was quite rich already even though he didn't know exactly how rich. Jit estimated the cages of crystals to weigh in at five hundred kilograms or more. Getting what they required out was going to be a challenge too. They sat around the table late into the night just talking and planning their new lives and nearing midnight Jit and Limtom excused themselves and went to bed.

....

Arrill remained up a little longer and went out to talk with Ladone who was on the bridge. She asked him what he was going to do when this was all over and if he would buy his own ship. He told her the first thing he wanted to accomplish was clearing his name and seeing if Leearnah was out of a coma. Then he'd like to find the person responsible and inflict the same treatment on him. They talked for a while longer, with Arrill enjoying Ladones smooth and calm voice which soothed his pain even after such a length of time. Soon though tiredness became greater than the will to stay awake and he bid her good night and waited for the lift to return. As he did so he thought about the fact that he could buy whatever he wanted now but tossed with the idea thinking it would be better to stay with Jit and Limtom if they were okay with that. They were like a family now and he was an orphan who had no one in his life except them. He'd never known who his parents were. When he walked past their cabin door, he thought about them snuggled up together, and a sharp pain bit his heart as he thought again of Leearnah. In his cabin, he kicked off his footwear and undressed then slid into bed and lay there looking up at the ceiling thinking about what was ahead for a while before sleep carried him off.

....

By 8.00 am Jit and Limtom were on the bridge. Ladone awaited them and they all passed greetings per usual. Arrill was still not up but Jit knew he would be soon. He looked out at the mist covering the ground like clouds and the side of the mountain range which basked in the sunlight. He stared at the mountain in front of him and marvelled at the secrets it contained and wealth beyond imagining. He wondered if there were other such places scattered amongst the stars that hid secrets like this. Anything was possible! Thoughts of the Suevons returned and he contemplated how long it must've taken them to acquire what they collected and where it all comes from. He guessed with a thousand year life span one could do much and four could do even more. Arrill was soon topside and they greeted him and told him the coffee pot was on the console. With a cuppa poured he joined them at the window.

'I don't know about you pair, but I still can't believe we're impossibly rich' said Arrill out of the blue.

He smiled at them and looked out the window and Jit thought how right he was. When they finished their cuppa, they went to have breakfast then prepared for the trip over to the cleft and start bringing some of their spoils back. They agreed to take just one cage full for now and when they arrived in the cargo bay Jit went to get duffle bags capable of carrying one hundred kilograms. They would only carry fifty though and Limtom whatever she could manage comfortably. They had plenty of time and there was no need to rush. They were soon floating across the gap between the ship and mountainside and arriving at the cleft Arrill entered first followed by Limtom and Jit bringing up the rear.

When they reached the pedestal Arrill had to perform the same action as before and soon the obstacle sucked back and hinged into the wall like it belonged there. He then did the same thing again and they could hear the sliding of stone on stone echo from the way ahead of them. At the vault, Jit thought how appropriate the name for it was. They picked the closest cage and opened the top and slid out crystals and loaded bags until the weight was manageable for each of them. With the first lot loaded they began the trip back out which proved to be quite an effort. However, they soon had the first lot at the ship depositing them on the floor and going back for the next haul. By midday, they had half a cage over on the ship and they stopped to eat and rest. Despite Jit working out he was still feeling the work and wondered how Arrill was coping. Limtom seemed okay and although she carried less weight, it wasn't a great deal less. She was surprisingly strong for her small frame. With lunch over they finished their drink then Jit asked Ladone to move the ship as close as possible to the cleft cutting the distance and making it a little easier for them. They then trudged down to the cargo bay and strapped into their packs and set off once again beginning to feel the workload.

As Jit hovered over, he ran ideas through his mind on easier ways of transporting the crystals which they could use next time. The main problem was the narrow passageways and steps, not to mention the hologram gap. He figured something like a stretcher that could be lowered to fit under the gap yet capable of carrying a good load would be the best option but that still left the stairs to get past. Back in the cleft, they followed the same pattern as before and each time they arrived at the pedestal they had to go through the opening procedure. It took them until close on dark to remove just one cage full of the crystals and the cage itself broke down into one piece by folding up which made it possible to take out. They were exhausted by the time they finished but before them lay a cage full of the crystals looking different in the full light of the cargo bay. To look at they were clear with what seemed like frozen smoke a slightly dark colour trapped inside them. Their diameter was around seven centimetres and they ranged in length from thirty to forty centimetres. They had eight flat sides that made up the diameter with a point at one end and the other cut flat. To touch they were cold but smooth as glass and weighing around five kilograms each. All stacked again in their cage and secured they went straight to their cabins to shower and change. By the time Jit and Limtom arrived on the bridge, Arrill was talking to Ladone and told them he was heating leftover pizza for dinner. Despite the shower perking them up at first, they soon started feeling the strain of the day long work catching back up with them and making conversation strenuous. When they finished eating, they cleaned up and made a drink then went out to the bridge to discuss what their next course of action was to be. Jit and Limtom managed to stay up until nine thirty before they could remain awake no more and bid Arrill and Ladone good night and went to bed. Shortly after they left Arrill decided to do the same and on his way to the cabin found his movements stiff and painful.

…………………………………..

When Jit woke in the morning the first thing he felt was reluctance in muscle co-operation. He was stiff and sore and wondered how Limtom would feel and even more about Arrill as he didn't exercise at all. He'll probably need to be scrapped out of bed with a spatula and wheeled around on a stretcher for a day or two he mused to himself. The time was 7.00 am and Limtom lay still as a dead person with even her breathing barely audible. Jits estimation of five hundred kilograms per cage was off by two hundred kilos with the total at seven hundred. It took its toll on her light frame but she did the work without one word of complaint and kept up too. He soon fell back to sleep favouring the still motion and didn't wake again until after 8.00 am. It did nothing to quench the stiffness when he moved again. Limtom had woken him and they made light conversation while snuggling with the talk being how they both ached from the previous day's work. A short time later they rose from the bed and dressed then went to the galley. On the bridge, Ladone stood in her usual position and welcomed them.

After greeting her back Jit went to make coffee while Limtom remained on the bridge talking with her. Limtom was laughing at a comment made by Ladone with Jit not quite catching it when he returned from his task. He passed her a cup then went to the front view window to see what the day was going to bring. The sun shone brightly with another glorious day unfolding before him and below he could see wild cattle grazing on the grasslands. There was barely any mist this morning with only a few wisps strung around the bottom of trees like ribbons. The morning shadows raced to the foot of their creation as the sun climbed higher into the sky and warmed the day at the same time. Sometime after nine, they heard the elevator summoned and soon Arrill showed up with pain etched on his face. He greeted them all still standing on the lift platform fearful to move due to the dire consequences. Jit had to work at stifling a laugh while he observed Arrill make it to the console where he leaned on it heavily and waited for a moment. Jit poured him a cuppa and passed it to him and while Arrill took a sip he told him he was going to start working out with him and Limtom from now on. He was so stiff from lactose build up he could barely raise the cup to his mouth and drink.

In slow motion with a cup in hand, he made his way to the seats looking out the front window, and sat down letting out a sigh of relief as he did so. The previous night they'd agreed to go back to Limtom's place first before leaving for Geelok, so Jit told Ladone to set a course for the Pepplplant Estate. Limtom went on Link and called Shalby informing him they would be there by midday to which he said he'd be expecting them with lunch ready. The view out the front window changed from a looming mountain range to meadows and lakes peppered here and there varying in sizes but all the same azure blue reflecting the sun's brilliance. Ladone lifted the ship to a three hundred metre height which gave splendid views of the landscape as it rolled by beneath them. As they progressed, they could see in the distance dark ominous clouds that lit up at certain intervals from lightning. By the time they arrived at the Estate, the cloud formation was closer but for the moment the sun still reigned. It was closing on 1.00 pm when they arrived and once again the ship covered the place with her looming shadow even at three hundred metres.

They all went down to the cargo bay and took the shuttle down as there wasn't enough room below to land the ship. Shalby could be seen standing on the ground looking up and watched them land then came closer to greet them when they exited the shuttle. Limtom was first out and hugged Shalby hardly able to contain her excitement at seeing him. Jit and Arrill greeted him with a handshake and he commented Jit on the impressive ship yet again. Jit offered to take him up later and show him around to which Shalby said he'd like as he'd never seen the inside of a Windchief. In the house, they made their way to the courtyard undercover area to take their lunch. He and Arrill sat in their usual seats while Limtom helped Shalby bring lunch out. Whilst eating they discussed plans they'd talked about and checking that Shalby would be okay with the arrangement. They had also discussed keeping their find between themselves even if Shalby could be trusted. The fewer that knew the better was decided. Limtom was fine with the idea and very understanding. Shalby said they could take as long as they liked because he had things under control and at the very least could contact her if need be.

The conversation shifted to matters concerning Limtom's affairs with Shalby bringing her up to speed on what was going on. Jit and Arrill listened in and Jit wondered if Limtom was still interested in the matters as he could sense her disinterest in the dealings. All this was thrust upon her from a young age and now that she'd tasted the life he and Arrill lived he felt she no longer cared for her old life preferring her new one instead. During their dialogue, the sun suddenly paled and hid behind the distant clouds that had snuck up and gathered overhead. In the not too far distance, the rumble of thunder could be heard and they decided to take everything inside as it was imminent that rain was going to come. The breeze started getting stronger too Jit noticed and they could be in for a wild storm. He remembered the last one which funny enough was where they just came from. He also remembered the lightning strike on the ship that day and wondered if it would happen again. By 3.00 pm the clouds were so thick and dark that it seemed like 6.00 pm and the winds had gained in ferocity battering the garden outside with no mercy. Then the rain came and with the force of the wind, it struck the big glass windows attempting to break them and thundering away in the process. Jit couldn't hear himself think it was that shattering. They went to the kitchen to make tea while the tempest unleashed its fury outside and when it was made, they had to retire to the lounge room in the centre of the place where the noise was the least. As they talked Arrill was reminded of the sandstorms on Geelok which made the same sounds from the haunting wind sounding like a banshee trying to find a way in.

Limtom and Shalby stated how they'd not experienced a storm this savage before and things could be heard outside being hurled around and smashing against the house walls. They continued in conversation having to speak a little louder than usual as the afternoon passed by and the storm outside didn't diminish in intensity at all. They listened to Shalby share a story about a time when he was in the jungle on a planet he knew only as "target zone," and how the weather there one night was like it was outside now only he was exposed to it. He told them all he could do to not be carried away was lay face down flat on the ground and wait for it to pass. He finished by telling them it was the longest four hours of his life. Jit tried to imagine being in a fury like this and figured he'd never forget it either. He was startled out of his reverie when a cat jumped onto his lap scaring him quite a bit as he didn't know Limtom had any pets. It purred as it found a comfortable position to settle then went to sleep. They continued talking until dinner time and by then the cat had gone to find another spot to sleep. The intensity of the storm had calmed a little as night time fell but it was still wild with crazy winds. Shalby went to prepare dinner refusing help that was offered so they remained in the lounge talking until it was served.

When dinner was over, they sat around talking, meanwhile outside the wind was losing its sting and slowly diminished in intensity. They decided to leave going until the morning by this stage and when dessert was over, they indulged in some fine Port. Jit and Limtom decided to share a cigar while they continued talking about the following day's plans. By the time they were all ready for bed it had crept just past 10.00 pm and outside the storm had passed with only light rain falling. Arrill decided to go to his cabin on board the ship to sleep so bid them goodnight and they soon heard the shuttle lift off and make the short journey to the ship. Shalby was next to go and after he farewelled them they went to bed too. As Jit lay in bed with Limtom cuddled up to him he thought about the trip back to Geelok. It was about an eleven or twelve day journey away from Spollee. While he thought about how quickly the time had passed since taking on this quest, he became drowsy and as he went under his last thought was about the vault of prosperity and how very prosperous it made him.

....

When Arrill landed in the cargo bay he shut everything

down then took the lift to the bridge and greeted Ladone who awaited his arrival. His movements flowed a lot better now but he was by no means over the pain yet. He talked for a little while with her before he bid her goodnight and went back down to the cabin level. He lay under the covers with his arms behind his head thinking about his position now that he was wealthy and suddenly Leearnahs brother seemed a lot less intimidating. Soon sleep gathered him and pulled him away and his last thought was Leearnah and how he longed to see her again.

……………………….

It was around 8.30 am when Jit and Limtom rose from the bed. After they dressed Jit watched Limtom pack some things for the long journey away. He told her not to bother with too much because they could always buy what she needed. Some of her things were still on the ship so with a light bag filled they set off for the kitchen. When they entered the room, they met up with Shalby and Arrill who were already up talking. While they talked Arrill informed Jit that he already took Shalby up earlier on to have a look around the ship. Shalby nodded and said it was as fine a ship inside as it was outside. They then talked about the Windchief for a while before shifting to other matters and at the same time having breakfast. This would be their last meal with Shalby for a while because this trip would keep Limtom away the longest time yet. They hadn't discussed what to do after they sort matters out between Arrill and Leearnah. While Jit sipped his coffee, he looked out the large glass windows into the courtyard area at the upheaval the storm left in its path the previous day.

It was around 11.00 am when the last goodbyes were exchanged, and they walked out to the waiting shuttle and lifted off. In the cargo bay, Jit landed the shuttle beside the other one then they took the elevator up to the bridge to see Ladone. Limtom got off at the cabin level and went to drop her bag in the room then joined the rest of them. While they talked Ladone prepared for leaving Spollee and once clear of the planet she moved the ship to galatial speed. On the monitors above the front windows, they watched Spollee quickly become just another particle of the dust that made up the galaxy and up ahead they could see clear space looming predictably in front of them. Ladone informed them she calculated twelve days to their destination which was the longest time Jit had been cooped up in the ship yet. With that said they settled in for the long haul and Jit asked Arrill if he'd contacted Fryppe at all.

At the mention of it, he jumped to the console and called him up. Soon his face filled the big screen and it was good to see him again. They conversed with Fryppe for an hour and he insisted they drop in when their business was done and stay awhile. They told him they would stay in touch as they weren't certain what they would do after setting things straight for Arrill. By the time they finished talking to Fryppe, it was past midday, Spollee time, and Jit and Limtom went to make lunch. Partway through the afternoon, Ladone told them they were about to enter clear space and they felt the shift as the ship moved to full velocity. Limtom went to look out the front window as she was still mesmerised by the effect of knowing you were moving but looking like you weren't. Jit joined her and they held each other while looking out at the stillness. Arrill told them he was going to the library and read some more journals which he now had plenty of time to do. Before he did Jit told him he was going to the gym and Arrill said maybe in the next day or two he'd join him as he was still recovering from yesterday's workout. Later on, Jit and Limtom did go to the gym and put a good hour in, despite the hard day's work the previous day. When they finished, they went to their cabin to shower and change then Limtom unpacked her bag loading up the drawers again. With everything settled they returned to the bridge. Unexpectedly the time had crept to 6.00 pm and hunger motivated Jit to go and prepare dinner. The buzzer soon informed him his dinner was ready and he called out to Limtom then asked Ladone to summon Arrill. In a short while, they were sitting around the table talking about what Arrill had read in the journals which were mostly about daily activities on Cartergole. When they were done and cleaned up Arrill decided to go to the games room for a time out period while Jit and Limtom decided to go to the theatre and catch a movie. They took the lift down together then split off in their chosen ways. While she chose something from the vast range, he went over to the wall panel and selected champagne to have while they watched the movie.

She picked a story about a male and female thief that met whilst trying to steal the same item and fell madly in love. They went on to become the best thieves of all time and were never caught in any of their work leaving the authorities frustrated in their pursuit. It was a long movie stretching to nearly three hours and at the end of it, they'd long finished the champagne and were feeling ready for bed. Before going to their cabin, they went to see if Arrill was still in the games room but on poking his head in Jit found a dark room void of any activity. He told Limtom he must be back in the library and from there they went to bed.

....

In the games room, Arrill walked around the machines seeing which one jumped out at him, and finally settled in front of a hidden object game. The idea was to find the hidden objects until all were discovered and then you could move on to the next level. If you completed each level in a given time it would unlock a secret area to challenge your skills with greater difficulty. Although the game was absorbing, he found thoughts of Leearnah springing up more often now that he was on his way back to Geelok. For a while there he'd almost forgotten his old life, whether deliberately or out of distraction he wasn't so sure, but it felt good. Now going back bought feelings he was glad to have forgotten. He stood from the machine defeated by the lack of concentration and went to try a racing game which although he wasn't good at, had the power to distract him from his previous thoughts. He managed an hour or so in the room before he'd had enough and left, deciding to go back to the library to read some more journals.

As he passed the theatre room, he wondered what Jit and Limtom were watching. He was happy for them and could see they had a special and potent bond between them, just like he and Leearnah once had. If it wasn't for Leearnah he would never have gone back to Geelok at all he reckoned. In the library, he went to make coffee first then picked up reading where he left off. The entries didn't cover every day of activity on Cartergole, or Yuplar as the Suevons called it, and seemed more targeted at special events or significant accomplishments. After a while, he felt his eyes become weary from reading and set the laptop aside and returned his cup to the sink then made his way to bed. The time had crept up to midnight. As he drifted off to sleep his finishing thought for the day was, every passing hour bought him closer to Leearnah.

……………………..

It was around 8.00 am when Jit and Limtom stepped into the hallway and made their way to the bridge. On deck they greeted Ladone who looked splendid in a long yellow flowing dress that passed her knees, and on her feet, she wore dainty gold shoes that suited her petite small feet. A medium sized red hat sat on her head tilted at an angle and she wore white silk gloves that stretched right up to her elbows and fitting so snug it looked like she'd dipped both arms in white paint. Of course, that got Limtom talking about clothes and while the girls did so he went to the galley. Not more than five minutes later he heard Arrill arrived on the bridge and greet the girls. He then entered the galley and said hello to Jit and took a seat at the dining table allowing the last of the drowsiness to leave him. Whilst having breakfast Arrill disclosed to them that he came across the names of the other two Suevons who made up the four that arrived on Cartergole. They were, "Dirk Zergoid and Jiltong Kerr." Jit repeated the names quietly to himself in an attempt to remember them then wondered why they weren't recorded in the Temple with the other two names. Arrill continued and updated them with more material he read and highlighted the more important things with a little more detail. Later, they went back to the bridge with Arrill continuing onto the library to find out more from the pages of the journals.

Jit, Limtom, and Ladone set up the console for some card games which they played until the Link signalled a call from Shalby. On returning from her session Limtom relayed what the call was about. There were some matters that only she could confirm and allow. Back at the game, Jit was in front for a change with Limtom close behind followed by Ladone. They played until midday before stopping for a lunch break. Jit was still in front and thought it good to quit while he was ahead. While they ate Jit asked Arrill if there were any more interesting developments in his readings. He told them that as he slowly made progress through the journals, he was becoming more and more aware of the growing animosity between the two couples. He concluded so far, that as they were in their present situation due to an unforeseeable accident, they were never good friends, to begin with in the first place. They just worked together and went home at night having nothing more to do with each other but on Cartergole where they were stuck living together, things seemed to be mounted to an explosive conclusion.

Considering that they lived so long the dislike between each couple took a long time to manifest. Jit tried to imagine living a thousand years which could be either good or bad. When they finished eating, they cleaned up and Arrill returned to the library while Limtom and Jit went to the gym for a light workout. As they were doing a light routine, instead of the usual hour they pushed it up to two hours and at the end of the time, they were exhausted. Content with their performance they went to their cabin to shower then lay down for a nap. When they woke the time had escaped to after 5.00 pm and they made their way back to the bridge where only Ladone awaited them. Arrill rejoined them later and they sat around talking about what they might do when all this was over with many options open to them now that money wasn't an issue anymore. And not only did they have money, but they also possessed charts to a large part of the Universe giving them the freedom to go to otherwise undiscovered places. Even if they had a thousand year life span they would not see very much of it. Jit knew one thing for certain when they were done with Arrills business, he wanted to see the Jorphas and find out some things, like updating to the latest Windchief and transferring Ladone to the new ship.

If that was not possible then he contemplated asking if it was possible to update the ship they had with the latest drive system so they could achieve the same velocity as the new ships. There had to be a way and he knew with enough money changing hands anything was possible. The Jorphas used a large quantity of Chelinah Crystals in their work so he figured he had a good bargaining chip to begin with. Soon the buzzer announced dinner to be ready and while they ate, they continued chatting about their futures. They discussed the possibility of finding the planet the Suevons went to call Stellstone and see what they might find there. First, they'd have to find the charts that showed how to get there, and then it would depend on how far away it was. Even with a new Windchief four it could take a long time. Maybe longer than they lived Jit thought to himself! They were so caught up in the discussions that the time slipped away unnoticed crossing 10.00 pm unrestrained. However, weariness exposed it and Jit and Limtom bid Arrill goodnight and went to their cabin. They were soon in bed and while sleep crept up on them Jit wondered about the Suevons and where they went and what became of them.

……………………..

Arrill stayed up a while longer and selected a fine old scotch from the wall menu. It soon appeared for his pleasure with ice already in it shaped in an octagon fashion. He sat back at the table thinking about all that was discussed during the night and from what he could put together, Jit gathered he would be staying with them. He liked the idea of that as he had nowhere else to go unless things changed when he caught up with Leearnah. Just the thought of her name sent him into deep thoughts of their time together. He still wasn't certain why she left him, nor did he care at present. All that mattered first was to see her and make sure she was okay then clear up the misunderstanding that had arisen between him and her brother. It would help greatly if she was out of the coma so her brother could hear the truth from her. It all seemed like a mountain looming in front of him the whole ordeal and he wondered if he should forget the matter entirely. It was an easier option, but he knew he was just kidding himself. He had to know if the love of his life was okay before he could move on. He finished his drink and decided to head down to his cabin and go to bed. When he arrived, he was soon tucked up and feeling the effects of the scotch which by now had numbed his body in preparation for sleep. As he went under a smile formed on his face thinking that maybe he and Leearnah would become one again and the four of them could go and look for this place called Stellstone.

……………………..

The days rolled one into another and on the sixth day and halfway through their journey Arrill told them some more news about the Suevons he'd uncovered. This new revelation came while they were having lunch and he went on to tell them that all the Chelinah crystals in the vault were harvested on Cartergole. The ground on the planet was perforated with varying size holes and some were enormous and it's from these places they harvested the crystals. According to their exact words……

"The planet is infested with them."

It was a long time ago when all this happened, and Jit wondered if the haul in the vault was all of them. It certainly seemed like it to him.

'If they harvested them on Cartergole, why would they transport them all the way to Spollee?' said Limtom.

Arrill suggested the idea may have spawned from their hatred for each other with one couple hiding their spoil on Spollee. Exactly why they picked Spollee he wasn't sure, at least not yet. This also meant that there was a possibility another haul the same as they had laid out there somewhere hidden by the other two Suevons. He hoped to find out more as he kept reading but there was still a lot of material to sift through. Some of the journals contained more entries and because of that, it was not possible to predict how long each journal would take to get through. Arrill then went on to tell them he believed there was still more crystals on the planet that had not been harvested because they weren't found yet. Jit couldn't possibly imagine needing more than they already had and wondered if Wisplok knew what he was sitting on. When lunch was over, they cleaned up then went back to the bridge. Jit went to the front window and looked out and far away in the distance he could make out spots that were galaxies a long way away still. The spots he looked at seemed so small yet in their midst, each galaxy was a mini-universe. He then pondered what mode of transport the Suevons had to get them about the stars as they did. He was intrigued by them and if the chance presented itself would like to find where they went and if they had offspring. Limtom sidled up beside him and they stood together staring out at the vast blackness in silence for a while then they went back to the console where Arrill was talking with Ladone. The day passed as the previous ones and they continued staying on Spollee time which would only change when they entered Geeloks orbit.

By the tenth day of their journey, they could see the galaxy which held the moon in its sprinkling of dust as they moved progressively towards it. Arrill hadn't uncovered much more of interest in the journals with most matters referring to politics and tradition. He had no doubt there would be more of interest, but he just had to wait until he came to it. He was committed to reading each journal one by one until he'd read them all and despite long days of reading, he still had many to read through. The Suevons were on Cartergole for a few hundred years so a lot of information was gathered in that amount of time. Then there were days where he was fed up with reading and did other things to give himself a break. He started training with Limtom and Jit which at first hurt a little, but with a week of it up his sleeve, he was now okay and liking it. The days passed as normal with activities found to occupy them all until the day came when Ladone announced they would be slowing down to galatial speed meaning they were through clear space once again.

....

Back at Geelok

It was just past twelve days when they arrived in Geeloks orbit and the time on the moon's surface was 1.00 am in the morning. They discussed whether to land the ship at Arrills cave or just take the shuttle and they settled on taking the ship down as there was plenty of room to land. Being out in no man's land they would not be seen either. That being the case Jit instructed Ladone to make it happen and Arrill set the beacon for her to home in on. All of them were looking forward to getting outside and stretching their legs too. When Ladone bought the ship close to the ground the underside lights lit up the area and all they could see was sand everywhere and Arrill told them the entrance was more than likely covered due to the storms that could pass through. Jit told Ladone to leave the ship at one hundred metres and later when day breaks and they could see better they would land then. In four hours daylight would break which meant if they were still on Spollee time, dinner will become breakfast Geelok time. Jit and Limtom decided to go and have a nap for a while in the hope to diminish fatigue at the end of their first day back on Geelok. They managed to nap for three hours before they returned to the bridge. Ladone was there to greet them and Jit asked her where Arrill was. Expecting to hear he was in the library she instead informed him he was in the gym. That day of work not so long back seemed to change him in ways no one could, and Jit also wondered if Leearnah might have something to do with it.

He and Limtom looked out the window where the day was just breaking. Jit wondered how Arrill managed to live in a place like this for as long as he did. It was certainly a great place to hide from anyone. As the day brightened all that could be seen was sand in every direction. When he finished his drink, he went to check the monitors showing the underside of the ship to see if they could land. Whilst he was doing this Arrill came back onto the bridge and they decided to leave the ship suspended and take the shuttle down. Arrills transporter should fit into it and they could bring it up to the ship that way. All Arrills things would fit in his transporter as he had little anyway. While they waited a bit longer for the daylight to increase, they had breakfast and around 8.00 am they went down to the cargo bay and took the shuttle to the surface. When they stepped outside the heat from the sun was already noticeable despite it still being early. Jit watched Arrill press a button on a device he pulled from his pocket then could hear a sound that increased in intensity until a tube protruded from the sand near where he stood. He brushed away the sand and opened the lid on top of the tube and inside attached to one side was a ladder system for descending into the cave. Arrill told them he used the tube often when he would return from Arczepp and the place was rearranged.

The tube was a telescopic arrangement with the ladder being the same too. In the cave, Arrill knew his way around in the dark and soon had the lights on bringing daylight to the place. It was nice and cool in the cave and everything sat as it was when he left it. At the main exit door, Arrill exposed a panel that had switches in it and he manipulated them until a hissing sound could be heard building up. He explained to Jit and Limtom that the door had high pressure valves that would clear the doorway when he released the built up air. He then pressed a button and from the other side of the door they heard a thud then the hissing returned while the pressure built up again. Arrill did this three times before a light and siren indicated a clear way. Next, he depressed a yellow button which allowed the door to slide down into the ground letting light and fresh air into the cave. They commenced loading Arrills belongings into the vehicle and in a few hours they were ready to drive it into the awaiting shuttle. Before boarding the transporter Arrill looked around at the cave that was his sanctuary for so long and felt like he was abandoning a friend. He consoled himself by the fact he could return whenever he wanted and then drove out to the shuttle punching the remote lock on his way out of the cave allowing it to seal up again.

The transporter fit into the shuttle with ease then they lifted off and were soon entering the cargo bay of the ship. Once they were in Arrill removed the transporter and parked it out of the way and secured it then they all went up to the bridge to greet Ladone and have lunch. While they ate, they discussed plans for their trip into Arczepp. They tossed up whether to take the ship back out to orbit and return with the shuttle as Jit did when he first came which would attract less attention and they chose to do that. Next, they talked about finding Leearnah and it was agreed that Limtom would go into the hospital to ask about her and track her down. She was going to go with the assumption that she was a long lost friend of Leearnah and as she'd never been to Geelok, no one would know any better. When Lunch was over, they cleaned up and then returned to the bridge where Jit instructed Ladone to take the ship out into orbit. They stood at the window as the ship ascended watching the landscape shrink below to an ocean of sand until they were in position looking down at the moon itself. It was a barren place thought Jit and wondered again why anybody would choose to live there when there were countless other places more pleasant to call home. Visions of Kelpuk came to mind and he wondered what Limtom would think of the place. It left a lasting impression on Jit.

With the ship settled they informed Ladone of their intentions then went down to the cargo hold to board the shuttle and head down to the surface. Jit noticed Arrill seemed to be taking this all in with a different attitude than he expected. He didn't seem the jumpy nervous type he was when he first arrived here. Arrill took the shuttle down and as they entered through the atmosphere, they went over the plans discussed during lunch. With clearance given at the Port, they landed in one of the bays beside where Jit first landed some weeks back. It was early afternoon by this time and when they exited the shuttle they walked to the "Vehicle hire desk." With money no problem they hired something a little better than what Jit hired previously and were soon on their way into town. Arczepp was a growing town that seemed to draw visitors to it making it expand even more. Every day more people came and in the weeks, they'd been away Jit noticed obvious changes to the town. Buildings that were partially built when he first arrived were now finished and inhabited and in other places, new foundations were laid for yet more buildings. Shops that were vacant now sported merchandise to suit the influx of new people. More people roaming around the streets were quite apparent too. For a desert moon, it still eluded Jit what made people want to come here let alone live here. Outside of the city was a barren hostile environment that could send sandstorms that were unpredictable and capable of killing anyone not prepared for them.

They drove to the hospital which Arrill knew was the last place Leearnah stayed and showed Limtom so she would find her way then he sent a coded message to Neeok informing him he was on his way there. They parked in the back area Arrill used to park in and both he and Jit got out and Limtom took off to see if Leearnah was still in the hospital. Jit followed Arrill through hallways until they eventually came to a private lounge area where he took a seat while Arrill went to make them a drink. They were partway through their drink when the door opened and Neeok entered.

'It is good to see you again old friend' he said to Arrill as they embraced briefly in their greeting.

Arrill returned the welcome then introduced Jit. Neeok recognized him from before and shook his hand as they exchanged warm greetings too. He made himself a drink and joined them in talks filling Arrill in on what had been going on since he was last there. Neeok had no idea Arrill had just returned from being to three different galaxies far across clear space. He went on to ask him what news there was of Leearnahs brother and his whereabouts. Neeok told him that he hadn't seen him since the last time Arrill was in, nor had he heard anything about his whereabouts. It was almost as if he'd left Geelok altogether. Arrill knew Zarp to be cunning with contacts in many places so he was certain that one of his ears would be lurking about somewhere not far away. Neeok couldn't relay any information about Leearnahs state of being or movements. For that, he would have to wait for Limtoms report. When Arrill was caught up on all the news Neeok asked Jit what he did giving Jit the floor for a while. While he elaborated Arrill got up to make them another round of drinks and couldn't help thinking what Limtom was turning up.

....

Limtom was a little nervous as she drove to the hospital barely noticing the trip and seeming to just appear at the establishment. Parking was plentiful and she found a spot closest to the entrance then stepped out of the vehicle and brushed her clothing and checked herself before walking towards the entrance. The doors opened automatically as she approached them, and a gush of cool air mixed with disinfectant greeted her as she passed into the foyer. The place was busy with stretchers being whisked around carrying patients and nurses with caps on walking briskly to their destination. She looked around and soon found the main information desk and headed in its direction. People looked at her as she passed through the waiting area with not one face smiling or looking pleased with being there. It seemed all hospitals were the same no matter where she went. When she approached the information counter, she talked with a pleasant young nurse who was polite and had a kindly disposition about her, making Limtom feel at ease right away. She was a little shorter than she was and had a pretty face with deep blue eyes that sparkled like jewels. She ruffled through files after Limtom told her the name of the patient she came to see, not asking her relationship to the patient at all. Soon she made a sound of victory and read through a folder then looked at Limtom and told her Leearnah had come out of the coma a week ago and was in rehab. The rehab was in another wing of the hospital and she instructed her on how to get there making her repeat it back so she was certain she wouldn't get lost. Limtom thanked her for the help and went to look for a Link booth to call Jit and Arrill and found one close by.

....

Only moments after Arrill wondered how things at the hospital were going were they interrupted by one of the staff informing Neeok there was a call for Jit and Arrill. Neeok picked up a remote control sitting on the coffee table and pushed a button that switched on a monitor on the wall and Limtoms face appeared before them. She relayed to Arrill her findings and asked him what he wanted to do. He was thrilled that Leearnah was okay and asked Limtom to come back and pick him up. She said very well, and the screen went blank and he sat back to absorb the information and let it sink in. Leearnah was awake which meant she could clear his name. He also hoped they could rekindle their love for each other but that wasn't as certain. The talk shifted to the good news Arrill received and a short time later Limtom arrived and parked in the normal customer car park of the establishment. She no sooner entered the lounge and Arrill was rushing them off to the vehicle again to get back to the hospital. He thanked Neeok and told him they'd catch up later on then they left. Arrill walked out of "The Crossed Arms" like a normal patron just strolling out the front door with fear of Zarp gone altogether now.

He slipped behind the wheel of the vehicle to drive and they were soon on their way back to the rehab section of the hospital. When they arrived, they passed the entry Limtom took and continued to another entry, turned in, and followed a tree lined driveway that ran a little distance to the main entrance of the facility. Parking was plentiful and after doing so they walked to the wide front steps that allowed entry into the main building. Jit thought the place looked more like a library he was entering rather than a rehab facility. Inside the ceilings were high and the walls were adorned with all manner of objects further making the place seem like something other than a rehab institution. Jit thought the idea might be to make the patients feel more at home which it did because he felt like he was visiting one of Limtom's influential neighbours. People wandered around with some in wheelchairs while others used a stick. Some had no means of support not needing them as they hobbled along. Despite their conditions, most of the people smiled when they passed them on their way to the information desk. Limtom told them the place was a lot chirpier than the hospital she was at only a short time ago.

The information desk was a large square area in the middle of the floor allowing access to all four sides for service. The counters were cluttered with paperwork and books along with rolls of other paperwork. In between all this, there were gaps where one could stand to be served, or seen for that matter. A young male was the lone occupant of the square and on seeing them called out he'd be over soon and finished fiddling with the task at hand. True to his word he soon came over and asked them what he could do for them. Limtom spoke telling him they were there to see Leearnah Borche and that the nurse from the hospital sent her. She was using her maiden name which she found out from the nurse too. Jit could see Arrill flinch when her maiden name was mentioned but recovered just as quickly. The assistant told them to wait a moment then went to a phone and they watched his lips move in conversation but unable to hear what was being said. He soon placed the phone down and came back telling them someone was on their way to escort them to Leearnah. Arrill was just about jumping out of his skin Jit noticed, and placed a hand on his shoulder to comfort him. It was close to half an hour before someone finally turned up to get them and lead them to Leearnah.

This time a female assistant came and after a quick hello and apology for the delay, she asked them to follow her and turned to go. She wore a shortish uniform with shoes that squeaked every time she took a step on the mirror like floor. She also walked at a brisk pace with the three of them having to almost jog to keep up. They passed more walls laden with objects and paintings until they came to a large pair of glass doors that were open and beyond them lay a large courtyard exposed to the sunshine. It was beautiful, taking away your breath from the moment you stepped over the threshold. Forest size trees scattered the grounds looming high above everything else while still allowing the sun to reach down onto the grounds in patches of differing sizes. Gardens with shrubs of all colours gathered in clusters placed methodically for the best soothing effect. Pathways twisted with no set destination in mind and water features sprouted here and there at random playing fluid tunes. People were peppered around the place with some in small groups sitting on benches under the shade of the large trees and others sat in the open sunshine wearing broad rimmed hats to shade their eyes. The nurse that led them to the courtyard pointed in the direction of a woman with her back to them in a wheelchair and then left with other duties to perform.

Jit and Limtom waited for Arrill to proceed but for a moment he seemed to be frozen where he stood.

'Are you okay ole friend?' said Jit as he gripped his shoulder.

Arrill nodded then squared his shoulders and sucked in a deep breath and strode forward along the stone path in the direction of the wheelchair. Jit and Limtom followed close behind holding hands as they did so with their hearts gaining momentum from the tense and long building moment that was about to unfold. When they were close, they could see over her shoulders and saw she had her hands clutched together with a blanket over her lap deep in thought and not hearing them until Arrill spoke her name.

'Leearnah.'

She wheeled around slowly and as she did her injuries became visible. She had a long scar above her right eye and an equally long scar across her left cheek. Her lips quivered and tears began to fall from her staring eyes as she whispered his name then stood reaching out for him. It quickly became apparent she was blind as well and Arrill pulled her into his hold where she completely let go and howled her grief out. The moment was so emotional that Limtom turned into Jit's chest where she began to weep unable to stop herself. Jit found himself working hard at keeping his emotions in check but failed as a tear slid from his eye, rolled off his cheek, and dropped onto Limtom's head. They decided to leave them to talk and Jit signalled to Arrill that they would wait in the vehicle and turned to leave. Limtom was still sniffling and wiping her eyes on the sleeve of her top as they moved back inside the building and returned to the carpark.

Having no idea how long they might have to wait Jit led Limtom by the hand until they found a café where they could get a hot drink. With a drink in hand, they returned to the vehicle and sat on a wall where he put his arm around her. She sidled up to him and they remained silent sipping their drink with the experience that just passed strong on their minds. Partway through his beverage Jit felt like a smoke and rolled one up for both and passed one to Limtom. While they drank and smoked Jit talked about Leearnah, telling Limtom the story of how she and Arrill first met. It was some years back now, but the story went like so... Jit's vehicle was at the mechanic workshop this day and he had to look at a new place to rent. Arrill being his closest friend offered to take him to view the place where they were to meet the agent on-site at a prearranged time. They arrived on time, but she was ten minutes late and from the moment she stepped out of her vehicle and their eyes met Jit could feel the magic crackle in the air such was its intensity. He told Limtom he never thought they would separate and was astonished when he was told by Arrill who never went into detail about the matter. He still didn't know why they ever split up. He pulled Limtom close to him feeling that he could never live without her and knew only death could separate them now. He didn't need to ask her if she felt the same way because he could feel her commitment in the way she held onto him. She clutched onto him at times like her life depended on it and it made Jit feel things he couldn't describe in words. It was truly as if he'd known her for all time, and they'd once again found each other.

The time was moving on and Arrill still hadn't returned and they were both getting hungry. He told Limtom to wait in the vehicle just in case Arrill showed up while he went to find something to eat. While he was doing so he heard his name called and looked over to see Nisteeva and Kalisafah, the two Jorpah girls he met when he rode with Ishmak to the outpost. They were so excited to see him and asked him if he'd found his friend which Jit told them he had. They then asked him what he was up to and if he wanted to spend some time with them, but he told them he was with someone and was just getting a bite to eat. They talked for a little while longer before he bid them farewell then continued with what he was doing. Geelok always had something open and he finally settled on a hotdog stand where the attendant claimed to make his sausages to an old style mamma's recipe. He seemed genuine and admittedly the hotdogs smelt irresistible but that could've been due to hunger. However, he took two and then went back to where Limtom was waiting. When he approached the vehicle, he pulled a face at the window making her laugh and poke her tongue out at him. He jumped in and kissed her first meanwhile the smell of the hotdogs filled the cab in moments.

'They smell marvellous' she said to him as he passed her one then unwrapped his and hooked in.

Marvellous was an understatement he thought as he polished off the hotdog in little time. He looked at Limtom who relayed her approval with just a look then he went to get two more. The guy smiled when he saw him walking his way and started preparing the next order for him. Jit told him they were the best hotdogs he'd ever tasted and was soon on his way back to the vehicle again. Two should do the trick just fine he thought as he made his way in the fast diminishing light. Already the streetlights came on and shop windows lit up to do the sun's work for the night and changing the mood of everything. He sat back in the vehicle where Limtom sat listening to music from the radio and passed her another hotdog. While they ate, they made small talk about nothing in particular. By the time they finished eating the second hotdog, it was completely dark.

Surely Arrill couldn't be much longer he thought to himself and he just finished the thought when he saw his silhouette come toward the vehicle. He seemed to be in a good mood by the way he moved, and he soon entered the cab with his first words asking what they'd eaten that smelt so good. Then he told them he was starving. Jit started the vehicle and they drove to where the stand was so Arrill could get a feed. He watched Arrill make conversation with the guy selling the hotdogs and he looked to be in good spirits considering what happened earlier on. He wondered what his friend might do now that he's caught up with Leearnah and hoped he would stay on as he considered him family. Back at the car, he jumped in and they drove back towards the Port. As they went past a motel of repute Jit suddenly swung into its driveway and decided to spend the night in different lodgings. They booked accommodation in luxury suites that were joined by an internal door giving them their privacy but still close together.

The payment was made by Limtom and passed her Platinum card to the desk clerk who looked at her like she was royalty. Only the very wealthy carried Platinum cards. In their rooms, they looked through clothing catalogues for going out and when their choices were made, they called for the assistant to fill the order and book it to the room. While they waited for their new clothes to arrive, they made tea and discussed their plans from here on. Arrill told them that Leearnahs brother hadn't been seen for a while because he was off-world looking for the creep that beat his sister up. He was the first one called when she woke from the coma and she told him everything that happened, which set Arrill free at last. He then told them that her blindness was temporary, and it was a side effect the female Chungahs suffer if hit about the head too hard. Her scars would heal and with time would all but vanish. He saved the best news until last telling them they were getting back together again. Being as sensitive as she was Limtom started to weep into Jit's shoulder once more at the news and Jit extended his hand to shake Arrills telling him how happy he was that his wife came back. Despite all that happened Jit knew Arrill and Leearnah were meant to be one just as he knew the same of him and Limtom.

Their clothes arrived after the given time and they showered then dressed and went out for the night to celebrate. Now that Arrill was free to roam without looking over his shoulder they decided to go to the Crossed Arms to start with and see what happened from there. They hailed a cab from the footpath and being plentiful in supply they were soon riding to Neeoks establishment. When they arrived, they were told Neeok was having the night off, but he did leave instructions concerning them all. The badge on the bartender's shirt read, "Paul" which was a name Jit had never heard before. He looked over to another bar staff and nodded then wiped his hands on a teatowel and flicked it over his shoulder as he led them to a private booth towards the back of the room. It wasn't all that private when he stopped in front of the booth then asked them what they would like to drink. They took a seat and ordered then he left scribbling on a pad while returning to the bar. Quite a few people were sitting around with some standing at gaming machines that were in the middle of the floor creating an island of people and colour. The building inside looked more like a wooden ship. It had huge lumbering pieces of wood crossing each other supporting the top of the structure and Jit saw places where the wood was wide enough to nearly sleep on and wondered where the timber came from as trees were scarce on Geelok. Giant round wooden posts sat in strategic places with tables built around them and patrons sitting with smoke curling into the air from ashtrays that were heavily laden.

Their drinks soon came and while they drank, they talked more about what they were going to do. Arrill told them that Leearnah was ready to leave and that they would have to get themselves sorted out which he had no plan for. Jit told him straight up that he wanted them to stay with him and Limtom for as long as they wanted. Limtom was nodding eagerly and telling him to stay and they soon had that matter settled with and agreed upon. Jit knew Leearnah well enough to know beyond a doubt that both Limtom and Ladone would love her. They stayed long enough to have another drink then they decided to go walk the streets for a while and see what they might happen upon. The place looked different at night with all the bright coloured lights vying for the passerby to enter their premises. The crowds were beginning to build as the time just passed 8.00 pm according to the large clock in the centre of a park they passed. Vehicles were everywhere picking up people or dropping them off while inpatient motorists beeped horns in protest.

Most of the crowds they saw were cluttering into an entrance that looked more like a subway entry, so they walked that way to investigate. As they approached closer, they could make out a word stretched across the top of the entry in a cloister which read, "Undertown." They walked towards the crowds then followed them inside taking a wide flow of steps to the basement of what they thought was a building but when they reached the bottom, they were stunned at what they saw. The whole of the town's underneath was hollow and there was another town altogether down there. This served as the town before the force field spires were built to keep the sandstorms at bay. The crowds dispersed in all directions and they just followed their instincts looking as they walked. It was amazing under here thought Jit as he took in all the different goings on. It was like a market atmosphere but on an extensive scale with more people around the place than up top. It seemed he might have discovered why so many came to the moon then wondered what else lay undiscovered. Performers entertained street dwellers with all kinds of dazzling tricks and feats of balance while some played instruments that Jit had never seen before. Food vendors roamed everywhere with anything you could think of available and Jit thought about the hotdogs of earlier on suddenly craving another. Stalls catering for every desire were to be found with things available that could not be purchased up top. There were drinking houses and clubs with restaurants that boasted fine cuisine in bountiful supply. They happened upon a nice little outdoor alfresco style café bar and took a seat with service arriving shortly after they did so.

They watched electric two wheeled vehicles darting about carrying people and cargo around with some loads impossibly staying put. When they finished their drinks, they got up and walked around some more and came upon a dance floor where Jit took Limtom for a few dances. Arrill sat at the bar and watched them before a conversation with a drunken guy next to him struck up. They'll talk about the most amazing things he thought to himself. The guy was telling him, his wife told him she thought about his best friend when they had sex. He then asked Arrill what he should do about it and he told him he wasn't able to assist in the matter and left to sit elsewhere. He ordered a drink and sat at a table watching Jit and Limtom who were having a great time and thought about himself and Leearnah soon doing the same. By the time he finished his drink, they appeared beside him taking seats whilst breathing heavily from the dancing. They watched other people dance and hung around a little and the next thing on their minds was something to eat. The choice was limitless, and they eventually settled on something called a "Decklar" which was a flat fired dough rolled up with spicy meat in it and salsa that leaned on the hot side and plenty of gooey tasty cheese. It was sensational and despite its size, Jit put his away with little effort. The hot sensation of the food mixed with the drink was giving him a euphoric feeling increasing the experience of Undertown. When they were content, they agreed on wandering around some more to see the whole place while they were down there. Some establishments they walked past were sleazy looking with guys standing around out the front who hadn't seen a bar of soap in a long time. Only the distance saved them from the smell they must've harboured. Limtom squeezed close to Jit as they walked past looking straight ahead and picking up her pace a little. They were in Undertown until after midnight before they decided to head back to the motel and get some sleep. When they exited and were back up top again, they hailed a cab to take them back to their lodgings. The streets were quiet at this hour but where they'd just come from everyone was still in party mode. On arriving at their destination, they were soon carried up to their floor in the glass lift that awaited them in the foyer. At their rooms, Jit and Limtom bid Arrill goodnight and entered their room and a few steps further along he entered his room.

…………………

Both Jit and Limtom woke at the same time and were soon up to begin the day. They wondered how Arrill was going then went to knock on the door dividing their rooms. It took two attempts before they gained a response and when he came out, he looked to have only just got up. He made a welcoming sound which included he'd be ready soon then went to accomplish the mission. While they waited Jit made coffee and they sat on the balcony to have it overlooking the town. The day was clear and sunny with a breath of cool wind trickling past the warmth of the sun. By the time they finished their drink Arrill presented himself and looked sharper than usual. He told them he'd get a coffee later and with that said they exited the room and went down to the foyer. After fixing up the bill they went to the car park and within a short time were on their way back to the rehab facility. On arriving they parked in the same spot as the previous day then went to the get Leearnah as she was approved to leave today. A nurse soon turned up with her in a wheelchair and when they signed papers and listened to her care instructions they were on their way. Although she was still unable to see she hugged Jit warmly and embraced Limtom too. The wheelchair was left behind as she could walk and just held onto Arrill while they went back to the vehicle. It was a great sight to see them together again Jit thought. From the rehab, they decided to go to her brother's place with Arrill informing her of the newfound plans along the way. Although she was still blind Jit could sense her excitement at the adventure and her happiness at being with Arrill again.

They soon arrived at a leafy tree studded street with opulent homes gracing the roadside varying in sizes from huge to even huger. Zarp was not short of money and as they approached a wide set of double gates Jit stopped at a speaker which Leearnah spoke into then the gates swung open allowing them entry. The driveway was made of white gravel that nearly blinded the three of them crunching loudly as they wound around manicured gardens with gardeners tending them and looking with suspicion at the unknown vehicle. They soon arrived at a palatial entrance to a three storey mansion with an exotic sports vehicle sitting to the side sparkling like a jewel in the sunshine. It was stunning to look at and oozed wealth and flamboyancy in its silence. Arrill led the way with Leearnah clutching onto him while Jit and Limtom followed behind. They ascended the steps that started wide at the bottom and narrowed at the top then spilled onto a pathway leading to the front doors. The door was opened on their approach by an immaculately dressed servant that stood no less than seven feet tall Jit thought. He greeted Leearnah with a note of concern in his voice then the others and led them inside. The servant's name was "Mutteel" and she asked him if he could lead them to her room which she'd been using since she and Arrill parted company. Her room was on the bottom floor and when they arrived Mutteel left them and they went inside to help pack what she needed. It was spacious inside with a large floral patterned lounge that Jit and Limtom sat on while Arrill followed instructions to different drawers and emptied the contents she wanted into a suitcase. As Jit watched them work together it seemed like they'd never been apart with Arrill almost reading her mind as to what she wanted. One bag she filled with clothes while another she filled with personal mementos and keepsakes. When she had all she wanted they went back out to the front door and were intercepted by Mutteel before reaching it. Leearnah left a message for him to give to her brother when he returned and they hugged each other then went back to the vehicle and prepared to head out to the Port.

The time was closing on midday and all of them were hungry, so they decided to make a stop in town for a bite to eat before continuing. They found a nice little eatery that was busy with people and took a seat. While they ate and made conversation Leearnah told them her sight was beginning to come back as she could now see a bright blur compared to before when there was only blackness. Arrill filled her in on what had happened since he and Jit caught up again. The conversation lasted right through lunch and when they finished, they continued to their destination as before. In the allotted time they arrived at the Port and soon pulled in at the vehicle hire compound to return their ride. With paperwork done and completed they walked to the shuttle where they all strapped in and Jit lifted off and aimed for the Winchief that awaited them in orbit. He entered the cargo hold and manoeuvred the shuttle into position beside number one then shut her down and they all hopped out and took the lift to the bridge. Ladone naturally waited for them in her usual place and once the greetings were exchanged Jit introduced Leearnah and told her she and Arrill would be staying a while. She was delighted at the idea that there were two females she could chat with and admitted she was quite fond of Arrill and glad he was staying on. While the girls chatted amongst each other and Leearnah settled in, Jit and Arrill talked about their plans and concerns. They then listened to the girls that were locked in conversation about the ordeal Leearnah had been through. Despite the cuts on her face, she was still a very attractive woman and the attack on her person did nothing to change her great personality. They remained in orbit around Geelok for the present discussing what they were going to do, and the afternoon slipped away quickly then dinner time was upon them. When dinner was ready, they ate and continued talking and agreed to make their way to the planet of the Jorpahs which was called, "Kallak." It was situated in the fifth galaxy which Jit estimated would take two or three days to arrive at.

He instructed Ladone about their plan then she set the ship for their destination and they were soon departing once again. When the meal was finished Arrill and Leearnah went to get her bags from the shuttle and get her settled in while Jit and Limtom cleaned up then went to look out the front window. On the monitors above the window, they watched the shrinking moon of Geelok wondering if they'd ever see it again. They soon shifted to galatial speed and the stars drifted by lazily as they streaked along in silence. The evening began to get late and Arrill and Leearnah hadn't come back to the bridge, so Jit assumed they were likely to not see them until the morning. Limtom suggested a movie and as the movie began, he thought for a moment about everything that had happened in the last couple of months and felt like his life was a movie. During the action, they felt the shift to full velocity as the ship entered clear space once more. When the movie finished some hours later, they were so comfy and stunned on Abbeymoss they remained on the sofa for a couple of hours longer before they rose for bed. Jit had to just about carry Limtom she was in such a state. In their quarters he pulled the covers over her and kissed her then decided to go up to the bridge for a last look before retiring too. He stood there for a little while thinking about what lay ahead and what it would be like travelling four times faster than they were going now. After a while, the Abbeymoss weighed down on him and he decided to go and join Limtom.

....

The bridge sat in silence with low lights glowing and some moving to a rhythm of their own then the speaker crackled a few times before the words, "*side of the moon*" were heard accompanied with a tune then crackled away until silence remained alone again.

The End

www.ingramcontent.com/pod-product-compliance
Lightning Source LLC
Chambersburg PA
CBHW050921030726
47503CB00007BB/2413